GARY LOVISI

lives in Brooklyn, New York, and is editor of a number of magazines, including *Hardboiled*. He publishes books under his own Gryphon imprint and has written dozens of shorts stories, many of them featuring hard-boiled PI, Vic Powers. His début novel, *Hellbent on Homicide*, was published by The Do-Not Press in 1997; *Blood in Brooklyn* is the second, and the first to feature Vic Powers.

First Published in Great Britain in 1999 by
The Do-Not Press Ltd
PO Box 4215
London SE23 2QD

A paperback original.

Copyright © 1999 by Gary Lovisi
The right of Gary Lovisi to be identified as the Author of
this work has been asserted by him in accordance with the
Copyright, Designs & Patents Act 1988.

ISBN 1 899 344 48 9

British Library Cataloguing in Publication Data.
A catalogue record for this book is available from the
British Library.

All rights reserved. No part of this publication may be
reproduced, transmitted or stored in a retrieval system, in
any form or by any means without the express permission in
writing of The Do-Not Press having first been obtained.

This book is sold on the condition that it shall not, by way
of trade or otherwise, be lent, resold or hired out or otherwise circulated without the publisher's prior consent in any
form of binding or cover other than that in which it is published and without a similar condition being imposed on the
subsequent purchaser.

h g f e d c b a

Printed and bound in Great Britain by Caledonian
International.

BLOOD IN BROOKLYN

GARY LOVISI

BLOODLINES

Chapter One
BROOKLYN, NEW YORK, 1994

There was a time not too long ago when I had a life. A real life.

The kind of life where you can hold-your-head-up-when-you-walk life. I had even been a cop, once. Now I was a private eye. Sort of. Did other stuff too. Did stuff I never would have dreamed doing. Involved in unbelievable things with real bad people.

It just happened.

Sometimes you get on the hellbound train and you never know where it will lead or how long the ride will last.

It lasted a long time for me.

Now, don't get me wrong, I'm not saying I didn't enjoy the ride at times, or at least parts of the ride, but I didn't want to board that particular train again for a long while. Maybe never again. I'd had enough.

I figured my life had just about run its course. That now I could go back home, pick up the jagged pieces of my shattered personality, resurrect my go-nowhere existence and try to make something of myself.

That's what I figured.

So I started looking for work.

I was a guy who was known by people in the know. They'd come to me. I'd let it be known I was back in town and looking for action. That's the one thing New York will never run out of. It's like one big fish tank full of piranhas, all of them eating each other up. Always hungry.

As it turned out the job that did come my way seemed like easy money. Usually, I'm suspicious as hell, and skeptical of everything, but I figured I'd been through the meat-grinder so much lately that the scales just had to turn in my favor at least once. At least a little bit. You know what I mean? An easy break. At least, that's what I figured.

The job was in Brooklyn.

I should have realized it would be bad.

Brooklyn, New York. It used to be something once. That was, back when I was a kid, and even more so when our parents were kids. Now it's just a dead-end town. Three million souls jammed into a third-rate, second-class section of New York City. A city which has itself become another synonym for cesspool, no matter what anyone says to the contrary Oh sure, its come back a bit lately, but even that won't last. But for those who live and work in Brooklyn it is always worse, and go- nowhere for most of them.New York City, still the greatest city in the world is just across the river. It's only half a mile or so, just a walk over the Brooklyn Bridge actually, but in a lot of ways it might as well be on another planet. Mars, Pluto, maybe even Never-Never-Land to most people who live in Brooklyn and the outer boroughs.

But enough of that New York pessimism.

I had a life now. Finally. It was all because of Gayle. She'd quit the business after what had happened a few years back. I can't talk about it now. She stayed home, cooked, cleaned house. It was cool. We were living the fantasy. We were even thinking of having a kid. Maybe afterwards, Gayle would get a real job, like where she didn't have to go and kill anyone. Maybe do something honest, or relatively so? Maybe work as a private eye for some shysters I knew? Or maybe we'd both go private together as a husband and wife team? Now wouldn't that be cute?

Vic Powers and Gayle Armstrong, private eyes! Why, in a lot of ways Gayle is a lot tougher than I am. Maybe even crazier. Hard to say about that last one, but the fact that she stuck with me so far has to mean something. It's not just love. It's kinda, like, we belong together. She's certainly smarter than I am, and a whole lot more dangerous if you happen to get on the wrong side of her. Like the guys who stole her kid. But I don't want to dwell on all that now.

When I think of it, it gets me crazy and then I think of how much I love her, how much she means to me, and it drives me nuts to think of all the hell we'd been through. She's an extraordinary woman and I know I don't deserve her.

So these were the dreams and thoughts I had in my head back then, fantasies of some sorta Mr and Mrs North for the nasty nineties, a Donald Lamb and Bertha Cool for the tail end of the stinking Twentieth Century, maybe even Nick and Nora Charles for the... ah... Now, who the hell was I kidding? No way we'd turn into people like those fictional detectives. We worked in the real world and the real world is nasty and evil and full of shit. We were two of a kind, Gayle and me, individuals, not characters made up by some screenwriter. Some guy who'd never experienced the shit, felt it deep in his bones. We felt it. Faced it every day. And if you don't know what I'm talking about you don't know life yet, my friend.

We were two maniacs on the loose. We like to hurt the people who like to hurt people. It's a kind of lifelong thing with the two of us. We'd been doing it for the longest time by ourselves, before we ever met, not really figuring it out totally. Now we understood it better, we did it together. Ridding the world of the slime that creates the evil, nurtures it, feeds it, and then tells us all it does *not* exist. The slime people who feed off the souls of the innocent. You see, it s the bad guys we love to mess up. I can't help it. That's just the way I am. Gayle's the same way. More so now since, well... since what happened with her son...

We're two peas from the same pod. Toxic waste and pure poison to the skells of this world.

I was happy. I finally got a job.

The job was in Brooklyn.

I should have known.

They say nothing is simple in Brooklyn. And more often than not they're right. It's a town where anything can get out of hand and explode in your face.

Crossing the damn street can be as dangerous as taking a dive off a mountaintop, with more fatal results sometimes. In some neighborhoods, if there ain't a dead body or two found on the street by sunup Saturday or Sunday, some people figure it was just a real dull weekend. They might be figuring that maybe the 'hood might of lost some of its excitement. And that's in the 'good' neighbourhoods.

I got a tip from Jack the Skell. Jack was an overweight, brain-dead postal worker who played the ponies like a fiend. He probably could have bought a chunk-size piece of Aqueduct racetrack with all the money he'd blown there over the years. Now all he had was a go-nowhere job and a basement apartment with a cot by an old noisy boiler. I could relate, except for the fact that Jack the Skell was a first class scumbag. He had a big mouth on him, if you had the cash on you to make him sing. The day Jack sang for me I wasn't paying. I didn't even want to hear what he had to say. I wasn't interested. I didn't want Jack the Skell anywhere near me.

'Hey, Vic. I got something for you,' he said in that raspy smoker's voice of his. Always with a cigarette dangling between his lips and an angle in his mind to get more cash out of some mark to blow at the track. I walked away. Ignored him.

He came on stronger than ever.

'Vic, man, come on. You'll wanna hear this and it won't cost you nothing.'

I sighed. Turned. Looked Jack the Skell in the eyes as he slowly and inevitably closed the distance between us.

'Really, man, what I got here...' Jack said, all of a sudden getting real quiet and looking around furtively, then whispering to me right there at the corner of 86th Street and Twentieth Avenue as if we were in the middle of church or something, 'This is really gonna blow your mind.'

I said, 'Okay, Jack, spill it if you want, but I ain't paying you a dime.'

He said, 'Vic, this is a freebie, you're not going to believe this shit, but...'

It was just about then that the bullet slammed into Jack the Skell's forehead. A tiny red dot instantly appear an inch above the spot right between his eyes. It got bigger. Fast. Jack was real surprised. So was I. And then the blood started to spout from his head like from a fountain as he sank down to the concrete like a balloon with all the air let out of it.

Another shot rang out, this one hit and split Jack's head like it was a big ripe tomato that had been thrown up against a brick wall. I looked to see where the shots came from. I scanned the doorways of the stores across the street, the windows, roofs, passing cars. Nothing.

Jack fell down dead, making a mess all over the concrete. All over my shoes. Jack the Skell. Scumbag. Blown away the one time in his life it appeared he actually tried to do someone a good turn.

Blood all over the street now.

Blood all over Jack the Skell too.

Blood in Brooklyn.

It was only the beginning.

While I waited for the ambulance and the cops I wondered what the hell Jack the Skell had been trying to tell me.

Thing is, it must have been pretty important shit for someone to blow him away in broad daylight, and right in front of me and a crowd of shoppers on 86th Street no less. I felt highly insulted about that. I figured Jack had been followed, that someone must have been watching him like a hawk. The minute it looked like he was going to spill the beans he was popped. Quick and professional.

The thing that got me thinking was that Jack was strictly a low-level guy. He never came across heavy-duty info, probably wouldn't even know it if he did. That's the thing, and that's what I figured could have happened. It was a hunch. And there was something else. It was most unlike Jack the Skell to give up anything valuable for free. Sort of against his religion, you might say. Info was his trade. He wasn't great at it, but he made ends meet. If he ever knew something that was heavy-duty he would milk it for all it was worth – unless he didn't know what he had.

I figured Jack the Skell might have been onto something big. Maybe he had some big-time tiger by the tail, stuff he wasn't sure of and had no idea how serious it might get. Either that or he did know what it was and it scared the shit right outta him. That kind of gave me a chill, wondering what it might be.

I watched as they picked up Jack from the sidewalk. A piece of skull here and a blob of brains there. Threw it all into a big black bag as the cops tried to keep the crowd back from enjoying the show. Cops telling them, 'Now there's nothing to see here, folks'. Nothing to see when a guy's head has been splattered all over a sidewalk of their neighborhood. Give me a break!

One of the better detectives, a guy I actually liked name of Fortuno, came over, scratched his head: 'Powers, what the hell happened here?'

I told him. He didn't seem impressed.

'And you say he never got a chance to tell you what he wanted to tell you?' Fortuno added, watching me closely.

'That's it. He never got it out,' I replied.

'And of course, you have no idea what any of this is all about, Powers?'

'That's right, Fortuno. I can't read minds and Jack ain't talking any more.'

He nodded, then was called away by a uniformed guy. I walked across the street to watch the show. Sorta get the big picture. Mingle with the crowd, watch them, looking for... what? I didn't know exactly. Maybe a face, some eyes, a nervous twitch that might tell me something. Maybe the killer was in the crowd watching the results of his work? It wouldn't be the first time. Happens all the time with pyros. Sometimes with killers too. I looked. There was nothing.

Of course it could have been that Jack had opened his big mouth just once too often. Or opened it to the wrong guy. Snitches never live too long even under the best circumstances, and snitches in Brooklyn could go down awful fast. In the end, I went logical, had to really, and put it down to some payback because of Jack's big fucking mouth.

I figured wrong.

Then I forgot all about it. Filed Jack the Skell away with all the other dreck.

A week later I was busy again. I'd gotten a case. Not much of one, but it was money. And it was fairly honest. I had to find a woman's husband who skipped on alimony and child support. The snake owed his wife $15,000, owed his kids $25,000. Hadn't paid a dime in over five years. I tracked him down, found out now he was a preacher in a church in Bay Ridge. I was there Sunday morning in the crowd while he was giving his sermon. Fire and brimstone. Talking family values. It made me want to puke.

I made sure it was him, then I left, disgusted. I waited for him outside the church on the steps with the message, an envelope from his ex-wife. I didn't know what was inside the envelope but she wanted me to find him and give it to him. Said it was important. After I did that I was done. Seemed simple enough. Not in Brooklyn.

After the Sunday service was over and most of the people were gone I walked over to Reverend Johnson. He sent his wife and kids away. New life, new wife, new kids. How nice. He motioned me down the steps to the sidewalk.

He said, 'How did you find me?'

'That's my job. That's why I get paid.' I handed him the envelope. 'This is from your wife and family – the ones you left behind.'

He gave me a dark look.

He reached for the envelope. Smiled at me, like, well like he was humoring me by accepting a letter from his ex-wife and kids. Like, whatever *they* had to say to him was all some big joke. He didn't give a damn. Couldn't care less. It was just a little show he was doing. I knew it and it pissed me off.

I didn't say a word.

He tore open the envelope with a snick along the edge. It was a ripping sound. It seemed to be all around us.

That's when it happened.

This time it was just one shot. Short. Sharp. A killing blow that tore open the reverend's chest, ripping out of his back like a cannonball, arterial blood spurting out all over the place.

He screamed and died as his family rushed over. I watched him drop, falling on his face. He never got to read the letter. His back was opened up with a hole big enough to drive a truck through. By a dum-dum bullet.

I looked for the shooter but it was like the world had eaten him up. Swallowed him whole. I only got a general direction on where the shot had come from, somewhere behind me where there were a dozen stores and apartment buildings. A hundred possibilities, but I knew the shooter was sure to be long gone by now.

Once again a man had been killed right in front of me.

Once again there was blood in Brooklyn.

Chapter Two

NORFOLK, VIRGINIA, 1964

They say a guy can be haunted by his past. I could see how that could happen. Hell, I was haunted by my past, present, and future. All rolled up into one stinking mess I couldn't see any way out of.

I went back in my mind, all the way back to Norfolk, Virginia. My brain sifting through the fog of time.

It was 1964 again.

It was kind of fun to be twelve again. I remember it like it was yesterday. There was election fever in the air back that summer. Barry Goldwater getting ready to be trounced by Lyndon Johnson. Everyone shouting 'All The Way With LBJ'.

What a bunch of jerks. They all voted for Johnson and he was promptly elected and sent all their sons off to go fight and die in Vietnam. But only the poor and black ones. Not the elite. Never the elite!

The World Series was going to be the Yanks again for sure. No one knew who the Nationals were going to put up yet, but it looked like the Cardinals. Did it matter? Everyone, but me and my brother hated the Yankees back then. This year they couldn't lose. Or so I thought. Of course the previous year must have been a fluke, Koufax and Drysdale had been just unstoppable on the Dodgers. But Hell, the Yankees had Mickey Mantle! All the Cards had was Stan the Man. Ricky told me that was enough. Me and my brother couldn't believe that.

It was just another end to another long hot Virginia summer, dozing away as the new school year came upon us. Like it did every year.

Soon I'd see all the kids from the year before, everyone tougher, meaner. Baseball cards and comic books making way for penny-loafers, Banlon shirts, trying to be cool, cigarettes, and of course, girls.

Of course girls had been around all the time, but for a lot of us guys it was the first time we really noticed them – or at least noticed them in that *special* way. Or at least, admitted that we noticed them in that special way. You'd a thought they'd dropped from outer space or something. Just landed on the Earth. Our Earth. Invaders from Mars. But they were okay once you got to know them. Usually.

What the hell, we were just kids. And pretty stupid and naive ones at that.

We used to pal around a lot that July and August before school resumed. The same way we did the previous June. Playing kickball in the school yard or street, talking and telling lies about what we did on summer vacation, bragging about all the secrets we knew about adult things like sex, when in reality none of us knew a damn thing about it at all.

But there was one kid who knew a whole lot. Maybe too much. And he wasn't talking.

That summer I made friends with a new kid down the block named Cliff. He was an okay kid but a little weird. Like so damn serious and so damn tough that everyone knew never to mess with him in any stupid way. One of the reasons we became friends was that I understood that and even respected it to a degree so all was well between us.

We got along okay too, hung around together, talked, played catch a lot those few weeks at the tail end of summer just before school started. I figured he wasn't a bad guy and we became buddies.

When school started I told Cliff I'd walk with him in the morning to class. Meet him at his house at 7:30 sharp, show him around. Introduce him to the kids, let him know who the bad guys were, show him how to avoid the older kids who always hit down on us younger ones. I didn't want to scare Cliff but I didn't want him to get smashed either. Things like that always happened the first day to new kids.

For some reason that didn't phase Cliff at all. He just wasn't concerned. Not concerned that the bad kids or some of the older kids were only just looking for fresh meat to pick on, to beat up, to smash into the dirt. Cliff just smiled like he couldn't care less. It bugged me. I told him to watch out, everyone in this school fought with everyone else. There was no reason to it. And most kids changed sides more often than they changed their underwear. Fighting was all that went on back then.

I wasn't a small fry, but I wasn't no big tough guy either. Anyway, none of that mattered because there was always someone bigger. Always someone tougher. And always someone crazier. Just like today. If not, there were plenty of kids there to jump you and beat on you in packs. No matter how good you were, how tough you were, you could never win a fight when it's five or ten against one. And that's just with the kids your own age – the big kids were worse. Four, five, six years older, that much difference in age means a hell of a lot when you re a kid. With me being just twelve back then, and barely in junior high, I didn't want no trouble from one or more sixteen to eighteen year old high school thugs. They'd throw you a beating you'd never forget. For sure hurt you bad physically. Mentally they'd smash you into the muck and laugh all the time they were doing it.

I remember telling things like this to Cliff. I knew that since he was the new kid, out-of-town Navy brat, they'd all be after him.

I said, 'You really got to watch what you say to these kids, if you don't want to get a beating.'

Cliff just shrugged, said, 'I don't care.'

I said, 'You'd care if you'd seen what's s been done to some of my friends around here, some of the other kids at school when the bad guys or the big kids caught them alone.'

'They won't bother me.'

'Oh yeah?'

'Yeah. That's what I'm afraid of,' he replied.

He was serious about it. Cliff was always serious. 'I don't understand what you mean, Cliff.'

Hell, I was only twelve back then, it's not like I could be expected to understand a lot of the shit the world had in store for us all. I let it go.

Cliff just smiled, said, 'Wait for tomorrow.'

Tomorrow became the here and now faster than yesterday had disappeared into memory. It was the day we all dreaded. The first day of a new school year.

A group of us were going to walk to Azalea together. That was the junior high school that was about three miles away from our homes. We were big, tough guys this year, finally. Seventh graders and in junior high. But it didn't matter. Laying in wait were most of the morons and troublemakers that had made all our lives miserable last year when they used to come down to our elementary school and beat us all up for fun. Or sometimes they'd set the place on fire, they liked to set fires. Other times they'd rampage the halls and trash the rooms.

Those were the kids we all called the animals from Azalea – the eighth and ninth graders – and now me and my friends were going to the same school as our worst enemies and we'd be seeing them there every single stinking day.

I tried to explain this all to Cliff the night before one more time. I tried to let him know what he was in for – what we were all in for. I said I'd stand by him, do the best I could to help him out but not to expect much from the other guys. They were all scared. Hell, so was I. But I wanted him to know that whatever happened it would be worse for the new kid. It was always worse for the new kid.

That morning I went over to Cliff's house but he wasn't out yet. I would have rung the doorbell but I didn't want his old man to answer. That guy scared me. He was a Chief in the Navy, and tough-shit mean. I thanked God he never seemed to be home. I didn't want to press my luck by ringing their doorbell. With my luck I'd probably catch him the only day he *was* home. So I waited. Patient. For a time. I didn't want to be late the first day, so I finally had to run up to the door to ring the bell. That was when Cliff stepped outside.

Something was very wrong.

Really weird.

Cliff stood there looking at me with a stone face like he wasn't even alive anymore. Like he was a robot or something. His eyes were black as coal but looked as though they threatened to burst into flame at any moment.

He had lipstick on his lips.

Like a, like a… girl.

His lips were painted red like everyone's mom, like the older girls at school. In his hair there were two pretty pink ribbons.

Pink ribbons?

It was all wrong. All weird.

'Don't laugh.' His voice was like a cold blade of ice that cut right through me.

I didn't laugh.

I didn't know what to do. What to say. Or what the hell to think. It wasn't funny. It was just real weird. Scary. This wasn't the Cliff I knew.

Of course I was just a kid back then, I didn't know anything about sex and stuff. Certainly not much more than the barest fundamentals. We did have a name for it though, we'd razz guys and call them sissys or fairys, and a few years later we'd call them fags or faggots but we didn't really know what the hell it was really all about. And it was after all, damnit, back in 1964 before anyone knew much about anything like this. All we knew back then was that it was a bad thing. So you'd use the words to hurt others, or defend yourself. But I just couldn't believe my buddy, Cliff, was a sissy or a fairy, or anything like that. It just didn't make sense to me.

Something was very wrong back there in 1964 but I didn't realize it until years later. And it had nothing at all to do with being a sissy, fairy, or faggot.

Which Cliff wasn't.

It was something worse.

I looked at Cliff, and I felt very sad for him, because I knew, even way back then, that there was more to this than met the eye.

I said, 'You can't go to school like that, Cliff!'

He said, 'You don't know how it is, Vic. I have to go and I have to do what I'm doing.'

I said, 'Come on, listen to me, you can't do this.'

And Cliff just said, 'Shut up, Vic', and began walking.

I didn't know what to say and knowing Cliff a bit I figured it was best to shut up for a while.

On the walk to school, before we met any of our friends, I figured I'd try to talk to Cliff and straighten him out. Find out what the hell all this was about. I knew that if the bad guys or the big kids ever saw him with lipstick on his lips and those pink ribbons in his hair they'd really beat the shit out of him. I didn't realize it at the time, but that was exactly what Cliff wanted.

Chapter Three

BROOKLYN, NEW YORK, 1994

I put Cliff and our childhood days out of my mind now. I had other things to consider in the here and now. I had a meeting with NYPD detective Fortuno outside the Federal courthouse downtown on Tillary Street, across from the remains of what had one been the old Brooklyn General Post Office.

That old post office at 270 Cadman Plaza East was an interesting building. I'd worked there temporary for a few months in-between 'Nam and the cops back in '72. It was a huge and ornate granite edifice, over a hundred years old, a genuine landmark of the borough. It took up an entire block of primo real estate in the most crowded business section of Brooklyn.

The part I liked best about it was the huge ornate tower where they used to hang prisoners in the old days. Closed to the public for decades, the tower was said to be haunted, but if you ask me the entire building was haunted. Haunted by all the postal workers who had worked there, lived there, and died there since before Brooklyn was a part of New York City.

Three weeks had passed and business was going from bad to worse. Fortuno had just appeared in a court case, said there was something on his mind that he wanted to talk to me about. About the murder of Jack the Skell and the Reverend Johnson. Both were still unsolved. Things that seemed so clear at first just didn't add up.

'So, what's up, Phil?' I asked Fortuno.

We were in the park across from the old Federal courthouse off Cadman Plaza West that has since been torn down. The park was a huge area filled with coffee-drinking office workers, kids out from school, and oldsters feeding bread to the millions of fat pigeons that owned the place. With pigeon shit all over everything.

Weeks before, John Gotti had been arraigned in the Federal courthouse across the street, black protesters starting a riot with the cops for his release. A big media circus and publicity event. Only in Brooklyn would black militants march for the Godfather of the Mafia and proclaim his innocence.

I looked across Tillary Street at the old General Post Office where Jack the Skell had worked for twenty years. I looked back at Phil. He had on his confused cop face.

He said, 'Vic, you're not going to like this.'

I shrugged, waiting for the other shoe to drop; it seems to be a lifelong situation with me.

I said, 'I don't like it already, Phil.'

'I been thinking about those two unsolved murders that you witnessed. I been asking around.'

I shrugged, laughed.

'Cops will do that, Vic. Sometimes. Anyway, at first I

figured Jack the Skell had someone after him, someone he'd figured. You know I like digging, Vic.'

'I know, Phil.'

'Someday, I'll dig a little deeper on you too, Vic.'

I swallowed, hard, said, 'So, are you going to talk to me, Phil, or just bust my balls?'

'You were a good cop once, Vic.'

'No I wasn't, Phil. Larry was the good cop. I just went along for the ride.'

'I've heard some talk about that ride, Vic.'

I didn't say anything.

'Thing is, Vic, when you take a ride on the hellbound train, if you got your eyes open, you'll notice that sometimes you ain't the only passenger. Get what I'm saying?'

I nodded, but I didn't have the faintest idea of where he was going with all this, and I liked it even less. But that's a lot of crap too, ain't it? I mean, I been on that train. Took too many damn trips. I can't even remember how far back it was when I first heard *All Aboard!*

It was a long time ago. Like when I was a kid.

Shit. I hated thinking back.

Phil watched me with his cop face. I hated his cop face.

'Come on, Phil, what the hell is this all about?'

Phil laughed. 'I always liked you, Vic. You know that? You're a crazy bastard but in your own twisted way, an honorable man. Usually. Or at least, sometimes. Hell, these days even a little honor goes a long way. With me. Look, I checked into those killings. On the surface they seemed to say one thing. You know, the logical thing. That's what I thought. I'm not so sure now. Sometimes, Vic, when dealing with crime, the logical thing can seem so real, so right, but the truth may be as far away from reality as Santa Claus. I seen it, here and there, on the job over the years. You know what I mean?'

I shivered in the warm sun. I knew.

'Vic, you know what I found out?

I nodded.

'Nothing.'

I kept walking, Fortuno had to work to keep up with me.

'I mean, there ain't shit or shineola anywhere on this. It don't make any sense at all.'

We walked over to the Brooklyn War Memorial, a huge marble monument that looked like a cross between the Parthenon and the Lincoln Memorial. Brooklyn-style. We walked over to a cement statue of a big naked guy holding a sword. It's a spot where gay boys meet at night, some of them selling themselves to old guys driving up in cars. When there ain't no sex action they steal the cars of night workers parked on Cadman Plaza West or Tillary Street at night. Or break in and rip off car radios, air bags, CD players, to buy drugs. It was a warm Brooklyn fall day. The perfect day for a walk and a talk.

I walked fast, Phil talked fast.

'I mean, Jack wasn't the most popular guy around but he was just low-level, even sorta tolerated by the boys, if you know what I mean. If someone had it in for him, it wouldn't of been a public hit like that, Vic. The guys he played with, if they were mad at Jack the Skell, Jack would have just disappeared, like off the face of the earth. Maybe end up in the cement foundation of some building, maybe turn up in a week or so in the trunk of a stolen Caddy. Deader than hell, and made up the way the mob likes to send its messages.'

I nodded. A bullet in the brain, and his cock cut off and shoved down his throat. Or up his ass. That kinda thing sends a definite message: nasty people were very pissed with the dead guy.

Phil was making sense.

'And I been checking, Vic. If someone with juice really had it in for Jack I would have heard about it by now. I might not be able to get an indictment, but I'd sure as hell have a suspect. There would at least be a hint in certain circles.'

'Yeah. So you got nothing.'

'A lot of nothing. And it ain't even like everyone's clamming up, like usual. It's just that no one gives a shit, because no one knows anything. It's, like, weird.'

'Okay,' I said. We walked through the trees to a more secluded end of the park. 'What about the Rev? Was it his ex? She was mighty steamed over all that money owed her.'

'That goes without saying, but now that he's dead she won't see a red cent. She had a real case, Vic, could have collected something on this. It doesn't make sense her offing him.'

'At least not *before* she got the money,' I offered.

'That's just it, Vic. After she got the cash – some big settlement he'd pay to stay out of jail, or to keep his name clean – well, then maybe. Not before.'

'What about the note?' I asked.

'The note you were to deliver to him from his ex-wife? Yeah, I saw that. The Rev never got a chance to read it. Did you, Vic?'

'No,' I said, 'but I was wondering about it.'

'No big deal, you know what it said?' Fortuno laughed, enjoying what was to come, 'You'll get a kick outta this, Vic. The wife wrote she'd turned lesbian! She wrote the fucking guy a note saying that he was such a lousy fuck he'd turned her into a cunt-lapping, bull-dyke lesbian! How you like that shit?'

'Was it true?'

'No, and when I asked her about it, she said she did it only because she wanted to hurt the stupid weasel's male pride for leaving her and the kids.'

I shrugged, 'No loss, he was a real asshole.'

'The wife is cute, though. Tough woman.'

'And where does all this lead you, Phil?'

Phil Fortuno looked me in the eye. 'That leads me to you, Vic.'

I just laughed. But real uneasy.

He shrugged. I didn't know what the hell *that* meant!

I said, 'Phil, in case you don't remember, I was with both guys when they were killed, no way I could have done the dirty deed. And if you think I hired someone, you're nuts!'

'Now, Vic, I didn't say that.'

'Then what the hell are you saying?'

Phil Fortuno shrugged, apparently unconvinced, perhaps a bit confused, playing the cop game with me. 'Vic, is there, like, maybe, someone after *you*?'

I had to really laugh at that. 'Take your pick, Phil. The usual crowd, plus a bunch I can't even tell you about.'

Phil Fortuno was quiet for a long moment, thoughtful. So was I. We walked in silence. I was thinking about Gayle, getting home to her later and rubbing my face all over her body. Wondering if she was wearing that short-short skirt. Not caring if she did or not when it came right down to it. Thinking about the two of us maybe taking a trip out to the Island for the weekend.

I didn't know what Phil was thinking, but he sure had something on his ever-loving cop mind, something bothering him about those killings. I just smiled at him, thinking, 'typical cop'. I know, I been there, but half a dozen people get killed every day in Brooklyn. I mean, like, what's the big deal?

But I knew Phil was a real cop, a cop's cop, and I remember that Larry had liked him a lot. So did I. And I knew that Phil, being a good cop, once he got something in his craw wouldn't let go until he solved it or it ate him up. A bad way to be. Except for a cop that wanted to get shit done. In that way, Phil was a typical cop. I'd been a cop too once, but hardly typical. But I understand how it is.

I was going to tell him not to make a big deal over it. Murder happens. Especially in Brooklyn. These two killings were unrelated, they were unsolved, and they'd probably stay that way. He shouldn't bust his hump over it. Maybe it was time for Phil to move onto some other murder. I figured the dead body cases must really be piling up if Phil was stuck on these two killings. I mean, Jack the Skell wasn't exactly high on anyone's list of priorities. And the Rev case was stalled.

The Brooklyn DA, another politically-connected hack, trying to make the case against the ex-wife when there was nothing to make. The case was full of holes and the DA would have been laughed out of court if he tried to pursue it. But there seemed to be some political mileage to be made from it so who knew where it would lead. Or when it would all end.

I was thinking of all this junk as we walked, looking at Phil Fortuno's dark face, large rings under his eyes, eyes that were red probably from loss of sleep and overwork. I noticed a red spot there between his eyes. It was so tiny. It was so small, so red, then I realized the red was blood, the blood spot growing as I watched. My shock instantly was mirrored in Phil's face as his eyes opened bug-eyed. Fear and confusion mingled with pain and anger as I pulled him to me and down to the ground.

I tried to cover him, to help him, but Phil was not talking. Instead he was groping for something in his jacket pocket. He pulled out an envelope and with his dying gasp pushed the crumpled paper into my hand. He smiled at me then. The smile frozen on his face. Goddamnit! Tears came to my eyes and I screamed.

'No! Phil! No!'

He never heard me.

I looked for the sniper but couldn't find a thing.

Lots of people came over. Cops came over and hassled me until they realized what had gone down.

The shot had been silenced, a small calibre bullet, and there was something else, it was a professional sharpshooter job. For sure.

The park had been full of people. Walkers and talkers, kids all over the place, ladies with strollers, dogs walking their masters, businessmen, lawyers from the courts, their secretaries eating breakfast, people buying hot dogs and Italian ice from vendors, trying to get out of the warm September sun. The trees leafy and green, swaying in the gentle breeze. And no sign of the sniper anywhere.

Phil Fortuno had been one of the good guys, one of my only friends these days on the cops. Now I felt I understood what he'd been trying to tell me, what he thought he had figured out about the killings. I knew that it had to be a progression, that the killer of Jack the Skell, the killer of the Rev, the killer of Phil was actually *my* enemy. Not theirs. A killer who figured he could do me the most harm by hurting the people around me – and as a logical extension of that, hurting the people I loved, and who loved me.

I was being haunted and hunted by some kind of progression killer! And I didn't want to think about where that progression would lead.

I got the message now. I gave my report to the officer on the scene, then I knew what I had to do.

I knew *what* the message was.

Murder.

Now I just had to figure out *who* the messenger was.

In the meantime I had to get home, get Gayle, and get the hell out of town.

I looked at the envelope Phil had given me. It was white. Sealed. No address or outside marking. I wondered where, how, he'd gotten it.

I opened it. Expecting a letter, or something.

There was nothing.

It was empty.

No, wait, it wasn't empty.

Inside were two little strips of cloth.

I took them out. Held them in my hand.

They were two little faded ribbons.

Pretty little pink ribbons.

'Cliff!'

Chapter Four
NORFOLK, VIRGINIA, 1964

He was serious. So damn serious. Always serious. He never smiled. He never laughed like a normal kid. Only that crazy Cliff-laugh of his. Like when he saw suffering. He thought that was cool. When he hurt someone or something, that's what he liked best! I think that's why I went after the scumbags of the world, I understood them, from since I was a kid. From Cliff. How evil they could be. How they love to destroy. I went to the Cliff school, and learned a lot back then. And graduated too. If you got out with your life, that was graduation. It's called survival.

Cliff just burned. And waited. And when it was time, he acted.

That was Cliff.

He was the first real psycho I'd ever met. Maybe not the worst, but definitely the first in a long line. We took a ride on the hellbound train way back in 1964. He was the engineer of the damn train. Or maybe the ticket taker. Well, something. Maybe it was just *his* train? I think that's what it was. It was Cliff's train.

He asked if I wanted to take a ride with him and I didn't figure anything bad about it back then. Cliff smiled, said, *All aboard*, Vic!'

And like a fool I jumped on board.

Cliff was bred and raised a certain strange way by his old man. The hard-ass Navy Chief who I hated. Who scared me whenever I saw him. Scared me bad. He scares me even now.

He reminded me of another guy, one who caught what I call the 'evil disease', years later. My own old man.

I don't know where pop had caught it. Maybe he caught it from Cliff's dad? Like it was some kind of bug you could catch like a virus? Like maybe it was just making its merry way through the suburbs of Norfolk, Virginia in 1964 like the damn plague.

I don't know.

I try not to think about it.

My own dad was dead now. I'd made sure of that.

So I could imagine how Cliff's crazy old man must have scared him. And yet, Cliff and him hung out together all the time when his dad was in port. Back then I was just a kid of twelve, I figured it was nice that Cliff could hang out so much with his old man. They were buddies. They had a rapport. Or something. I didn't know that it was a damn curse on the kid that would follow him around for the rest of his life.

It was a curse on the world too.

Like I say, being a snot-nosed kid of twelve back in 1964 I didn't figure out any of this stuff. I only knew something wasn't right. And it scared me.

Cliff said for me not to be scared.

Cliff said *he* was never scared.

Cliff laughed, said, 'Now we'll have fun. Watch this, Vic,' as the big kids came down the block. They noticed Cliff was wearing red lipstick and had pretty little pink bows in his hair. And they came on over.

My guts churned, I picked up a metal garbage pail cover and stood next to Cliff.

There were ten of them. Big kids. Looking for a fight. Fifteen and sixteen year old high school kids. They were bigger than us. Meaner. Some had hair on their faces. Some of them shaved. Like men! They smoked cigarettes. They wore dirty jeans. They were supposed to be in school, at Norview or out at Lake Taylor. This wasn't their territory. They shouldn't even be here. They were here for one reason, and one reason only.

'They're going to throw us a beating, Cliff,' I whispered, scared.

'I don't think so, Vic,' he said.

I said, 'If we run maybe we can get away.'

'Run? I'm not running, Vic, I'm gonna fight them.'

Now I was really scared.

The enemy moved in but Cliff held his ground.

I said, 'But we don't have to do this, Cliff!'

'I do', he said, and then he looked at me smiling, and added, 'so what will it be, Vic? You sticking? Or running?'

I sighed, and boarded the train.

There was no turning back now, the big kids surrounded us, jeering and laughing, blocking our escape.

Cliff said, 'Come on faggots, pussies, see if you can kick my ass!'

Not what I wanted to hear from Cliff at all just then.

Then again, it didn't matter, we were going to get the

crap kicked out of us anyway, it was really just a matter of degree. Back then, we never thought about getting killed, actually dying. That was TV stuff. But it could have happened. Easily. I saw one guy had a knife, others were picking up sticks. I held onto that metal garbage pail cover, ready to knock a few heads off with it before I was brought down.

I told Cliff, 'Come on, let's charge them!'

He said, 'Wait, let them come to us. Stand behind me Vic, I want to show you something.'

I didn't say anything, but Cliff moved in front of me, egging the big kids to move against him.

And they came forward. Playing with him, seeing his red lips and the pretty pink ribbons in his hair and calling him pussy and fairy, saying how they were going to fuck Cliff up the ass, cut his cock off, and shove that up his ass. How they were going to beat the shit out of both of us, calling us faggots and shit like that.

I didn't appreciate their words, and they sure as hell weren't true, but I was too scared and in no position to do much about them. I kept thinking, maybe some of our friends will come along and help us out of this? Maybe someone, an adult, a cop, anyone, would save us? Then again, I knew the truth – Cliff and I were goners.

Cliff kept taunting the big kids, and they taunted him right back. All the time they moved in closer. A kid named Paul, bigger even than the others, led the attack, and then all ten jumped Cliff.

From then on it was crazy. The train was out of control, jumping off the tracks, running at full speed like a bat outta hell.

The big kids were all over Cliff, and a bunch of them had him down, punching and punching like it would never stop. A couple came at me and I smacked them around with the metal cover, some of them fearful to come closer, but not really paying attention to me that much. They were really after Cliff. They wanted him bad. And they were getting him. Taking a piece at a time. Hitting him, throwing punches all over his body, using sticks and fists to lay into Cliff like I'd never seen anyone get a beating up to that time, and damn few beatings since, even to this day.

Cliff was a stone, taking it all. Down and bloody. The kid with the knife had cut him a few times, nothing so bad really, it was a tiny blade, but it sure looked bad. In the meantime they were still beating and punching.

Cliff just lay there, taking it all.

I shouted, hysterical, 'Get off him! Leave him alone!' slamming the garbage pail cover over the head of the kid with the knife, knocking him down. Then I hit him again, as hard as I could before I hit his friend, and then another kid next to him. One after the other. Hitting, banging, slamming, yelling to the big kids to leave Cliff alone.

'Get off him! I'll kill you all! Get the hell away from us!'

I couldn't fight them all off of him. There were too many and they just got more pissed and finally all came after me. In no time they had me down and were knocking me around.

'Cliff!' I shouted, 'Run away!'

I saw him on the ground. Just laying there. A stone, so serious, dripping his own blood, pus, vomit.

Then I saw him look at me.

And he... smiled.

While the big kids beat me, pummelling every inch of my body as I tried to dodge as many blows as I was able – I heard Cliff call out behind me, 'See, Vic, I told you this would be fun.'

The kids beating me up stopped for a moment and we all looked at Cliff. He was standing a few feet away from us. He was a bloody mess, but he was standing and he had that very serious Cliff-look. I was getting to know that look and it spelled danger. There was fire in him now, blood dripped from his nose, from his ear, from his eye – the one that was able to stay open – and then he came closer to me – closer to the big kids who were all over me.

The big kids saw him and were taken aback. Cliff looked bloody terrible, but also scary. There was something about him now that scared us all.

Cliff went right up to Paul, the biggest big kid, their leader and said, 'You hit like a faggot! Don't you know how to hit like a man? Let me show you pussies how to really fight!'

Well, Paul was surprised as all hell. So were we all. No one knew what to do or say.

Suddenly, Cliff was on Paul like a panther. Fast. Hard. He went right for the face and throat. Hitting Paul again and again. I heard a sharp crack, then Paul went down choking, trying to get his breath.

Well that did it. The other big kids were on Cliff in a flash, and he was on them right back. Just as fast and hard. Like a whirlwind. Looking like he was having the time of his life. Punching and kicking and hitting them in places that sent each kid down to the grass in pain. I saw more broken bones and bloody noses that day than I've seen in a year of Brooklyn bar fights. Cliff was after blood, he was insane with the fight, he was a fucking twelve year old boy and he was a stark raving madman kicking the shit out of ten kids who were all bigger than he was. He knew precisely where to place each blow to obtain maximum damage on his enemy. I don't know where he learned to fight like that, but he seemed to know every move, every trick in the book. And many that weren't in any book.

It happened so fast. I watched, stunned. Most of the big kids eventually ran away. They actually ran away! Scared. Three were on the ground unable to run, one with a broken bone, another with a broken nose that was bleeding like Niagara Falls, and then there was Paul. He was unconscious.

I watched as Cliff took out a scissors. I didn't even know he had scissors. I remember wondering, why did he have scissors? Why hadn't he used them to protect himself? I sure would have. I didn't understand back then. I had no idea what was actually going on. I thought Cliff and I were in a fight for our lives. I know *I* was. The ten big kids thought they were going to have an easy beat-up spree. At our expense. They didn't. What looked like an hour of fun and games for them turned out to be just a set-up. *They* were the ones that never had a chance.

Cliff walked over to Paul. Paul was unconscious. I thought Cliff had killed him, but I didn't care that much back then after all the beating we'd taken. I figured the hell with Paul, and all the big kids. Anyway, he was still breathing so how bad off could he be? It wasn't like he was bleeding, like the other two kids laying on the ground. Both of whom were whimpering in pain.

Then Cliff went over to Paul and began cutting the hair from his head. Like, giving him a haircut. I couldn't believe it. In five minutes he'd reduced Paul's head of longish hair to a bald, sickly white, unevenly crew-cut dome. It was a mess. Like Paul was some escaped mental case or something.

Cliff kept the hair and put it in his pocket.

Even back then he was collecting trophies.

Next, Cliff went over to the other two kids. Ernie was the guy with the broken nose. A lot of blood, and there was also something wrong with his foot.

Cliff looked down at Ernie and smiled. It was a terrible thing to see. Ernie was scared. So was I.

'What do you want?' Ernie muttered, between sobs of pain.

Cliff said, 'Tell me you love me and that you want me to fuck you up the ass.'

It would have been funny if Cliff hadn't been so serious when he said it. So crazy-serious.

Ernie turned white, didn't say a thing.

Cliff smiled, moved Ernie's leg so that it was wedged between the street and the curb, then jumped up and down on it until there was a resounding crack.

Ernie screamed, shouting, 'You broke it! You lousy bum!' He cried in agony, and I saw a bit of white bone protruding from his leg.

Ernie was in terrible pain. Screaming now. Cursing. Panicky. Blood all over.

Cliff nodded, like it was good, then he went over to the other kid. This was Joe, big but not too smart. He had a broken leg, had been laying still but after what he'd just seen done to Ernie he was scared shitless now.

Cliff grabbed Joe by the throat, holding him tight with one hand, while his other hand covered his mouth and nose. Holding it hard and tight. Joe, who had struggled at first, now lay silent and still. Sweating and whimpering. Waiting.

'Leave him alone, Cliff,' I said.

'Shut up, Vic!'

I saw that Cliff lived for this. This was his thing.

He told Joe, 'If you don't tell me that you love me and want me to fuck you up the ass right now, I'm going to stick my fingers up your nose and rip it right off your face!'

'Cliff!'

'Vic, this is what happens to losers! You think if they won they'd have treated us any better?'

I didn't say anything. I wasn't sure about things like that back then. But Cliff and me were friends so I stood by him. Looking back on it now I realize that the big kids weren't as bad as they seemed. Not as bad as Cliff made them out to be. Hell, they weren t nowhere near as bad as Cliff! They were bad. But Cliff was something else. Cliff was... just so beyond them.

I didn't know what the word for it was back then. The word for it in the bible seemed so remote, unreal, like it wasn t something that could really be happening today. But it was something I've found in daily life, every damn day. Strong and fierce as ever, and more personal than the old words written in the bible. It's with us every day if you know life. It's out on the street, in the schools, on the news every night. The enemy. Stronger and meaner than ever.

Finally Joe said what Cliff had wanted him to say. After he said it, Cliff dug his fingers into Joe's nose, pulled as hard as he could, and blood gushed out all over the place. Joe screamed while Cliff kicked him and cursed him.

'Tell your friends, they ran away today, but I'll find them! I'll get every one of them! They think they can run away from me but no one – *no one!* – ever gets away from me!'

Then Cliff laughed at him. A vicious laugh that scared me even more than the fight had. I mean, back then, it was just kids. Fights were every day things. Punches and kicks, a few bloody noses and maybe a broken bone.

Rough stuff to be sure, but not nasty, not deadly. Not sick like this. Even the big kids weren't that bad. This was different. This was something I'd never seen before. I knew that Cliff really liked it a lot. He grooved on it. The hurting. The torture. It was his thing. I only learned later on when I grew up what it was.

It's called evil.

Cliff was really into it.

That had been the first of many rides on the hellbound train for me. I began to think, maybe I had a lifetime ticket or something? I mean, I've taken trips on that damn train way too many times in my life. But back then with Cliff, that had been the first time. They say you always remember your first time. In all things. I certainly did. A fun little journey, compliments of Cliff, way back in 1964.

★

Now I was back in 1994, and Cliff was bringing the train into the station once again. I saw him at the controls, easing the train down the tracks. Towards me. And me having no choice. No choice at all now.

I heard *All aboard!* somewhere in the back of my mind once again and thought, if I can't get to Gayle in time and get us both the hell out of here...

I didn't even want to think about it.

I rushed home, my thoughts full of a dead cop and a mounting pile of corpses. A Progression killer, and that progression just naturally leading to my wife, Gayle, as a target.

And I thought of Cliff, thirty years later, now a grown man. What would he be like? What would he be capable of?

Monster was the only word that fit.

And monsters are capable of anything.

I froze up, scared shit for Gayle, driving like a maniac back to our small apartment in Bay Ridge. I took the spare gun out from under the dash where it was hidden. It wasn't legal but I didn't give a shit. I parked the car in front of the small house. So far everything looked cool. I took a deep breath, shielded the gun with my body as I ran up the steps and into the hallway. No one was there. It was a warm September day and no one was out. Air conditioners going all over the place.

I thought, okay, maybe I'm jumping to conclusions.

I knew I wasn't. Not where Cliff was concerned.

I left the elevator and took the steps three at a time. Got to my door, opened it slowly, gun in hand, ready to kill anything that got in my way.

I didn't hear anything.

The lights were on, the air conditioner going softly in the background.

No Gayle, saying, 'Is that you, honey?'

I got nervous and called out. 'Gayle?'

I entered the living room. Looked around carefully. Everything looked just as I'd left it. But that didn't mean anything where Cliff was concerned either. I looked in the back bedroom, the spare room, the master bedroom. No sign of Gayle. I thought: maybe she's out somewhere. Shopping? Something?

Then I saw the two pretty little pink ribbons laying on the kitchen table.

And I knew.

Gayle was gone and Cliff had her.

Chapter Five

BOCA GRANDE, NEW MEXICO, 1990

My mind was time-tripping again. Thinking back. Remembering. About how I'd met Gayle.

I left the car back there. On the dirt road outside Boca Grande. The New Mexico sun would probably melt the damn thing into slag before I could ever get it fixed. It was just as well. It was too hot to fuck around with the thing, better to just leave it and walk. But was it hot! I mean, it was like those Foreign Legion movies where the desert guys look up at the sun and it burns right into their face. It wasn't like the sticky, slimy New York City heat I was used to – here there was no moisture at all; which was good, because it must have been over one hundred degrees, easy. And that was in the shade. Still and all, it was pretty rough, not what I was used to; unrelenting heat, coming at me in searing waves of burn that hit me like a hammer. This was the south-west, where the sun gets its revenge on us northerners.

I was walking through the desert and toward town. It was along a thin strip of highway that led to Boca Grande. Big Mouth, in English, or Anglo. Nice name for a town, if you like a pimple on the ass of a shit pile. It was a small sleepy hamlet of oldster retirees, Mex poor, and farmers with guts so big that you just knew when they took a piss they couldn't even see their weiners. Most of them fat, good old boys who probably hadn't even seen their weiners in years. I figured they hadn't much use for the damn things in a place like Boca Grande. It was too much a home-town place. No action to speak of. I didn't like it but I figured to stay a while. I needed to recharge. Regroup.

I'd been through a lot of heavy crap the last year or so. Beat-up, burnt-out, drugged-up, wore-out, damn near killed myself a dozen times – killed a dozen damn people back along the way. Don't worry about that though, it was no one you'd want alive anyway. Drug dealers, mob guys, a crooked cop… I didn't even want to think about the Lovely Sisters… and lastly some little twisted lunatic psycho bitch that tried to kill me in a no-tell motel back in Ohio.

She'd really pissed me off. Now she's doing the eternal sleep in a dumpster and good riddance. It had been self defense: she'd tried to murder me in my sleep, and when I woke up and caught her at it, she tried to do it again. One of those single-minded types. Persistent, for shit-sure. It had been self defense. But no one would have believed me. So I just let it be. We all must move on. So I moved on too. I moved just as fast as I could these days.

I was sitting in one of those small eateries, at an outside table, under a big, once brightly-colored, but now badly faded, awning. Sipping a beer, waiting for the waiter to bring me my food. I was thirsty, and hungry, and tired, and thirsty all over again.

As I sucked down the first of many beers I looked over the dirty town square of Boca Grande, the small dun-colored buildings, and the rugged, deeply furrowed faces of the locals. They eyed me back, wondered. I looked back at them, winked. They smiled and moved off.

Not bad people. Not bad at all. I was getting to like this place. No one here seemed to bother anyone. Amazing in America these days. But I knew it couldn't last.

Then *she* had to come and ruin it all.

Or so I thought at the time.

I didn't really notice her at first. What I remember first off was the click of her high heel shoes on the wooden planks of the sidewalk. Click-click. Click-click. Coming closer. Short, meaningful strides, a serious walk, a power walk if ever there was one.

I sighed. I smelled trouble.

Then I saw her.

It was hard to explain. I liked her right off. Right away. She was deep. I could see that. An authentic *woman*, not some hot little vacant chippie, though she was certainly pretty damn hot in her own way. I could just tell she was a multifaceted person, intelligent, educated, sharp, but I could see that there was a light, fun side to her, a laugh-at-herself, laugh at the world, devil-may-care attitude. A sense of humor. Even better, there was a deep and serious womanly warmth about her. She cared. About people. About ideas. About herself. Maybe even about me. I could tell these things from that one look, or at least, that's what I felt about her.

Or that's the image she showed me.

Was it real? Fake?

I know she was dangerous. A real R.I.S.K. for sure.

It was one of life's weird little things. I knew I'd have to find out about her, find out if I was right or wrong about her. Eventually, I'd have to know. Hoping I'd discover that I wasn't wrong, and even more nervous of what that might mean.

I also felt something else. She was a serious pro and in the business.

And that got me scared. Here was real danger. I knew I should stay away from her.

All I could do was look at her and smile as she came over.

'My name is Gayle. Gayle Armstrong. I'm new in town. Do you mind if I join you?'

I told her, 'Look lady, I don't know who you are or what the hell you want but you'd just better get the fuck away from me!'

I laugh when I think about it now, years later.

It was so touching. It was our first words.

She'd just laughed too back then. Ignored my words. Sat down. Looked deep into my eyes and said, 'The little psycho bitch you threw in the dumpster? You were very lucky, Vic. She's done three guys that I know of.'

I didn't know what to say. I couldn't figure out how she knew. 'Who are you?' I asked.

'Oh, don't worry, I know it was self defense. I'm private, I was tracking her for a client. See, you weren't the only guy she'd tried to murder in his sleep. That was Delilah's thing. She just wasn't successful with you. I'm working for the family of one of the guys she *was* successful with.'

I sighed. The waiter brought my food. By now I wasn't hungry. I ordered another beer. I ordered one for Gayle. I figured that we had a lot of stuff to talk about. I don't know how she knew so much, but she sure as hell knew it.

I smelled trouble all over the place.

She wanted me to do something for her.

I said, 'So? What is it? What do you want me to do?'

She just laughed, smiled, it was nice to see. She said, 'My, you're so serious. Are you always only interested in business, Mr Powers?'

'Look, lady, you seem to know an awful lot about me. Knowing that kind of stuff about some people would be a sure guarantee of a trip to the bone yard for you.'

'But you're not like that, Mr Powers,' she said.

'Don't be so sure,' I replied.

But she was sure. She was so damn sure. Sure about me. I kinda liked that, but it was still bad news when they know you too well. Or think they do.

I laughed, said, 'You think you're going to rope me into something and you're sure as hell not. Understand? After I finish this beer I'm getting up from this table, getting out of this stinking town, and I'm never going to see you again. And I'm warning you now, lady, stay the fuck away from me!'

She laughed back, not giving an inch, not intimidated at all. 'I know all about you. That's why I'm here. After you finish your beer, I want you to come with me to my hotel room. It's just across the street. I want five minutes of your time. I want to tell you something and show you something. If after five minutes you want to leave, you can go away and I'll never bother you again.'

I sighed. She looked so nice, long blonde hair, big eyes, so stern but soft, but I could see that hardness in them just the same, like steel ball-bearings.

Damn!

She had on a tight short dress, dark colored, a pretty

top, she looked businessy, not sexy, but she was sure-damn sexy in a smart way. She was classy. Not fake high-class, but classy all the same. She could sling hash in a Skell joint and make the place look like the Ritz.

I didn't like this one bit. I knew I had it bad. And while I knew it was best for me if she just went away and I never saw her again, I didn't want her to go away.

'Look, I don't know what you have in mind. I'm not a cop anymore, far from it, and I'm not private, not really. I can't help you out. '

'Please, Vic, just give me five minutes. Let me say my peace and it'll be up to you to do whatever you want,' she said softly.

'I, ah, look, Ms Armstrong...'

'Call me Gayle, Vic.'

I sighed again. Doing that too much lately. I downed the beer in a long chug. It was already warm and tasted lousy. I got up to leave.

'I'm sorry, Gayle,' I said, and I walked away from her.

She got up and came after me, 'Vic, don't be such a hardheaded fool! I need you!'

'Lady, I don't even know you!'

'But I know you, Vic. I know you, maybe even better than you know yourself.'

I stopped, looking at her head-on, in the middle of that damn street in Boca Grande, 'You don't know shit!'

'Yeah? That's what you think! I know you're not the murdering creep you think you are. I know, that as twisted as you are, you'd never, *ever*, do anything to hurt me. And Vic, I know something else. Something that you'll never admit. I know you want me, want me more than even you know – but you're just too damn pussy scared of me to admit it!'

'Fuck you, Gayle!'

'No, fuck you, Vic! Run away! I need you, Vic, and now you're going to run away?'

'Oh, Jesus Christ!'

I stood there. Looking at her. She looked so beautiful. The hot sun playing off her face and eyes and all that light blonde hair, and then she smiled, and I just knew I was in trouble and I'd lost it.

I sighed again. 'What's your room number?'

'It's number three, Vic. Come along with me and I'll show you.'

Chapter Six

BOCA GRANDE, NEW MEXICO, 1990

I had planned on only giving her five minutes. And that real grudgingly.

Man, what a jerk I had been! Here was the one woman I knew I wanted to spend the rest of my life with, and to my Stupid warped way of thinking back then I was only prepared to give her five lousy stinking minutes of my miserable precious time. Life can sure be weird at times. Damn silly, too.

When we got back to her room Gayle sat me down in a chair by the table in the kitchenette.

She said, 'Thanks for coming, Vic.'

I laughed, said, 'You didn't give me much choice.'

'I know. I can be so hardheaded sometimes. Like when I see a man I like. If I want him, I'll usually get him.'

I didn't say anything.

'But that's not why you're here, Vic. You're here because I want to tell you something, and show you something. And because I need your help.'

'Okay, so let's get down to it.'

Gayle walked over to a dresser and took out a large manila envelope. She opened it and took out some eight by ten photographs. She put one down on the table in front of me. The photo showed an old man with some indistinct but very ethnic features to his face, white hair, piercing eyes.

I recognized the face. A very bad man.

'You know him, Vic?'

'No.'

Gayle smiled. I got the feeling she could see right through me. Read me like a book.

Knew that I was lying, but was going to go along with my little game for the moment at least.

She said, 'His name is Alberto Constintine. He's very powerful, very influential, but in a behind-the-scenes kind of way. He's also a very vile and evil man. He's the man who recently bought my contract from my former employer. Now he's my boss. I work for him.'

I'd heard of the Constintine group. Bad people, shit-deep in a bunch of rackets that were full of bad people.

'Never heard of him,' I said.

Gayle just smiled, said, 'Oh, Vic, that's what I like about you. You play the hand to the end, whatever's been dealt you, bull it through like a typical hardhead even when the game is up.'

I didn't want to start in by saying I had no idea what in the hell she was talking about – especially since I think I did have an idea what she was talking about and that she might have been right.

This Gayle Armstrong had class, and she had style, and I was beginning to understand why I liked her.

Then Gayle took out another photo. Set it down carefully in front of me. Almost lovingly. It was a body shot. Looked like a boy of about two or three years old. Cute as the dickens. Blonde hair like Gayle. Blue eyes like her too.

'Your son?'

'Joey. He's going to be four next month.'

'Nice kid,' I said.

Gayle didn't say anything. It was strange. Her silence.

I was waiting for her to continue but she couldn't seem to be able to go on. I could see that she was losing it. She was under some tremendous pressure, terrible strain, impossible stress. Like a boiler ready to burst. She wanted to say something but the words just wouldn't come out. And then the tears came. Her eyes grew big and red and tears ran down her cheeks. But she didn t cry. She didn't say a word. She just pulled out another photo from the envelope and set it down on the table in front of me. This time it was a photo of someone I knew very well.

It was me.

Me!

I looked at it. A surviellance close-up. Caught somewhere in NYC.

A photo of me!

Why did she have a photo of me?

I began to get a very bad feeling about all this.

Constintine? The boy? And me?

I didn't want to figure this the way that it looked to me just then, but it sure looked like Gayle was kinda giving me a message. A weird message. And at least part of that message said that Constintine had put my ass under contract and that Gayle was to perform the hit.

I really didn't want to believe that. I thought, hey, maybe I'm just jumping to conclusions here? But I wasn't. I knew what it was. I hoped it was something else but I knew what it was. I actually liked Gayle. I didn't want her to try and kill me. I didn't want to have to kill her. I hoped there was something else to all of this. There damn well better be something else here!

There was.

It was about the boy.

I said, 'Okay, Gayle, you'd better spill it all. No more bullshit '

Then she started talking. Real fast. I could see how hyped up she was. How scared. But not for herself. Not for anything she feared I might do to her. She didn't seem to fear for herself at all. Which in her position, seeing as how she'd practically admitted she was out to perform a hit on me, could be seen by some to place her in a bad situation. Like she'd be dead before she hit the floor.

But Gayle was right, about me, and about a lot of things. She'd told me I wasn't the type, and that I'd never hurt her. And the funny thing is she was so damn right.

The five minutes I'd given her were up. I said, 'Look, try to relax and tell me the whole story from the beginning.'

'I need your help, Vic!'

'I know, Gayle.'

'They've got him!'

'Calm down. Sometimes it helps if you take a few slow deep breaths.'

'I know. Believe me, Vic. This isn't the first time I've let it affect me like this.'

'I know,' I said.

'I just can't help it sometimes,' she said.

'Just tell me about it.'

She tried taking those slow deep breaths. Calming down, the tiny beads of sweat disappearing off her face.

In a few minutes she was more steady. I opened a can of coke from the hotel's wet bar. Gave it to her. She didn't drink it, just held the can. Held it just to be holding onto something.

'First off, you lied to me back there, Gayle. I want the truth, the whole truth.'

She was thinking. A bad sign.

'You can be one nasty fuck sometimes, Vic!' she said.

'Ah, thanks. I try.'

'No you don't, Vic. You don't even have to try.'

I sighed, 'Yeah, I guess you're right. It comes sorta natural to me. When I gotta put up with bullshit. Know what I mean?'

'Yeah, I guess I do. I'm the same way sometimes. Hell, who am I to complain, I kill scumbags for a living, to put food on the table for me and my son, so I guess I shouldn't be playing that pot calling the kettle black bullshit.'

'Yeah, Gayle.'

She nodded.

'You were following *me*, not Delilah, right?' I began, trying not to accuse her, but serious now for what I needed most. Truth.

She took a deep breath, said, 'Don't hate me, Vic.'

'I don't hate you, Gayle. Just tell me.'

'You were supposed to die out in Ohio. They wanted it done anywhere out of New York State and that was where I picked up your trail. I'd been looking for you for weeks. Caught up with you in western Jersey, and watched you for a week. Wire taps. They gave me a file on you two inches thick. It made interesting reading on lonely nights before I picked up your trail. I didn't know that you'd been a cop once. So had I, Vic. And we'd both quit. You forced out, me leaving because I couldn't take the bullshit and corruption anymore.'

I sighed, 'But how did you get involved...?'

'In this business? Not that hard, really. Some bad people had some stuff on me. I'd made a foolish mistake years back when I was young. Now I had a new baby boy. My employer threatened to expose me if I didn't work for him. I had to do what he told me. I thought about it. The pay was good, as opposed to some sure jail time if I didn't do what they wanted and they told on me. But the jail time didn't bother me. What really bothered me was the idea of losing my son. If I was arrested they'd take my son away from me. For sure. I couldn't deal with that. So I shut up, took the money, and kept my son.'

She stopped, took a drink of soda. Remembering.

I shrugged, no sense now in stupid recriminations. 'I can understand that,' I said, not even able to tally up all my own mistakes, stupidities, screw-ups over the years. Who the hell was I kidding – even over the last few months!

Gayle put the soda down, 'I would get a call once in a while for a job. Not very often. They saved me for special events. They were all hits on local thugs and mob guys. They were real scumbags. I didn't mind. I felt I was doing society a favor by offing them, and the money was good. When I got the call for the hit on you I refused. You weren't a part of any mob, and you'd been a cop. I couldn't do that. I told them so. It was a big mistake.'

'You can't refuse these guys,' I said. Remembering how they worked, how they thought.

'No. Constintine wouldn't hear of it. That night when I went home, Joey was gone. Insurance so they could be sure I would do the job.

'To kill me?' I said.

'Yes, Vic.'

I swallowed hard. Not because of Gayle's admission

that she was supposed to kill me, but because of the kid, Joey. I didn't want to tell her what was really on my mind about that. Often, when certain events are set in motion, they can't be called back. Not forgiven. Not forgotten. Threatening someone to do a job is one thing, insuring they do it by kidnapping her son is quite another. It can't be let go or forgotten by those involved. Either side. It's almost a law of nature, like some kind of mathematical equation. Just as sure. Just as true. And once shit is set in motion it finds its own level to settle down into alignment. Shit was in motion now. With Gayle. Now with me. And with her kid too. That was worst of all. I didn't want to tell her what I really thought about it.

I didn't say anything. Gayle said it for me.

'You're a good man, Vic.'

I said, 'There's gotta be a way outta this.'

'You're good for not telling me what you really think. But it s okay, Vic, I'm a big girl. I know how things work.'

'Then you know? Even if you kill me?'

She smiled. Crooked, forced, sad. 'I'm not going to kill you, Vic. Ever. I understand. I know. Joey is probably already dead. And so am I, whether I take you out or not.'

I nodded, 'It's the way they work.'

I walked over to her, held her in my arms. She began to cry, and so did I. We held each other a long time. Together. Tight. Our hearts beating against each other. Strong. Fast. Powerful. Two hearts beating together. As one.

'Will you help me, Vic?' she whispered.

I said, 'Gayle, the five minutes you asked me for was up a long time ago.'

'But you're still here.'

I smiled, 'Yeah, baby, like you say, I'm still here.'

★

I helped her.

I did the best I could.

It didn't turn out to be good enough.

We both took care of Constintine. That wasn't as hard to do as you'd think. Or even as hard as Constintine and his guards thought. Surprise on them!

Joey was a different matter. I honestly figured him for dead but we never found a body. Not surprising. Even in the mob killing a kid is taboo. Or at least, it used to be. I figured the body would show up, sometime, maybe a few weeks from now, maybe a few months from now, maybe in a few years they'd find some bones somewhere and identify them? Maybe not.

It was a waiting game I didn't want to play, and I didn't want Gayle to be playing it either.

It wasn't easy.

Some of Constintine's people remembered the little boy, the cute little boy that was a 'guest' for a few days, then all of a sudden he was gone. Never seen again.

One guy admitted to me in a bar that he'd been ordered to kill the kid, but later while I was strangling the life out of him, he began to deny it all. Said it was just a story. He was trying to play the tough big shot. Some big shot, bragging about killing a kid! I asked him where he'd thrown the body, and when he didn't answer me I broke his neck. Snapped it with a resounding crack.

Gayle and I checked all the area police and missing

persons, all the Social Service agencies and adoption centers, everything we could think of. We looked through reams of heartbreaking photos of dead children discovered throughout the country. No Joey. He had just disappeared.

It tore Gayle apart. And it tore me apart to see her torn apart like that.

It took us years to get past Joey. Even then we were never fully past it, he was always with us. But we both knew we had to go on. We mourned and moved on. As best we could. It wasn t easy, but it had drawn Gayle and me together since that first day in Boca Grande, and we still held together as tight and strong as ever. At least we had each other, and in a stinking, lonely, lousy world such as ours, having someone who loves you and who you love is a lot more than most people ever get.

Now Gayle and I were talking about having our own child. I figured, hey, maybe I'd have a son. A little Vic junior! Oh my God!

Except now, Gayle was gone.

Taken from me. Just when we'd both gotten our lives in some kind of order, along had come the murder of Jack the Skell, The Rev, and Fortuno. And now Gayle was gone.

And Cliff had her!

And there was nothing I could do about it now. I sat down quietly at our kitchen table. The same table where Gayle and I had eaten a thousand meals, the blank whiteness of the table top so clean, so pure, so empty, but in the center were two little pretty pink ribbons.

Cliff's calling card.

I waited.

I knew the phone would ring. Sooner or later.

I knew that scumbag would get in touch with me.

Chapter Seven

NORFOLK, VIRGINIA, 1964

I tried not to think about things. Trying to keep my mind free and loose, in the here-and-now. I didn't want to think about Cliff. What he had become.

I didn't want to think about Gayle. Or the incredible danger that she was in.

I didn't want to think about what the hell Cliff's sick little game was either. Or what the hell I was going to do about it. But I couldn't help it. Cliff had killed three people so far, all brazenly, arrogantly, right in front of me. Now he'd kidnapped my wife. I couldn't understand it. Couldn't figure his game or why he had it in for me after all these years. Obviously though, he did have it in for me. I just couldn't figure it yet.

I knew I'd have to go back. Look at it all again. See it all again. Relive it in my mind. I hate doing that. I hate going back there.

I tried to put it off. I sat there waiting for the phone to ring. Cleaning my gun. Cleaning it again and again. Finally, my mind began tripping back in time. To when Cliff and I had been kids. Best friends. To what had happened so far back long ago between us. To make us enemies.

There had been a blow up. I remember now. We'd been friends. And after the fight with the big kids, after I'd stuck with Cliff, taken a beating and given a beating alongside him, Cliff told me I was okay in his book. His book? The book of beating?

I don't know, I never minded a good fight, not even today, and when we'd been kids back then that's all we ever did. Fighting was a way of life. But with Cliff it was different. It was his god. Even back then. There was something very wrong with Cliff.

He was a monster in training.

Of course, the next day after our fight with the big kids, the first thing Cliff did was go after the other seven big kids, the ones that had run away. I went with him. After all, they'd jumped both of us, and hurt each of us badly. These guys deserved what they got from us. They had it coming. Maybe they even deserved Cliff.

We ambushed them. One by one. Tracked them down, jumped them, and then beat the shit out of them. It was business-like. I usually just hung out while Cliff did the work he loved doing so well. Sometimes I'd fight the kid's friend, or hold back other kids from interfering with Cliff. He didn't like interruptions.

Cliff ended up giving each of the kids a good beating. And afterall, it was only what they each deserved. What really bothered me was that once they gave up, once they surrendered, well, that was when Cliff really swung into action. That was when the beating really began for him.

His fun. And it was terrible. Sickening. There was no honor or mercy in any of it.

By that time we'd caught six of the seven and I was sick of it all. I figured we were finally at the end of the situation. That is was finally all over. I never realized that it was only the beginning. That now the hellbound train was headed in a whole new and much more nasty direction and that Cliff was sitting at the controls up in the cab with the throttle wide open and full speed ahead.

The seventh big kid was named Mikey. Mikey was a little weasel no one liked and no one feared. He was hardly worth our trouble and I tried to talk Cliff out of going after him.

'Forget it, Cliff, he ain't worth it. He's nothing.'

'He hit me, Vic. He hit you. He was in on the fight from the beginning. You know that. You should know better. He wanted to fight and beat us up, and his side lost. Now he's got to be made to pay.'

'Why don't we just drop it? He's nothing.'

'More the reason, Vic. Teach him a lesson,' Cliff laughed. Still serious. Anticipating. Giving me that Clifflook of his that I knew only meant trouble.

I shrugged. Back then, maybe Cliff was right. Hell, maybe he was right for today too? I mean, a lot of little weasels mouth off or do all kinds of lowlife crap to hurt people because they know they can get away with it. Because they got the law, or might, or money, or daddy, or the boss on their side. Usually there's no one mean enough, bad enough, or with balls enough to fuck them up for all the damage they do. Too bad. They deserve it. Someone like that, might teach them to be a little more careful, a little more respectful. You know what I mean?

So I said, 'Okay, Cliff, I'm with you. Let's fuck him up and then it's all over.'

I figured then it would be over and we could all get together and play ball, like we did every year at this time.

Cliff just laughed.

He wasn't interested in sports.

I didn't realize something Cliff knew so well. Nothing is ever over, nothing ever ends, when you're a lunatic. The craziness had only just begun.

★

Mikey was scared. He was hiding. He sent his fifteen year old sister to talk to me, try to talk me out of what Cliff and I were going to do when we caught him alone. Namely beat the living shit out of her brother.

I liked Mikey's sister, but I told her Mikey had to get the beating. He deserved it. It was right that he got what was coming to him. She understood. Kids were like that in those days. She just told me not to hurt him too much.

I told her I'd just smack him around a little. Sort of set him straight.

'And watch Cliff, okay? Please? You can beat up Mikey, Vic, I don't mind if you do that. But don't let Cliff go near him. He's not like you.'

I asked what she meant by that.

'Vic, I like you, but you can be bad sometimes. But that s okay. That's normal. Almost. Cliff is different. Much worse. He *likes* to hurt. He enjoys it. Enjoys it too much. I've seen him in fights. He fights harder when a kid gives up. He's an evil bastard and I hate him!'

A couple of Mikey's friends tried to talk me out of catching Mikey and beating the crap out of him. I could have gone for forgetting the whole thing, it was getting to football season and I'd rather play sports than fight any day.

Not Cliff. Fighting was Cliff's sports. Cliff told me one day that what he really wanted to do was to beat the Shit out of Mikey, then each one of Mikey's friends, then his sister – then his mother and father!

He was serious.

It was like we were at war or something.

It was getting weird.

★

I made it known to Mikey through his friends for him to come out and get it over with. Take his beating and end it. I never heard anything back.

Mikey was laying low. Scared shit now. With Cliff after him, I couldn't blame him. Always staying in the house. Only going out with his mother or father, usually quickly into the family car. Always being driven by one of his parents to school, then picked up at school by them at the end of the day.

Cliff was boiling over. 'Mikey thinks he's going to get away from me, Vic. Well, he'll be running and hiding until he's a hundred years old!'

Cliff and I watched and waited.

So did half the students in school.

Mikey, being the puniest and youngest of the so-called 'big' kids was really just a 'small' fifteen year old in nineth grade at our junior high school.

But the teachers were watching, especially the gym

teachers, all big tough guys, making sure nothing happened in their school. And with Mikey's parents driving him and picking him up each day from school, everyone figured Mikey was safe and no one could touch him.

I laughed about it. So did Cliff. And we waited.

'There's got to be a way to get him,' I told Cliff one Indian summer night, sitting on my porch. He was busy catching the last bumble bees of the year with his cupped hands. Big, black, nasty-looking bees that looked as if they could sting you to death. Cliff said that if you cupped your hands together fast enough, surrounded them by the darkness of your hands quickly enough, then shook your cupped hands, you'd rattle their cage so much they wouldn't be able to sting you.

Cliff would always smash his hands together and pulverize the bees into mush after he caught them.

Cliff said, 'When I want him, Vic, when I *really* want him, I'll just go in there and get him. And nothing will be able to stop me!'

'You mean in his house? Go right into his house with his mother and father there and get him?'

Cliff smiled, smashed another bee, said, 'Just watch, Vic.'

★

That day came sooner than I thought. It was a few days later. All that morning Cliff had been playing with his bugs, like he did a lot lately, using a can of lighter fluid, spraying them with a drop or two of the flammable liquid and then setting a match to them. Laughing as they spun around the sidewalk in pain. Cliff did bees, ants, a praying mantis, tons of Japanese beetles, a few wasps, earthworms... you get the picture. He had his own little insectoid Auschwitz death camp there on the driveway. All the various bugs, smashed up, with legs cut off, heads cut off, appendages set in piles, some set on fire, others drowned in cups of water, more stepped on and made into bug mush soup.

That wasn't the weirdest part though.

What was weird was how all of a sudden he just got up and ran down the block.

To Mikey's house!

With a can of lighter fluid!

Cliff was ready.

It happened so sudden I didn't know what was going on but I ran after Cliff and watched in astonishment as he walked right *into* Mikey's house. Like he lived there! Just opened the unlocked front door and walked right the hell inside!

I followed, standing by the door, looking inside, watching Cliff walk into Mikey's living room.

Mikey was on the sofa watching TV. His sister and mother were there too. No father. Probably at work. A baby lay in a crib off to the side by the dining room table.

The mother noticed Cliff first, screamed, 'What are *you* doing here!'

Mikey's sister jumped up. Startled. Fearful. Ran toward Cliff, shouting for him to get out of their house. Warning her brother to get away.

'Run, Mikey!'

Mikey saw Cliff and froze, yelled, 'Oh, no! Get out! Mama!'

Cliff moved forward like a tank. He punched the sister, sending her sprawling down to the floor. Hit the mother. Pushed her away. The mother full of anger and screaming, shouts of pain and fear. Then Cliff was on Mikey, his hands on his throat, pounding his head into the wall behind the sofa. Pounding his head even as Mikey tried his best to fight him off.

Mikey's sister got up, shaking, screaming, running to Cliff to try to pull him off her brother. By that time Mikey's mother was behind Cliff, slamming him mercilessly with the hard handle of a broom. On the back. On the head. All over his body.

Cliff hardly noticed.

Mikey's sister shouted, 'Vic! Help me!'

At that point I'd had enough. I figured Mikey had had enough. And Cliff had gone too damn far.

'Cliff! Come on, stop it!'

'Shut up, Vic!'

He didn't even look at me. Too engrossed in beating in Mikey's head.

I knew I had to do something, something I really didn't want to do. I had to mess with Cliff. I had to pull him off Mikey.

Cliff had always told me, 'Don't ever mess with me, Vic. You don't mess with me and I'll be your best friend. You mess with me and I'll be your worst enemy and I'll never forget. Never!'

I'd said, 'Sure, Cliff, you know I wouldn't mess with you.'

He'd liked that answer.

It hadn't been a big thing to me back then.

Now it was.

Now I was going to do the unthinkable. I was going to mess with Cliff. I went over and tried to pull him off Mikey.

It wasn't easy. Cliff had a grip, and an anger that

wouldn't allow him to give up. He fought me all the way.

'Get out of here, Vic!' he shouted, pulling away from me.

'Let him go, Cliff! Let him go!'

'You're messing with me, Vic!'

'Come on, Cliff!'

'I'm warning you! You're messing with me!'

'Shut up, Cliff!' I said, 'Let him go!'

I felt the arm I was pulling on give way, then a hard fist landed in my face knocking me to the floor. It hurt like hell.

'Nobody messes with me!' Cliff screamed, once again back to work pummelling Mikey's head.

I was up again, and back to work on Cliff just as quickly. Angry too, now. Punching and pushing him off the smaller kid. Finally getting Cliff to release Mikey, pushing Cliff off the sofa to the floor where he landed with a loud thud.

The mother and sister both went over to Mikey, crying, screaming, cradling his head in their laps; threatening to call the cops but too scared and upset to even do that. In real shock. Terrorized. They pushed me out of the way. I turned and looked down at Cliff, but he wasn't there.

I looked over at the picture window in the living room, then over by the open front door. Cliff wasn't there. He didn't seem to be anywhere. I turned and looked behind me, inside the house, by the dining room table. And I saw him then, by the table, and by the table right next to him was a small crib with a baby in it.

I didn't think much of it at first. Trying to get myself together after the fight, worrying about Mikey's mother going hysterical, calling the cops, my parents, stuff like that going through my head. Then I realized. I saw the can Cliff held upended in his hand, the fluid streaming down onto the tiny form in the crib, the match that Cliff now lit with his other hand.

'No, Cliff!' I shouted.

'You messed with me! Nobody messes with me!'

The mother and daughter both screamed, they forgot about Mikey as they turned and saw Cliff by the baby. Their newest horror. They freaked when they saw what was going to happen, but Mikey's sister knew Cliff, she wisely held back her mother from doing something stupid, like running after Cliff and forcing him to drop the match into the crib.

'All I have to do is drop this match and Mikey's got a roasted brother,' Cliff warned, sending a chill through us all.

No one there doubted for a moment that Cliff was capable of such a terrible act.

Mikey was too far gone now to respond. The mother just screamed, 'My baby! My baby! Don't hurt my baby!'

Mikey's sister looked at me, said, 'Vic, do something. He's your friend.'

He was my friend. I began to realize that Cliff was also my responsibility. At least in this situation. I couldn't let it go any further.

The hellbound train needed a derailing. Right away.

I moved closer, said, 'Come on, Cliff, this is crazy. Let's just get out of here. Come on!'

'Fuck you, Vic!'

'Come on, we got Mikey. You got him good.' I moved closer.

He ignored my words, his eyes burning with fire for me.

'You're a traitor, Vic!'

I moved in closer.

'Cliff, we're buddies, remember? I was the only one who stood with you against the big kids. The only one, Cliff!'

'Don't come closer, Vic. You're the cause of all this. I should be burning *you*!'

I gulped nervously. I saw him plain now. Crazy. Evil. Out to hurt just for the sake of hurting because it was fun. I hated that so much.

'Then come on! You lousy stinking faggot! You too scared to fight me?'

I'd found the right button. I'd called him faggot. He went berserk then. He came at me with the can and the match. Trying to get at me and spray me with lighter fluid, trying to set me on fire while I ran away from him, out of the house, out onto the front lawn. Waiting for him. Getting him away from the baby.

He fell for it and came running after me.

Once he came outside on the steps he saw me standing a few dozen yards away with a baseball bat in my hand.

Ready.

He threw the can of lighter fluid in the bushes.

The door to Mikey's house slammed shut behind Cliff with a resounding whack. And then was locked.

Cliff just laughed.

He looked at me and laughed.

I held the bat tight, waiting for him to attack, but he just stood there laughing at me.

'Hey, Vic, I told you this would be fun, didn't I?'

I was ready to bat his head down the block if he came one step closer. And I told him so.

He just kept laughing, said, 'Come on, Vic, calm down. I'm not mad no more.'

I knew I could never trust him again.

'I said, 'You sure you're not mad, Cliff?'

'Sure, Vic. Hey, wasn't that great fun?'

'Yeah, Cliff, it was a lot of fun.'

I never stayed with Cliff much after that, and I never turned my back on him ever again. We sort of grew apart. I guess I was the only person who ever stood up to him, the only person who ever tried to stop him, and backed it up by putting my ass and fists on the line. The only person who said what he was doing was wrong. For some people, hearing they're wrong is the last thing they want to hear. The worst thing you can ever say to them.

When Cliff's old man was transferred and the family had to move a month later I was happy that I'd never have to see him again.

That's what I thought at the time.

I couldn't help remembering back on it now. I'd messed with Cliff back then, stopped him from doing something he had wanted to do. I don't know if he would have really set that baby on fire, but if not then, that kind of thing was just a matter of time where Cliff was concerned. He was on a certain path. Making the world pay for what his father had done to him. What his father had made him into.

Now thirty years later he was a full-grown, adult... monster.

I'd messed with Cliff back then and I knew that for all the times he told me that he wasn't angry, that he didn't blame me, that he didn't hate me, the events of that day were burning inside him.

Still burning all these years later.

I was a traitor. It's true. I was a traitor because I had gone against my best friend, taken the side of our enemy against him, and stopped my friend from setting fire to a baby.

Treason never felt so noble.

Chapter Eight

BROOKLYN, NEW YORK, 1994

So I guess that had to be it. At least, some part of it. Of course it was all totally crazy, thirty year old crap that had happened with kids in another life, but then that was Cliff for shit-sure back in 1964 when he had been only twelve years old. Now he was 42, thirty years older, wiser, more dangerous than ever, and just as shit-sure more crazier than he had ever been. It sent a chill through me even to think about what he must be like now.

And now he held Gayle captive while I was sitting alone at our kitchen table with my thumb up my ass. Doing nothing. Waiting. Having no idea where to look for Cliff. What he wanted from me. How Gayle was. Nothing. Waiting. Waiting for what? Waiting for the damn phone to ring. Knowing Cliff would call, after he let me stew a bit, of course. Sitting there alone in the dark, quiet, cleaning my gun. Anticipating usage. Fearing for Gayle. Fearing the worst, and telling myself that it wouldn't happen, that Cliff really wanted me. That he needed Gayle, alive, to get back at me. Thinking how logical that all was. That she was safe for the moment, at least. Not even wanting to look into the future more than a few minutes. So fearful of what awaited Gayle and me there.

You see, it was like it had been years before, when Gayle's son, Joey, had been kidnapped. It was all the same. Once events of a certain magnitude are set into motion they can never be called back. Eggs can't be unbroken. Some things can never be forgiven. Some things can never be forgotten.

Cliff was heading down the tracks in the hellbound train straight towards me, and here I was waiting patiently by the phone, hoping desperately for his call, a call from a monster who held captive the only woman I've ever really loved. A call that would tell me where, and when, and how I could get back on that damn train with Cliff once again. And maybe, I prayed, be able to save Gayle. Somehow. Maybe save myself too. For I knew I was the focus of Cliff's anger, the eventual target of his plan, whatever that might be. None of that bothered me as long as it didn't hurt Gayle. As long as she came out of this without any injury.

I felt the train roaring down the tracks at me as I thought about all these things. Puffing evil dark smoke, Cliff in the cab laughing like a maniac.

I almost thought I could hear the whistle on the damn train, so loud and strong, as it barrelled down on me. Loud, shrill, demanding attention.

I jumped.

It was the telephone.

It was ringing. Demanding attention.

I took a deep breath. Picked up the receiver. Said, 'Yes.'

There was a dark silence at the other end. Almost like a void. Ominous, but I could tell someone was there.

Finally, 'It's me,' was all that Cliff said.

'I know.'

'You been waiting?' he asked. Cold, hard, like a machine, not really interested, not really a question.

'Yes.'

'You knew I would call?'

I said, 'Yes, Cliff.'

There, I'd said it. Said his name. Like saying the name of the devil. A normal kid's name, had become an evil name. The name of an evil creature.

I tried to stay calm, tried not to let the fury and rage I felt creep into my voice – or at least tried not to let it creep into my voice any more than necessary. Cliff was weird, hearing fear might egg him on, embolden him, or maybe scare him off and make him do something even he didn't want to do. Yet. Like kill Gayle. He was like a starving man with too much food when it came to suffering. Show him a little suffering and he'd want to see more. Do more. I thought of Gayle as the captive of such a person. I knew what I had to do. I just had to be very cool, very careful about everything.

It wasn't easy for me. I was just as crazy as Cliff at that point. So full of anger and rage and helplessness I couldn't think straight.

'It's been a long time, Vic.'

'About thirty years, Cliff. I thought you'd forgotten all about me.'

'Vic, Vic I never forget. You, above all people, should know that I never forget.'

I guess I forgot.

Me being stupid again.

I said, 'I know you have Gayle. She's never done anything against you, Cliff. Why don't you let her go and we can forget all this? I won't say another word. What's been done, is done.'

I swallowed. It was hard to be a weasel, even doing it for Gayle. But I'd do it gladly. My one friend on the cops, Fortuno, was dead not two hours, and here I was calmly trying to make a deal with his killer and practically pleading with him that I'd forget about everything, let it all slide, if he just let Gayle go. And meaning it! I hoped that if Fortuno was watching it all from somewhere in Heaven or Hell, he understood. I figured he probably did. Being a cop, he understood how it was when your hands are tied.

I just couldn't do otherwise. I loved Gayle so much, I'd do anything to get her back, give up my honor, my honesty, my pride, my life. Everything I had. Everything I could beg, borrow, or steal. Anything.

'Cliff?'

There was a loud click from the other end of the line.

The phone had been hung up.

I set down my receiver slowly. Wondering. Scared now. For Gayle. Scared now more than ever. This was bad. Obviously, I'd said the wrong thing. I'd tried to cut a deal with Cliff.

There was no deal to be cut, I was in no position to cut anything at all. I'd fucked up.

The phone rang again.

My heart skipped a beat as I picked it up.

'Do you want to try this again, Vic?' Cliff said, the hard edge of sarcasm in his voice, mixed with a venom and sadistic pleasure that I hadn't heard in a long time.

'Yes,' I said.

'That's good, Vic.'

'Cliff?' I said, 'What do you want?'

There was silence for a long time. I was afraid he was going to hang up on me again and maybe not call back. Ever again. That chilled me more than I cared to admit. It would have left me out in the cold and Gayle at his mercy. Perhaps even make her expendable? Because if Cliff couldn't use her as leverage against me, which was obviously his goal, then she'd be useless to him. An impediment he'd do away with at the first opportunity. So I just sighed, said, 'Okay, Cliff, I'm ready. Talk to me.'

'Now that's better, Vic,' and his voice suddenly grew jaunty, victory flowing through it like thick syrup. It was disgusting to hear.

I held the grip on my gun until my knuckles shone white, and sat quietly listening to Cliff's breathing through the phone line. Calm, measured, machine-like. So in control. Of himself. Of Gayle. Of me. I cringed, rubbed my forehead trying with little result to alleviate the pressure that had built up there over the past few minutes, and that threatened to burst through my skull.

I waited.

It didn't take Cliff long to set the train in motion.

'Now listen very carefully, Vic. First off, I'm going to start by telling you the rules,' he said. Pausing for effect. For it to sink in.

And I thought, what 'rules'? What the hell was he talking about? What did he really want? Where was Gayle? How was she? If he hurt her in any way nothing in this world would be able to stop me from ripping his black heart out with my bare hands!

'You there, Vic?'

'Yes.'

'That's good,' he said, 'I wouldn't want you to mess up. Don't mess up, Vic. Listen very carefully. Now here are the rules. Just like in a game, Vic. A game of life and death. You understand?'

'I think I do,' I answered.

'I'm sure you do, Vic. You had better.'

'So let's get down to it. What's this game? What the hell do you want from me?' I asked, impatient, angry, getting stupid again in spite of the fact that I knew better.

Cliff just laughed this time. Enjoying my obvious suffering, my rampant panic and confusion, 'Vic, you're getting ahead of things. Like you always do. Now are you ready to shut up and listen?'

I took a deep breath. Exhaling slowly.

'Yes,' I said, swallowing my pride. Trying to play this smart, and finding it very hard to do. Not my nature at all. Wishing I was someone else. Someone who would know how to handle something like this. For Gayle's sake. Trying to forget how much I hated Cliff, how much I feared for her.

'That's better. Now for the rules, Vic. I'm going to play a pre-recorded tape. Listen to it very carefully.'

There was silence and a pause, then a click. Then Cliff's voice came over the phone again, this time slightly tinny, as from a recording.

'The rules. You have twelve hours to save your wife's life. She is now being held captive in a location that will be disclosed at the end of this tape. In your attempt to rescue her you may not use the telephone, may not go to the police, may not seek any outside help in any way. You can not use the subway, trains, bicycle, bus, your private car, taxi, friends. You must remain on foot at all times, you must remain in the open out in plain view at all times. Understand? You are being watched. If the watchers loose sight of you for any reason, or you are found talking to anyone, passing messages, writing anything, this will be reported to me and your wife will be killed. Immediately and painfully. Believe me when I tell you this.'

I believe him. This was Cliff. I believed him.

The tape continued, 'You have twelve hours to get out of Brooklyn and down to the Brooklyn Bridge where your wife will be held and waiting at 3am. She will be brought there at precisely 3am. If you are not there to save her she will be dead at 3:01am. Dead, Vic. Understand?'

I nodded in spite of the fact that it was a recording.

Once more, Cliff on tape: 'So that we can be in constant contact there is a small radio headset in your mail box in the lobby. Use it. I'll contact you through it.

'And that's it, Vic. You have twelve hours to get to Gayle and save her. I'll be watching you all the way So don't mess up. Understand?'

There was another pause. Another click and a new tape obviously running, now coming over the phone.

Then Gayle's voice this time.

'Vic, Vic it's me. Don't do it! Don't do anything this sick fuck says! I love you, honey! Vic, I love you so much...'

There was the loud sound of a slap.

I jumped.

'Bitch!' Cliff's voice on the tape now.

'Go to hell!' Gayle's defiant voice. A loud scream then. More slapping. More screaming.

The tape ended.

The machine clicked off and it was quiet for a minute.

Another long pause.

Cliff came back on the line now. Real-time. Live.

'That was from an hour ago, Vic. Your wife is very uncooperative. A real hardheaded pain in the ass. Just like you.'

I was burning. My heart racing like a herd of wild horses, stampeding with rage.

'You slapped her.' It was not a question.

'Yes, she is…'

'You slapped her.'

'Yes, Vic, I…'

'You slapped her!'

'Now, Vic…'

'You slapped my wife!'

'Yes I did, Vic, because…'

'There's no going back now, Cliff. You'll pay for that. Pay real hard. No matter how this turns out in the end, no matter if you kill her, or kill me, you'll pay for that. And anything else you do to her. I swear it!'

Cliff laughed, 'That's good, Vic, I'm glad I have your interest and that you're fired up now to play our little game.' But I could hear a slight bit of concern in his voice. A tiny bit of nervousness lurking there far in the edge of the background.

'You're a monster, Cliff. I'll give you that. But you've made the mistake all monsters make.'

'And what's that, Vic?'

'You've woke up another monster, Cliff. Another monster that will never rest until you've been put down!'

I slammed the receiver down. Hard.

It was time.

I took my gun and put it in my jacket pocket, where hopefully it wouldn't get noticed. I left the empty apartment, finding the small radio right where Cliff said it would be. So Cliff and I could be in constant contact. How nice!

I went down the stoop and into the street, looked at my car, looked over the area, knew that Cliff could have someone watching me. Hidden. But where? Someone had put the radio in my mailbox, someone was working with Cliff for sure. Maybe more than one?

There were people all over the block, down at both ends, across the street, sitting on stoops, walking, talking, kids playing ball down the block, cars driving past one after the other. It was impossible.

I walked over to my car. Just before I touched the door handle I heard a slight ping and the rear window of my car shattered into a hundred pieces. Like a spider's web. Gun shot. Silenced. Someone was definitely watching.

Cliff's voice came over the radio, tinny but clear, 'Vic, don't even think about doing something like that again. Don't break the rules. Think of *her* before you do something stupid.'

I was in Bay Ridge. It was almost 3pm. The afternoon of a warm Brooklyn fall day. I had twelve hours to get downtown and reach the Brooklyn Bridge. By walking? It was more than possible. Easy really. No way it would take me twelve hours to get there. Even walking. It was a long walk but I figured it would take me two hours at the most.

I began to wonder what Cliff had in store for me along the way.

So I began the long walk. I didn't have a choice. I couldn't go to the cops, couldn't contact anyone in any way. I knew Cliff had me right where he wanted me. By the balls.

Now he would begin to twist.

What Cliff didn't tell me was that he'd be playing with me all along the way. Having his fun. Cliff-type special fun.

Chapter Nine

BAY RIDGE, BROOKLYN, 3PM

I walked and walked, down one stinking block, one lousy street after the other. People all over the place. Tall, short, Puerto Rican Spanish, old stock Norwegian, Italian, white, black, young, old. All types. All kinds of looks.

Which ones were working for Cliff?

The old man walking behind me? Was he following me? The young Spanish girl with the baby carriage? Was there really a baby in that carriage, or an Uzi? The tough kid on the corner looking me over, was he Cliff's guy, or just a tough punk thinking about ripping me off. Wondering how much money I had in my pocket.

I moved parallel to the punk, let him see the butt of my gun. Gave him a knowing smile. If he wasn't a cop he would turn his back to me and walk off.

He turned and walked off.

That didn't necessarily mean he wasn't Cliff's guy, though.

And what about the man with the little girl? What about the boy playing with the toy gun in front of the candy store? Was it a *toy* gun? Was the man next to him, the one who appeared to be his father, actually one of Cliff's men?

My mind was buzzing. I'd gotten myself in a real mess. Out in the open, helpless, where Cliff had me totally under his control. He could play with me all he wanted now. Fuck me up at his leisure. I walked, but my mind was thinking overtime. Full of fear and what was sure to come.

I figured the best way, the most direct way to get to the Brooklyn Bridge was to take Fourth Avenue straight down, a wide triple-laned thoroughfare I could walk to Flatbush Avenue, then take Flatbush down to the Manhattan Bridge on the waterfront. From there I could cut over a few blocks to the entrance to the Brooklyn Bridge.

All seemed simple enough.

Though the walk itself shouldn't take more than two hours, three at most, even without pressing it, something was very wrong about the whole thing. It was all too crazy, seemed so wrong. Crazy? Well, that was Cliff. The crazy parts were all his.

I felt I was being followed. After a while I noticed at least one car with a guy in it, holding back a block or so behind me. He was a young guy. Maybe another mugger? The area was full of them. They used bicycles, motorcycles, cars and vans. The old grab and run, or hit, grab and run.

For the past six blocks now I'd been followed by the young guy in the Toyota. Going slow. No rush. Always there. Sticking to me. Never turning off. A young guy. He even sorta looked a little like Cliff. Did Cliff have a son?

I realized that though we'd known each other as kids, that had been thirty years ago and I knew absolutely nothing at all about Cliff now. That was bad. I was missing vital information that could be of use to me.

I kept walking.

As far as the walk went, it was a gorgeous fall day, warm but not hot, typical Indian summer. A lot of people on the street, all over the neighborhood, going in and out of the stores, driving cars, parking, walking the streets all around me. And yet, it was quiet, calm, almost peaceful. Everyone going about their business, quietly, minding their own business. No one getting in anyone's way or in any one's face. Yet.

Like before a volcano erupts.

But I could feel the eyes on me. The radio was silent, but I knew Cliff was right there with me. Right beside me. Watching me through the eyes of his own watchers.

I had barely gotten to Fourth Avenue when the old lady came over to me. She asked me to help her cross the street. There was a lot of traffic and I could see that it made her nervous. Cars never give pedestrians in Brooklyn an even break, and if you're old, just forget it. In fact, if you're old and live in Brooklyn, better not even go out of the house at all. Lots of old people in Brooklyn never leave the house. Prisoners at home. Between the muggers and all the crazy drivers, all the hit and runs, an old person might as well wear a circle with crosshairs on their back. Living targets. Human game. It was so normal in some sections of Brooklyn that it was all but legal. Or seemed to be.

I couldn't do nothing for the old lady. I ignored her, walked away. I remembered the rules. Don't talk to anyone on the street. I walked faster, got to the curb, waited while a car passed, then another.

The old lady called out to me. Came up to me, shaking, nervous.

'Help me, please.'

She said she wanted me to cross her.

She latched onto my arm just as I began to walk away from her. I ended up dragging her with me. She was a weathered old thing. Eighty years or more of rough usage behind her.

I told her, 'Get away from me! Leave me alone!'

I tried to move off, dislodge her long, old fingers from my shirt sleeve. They were surprisingly strong.

I didn't want to hurt her, and there was no way I could make her understand she had to stay away from from me. I was about to push her away when she suddenly crumpled down beside me. I thought she'd had a stroke or something. You know, like old people get? But then I saw the red spot in her back, soaking through her coat. Wet and red and growing large.

'Goddamnit, Cliff!'

And now there was more blood in Brooklyn, dripping from an innocent eighty year old woman, drops of her old blood hitting the time-worn sidewalk, her blood sprinkling it with a lush red wetness.

I looked up, all around, trying to see where the shooter was hiding.

There was nothing.

Cliff's voice came over the radio, 'You break the rules one more time, Vic, and your wife dies. I don't have to tell you it will not be pleasant. Except for me, that is.'

'You lousy son-of-a-bitch!' but Cliff couldn't hear me. The radio was only one-way.

I tried to help the old lady best I could. She was losing

consciousness, going into shock. She didn't even know she'd been shot: she muttered something about a stroke or heart attack. I felt terrible, picked her up and carried her into a nearby shop. I set her down in a chair and told the kid behind the counter that the woman had been shot in a hold-up attempt. I told him that the kid who shot her had run away and was long gone now. I told him to call an ambulance immediately. I told him I'd wait outside.

I was gone in a flash. I couldn't stay there. The place would be swarming with cops before long. Walking away, I cut down one block, down another block, cutting over to the other side of Fourth Avenue. Still on my way downtown.

On the way I still noticed that same car behind me. Following. Like a shadow. With one driver.

Was it Cliff's guy?

It had to be. Didn't it?

I decided to try something. It was another stupid idea but I felt I had to do it.

I was walking down Fourth Avenue. I figured I'd turn off down 84th Street and get onto Third Avenue. Then come at the guy when he turned the corner to follow me.

It wasn't such a great idea, and I didn't know what I'd do with the guy once I got him. I guess I had some kind of vague notion that if this *was* Cliff's son, maybe I'd trade him back to Cliff for Gayle? It was something stupid like that. In desperate planning it seemed to make sense, but in practice it would be a mess. It only made sense to a desperate person without any real plan or any real hope. Which sure as hell was me!

In any case, Cliff didn't strike me as the kind of guy full of any fatherly concern for his son. That is, *if* the guy in the car was Cliff's son. Cliff had been raised a certain way, after all. I remembered back about Cliff's old man, back in Virginia in 1964. Crazy and evil and out of control. A terrible combination. Today Cliff was probably just like his old man had been back then. Only worse.

Of course, if the guy in the car wasn't Cliff's son, just some shlub he'd hired to do a job, Cliff wouldn't blink an eye about losing him. And Gayle and I would find ourselves in a lot worse position than we were already. If that was possible.

But I had to do something. Try something. Forcing Cliff's hand might cause him to change his plan, or alternate that plan. Even if I could affect his plan just a little bit, it might help me. Might help Gayle. I knew that if I didn't do something, if everything went the way Cliff had planned it, smooth and with no hitches, Gayle and I would both be dead and Cliff would be dancing on our graves. After a terrible death for Gayle, and no doubt, the same for me. That was Cliff's plan, and that's just the way it would all end up unless I did something to try to change it.

There was no hope for Gayle and me the way Cliff had set things up. This stupid, evil game of his was specially created to destroy Gayle and me. If I could change that game, perhaps throw a monkey wrench in it somehow, maybe at least I'd have a better chance to save Gayle. I figured that would be worth a try. I realized now that for all Cliff's insistence on rules, his threats against Gayle, he probably wouldn't kill her this early in the game. Not that he gave a damn about Gayle, or me for that matter, but a kill too early would spoil his sport, causing the game to come to an abrupt end before it had gone full swing. I figured Cliff didn't want that. He'd planned this, worked on it for a long time. He wanted to get all the gusto he could out of this before he ended it. His way. That was Cliff. I remembered him as a kid, he was an adult now, but he still wouldn't want his fun to be spoiled by ending the game too early.

So I turned right, walked down onto Third Avenue and then doubled back on my tracks. I watched from a hiding place between two cars on the corner as the gray Toyota came slowly down the block, slowed at the stop sign on the corner, and then began to make a right onto Third Avenue. I saw the car come close, the driver clearly, the unlocked door on the passenger side. In an instant I had that door jerked open wide and was in the car and at the driver before he knew what hit him.

The car took off in a loud screech across the street as my fist plowed into the driver's jaw, knocking him out. He slumped over the steering wheel and his foot fell away from the accelerator. The car jerked, slowed, rolled across the street. I slammed up the emergency brake and the car jerked to a hard stop on the other side of Third Avenue.

I took a deep breath full of relief, looking at the driver. He was sitting there, hunched over the wheel, out cold. He looked a bit like Cliff. I wondered if he actually was Cliff's son? Too bad if he was. For just a second I wondered what *his* upbringing must have been like. Then I looked for weapons, but I didn't find anything on him. No ID either. Something looked wrong. This guy didn't appear to be the one who had been the shooter of that old lady. If that was the case, it meant this guy wasn't the only watcher that Cliff was using. Unless Cliff was the shooter? Also possible, I guess. Who the hell really knew?

The shot that shattered the back window of the Toyota got my attention. It was silenced, just like the slug that had taken out the back window of my own car back in Bay Ridge. Just like the shot that had taken down the old lady back on Fourth Avenue.

'That was stupid, Vic. Do you think he is the only one watching you?'

I saw the radio in the car by the still unconscious driver. I lifted the mike, 'Cliff, you there?'

'Yes, Vic, I'm here. So is Gayle.'

I swallowed hard. Okay, here we go, I thought. I said, 'I've got your son, Cliff. I'll kill him, right here and now, if you don't let Gayle go.'

There was silence then laughter from Cliff. Real rich laughter. I hardly knew what to make of it but it didn't bolster my confidence or make me think this was going to turn out the way I hoped.

'Cliff?'

I began to panic. Maybe the guy I had *wasn't* Cliff's son?

Then again, maybe he *was*, but Cliff just didn't give a damn. That was also possible. And true to Cliff's 'character'.

'Cliff?'

'I'm here, Vic. You know, that's rich. It really is. And it took real balls, but then, what you lack in smarts, you've always made up with by having one big brass set of balls. Unfortunately, Vic, it will do you no good. Do you think I care, Vic? Really? You know me, or knew me a long time ago. I'm... worse now, Vic. Truly I am. So kill him! Go ahead! All it will do is just make me angry. And I'll just take it out on Gayle. I might not even wait for 3:01am to begin it. I might just tear into her right now. Wanna hear it? Harm my son. I'll do Gayle so good, Vic, you won't be able to handle it. You know what I mean? I think you do. I know how much you love her. I think I can guarantee it will be terrible. Just terrible. But I'll tape it all for you to look at later. I wouldn't want my old friend, my best old friend, to miss one wonderful moment.'

I was stone silent. There was nothing to say.

I had to bide my time. Hope there would be an opportunity. Hope something would come up where I could get at Cliff. It would have been more realistic believing in Santa Claus.

'Vic? Vic? You still there?'

'Yes, Cliff,' I said, full of numbness.

'You know how I am, Vic. You don't really want to get me angry, do you? Now leave my son alone, get out of the car and walk away. Walk back up to Fourth Avenue like you always intended. I'll meet you at 3am, Vic, at the Brooklyn Bridge. Don't be late.'

I picked up the mike and shouted into it, cursed, screamed, but Cliff had already cut the call. I looked at the guy slumped down behind the wheel of the Toyota. He'd been unconscious but seemed to be coming out of it now. He looked at me, groggy, totally dazed, uncomprehending. Trying to figure out who I was and what I was doing sitting in his car. It hadn't come to him yet. Before it did, I got out of the car, walked back across Third Avenue, up 84th Street and onto Fourth Avenue once again. I kept walking, feeling the eyes of Cliff's watchers still on me. Always watching me. Playing with me. Cliff laughing. Having the time of his life. I couldn't figure out what the hell was so interesting about me for them to be watching me, following me, doing what they were doing to me.

And Gayle. Maybe not being crazy, or at least, crazy-evil the way Cliff was, I couldn't fully understand or appreciate their motive. But it was there. Whatever the hell it was.

I walked more blocks, down to 62nd Street, and by that time I noticed a light blue Toyota following slowly behind me. One driver again. Different car. I couldn't tell if it was the same guy. He held back just far enough so it was a while before I picked him up. Once I thought I saw the glint of the sun off steel, on the driver's side of the vehicle. I figured that if it was the same guy he'd have to be packing now. Unless it was another guy. Maybe the shooter who had done the old lady? In that case, he was certainly packing. Which meant, that even with my own weapon, the watcher's car was off limits to me now unless I wanted to start a bloodbath in a neighborhood full of kids and innocent people.

I didn't want to do that.

So I kept walking. Talking to no one. Staying away from people. An old man came over to me asking a question, and I quickly walked away from him. I heard him curse me as I moved off.

A kid, maybe five years old, asked if I would help cross him and his little sister. The girl was probably two or three and I wondered where the hell the parents were. I told him to go get his parents and moved away. I didn't need no dead kids on my conscience. I knew Cliff and his shooter had already killed a cop, killed a Rev, killed an eighty year old lady. Why would they stop at killing a kid? I moved off as fast as I could.

An unshaven bum came up to me and asked if I had any spare change. When he threatened me, I pushed him down to the ground and walked quickly away. He cursed me in rich Spanish, never knowing that I'd saved his lousy life by not stopping and talking to him or giving him money. I crossed the street and froze. I saw someone I knew. A good guy by the name of Cotto, and he was walking over to me to say hello. I ignored him, and before he could come over, I found myself running away from him, down Fourth Avenue, over to the 60th Street side, running as fast as I could now. Running away from getting someone I liked, an old friend, shot down in the street by Cliff's mad shooter, running to get downtown, running to get to Gayle. Running and fearing what I would find when I got there.

Chapter Ten
FOURTH AVENUE, BROOKLYN, 5PM

I continued down Fourth Avenue, crossing over 60th Street, down into the Puerto Rican section. It was okay here, if you kept your eyes open. I figured I had about eighty blocks left to go in all, easy to do in a little over ten hours. There were sixty numbered blocks that went in order from 60th Street down to 1st Street, then about another two dozen named streets after that. That would take me down to Flatbush Avenue, from there I'd have another ten blocks or so until I came to the end of Flatbush Avenue. That flowed into the Manhattan Bridge. Once there, it was a walk of maybe five or six blocks over to the entrance of the Brooklyn Bridge. And Cliff. And Gayle. And maybe by then this circus of horrors would end and I could get off this hellbound train for just once in my life.

Somehow I didn't think that was going to happen.

I was very pessimistic about the future.

Living in Brooklyn can do that to you sometimes.

I continued my little walk. My head full of all kinds of crazy thoughts. I had a very bad feeling about all of this. My mind was so confused, so angry, so scared.

I didn't see the cops until they'd pulled up beside me, coming in real close. Real serious. I didn't think they could be out looking for me.

They were.

They were out of the car and on me before I could catch my breath. They held me down, said I was wanted for questioning in Detective Fortuno's murder early that morning. They'd been looking for me all day. I had to tell them about the gun. They frisked me, took my jacket, withdrew the weapon very carefully.

'Be careful, it's loaded,' I told them.

'Loaded and concealed, Powers,' one of the sergeants told me. 'Just what the hell were you going to do with this?'

I shut up like a clam.

They read me my rights and dumped me in the back of their prowl car. And I sat there and thought about it all. It seemed like it had all happened weeks, maybe years ago, but this was all happening in just one lousy day. I had to smile at that. Was I having one hell of a bad day, or what? I was so screwed up I could barely believe it.

I was arrested because of the illegal gun, then I was roughed up by a few of the guys. They were friends of Fortuno. They were angry he was dead. I couldn't blame them. So was I. These younger guys figured that since I was wanted for questioning in the homicide of a cop, I might have just naturally done the dirty deed. I had to explain to them, very carefully, that I wasn't the guy they were after. They sort of believed me after they'd used my face as a punching bag for a few minutes, then reminded me that I had fallen down the steps and hurt myself.

Right?

I nodded. I knew how it was. A lot of guys who get arrested often fall down and hurt themselves while in police custody. Thing is, most of them deserve it. I didn't, but I wasn't complaining, I had more important things on my mind.

Thing is, I couldn't be arrested! I had to be at the Brooklyn Bridge by 3am! Not sitting somewhere in a cell downtown!

I was brought downtown to the old Gold Street Station, Fortuno's old station house. These were his boys. That's why they were so pissed. I didn't blame them, but it hurt. I'd been a cop once, and I'd even killed a no-good crooked cop years back, but getting a beating from good guys who were Fortuno's buddies kinda hurt a lot more than physical pain.

They threw me in a cage. By that time it was 6pm. I had nine hours left but I found myself locked away in a local downtown precinct. In jail. There was no way out and there was nothing I could do but sit there and stew.

I stewed for an hour before a local cop named Willy Hernandez came in and talked with me. He was a buddy of Fortuno's, they'd been partners years back. He wasn't a bad guy. We knew each other, Fortuno had introduced us and said some good things about me. The one time in his life he'd ever had a good word to say about me.

Hernandez was pissed. I could see it. He hadn't been one of the cops who had beaten me, but that was only because he'd just got off duty and wasn't back at the station.

'I heard rumors you were a suspect, Powers,' he said carefully, looking me over and shaking his head disapprovingly. 'I see a few of the guys got outta hand with you.'

'They think I killed Fortuno.'

'I can't believe you killed a cop, Powers,' he said.

'I didn't kill any cop,' I said, gulped, tried not to think about the past and look guilty about it. I tried to tell Hernandez some of the truth. 'I was with Fortuno when he got it, but I didn't do the killing.'

'What about the gun? I heard they found a gun on you, Powers?'

'Yeah, but they'll check it out. It's clean. Honest.'

I could see Hernandez wanted to believe me. He was a good guy, and he knew I'd been a cop once. I told him that I had to get out of here. That it was very important for me to make bail and get out as soon as possible.

Hernandez said, 'You ain't going anywhere, my man, until you're arraigned and bail is set. Later.'

I said, 'How did you guys find me?'

He said, 'I don't know, I heard someone here got a tip.'

'Oh yeah?'

'Yeah, funny about that though, he said if we wanted to find you, all we had to do was cruise Fourth Avenue and you'd turn up.'

'Yeah?'

'Well he was right, wasn't he?'

I said, 'Yeah, he was right.'

Cliff again!

Now he had me just where he wanted me. Stewing in a jail cell with the muck of the city for company, sitting tight while the overhead clock ticked away precious minutes. It was now past 7pm. Night had fallen. It was getting dark outside my tiny window.

I waited another half hour until I was able to make a call. Tried to get my lawyer. He wasn't in, so I left a message on his machine.

Later on I spoke to Hernandez again, asked him to

speak to a bail bondsmen. He must have known *someone*? He said I hadn't been arraigned yet, bail hadn't even been set. I'd have to wait.

I told him, please, talk to someone for me.

He said he'd do what he could.

I never saw him again after that.

I think my lawyer was out of town.

I never heard from him either.

I was locked in a holding tank with a bunch of creeps and maniacs, but the biggest creep and maniac was out there, free and safe and still holding Gayle. And there wasn't a damn thing I could do about it now!

Time ticked away. The minutes flowing into hours. The arraignment was at 9pm, at the night court over in Boro Hall. I had a pimple-faced public defender who spoke with me for fifteen minutes and thought he knew my life story. I copped an innocent plea on the gun charge. First offense. As far as anyone knew. Told them I was a former cop. I told my PD not to go into detail.

'Mr Powers, what were you intending to do with that gun? You were apprehended walking on Fourth Avenue with a loaded and concealed weapon,' the judge stated.

'Your Honor', I said, 'this is all a terrible mistake. I had the gun sitting in the pocket of that jacket for I can't remember how long. I forgot all about it and didn't even realize it was there.'

'Mr Powers, it seems to me that weapon has substantial weight to it. You must have surely known when you wore that jacket that it had something heavy in the pocket.'

'Yes, your Honor, and I felt the weight there, but I never thought it was from a gun.'

'Your Honor–' (Pimple-Face stood up now) '–my client was not wearing the jacket when he was arrested. You can read that in the police report. Only when the police approached Mr Powers did he realize that he had the gun, and he immediately surrendered it to the officer in charge.'

The judge harumphed. The only law and order night judge in Brooklyn and I got him.

My public defender talked a lot about 'extenuating circumstances', mentioned something about some obscure case from years ago, and let it drop again that I was a retired police officer – but not that the retirement had been mandatory. The guy wasn't bad, as public defenders usually go.

The judge growled, said: 'Okay, bail is set at ten thousand dollars,' then slammed the gavel and barked: 'Let's go! Next case!'

★

Thing is, I didn't happen to have ten thousand dollars on me just then. Not even the ten per cent I'd have to put up, a mere thousand. No way I could get it. Not before tomorrow. By the time I could get the money, it wouldn't matter anymore if I got out of jail or not.

I thought of Gayle. I'd never get to her in time. No way now. She was as good as dead. Maybe even dead already? I had no knowledge, no way of believing anything Cliff told me. He could have taped her earlier, killed her right afterwards. Or killed her now. Later. Whenever he wanted.

They put me back in the holding tank and I sat down in a corner and began to cry silently to myself, thinking of Gayle. How this was all turning into one big shit like what had happened to her son, Joey. The same damn thing. There'd been no way to save Joey. No way to find him. Now there was no way for me to save Gayle either, and if I thought about it all realistically and logically, it occurred to me that where a guy like Cliff was concerned she was probably dead already. There was nothing I could do now. Short of breaking out of jail. And I didn't want to cause injury or death to any cops, because if I tried to escape, that's what it would take. The tears flowed from my face as I though about Gayle. I tried to keep the crying down, but it hurt so bad, I'm sure some of the guys in the cage with me heard. Thing was, most of the guys in the cage with me let me alone. I think they understood. They understood pain. Giving it and being on the receiving end of it. Sure, they'd rather be giving it. But a lot of them had been given plenty of pain in their lives. They didn't crowd me, and I kept to myself. Dreaming about the good times Gayle and I had had together, thinking about how much I loved her and how much I missed her.

When I'd first met her a few years ago in that stinking New Mexico town she'd told me she needed me. At that time I'd almost walked away. Turned my back on her. But I didn't. I tried to help her. Tried to help find Joey. As it turned out I hadn't been able to help her much. We never were able to locate her son, or even to find his body. He would have been five years old next month.

And now it was happening all over again, and this time Gayle was the victim. And I knew I'd probably never see *her* again either. Maybe never find her body. And if I did, I didn't want to think about what condition it would be in after Cliff got through with her. And just like Gayle and I had figured about Joey two years ago, I'd have to go realistic and figure that knowing Cliff, Gayle was probably dead already.

There was nothing left for me to do but go after her killers. Whenever I got out of here. And who knew when that would be? And where the hell would I begin my search? I tried not to think of any of that now. My head hurt so much I couldn't think straight no more. At that moment there was so much hatred and anger in me... a rage that I had never felt before. Never. Not when I'd killed that drug-dealing pimp Mendoza, not when I killed that child-raping bastard Robert Loring, not when I shoved a pillow over my own father's stinking face in the hospital and sent him down to hell where he belonged!

I was burning, sitting there in that lousy holding tank, with the sweat and filth, loud foul language all around me, dirty scumbags everywhere I looked. The scum of the earth for company – and yet any one of them was a more fit human being than Cliff would ever be. It was hard to stop the tears. Hard to try and be strong when everything was turning to shit right before my eyes. I told myself: okay, Gayle was probably dead, but at least I'd go to the ends of the earth to avenge her murderer. It was stupid fantasy, but it kept my mind together for another minute. And another minute after that. And that's what mattered.

I stoked the rage and anger inside me, but it didn't do any good. I kept seeing that pretty little face of hers, that smile, the blond hair and sparkling blue eyes, remembering the taste of those warm red lips, the feel of her body next to mine in bed at night. It was all gone. All lost to me. Forever gone.

I didn't hear the guy come over to me. I didn't see him when he was next to me. I don't know how long he'd been talking, or what he'd been saying. Making fun of me, most likely. Saying some stupid shit. Acting like he had balls in front of his boys. I only noticed him when I felt his hands on me, pushing my face into the wall of the holding tank. I watched as the latticed metal bars of the cell began to dig into my face.

'You be *some* white crybaby, my man. In here, you with the big boys now. The bad boys. I think I give you something *serious* to cry about!'

He was a big black guy. Stupid, but mean; and big enough to put the hurt pretty deep.

'Leave the man be, Ty, he ain't bothering no one,' one of the guy's bros said.

'Nah, come on, Ty, fuck him up! Fuck up the white boy!' another said encouragingly.

I didn't give a shit. Ty pushed me around. Trying to wipe the place with me. Not serious hurt, just bully-boy shit. It was nothing. He was laughing while he was doing it. So was most of his crew. I was still crying. He made fun. There was more laughter. I didn't care.

'You big pussy! Whitey here, nothing but a big pussy!' Ty laughed, using his big ham-like hands to push me around the tank. Growing bolder. Beginning to get serious.

'Fuck him up, Ty,' another guy urged.

I flowed. Like a leaf on the wind. I didn't much care about anything. I'd been hurt worse; worse than a two-bit thug loser like Ty could ever imagine. My mind wasn't in there anyway, it was with Gayle, and the black guy couldn't hurt me anymore than I was already hurting. Thinking of Gayle. Our love. Our life. It was all over now.

'Cliff!'

'What's your problem, white boy? The name's Ty, not no white fag name of Cliff.'

I didn't say anything. I wasn't there yet.

'I'll fuck you, white boy! Hear me! Fuck you right up the ass! Make you like it, too!'

I ignored him.

'Fuck your white woman whore too! I be gettin' that white wife of yours and fuck her up the ass, just like I will you!'

My mind came back then. Snapping back. Like elastic.

I turned and looked at Ty. Right in the eyes.

'You said something about my wife?'

'Yo' wife! I do yo' fuckin' wife, fuck her up her scrawny white ass!'

'You fucking piece of black shit!' I growled.

Then Ty went ballistic, and so did I. I was on him before he knew what the hell had happened, knocking him down and around that pen like he was a big fat rubber toy. He was shocked. His shock turned to fear soon enough. The sheep he thought he'd cornered turned out to be a wolf that was full of killing rage and anger and was beating the shit out of him. An out of control hurting machine that was out to spill blood, break bones, and kick ass like no one's business.

I had Ty on the floor of the cell, a crowd cheering the fight – it was all the same to them, entertainment to pass the time. I pounded my fists into his stomach and face. Pounding away on Ty like I was a jackhammer, busting him up all over his body; crying, screaming, shouting as I beat the hell out of him. 'You lousy fucking scumbag, you fucking piece of shit! I'll kill you, motherfucker! I'll kill you and kill you and kill you and kill you and kill you – Cliff! I'll kill you, Cliff!'

They had to pull me off Ty before I did kill him. It took six of them to hold me down and cool me off. I didn't realize all of what had happened. I thought I'd killed Ty. I thought he was Cliff. Or I wished he was. I couldn't tell just then, and I didn't care either. I forgot where I was for a moment, forgot what was going on.

It happens to me sometimes.

They picked up Ty and a few of his buddies brought him over to the other end of the cage. The part that was the farthest from my end. They sat quiet now. So did I. Ty was moaning, alive, but hurt. I didn't say a word. There was nothing to say. He was one lucky shitbag. Maybe he'd get the message and he'd get some manners. If not, he'd be another dead thug in a year or two. They don't last long. Those kind are looking for their own death, trouble is they'll keep on causing pain and trouble until put down.

Sorry to say, a good beating can be like real medicine to people like that sometimes.

The guards came by, asked, 'What happened to that guy?'

No one said a thing.

'Don't tell me he just fell down and hurt himself?' The guard laughed, then looked at me. Saw I was a mess. He knew I was the one who'd done the dance with Ty. He looked over to the other guys in the cage. I looked at them too. Gave them the *look*. They knew I was serious. No one said a word. The guard opened the cage, motioned two of Ty's buddies to bring out their friend. Take him to the Infirmary.

Then the guard came over to me. 'Hey, you Powers? Get over here. Time to go. You made bail.'

I got up. Gave the guys in the tank one last long look. The older guys knew what I was doing. Memorizing faces.

It was 2:30am. I still had half an hour. Nobody better get in my way now.

At the desk they made me sign some papers, gave me my money and wallet back. Not my gun. I wondered where the hell my lawyer was, or where Hernandez's bondsmen had gotten one thousand dollars to put up for my bail. I asked the desk sergeant. He slid a form my way. I looked at the name on the bottom of the form. it was signed 'Clifford J Jones'.

Cliff!

Again!

Still playing with me! Getting me pinched, then getting me out! All so he could mess me up some more. Just so I'd be able to play his sick freak game one more time before he decided to end it in his own evil way. With my death. And Gayle's death.

It was 2:45am by the time I got out of Gold Street Station. I ran out the door for all I was worth toward the Brooklyn Bridge a few blocks away. It was still possible for me to get to the bridge before 3:00.

Cliff had thought this through very well.

I ran like a fiend. Toward the Bridge.

Toward Cliff.

Toward Gayle.

Praying I would not be late.

Chapter Eleven

BROOKLYN BRIDGE, BROOKLYN, 2:45AM

I had fifteen minutes. I had to get to the Bridge. I had to save Gayle. I had to get Cliff. Make him pay. And I would. Maybe. But I was beginning to doubt it. What if Cliff tricked me again? What if he wasn't there? Worse, what if Gayle wasn't there? I didn't want to think about that. All I wanted to think about was getting to that damn bridge within the deadline.

Saving Gayle.

Getting Cliff.

It was near 3am, the middle of the night, when I reached the entrance stairs that led up to the bridge walkway. The vehicle part of the bridge beneath me was still busy this time of night, cars going into and coming out of the City after a long night out. A steady flow of traffic. Almost a 3am rush hour. I was on the walkway above. It's a fairly wide expanse that enables pedestrians and cyclists to go across the bridge. This time of night it was almost deserted. A cop walked away on the Brooklyn side, a couple of young lovers smooching it up by the rail, an old man with a dog, a guy on a bicycle coming at me, two black kids with a boom box, a homeless man pushing a wagon of old junk.

Were any of them Cliff's watchers?

Maybe *all* of them!

It looked cool. I didn't see Cliff. No Gayle, either. Nowhere. Then I saw the guy on the bike coming closer. He came on fast now, right up to me, held out a small walkman-type radio, like the one I had been given before by Cliff that I'd lost in the scuffle with the cops on Fourth Avenue.

The cyclist pushed the small headset on me, rode away, shouted back: 'Put in the earpiece!' Then he was gone, disappearing into the blackness at the other end of the bridge. I put the earpiece in my ear.

Cliff must have been watching from somewhere. I heard his voice: 'Very good, Vic. And you've still got two minutes to deadline.'

'Where is Gayle?'

'Over here, with me, Vic.'

'And where are you, Cliff?'

There was silence. I knew I wasn't going to get any kind of straight answer to that question yet.

Then I heard laughter.

Then the set shut off.

'Cliff? Cliff? Talk to me, damnit!'

There was no answer. I really didn't expect one now.

It all seemed hopeless. Cliff, Gayle – they could be anywhere. I had no idea where to begin looking, no thought on what to do to find my wife in the short amount of time that remained. Precious seconds ticking away.

Cliff was still just as evil as ever. And there didn't seem to be much else for me to do. Standing alone on the Brooklyn Bridge, looking like the biggest damn fool in creation, feeling like the biggest damn failure there ever was. Wanting to tell Gayle how sorry I was. I'd failed her. Again.

I was about to walk away – there was no sense hanging around. Nothing was happening. I didn't expect anything to happen. I was beat, in more ways than one. I was sure Cliff wasn't finished with me yet. That he would get in touch with me again. Call me later at home. Maybe tomorrow? Begin another sick game? Maybe even have me going through crap like this every single fucking day for the rest of my life? He'd like that. And if Gayle was alive or dead it didn't matter, it wouldn't matter, because I'd never really know the truth. Cliff would always have me by the ball's because he knew I'd always be hoping that she was alive and that I would always have the hope of being able, somehow, to save her.

'Cliff! You fucking scumbag!'

I looked out over the river that led to Manhattan. It was another world over there in the City. Here in Brooklyn, things were different, a less civilized world, a lawless world. It was my world. The frontier. I looked up at the sky, trying to find the moon and only finding the pitch darkness of the night reflected back at me. Everywhere there was blackness, desolation, loneliness; all around me, and inside me.

There was still the steady sound of traffic on the vehicle part of the bridge below me. The sounds of the City and the river surrounding me. The night was warm and breezy. I didn't know when it was that I became aware of the dust. Or whatever it was. Dirt, maybe? It was falling, in the air all around me. Very slight but visible. Drifting down upon me like a fog, light, unobtrusive, hardly noticeable, and yet it was there.

But it shouldn't have been there.

Not at 3am.

Cliff was a funny guy sometimes. Oh, not 'funny' in the comedic sense; 'funny' in the crazy people sense. He had weird ideas. Always did off-the-wall bullshit. I know he'd had watchers following me all day, reporting back to him on my every move. But there seemed to be something I'd missed. Something above me. The dust. It was flowing down on me from the darkness of the upper beams. That kind of thing just didn't happen, did it? I wasn't sure. Maybe there was a rat up there, or some bird? Or maybe it was a two-legged rat – maybe someone was up there. Probably one of Cliff's watchers. Maybe even Cliff himself.

I felt the eyes watching me now, too. Right over my shoulder. From up top somewhere. Someone *was* up there! They just had to be! I walked off, trying in my most casual way to see what was above me. All I saw was impenetrable darkness, thick, dark girders and beams, a black moon up there somewhere offering no illumination at all. All shadow and mystery.

For sure someone was up there. Watching.

It had to be someone.

Didn't it?

Who was he? Where, exactly in all that complicated mass of steel and cable, was he? I had no idea. But I felt someone was up there. I was sure of it now. And I was going to get him! And to do that I wanted to make it look like I had given up, like I was walking away. With my tail between my legs. Beaten. Hopeless. I could play the part pretty well. Had a lot of practice lately. So I walked back over to the Brooklyn side of the bridge, and to the beginning of the walkway. I don't know if I was being followed or not at that point. I hoped not. I wanted whoever was watching me to think that the game was over and that I'd lost. That I was going home. Beaten.

Instead of taking the steps down from the walkway, I climbed onto the stone masonry of the outcropping of the bridge, and lifted myself up to one of the horizontal girders. From there I lifted myself up to another girder, moving out onto the bridge, climbing cables and steel abutments, moving higher into the upper rigging of the bridge. Moving upward, inch by painful inch, my muscles aching, unused to this kind of severe work. My eyes trying to see in the blackness of the night. Looking for him. Whoever he was. The guy on the bridge. Unable to see a damn thing. Not knowing where my enemy was, but knowing that someone was certainly there. Still. Even after I'd made it look like I had left and gone away.

It was weird. Up that high, the wind that blew in such a gentle breeze down below me, was loud and powerful. Hitting me in the face as I advanced along the beams and girders, trying to slap me down, so I'd fall and kill myself before I ever found out who was up there. With every step I took, my eyes scanned the girders and beams before me, below me, above me as best I could. The darkness was inpenetrable, the field of vision limited in the extreme. Finding nothing, struggling to see through the obscuring blackness, I moved forward.

I continued moving slowly now. Careful. Scared. Nervous. I had no desire to fall off the damn bridge. That would be a real screw-up for sure. And the more I moved around up there, the less I saw. I began to wonder if I'd imagined the fact that someone might be up there at all. What the hell would anyone be doing up there, I though? Only a kook or an idiot would come up here. Like me?

Yeah. And maybe, like Cliff? I wasn't so sure now. Maybe my mind had just made up the whole thing? Maybe the few bits of dust or dirt that had fallen down upon me didn't mean a damn thing? Maybe a rat or a bird dislodged the dirt? Maybe the thought it *had* to be someone was something I *wanted* to believe, something I *had* to believe after I'd failed Gayle so miserably?

I didn't know.

I'd seen the dust. Falling.

Maybe it had only been caused by the damn foot or wing of some nesting gull? They were all over the bridge. Some fucking bird. Or a rat. Scurrying. Shaking loose the dust and debris that just naturally deposited in the upper parts of the bridge over the years. Or perhaps from the wind? It was strong up here, gusting. It could have been only the wind. Nothing more, nothing less.

I felt like a fool.

Perhaps Gayle was being murdered right now? Right this minute? Or maybe she was long dead? I had no way to know for Sure. Meanwhile, here I was on the upper stanctions of the Brooklyn Bridge walking around in the darkness, like some fool lunatic, looking for a guy that probably didn't even exist. Unable to do a damn thing to save my wife. Even if the guy did exist and was up there.

Then I saw something.

It was a little beyond the first tower. Near the center of the suspension part of the bridge. Just where I had stood below on the walkway minutes before.

There was a form. A shadow.

'Son of a bitch!' I whispered.

I moved closer. Carefully. Very quiet now. Trying to hide myself as best I could amongst the beams and cables.

There *was* somebody there!

I looked below. I thought I heard him laughing. I got

closer and heard that it *was* laughter. Evil laughter. I moved closer still. Carefully. The man's back was toward me but I was sure I recognized the voice. He was busy, laughing as he worked on something, looking at something that was being played back on a small VCR camera. Watching what was being played there intently. I moved around. Came in closer. Outflanking the man and coming up upon his left side. Quietly. Watching him carefully. Hoping that he didn't notice me.

I came in closer still. Quiet as a mouse. Finally I got a chance to see his face.

Cliff!

I held my breath. Chilled.

Suddenly, as if possessing some sixth sense, Cliff turned toward me, smiling matter of factly.

I froze. Stunned.

There was a gun in his hand, and he said, 'Well, Vic, it certainly took you long enough to find me! You're slipping, bro. If I didn't kick some dirt down on your head you would have thought the game was all over for tonight and went on home. Never found me at all.'

'The game's never over, Cliff...' I said, watching him, full of anger, my eyes on his finger, wrapped tight around the trigger of his gun. It was a six shot .38 Police Special.

'That's right, Vic, the game's never over, it never ends, until one of us is dead.'

'Where's Gayle?'

He laughed. 'Dead. Dead, Vic, but you knew that. Didn't you? You know how these things go. She's dead, just like her boy.'

'How do you know about her boy?' I barked.

'I know everything, Vic. I know things that you would love to know, but will never find out.'

Cliff laughed.

My blood froze. I knew he was right. I knew there were things he knew that I wanted to know but that he'd never tell me. Things of importance to me, maybe to Gayle, things that would die with Cliff, if I was ever able to kill him. Or be lost and forgotten, when he killed Gayle and myself.

On a hunch I said, 'What about the boy, Cliff?'

Cliff laughed. 'Vic, Vic. You'll never understand that...'

I never heard the rest of what Cliff had to say. I didn't care. I saw my opportunity. It wasn't much of one, and I'd end up eating a few slugs for sure, but it was the closest I'd been to Cliff, the best chance I had to bring him down. So I took it. I charged him, like a crazy out of control train, like a lunatic that didn't gave a damn anymore if he lived or died. I didn't care how many slugs I'd take at that point, all I cared about was one thing – there was Cliff – right in front of me! It might be my only chance to bring him down. There weren't enough bullets in the damn gun Cliff had trained on me to stop me before I got my hands on his throat and choked the life right out of him.

I knew that.

And one thing more.

Nothing was going to stop me now.

I screamed.

Cliff screamed.

The gun roared and I took my hits.

Chapter Twelve
SOUTH TOWER, BROOKLYN BRIDGE
3:30 AM

I didn't feel pain, just hard and sharp pressure, like jackhammer hits trying to push me backwards as I charged forward. I knew I'd feel the pain later. It would come on like a steamroller, rolling over my mind and every neuron of my brain. But that was later. For now, I couldn't give a damn. There was Cliff! I just charged like a berserk bull.

Right towards Cliff.

And death for one of us.

It was intense. Boom, boom, boom. Slugs hit my arm, and shoulder, one in my bad leg, another grazing my cheek snipping off a piece of my ear. Cliff was good, four of his six shots had found their mark, but they didn't stop me, they didn't even slow me down. I still kept coming at him.

I had to keep going: if I stopped, even for a moment I would be dead and that would mean that Cliff had won. I couldn't accept that. I didn't want Cliff to win. I didn't want to be kicked out of the world now and leave Cliff still alive with Gayle as his captive. That kind of world stunk. So I had to keep on going. I just couldn't stop. I couldn't allow myself to feel the pain. The growing pain as it began to surge over me.

I had to get Cliff!

Finally I was on him. Knocking the gun from his hand. The weapon falling down through the girders and beams of the upper portion of the bridge to clatter upon the vehicle roadway below. My hands knocking his out of the way, began pummelling his face, reaching like a fiend for his neck, grabbing onto his throat.

Squeezing.

Cliff fighting me off like a demon. Scared now. Hitting me hard. In the face, the neck, kidneys and spleen. The pain ripped through me with each blow but I would not let go. I would *never* let go now! This was the moment I had waited for. This was the moment I had dreamed of for so long.

Squeezing.

Squeezing the life out of Cliff.

Squeezing his throat for all I was worth. Lifting his head and bringing it down hard on the metal of the beam below us. Banging his head down on the steel as hard as I could.

Hard.

Bang!

Harder.

Bang!

Again and again.

Banging and squeezing.

Blood flowing from his nose and mouth.
Blood flowing from my face, my arm, my shoulder.
Blood all over.
Blood in Brooklyn.
My blood.
Cliff's blood.
So much blood it was impossible to tell which one of us was shedding it any longer.

I banged Cliff's head on the beam again, but Cliff just laughed at me like it was the funniest thing he'd ever had happen to him. The blood was pouring from his nose now, red drool from his lips, a stream from his ear or behind his ear from the bottom of his head.

He was laughing.

Cliff was laughing at me!

I was beating the life out of him, I was going to kill him right then and there in a few minutes, by my very own hands, and he was laughing at me!

It was like when we'd been kids. Cliff always laughed just before he really began to fight. He seemed to need the beating he initially received from his enemies. Perhaps to stoke the fires within him? Maybe as some form of penance for what he was going to do once he began to fight back seriously?

He laughed and it caused my heart to ache.

'She's dead, Vic! Dead! Like her son! They're both dead!'

'What are you talking about? Her son! What do you know?'

'What do I know? I know everything and nothing! Who the hell do you think worked for Constintine? Who the hell do you think it was who took up the contract from Constintine's replacement after you offed the old man? You asshole! You think you've got me and you're going to fuck me up now! Vic, you're the one that's going to get fucked up! All the way this time!'

I kept pounding Cliff's head against the metal 'I' beam. Trying to pulverize the back of his damn hard head into mush. I felt his hair wet with blood, hoping that his skull would soon become soft and brittle. I wanted to tear Cliff apart, piece by piece, even as my own blood poured out all around us.

'She's dead, Vic! Dead! Dead! Dead!'

He laughed. Unable to control himself.

'Cliff!'

'Yeah, Vic!'

'So are you!'

And I just squeezed harder. Tighter. My fingers digging into Cliff's neck, trying to enter his windpipe. Cutting, searing into his flesh. Blocking his rasping voice from saying anything more. Blocking his breathing, his sickening words.

'She's dead, Vic,' he shouted in a harsh rasping growl. 'Right now! While you're trying to kill me. My sons are killing her. Look, Vic, look!'

Then Cliff, with strength I never knew he possessed, and I had no idea where he'd drawn it from, grabbed my head and jerked it upward, so I could see above us up to the top of the bridge tower.

'Look!' he shouted.

And there I saw it. Three figures on the top of the tower far above us. Two male. And between then, a female form I knew only too well.

'Gayle! Gayle!' I screamed out.

'Vic? Vic! I love you, Vic!'

She'd heard me but couldn't see me.

'I love you, Gayle!'

Cliff laughed, 'I love you too, Vic,' mocking us, his

massive fist now slamming into my face like a battering ram, with a strength and power I could not believe, knocking me off and away from him. I was down and stunned, with Cliff standing over me. He came at me then and locked my head so that I could not move, so that one little twist would crack the bone, then jerked my head upwards so I could see Gayle.

'And now, Vic, say goodbye to your wife.'

'Cliff, don't do it. Please. I'll do anything. I mean anything!'

'I know, Vic, that's why you've got to know that no matter what you are willing to do to save your wife's life – I want you to understand that for as long as you live – it would never be enough. Bring that with you to your grave, Vic. Understand the knowledge!'

Then Cliff shouted to his sons above us: 'Do it!'

'No!' I screamed.

The two men suddenly pushed Gayle off the tower and I watched helplessly as she dropped down with a horrendous scream into the cold waters below.

'Gayle!'

Now I was on Cliff again. Breaking his hold over me, grabbing him, trying to knock him off the bridge. And in doing so, knocking myself off the bridge with him.

We were both falling.

Falling downward, with me on top of him, and all the while the two of us fighting to squeeze the breath out of each other.

Then we hit.

Hard.

Cliff landing with a loud *woooff*. The wind leaving his huge frame. Myself, barely conscious but still alive. Cliff below me, silent and still, dead or unconscious. He had made himself useful. He had broken my fall. I tried to move, but couldn't, trying not to sink into unconsciousness before someone came over.

We were on the roadway of the bridge below.

Right in the middle of traffic!

I heard cars breaking sharply, beeping horns, drivers cursing all around me, and headlights shining on the two of us.

I saw a face.

Looking down at me like he'd seen a ghost.

I said, 'Woman… jumped from bridge. Save her! Please!'

Then my mind went blank and darkness overtook me.

Dufour Editions
P.O. Box 7
Chester Springs, PA 19425-0007

Place Stamp Here

DUFOUR EDITIONS

Thank you for purchasing this book. For a free catalogue of our other titles that are available from better booksellers, please complete and return this card.

Name: _____
Address: _____

City: _____ State: _____ Zip: _____

Please indicate your areas of special interest:

- ☐ Children's Books
- ☐ Dance, Drama, Theatre
- ☐ History
- ☐ Irish Studies
- ☐ Slavic Studies
- ☐ Gay & Lesbian
- ☐ Literary Criticism
- ☐ Germanic Studies
- ☐ Poetry
- ☐ Religion & Philosophy
- ☐ Scottish Studies
- ☐ Classical History & Literature
- ☐ Welsh Studies
- ☐ Women's Studies
- ☐ Scandinavian Studies
- ☐ Crafts, Hobbies, Cooking
- ☐ Folklore
- ☐ Other _____
- ☐ Other _____
- ☐ Other _____

Chapter Thirteen
BLOOD IN BROOKLYN

Cliff was dead. That's what the people at the hospital told me a few day's later when I woke up and was able to understand what they were telling me. Good riddance, I thought. I hoped he was burning in hell.

'Burn brightly, Cliff!' I whispered to myself.

Cliff dead. More blood in Brooklyn. Blood that I had spilled. Blood I was happy had been spilled this time. A world with Cliff out of it was a much better place.

Meanwhile, I was a mess. Busted up inside and out. Weak. Hurting bad. The pain was terrible but the drugs helped. It was almost like the old days. About the drugs, I mean. Except I was too messed up to enjoy any of it and mostly just laid back and did a lot of sleeping.

And dreaming.

They wouldn't tell me about Gayle, other than that she was still alive. That was enough for me. In the beginning. That's all I wanted to hear right then. That's all I could have handled at that point.

Gayle had miraculously survived the fall from the South Tower of the Brooklyn Bridge. She'd hit the water and almost drowned, but now she was in a coma and in intensive care.

Cliff's sons were nowhere to be found.

Gayle and I were in the same hospital. As the days passed I grew stronger, healing day by day. Gayle stayed the same. Like in suspended animation. The doctors told me it might be a while before she came out of it. *If* she came out of it. Meanwhile, she wasn't eating, wasn't moving, wasn't talking. Just laying there like a lump. It was terrible to see her that way. Having a loved one in a coma is rough on the friends and family, rougher still on the person in the coma. Day after day there was no change. Or so the doctors told me. But I saw changes, and I didn't like what I saw. Gayle was losing weight. Her skin was growing yellow and dry. Her eyes looked dull. Empty. I couldn't believe it. A woman with so much life, so much energy, so much strength, and she looked like she was wasting away right there before my eyes.

I told this to the doctor.

He told me to wait, be patient.

I said, 'You *guarantee* she'll come out of it?'

The doctor just shook his head.

I said, 'I know – there are no guarantees.'

He offered to buy me a cup of coffee.

I told him thanks, but I wanted to be alone.

As soon as I was able I got myself into a wheel chair and rolled myself into Gayle's room so that I could be with her and sit by her side. I was there all night and all day. Right by her bedside. Holding her hand. Talking to her.

'Come on, baby,' I would whisper to her. 'We can get through this. We been in worse situations.'

But I couldn't think of anything worse than this.

I talked to Gayle all day long. Only she didn't answer, she couldn't respond in any way. We had good talks all the same. Sometimes I'd joke with her. Making fun. Being silly like she said I usually was when I was happy. Which was any time I was with her. And when I didn't talk to her I waited, hoping, praying that her eyes would open and she'd call out my name. Tell me to stop being such a worry-wart. Maybe tell me she was okay, and that she would soon be better. That before I knew it, she'd be wearing that little black bikini, the one she knew I liked her in so well.

I had to smile at that. But she never came out of it.

The days grew into weeks. I got stronger, able to walk again, to move around a bit. I was rusty for sure, but healing, getting near normal, or somewhat normal. I'd never again be in the shape I'd been before Cliff had shot me up. Cliff had messed me up for sure. Shot me up good. A lot of damage and a lot of pain, but I was coping. I'd been lucky really, the few places I'd been hit were messy but areas that were repairable with time, rest and drugs. And plenty of bandages.

Gayle was a different story. The fall had caused massive shock to her system. Causing it to close down. They fed her with IVs but she was still losing weight. Breathing shallowly now. It was a few days later that she contracted pneumonia. I freaked. That was a bad sign. I knew what it could mean. Her body was too weak to fight. The doctors were guarded but I could see they didn't hold much hope at that point.

'It's just a matter of time now, Mr Powers. Now we're at the point that if the drugs take hold she may come out of it. If not, she'll slip down lower, then we'll lose her.'

One of the doctors told me a couple of days later. 'I think you should prepare. I'm sorry, but I think you should know the truth.'

I got mad and cursed him, told him to do *something! Anything!* Like a jerk, I took it out on the doctor, but the doc was enough of a professional and a good guy to understand that.

When I went over to him later to apologize for my words he just smiled and told me to forget about it. 'Vic, we're all doing the best we can.'

I said, 'I know that.'

He said, 'I just wish it was good enough.'

★

Next day I had a meeting with the Brooklyn DA about the murders of Fortuno, Reverend Johnson, and Jack the Skell. They also asked about the old lady on Fourth Avenue. She'd died. I told them everything I knew. I told them what I knew about Cliff, his sons, and what this had all been about. Truth is, I didn't know all that much, and there were some things I didn't offer. No sense being stupid. Or opening another can of worms.

The upshot of it was Cliff was dead and it looked like his secrets had died with him. They were looking for Cliff's sons, but they really didn't have any idea who they were looking for. They didn't have any names. No description. No addresses. Nothing to go on. They tied it up in a neat little knot and shelved it as solved. More or less. At least, it was as solved as it was going to get.

That's when I decided to do some looking on my own. Especially for those two sons of Cliff's. The two who had thrown Gayle off the top of the Brooklyn Bridge that night week's ago. They had to be made to pay. Like their old man. And just as Cliff was now dead and burning in hell, the two sons who had tried to kill Gayle were headed for the same destination.

At full speed.

I wasn't going to waste any time or energy on them either. Gayle was still in a coma. I didn't want to be away too long. Vic Powers was quickly healing, getting stronger with each passing day. Now I was ready to do something about this entire stinking mess.

I let word go out to every scumbag, snitch, weasel, killer, and shithead I knew. I knew a lot of them. I wanted info on Cliff's boy's. I put a hefty price tag that no one could deny. It wasn't long before I got something.

★

I went after the older one first. He was the one I'd punched out in the car on Fourth Avenue months back. He was big and mean and dangerous as hell. His name was Rodney.

I tracked him to a bar in Greenpoint. It was very late at night. Almost the next day. I saw him sitting at a booth with a bunch of scumbags just like him, dressed to kill, drinking and eating, feeding their fat faces like they'd never seen food before. He had more than a few drinks in him. When he got up to go to the bathroom I followed him into the back. Into the darkness.

It was a small bathroom: two stalls, one sink. I walked in right after him, made sure we were alone and then quietly locked the door behind me. I drew my knife. I wanted this up close and personal.

The toilet flushed. The door to his stall opened slowly. Then I was on him. My knife at his throat, pushing him hard up against the wall, banging him into the cement cinder blocks of the bathroom wall. His head hitting the wall. Hard. Again and again.

He recognized me now through his drunken haze.

I smiled, said, 'Your daddy's dead but you boys are just as rotten. You threw my wife off the damn bridge. You hurt her. Now I'm going to hurt you!'

'No, don't do it!' he stammered.

'Go to hell, scumbag!'

'I'll tell you...'

'Fuck you!'

Then I brought the knife to stomach level, plunging it into Rodney's gut, hard and deep. Pushing the blade, the entire knife now, including my hand – deep inside him and upwards now. The blade cutting him to pieces with every inch that I pushed it inside him.

My other hand held Rodney's mouth so he couldn't scream. He was too surprised. Too scared. Too shocked at what was happening to him to do much of anything just then. I drove the knife still deeper, cutting upward, moving the blade, positioning it, while he was still alive, so that its tip now protruded from his chest. Right there, right before his eyes!

I looked deeply into Cliff's son's eyes while he was dying in my arms. He was still conscious, still able to hear my words. They were the last damn words he ever heard this side of hell.

'Fuck you, Rodney! And fuck your father! Now you'll

both rot in hell and it's my goddamn privilege to send you there!'

He gurgled blood. I drew out my arm, my hand. It was covered with my own enemy's blood. Warm and red.

More blood in Brooklyn.

This time it was good to see.

The blood of revenge.

The blood of justice.

I washed it off.

It washed off easily.

I opened the window of the bathroom behind the sink. It was small but I could fit and I crawled out of it and into a dark alley. I was gone before anyone from Rodney's table came by to ask what was taking him so long to take a piss. I went back to my place. Washed again and cleaned up better. I was tired. Still weak. Still recovering from my injuries, but I felt the best I'd felt in a long time.

More blood in Brooklyn now.

But it still was not enough.

★

The other brother, I found out, was also named Cliff. Cliff junior. Like the world really needed another Cliff in it!

I went after him right after I did Rodney. That same day, that same morning, before the news would reach him.

Cliff junior was younger, about eighteen years old. He lived with a hooker down in Red Hook. He was the shooter. Responsible for the deaths of Fortuno and all the others. Blew away an old lady on Fourth Avenue just to make a point. He'd also been the one, with late brother Rodney, who had thrown Gayle off the Brooklyn Bridge that night into the cold waters of the East River.

Cliff junior?

Nice guy. This one merited special attention.

I put the knife away. I wanted to use my hands on this one, but I was still weak, and I didn't want to give him any kind of chance. Besides, I wanted to get this over with quick, and get back to Gayle.

I picked up the Louisville Slugger. It felt good in my hand. Serious. There's something about a baseball bat that has nothing at all to do with baseball. Something primordial. I figure it goes back to the days of the cave men. I figured I'd use the Slugger to some good effect, give Cliffy junior a few good shots to the head, just to get him pliable. A few good shots to the head with a hard wood baseball bat can go a long way to softening up resistance from a scumbag enemy.

I figured I'd do it quick and hard. I didn't really have much stomach for this; all I really wanted was to be at Gayle's bedside holding her hand, whispering silly things into her ear. But certain things had been set in motion by Cliff and his two sons. And because of that, justice and rage and a bunch of dead people – Jack the Skell, Fortuno, The Rev, and that old lady on Fourth Avenue whose name I did not know – all called out for their fair share of justice. And revenge!

Cliff junior walked out of the apartment hallway, standing in the doorway. Obviously half asleep. It was very early in the morning, the streets cold and deserted. It was getting into winter. It was perfect for what I had in mind.

It was good. Obviously, Cliff junior hadn't heard

about Rodney yet. He was not observant. He had a cup of coffee in his hand. He was standing there, took a sip.

It was time.

I came out of the shadows from the doorway of the next stoop. It was batter up. Fast and hard. Me hitting a home run right upside his head just as soon as he stepped out of the doorway and onto the top step.

Bam!
Wham!
Slam!

And there was blood and brain pulp, wetness and mess all over the place. On the walls, on the steps, on my bat, on my face and arms. Cliff junior just looked startled, stunned, his body bouncing off the wall as I batted him back and forth. Finally, I grabbed his neck and pulled his head up to my face real close, so my eyes bore right into his own.

I said, 'You hurt my wife! Now I'm hurting you! Now I'm going to send you down to hell with your father and your brother – and you can all rot in hell forever!'

Then I administered the coup de grace. I brought the bat up and all the way back, then slammed it down with all my might onto the top of Cliff junior's head.

There was a resounding 'whack'!

A wet, pulpy sound.

I had cracked the wood of my best bat, but also the bone of Cliff junior's skull, shattering his head, splitting the bone. Blood and gray matter sprayed all over the place.

More blood now.

I hoped that would be the last of it.

Blood all over.

More blood in Brooklyn.

★

I washed my hands when I got back and cleaned myself up as best I could. Changed my clothes and went back to the hospital to sit with Gayle the rest of the night.

It was Friday night. There was a good movie on TV at nine o'clock. It was a love story, one of Gayle's favorites. I was glad we were going to watch it together. I remembered all the other times we had seen it. It was a thing with us. Whenever it was on, we tried never to miss it. It made me feel good that we could watch it together again. I held her hand, sitting next to her in a chair right up by her bed.

We had fun. Together. We were both quiet. Watching the movie together. Like usual.

I said, 'This is the best part, baby. When he realizes how much he loves her, that he'd been a fool for so many years and had never even noticed her when she'd been right there beside him for so long.'

Gayle didn't say anything.

I knew she got emotional about this part.

It was so much like her.

'I know how much you like this movie. It's kinda like us, you know?' I said.

She was still, quiet like a stone. Shallow breathing.

I rubbed her fingers. They felt so cold. I moved the blanket so that it covered her better. Give her some more warmth.

'Remember the last time we saw this? We missed the whole ending because we got all horny and started fooling around. That was so good. You were so hot that night, got me so hot. You made me laugh after, when you told me that I made you miss the movie.'

I laughed out loud. Remembering.

The people at the other bed looked at me like I was crazy. Then they turned away. They just thought I was some nut talking to myself. I wasn't. Gayle was with me. I was talking to her. She understood. She was right there with me, right next to me, sleeping. She was just sleeping. We were holding hands and she was sleeping.

But she would never wake up again.

I think I knew that now.

I whispered, 'Gayle, I love you so much, baby. Please, please don't leave me. I can't stand to be alone. I couldn't take it if you left me, baby. You know, you're my whole life? You know that? Please hang on. We can get out of this. I know we can.'

Her hand was so cold now. I rubbed it hard, trying to get the circulation flowing, to get some heat into it. I didn't really know what I was doing. Nothing seemed to help. I looked at her face, into her eyes. The eyes looked thick and glazed, her face looked cold and hard. Did it look blue?

I jumped up when the alarm went off on her hookup's. A dull droning from one of the monitors showed a steady flat line snaking across a nearby oscilloscope.

I didn't have to yell for the nurses and doctors. They were there before I knew what was happening.

They pushed me away. Closed off that section of the room with a screen. Other nurses rolled in a table with those electric shock clamps they use on people who've had a heart attack.

I heard someone yell 'Prep!'

Then someone yelled, 'Clear!'

Did Gayle have a heart attack?
Then there was a heavy thumping sound.
'No good. Try again.'
Another moment.
'Clear!'
Another heavy thumping, an electrical sound.
Again, 'Clear!'
Yet again, 'Clear!'
A long pause.
Silence.
Someone said in a low tone, 'He's just outside, doctor.'
'Please bring him in.'
A nurse came out to where I was standing.
'Gayle?'
'Mr Powers, the doctor would like to see you.' I followed her like a zombie.
'Mr Powers? Mr Powers, I'm over here.'
'Ah, why? Ah, no...! Don't do that. Don't do that!'
I saw one of the nurses pulling the sheet over Gayle's face.
'Don't do that!'
'I'm sorry, Mr Powers,' the doctor said.
I pulled back the sheet. Looked down on Gayle's face and began to cry. I hugged her tightly in my arms, holding her so close, so that we could never be separated, telling her how much I loved her and missed her and needed her.
'What am I going to do now?' I shouted.
No one could answer me.
The doctors and nurses left me alone.
I sat down with Gayle, holding her close to me all night long. We talked all that night, because now I thought I could hear her voice. She was telling me how much she loved me, how it was all okay now, that I

shouldn't fear because we'd be together some day. How we'd fought for our love, and how a love like ours could never die.

Even if one of us did.

Chapter Fourteen
TAKE THE BIG SLEEP

I bought the new car with the insurance money. From Gayle. Gayle was always good like that, watching out for others, even before she watched out for herself. It was a beautiful red Toyota Celica, fancy and fast. Fully loaded. My favorite kind of car, and Gayle's too.

When Gayle had been alive we used to go car shopping, looking at all the new makes and models, drooling, wishing we could afford this one or that one. Unable to afford anything because once we'd both left the business, we didn't have any more money and any new car was way too expensive for us. Hell, we couldn't even afford the insurance for such a car.

Now I had a new car, something Gayle and I had both wanted, something we'd both loved together. It made me feel a little bit closer to her. But not much. There was still a billion miles between us. She was dead. I was alive. Sort of. Gayle had been dead only six weeks but already it had been the worst six weeks of my life. I just couldn't take it anymore. I saw her face everywhere. I saw her face with me now, over at my right, sitting in the passenger seat of this damn gorgeous brand new red hot Celica. I wanted to talk to her. But if she was there, she couldn't hear me. And if she was talking to me, I couldn't hear her.

I drove onto the Belt Parkway and opened the car up. I had it up to 70 in no time, moving up to 80. Breezing down the Parkway, like a maniac, passing cars going 55 and 60 like they were standing still.

Cool!

I knew it wouldn't be long before I heard the sirens. Cops were always staked out all over the Belt Parkway, but I didn't give a shit about any of that now. I was doing 80, and now pushing it up to 90. I had an important date, an appointment I had to keep. I had to meet someone and I wasn't going to let anyone or anything stop me from getting to my destination on time.

A siren began to wail behind me a minute later, loud, growing louder and closer. I pushed the gas and sped up. Faster. Letting the needle on the odometer approach 100. Ahead of me, I noticed a helicopter dropping slowly downward, trying to hover over my general area. More cops, I knew. That was fine by me. They could watch. They could all watch. No one was going to catch me. Not now. I had my appointment and no one, no cop for sure, was going to stop me from keeping it.

I was going East on the Belt, toward Bay Parkway. I knew I'd never make it past that exit, certainly never get out as far as Knapp Street where I used to live out by Sheepshead Bay. They'd try to reel me in long before then.

I didn't care.

I blew past a stationwagon and a Caddy. Sirens from two or three police cars chasing me now, coming closer. Louder. The helicopter overhead probably setting up a road block up ahead around Knapp Street. That was fine by me too. No roadblock bothered me. No roadblock could stop me now. My appointment was firm. Set. In stone. It could not be broken.

That appointment was with the wall of the overpass right before the Cropsey Avenue exit on the Belt. It was a huge bridge than ran over the highway, with a long cinder block wall that was just right for what I had in mind.

The Celica was good. It was fast. It was pretty. Gayle would have loved it, but if She couldn't be with me to enjoy it, then I couldn't enjoy it either.

It was useless. Only a device. But a device that perhaps I could use to bring me closer to her.

Truth is, I was sick of life without Gayle. I just couldn't handle it, it didn't have any meaning for me anymore without her. It was annoying. The pain was too great. Neverending. I decided to end it. Finally. Get the hell out. Leave it all. Take the Big Sleep.

Cropsey Avenue was up ahead. I saw the wall and it looked like something was up there. I looked harder. There was something or someone standing there. It was a woman! She was beckoning me. Smiling.

'Gayle?'
'Yeah, baby, you know it's me.'
'Gayle!'
'You know I love you, Vic.'
'You know I love *you*.' I floored the gas.
'Vic, don't do it. You've got to stay alive. I want you to live. Live, Vic! Live for me, because I can't!'
'I can't do it, Gayle. I can't stand it anymore without you!'

She said, '*Oh, Vic, you fucked up again!*'

And I said, 'I know, baby…'

I hit that wall like a battering ram, but my aim, like everything else in my life, was off-center. I had hit at a jutting abutment, not head-on as I had planned. Even so, I crashed with a resounding thunderous boom, the tiny Celica smashing to smithereens, pieces of it seared, cut, thrown all over the highway.

I was flung up and outward. Shot out like a torpedo.

'I'll be with you soon, Gayle,' I muttered, knowing I was drowning on my own blood, my body torn apart, cut and slashed, blood all over.

More blood in Brooklyn.

My own blood.

My own life.

And the Big Sleep on the way.

★

Sometimes you get on the hellbound train and you never know where the ride will take you. Sometimes things can be set in motion and they'll take on a life all their own, a purpose all their own too. Or at least, it can seem that way sometimes.

Chapter Fifteen

RESURRECTION AND THE HELLBOUND TRAIN

When I opened my eyes there was no one there. There was only whiteness all around me. And fuzziness. White fuzziness. I thought maybe I was in Heaven. Hell? Who the hell knew where I was. Then it dawned on me. I was in the fucking hospital!

Again!

And I was still alive!

Damn it!

I'd tried my best to kill myself so I could be with Gayle and I'd even fucked that up!

I felt like such a failure.

All I wanted to do was die.

I would have unplugged some of the tubes and wires and things they had going into me but I couldn't move. I was in bad shape. Worse than before. I was hurting. Real bad. The pain was terrible. I tried to stay awake but my mind just drifted back asleep, my eyes closed and I fell into unconsciousness again.

It was like that for many days.

I dreamed about Gayle. We were together again. It was nice. I saw that we had an office somewhere now on the West Side. A damn PI office! Like we'd been planning. We were partners. I saw that we had a kid. It was Joey, Gayle's son. He was going to school now, a growing boy with a great laugh and smile. I saw him later in a baseball uniform. Was he on the New York Yankees? It wasn't a Met's uniform, thank God! Joey grew older. I saw where he brought home a girl friend for us to meet. A hot number. I told him, treat her good, Joey. Joey just smiled and said, 'Sure, Dad.' I watched as Gayle hugged the girl, asked her when she and Joey were going to have the baby. I said, ah, what baby? Gayle said she couldn't wait to be a grandmother. She said she didn't want to get too old, like me. I grumbled, said: hey, now, I can wait for that!

We all laughed.

That movie was on TV again. The movie Gayle and I liked so much. Actually, I didn't like it all that much, I thought it was kind of silly, but Gayle loved it, so I always watched it with her. It was always good when we were together. Sometimes I made silly comments about the film, like that it wasn't all that realistic, that real love wasn't like that in the modern world, and Gayle would just shush me like I was a big kid or something, or play like she was pretend-mad with me.

She'd say, 'You're being so silly, Vic.'

And I just laughed.

'You're so silly,' I said back to her.

I heard someone. It wasn't Gayle. She was saying, 'I think he's coming out of it, doctor.'

The smile left my face. I realized it had all been a dream. And I knew now that Gayle was still dead, that I was racked up again in the hospital after I'd tried my best to crash that new red Celica Gayle loved so much right into a wall.

And I just didn't give a damn anymore. Now all I wanted to do was die.

'Can't I just die?' I mumbled.

'What did you say, Mr Powers?'

'All I want to do is die! Can't you just let me die?'

'I'm sorry, Mr Powers, but I can't understand what you're saying.'

'I want to die! Let me die! Please?'

'Do you want to write it down, Mr Powers?'

There was a commotion.

Someone said, 'He can't write. He can't use his hands now, Cathy.'

The previous voice said, 'I'm sorry, Mr Powers. You're not able to write anything now, but if you could talk slower, maybe I could understand you?'

'Just let me die! Die! Die! Die!'

One nurse said, 'It sounds like he wants pie? Maybe he's hungry?'

'I think I understand you, Mr Powers. That's a good sign, but you can't eat anything solid right now. Maybe after you rest, if your doctor says it's okay, we might be able to get you a very small piece of pie tomorrow? Now wouldn't that be nice? Rest now. I'll be in to see you later.'

★

They wouldn't let me die. They did their best to help me, to put me back together, to mend me and get my body in some type of working order. It was a big job. And they did a good job, too, but I just didn't care anymore. Without Gayle it didn't matter to me. Without Gayle it just wasn't worth living.

Whoever said 'life is pain' was more right about it than he ever knew. We're each of us born in pain, and too many of us die in pain. And in between there's life, that for too many is just a succession of pains; various, sundry, one after the other. All right, so that's life. We're all in the same boat. I just didn't want to stay in the boat any longer. And the name of that vessel is the *SS Misery Loves Company*. But when you get older, when you've lived a life like I have, and when you've been privileged to know real love like Gayle and I had, you realize a few things. You understand how precious that is. And how truly rare and irreplaceable it is. And when it ends you miss it so much, having had it for a few wonderful years, you don't want to live the rest of your life without it. Life just becomes a pain and longing you can not bear. Or, one you will refuse to put up with any longer, if you're a hard-head like me.

I've never really been one to sit down and think about suicide, but it's sure haunted my tracks during my life. Down in Virginia when I was a kid, seeing things, realizing things no kid (and damn few adults) would ever understand. All the way up to today, wanting to kill myself. Years back when I was in that hotel room in Ohio with the razor at my throat before Delilah knocked on my door, I was going to do it. I did it when I charged Cliff on the Brooklyn Bridge months ago, knowing he was going to shoot me full of holes, but knowing too, that I was going to get him also. Finally. That had made it all worthwhile.

And, of course, driving that new red Celica into a wall on the Belt Parkway was just the latest stupid attempt.

Another pathetic failure.

The police said, 'The jerk was going almost 90mph when he hit that wall. Must of lost control of the damn car. All these older guys buy these fast cars and then can't handle them. Lucky for him he didn't hit that wall head on, that he was thrown from the wreck. Pretty messed up, though. Serves him right for speeding.'

The doctors were the same. Saying, 'You're very lucky, Mr Powers. A terrible car accident like that. I can understand though, that when you're going that fast it can be easy to lose control of the car. Don't feel so bad.'

I didn't say anything

I kept my mouth shut.

I thought only of Gayle and being with her.

As soon as I got well, I'd try again.

'Honey,' I whispered, 'I'll be with you soon. I promise.'

★

I was getting better. I had a few visitors. My sister. Her kids. I looked at each of them and kept thinking of Joey. Then trying to think back. What the hell had Cliff been getting at when he was talking all that crap to me on the bridge that night? I used the phone and called Willy Hernandez at the Gold Street Station downtown.

I wondered if he was still talking to me.

He was.

He listened to what I told him.

I had to talk slow, I slurred my words, I was still in a lot of pain. It took me a long time to get it all out.

'I'll see what I can do, Vic.'

'Thanks, Willy.'

'It's not for you. It's for Fortuno. He was my buddy, we d been partners once. He said you were a good guy and that I should watch over you. I figured he'd been drunk or stupid at the time he said it, but he made me promise. So, I'll see what I can do.'

Time passed.

Hernandez was the only cop I felt I could talk to now.

More time passed.

I figured, okay, that's the way things go sometimes.

Another blind alley.

★

I was getting better, feeling stronger. Healing up good. I was able to use my hands and fingers now. Move my arms, even my legs a bit. Everything still hurt like hell. Some broken bones, some bad burns. I still wasn't going to be winning any beauty contests anytime soon, or doing any Olympic sports either. But that was all behind me now.

All I wanted was to die.

Now I felt I had the opportunity again. I disconnected myself from all the tubes and machinery, cut off all the IV antibiotics and plasma, turned it all off. I was going to end it now if I could.

I felt myself getting weaker. Little by little. I figured it must be working. No one noticed. No one came to check on me for a long time until a young Jamaican candystripper came in and had a shit-fit that all my life support was down.

I smiled.

I told her, 'Please, I want to die. There's nothing left for me anymore.'

She didn't hear me. I was so weak I could hardly talk. She got the nurses and they reattached all the tubes and equipment.

'I don't know how it happened!' the Jamaican lady said, 'I came in and found him like this. He would have died if I didn't save him!'

'Nonsense, he's not dying, just a bit weak, that's all. Sometimes they're in pain, or dreaming and they thrash around and disconnect everything,' the nurse said matter of factly, 'No big deal, just watch him more closely.'

'I sure will.'

The nurse left. Then the candystripper came over to me and said, 'Don't worry, mister, I'll keep a good eye on you. I'll make sure you'll not be dying on me. Not by a long shot.'

And I just wanted to yell at her, to scream and curse her, until I saw the name plate on her uniform. It said, 'Ms Gayle.'

And I thought, maybe it was a sign?

So I just went back to sleep. And dreamed.

★

Willy Hernandez came in to see me the next day. He was dressed in civvies. He looked serious as hell. He had things on his mind. I was surprised to see him.

He said, 'Vic, this is for Fortuno.'

I said, 'Okay, Willy, I understand.'

'I been digging.' He got up, closed the door to my hospital room. Sat back down next to me. There was no one in the next bed today. 'Ah, some of the things you said I should look at. I looked. You're in bad trouble if it gets out. I know you offed those two boys. Cliff's sons.'

I shook my head. It could mean no. It could mean yes.

'I know you did it, nasty business, but I don't care about that. Something's come up. Something you should know about.'

I didn't like the sound of this, but Willy had my attention, for sure.

'Clifford Jones...'

I froze up inside.

'...he was reported DOA at Methodist Hospital. The night you and him fell off the bridge. Remember?'

'Remember? Of course I remember!'

'Listen, Vic, I don't know how it was done. Or why. But there seems to have been some kind of switch. I don't think Jones died – at least the body that was supposed to be his...'

'Come on! You're shitting, me! Right, Willy?'

'Vic, there was another body in his place. I think he was taken away from the hospital. I think one of his boys did it, replaced his body, probably killed some poor slob somewhere and replaced the body. I'm checking now to see if anyone in the hospital is missing. Porters, custodians, you know the deal. Vic, I think Clifford Jones is still alive!'

Still alive?
Cliff still alive?

I said, 'It can't be, Willy. We fell off the fucking bridge together for christsakes! He broke my damn fall. He was right under me. He was a bigger freakin' mess than I was. I wasn't even sure he was still alive after we hit and then days later when I heard he'd died...'

'He's alive, Vic. Somewhere out there he is alive!'

I was shattered. My heart beating a thousand times a second, ready to explode out of my chest like a rocket, alive once again with the old anger, the old hatred, the old fear.

The fear of Cliff.

'There's more, Vic.'

I sighed, feeling a real chill in the air now.

Hernandez gulped nervously, took a deep breath, 'There's something else I think you should know. I checked around on his sons, Vic. Jones had *three* sons, not *two*. Up until a few days ago Jones was living with this third son, probably recuperating from his own injuries.'

My muscles tensed. I made a fist that had all the veins in my arm popping like an iron bar.

'Vic, I asked around, the landlady, the neighbors. No one knows much but they all agree about the boy. He's about six years old. Blonde hair. Vic, he answers to the name of Joey...'

He didn't have to say it. The blood froze in my veins and my heart skipped a beat.

'...I think the boy may be Gayle's missing son. I think...'

'Cliff!'

★

Now I *wanted* to live.

Now I *had* to live!

To track down Cliff and his third son. To save Joey, Gayle's only child. To save the best part of the woman I loved, a part of her I did not want to become infected by Cliff or any of his evil ways.

And Willy Hernandez said, 'I'm sorry, Vic.'

And I just said, 'You hear that, Willy? It's coming. It's that damn train again. Coming closer, moving down the tracks toward me. See all the steam? Hear that whistle blowing? It's coming again. Coming closer. It's saying, '*All aboard*, Vic! *All aboard!*"

Willy said, 'Ah, I don't know what you're talking about, Vic. I don't hear anything, my man.'

'That's all right, Willy. I bought my ticket years ago. Now I'll just wait until the damn train pulls into the station.'

'Then what, Vic?'

'Then I'll take one more fucking ride!'

Violence Is The Only Solution

A VIC POWERS STORY
BY
GARY LOVISI

I believe in homicide. I've always believed. It's just the way things turned out for me. There was no choice. No alternative I could ever see. The choice was simple, kill the evil or let it devour you. And let me tell you, the evil has one hell of an appetite. Ever since I was a kid. It was always so damn hungry.

I've lived a while, done some things, been involved in some things. Killing has never really bothered me. Not all that much. As long as it was some scumbag who deserved killing that is, and Lord knows there's plenty of those.

I am always careful though. Usually. It's crucial. So I always make sure. Never break my Golden Rule. Never, ever kill an innocent person. Never! That's the one sure way to damnation. And that's a road down into hell you do not want to take.

My one law is this: if you're not sure a person is an 'innocent', then don't do it. Just don't do it.

Leave them alone, walk away. If you gotta, run away.

But that's all by and by what was on my mind lately.

I was beginning to get a mite testy with my country recently. stuff I'd found out about the Vietnam MIAs, two different CIAs fighting a secret war with each other and the dirty deals to open trade with the same people in 'Nam who had murdered our soldiers. Others doing worse: selling children for sex in Thailand. To American buyers. Sex tourists. I'd like to crack their heads. The sellers and the buyers. Put that whole market underground where it belongs... six feet underground.

I thought of crazy Jack Rodriguez blasting away at Congress a man who had originally been imprisoned unjustly, then had unwittingly discovered a secret book that I had mailed to the Washington Post. A book that had disappeared like it had never existed at all. I mean, Amelia Erhardt and Jimmy Hoffa had nothing on disappearances when it came to that damn book being lost and forgotten. And the information in that book? well, I knew now it would never, ever, see the light of day.

Then there was Rodney King, the LA Riots, Ruby Ridge, Waco, the OJ fiasco, Oklahoma City – all war cries in certain circles. Then there was a slew of recent court verdicts in trials that split the country right down the middle, splitting Americans against each other, not to mention a presidential campaign and fund-raising scam that was so crooked it made Tricky Dick Nixon look like a novice and a downright 'honorable' SOB by comparison! It was so bad it might even bring down another American president!

Of course, it was all common sense to see and to figure out, but common sense solutions didn't seem to matter much in America any more. Talk about the damn Snail Darter? Common sense was the real 'endangered species' in 1990s America.

My country had become a nation where one side was forever at war against the other, and everyone had to choose up sides to survive, and there was no one left honest enough to say the truth... or powerful enough to say the truth and get away with it... without getting screwed. So he or she wouldn't have their life and career destroyed. We were fast becoming a nation of sheep, where racists of every type – politically correct stormtroopers, self-serving hypocrites, and lying demagogues – bought their way to power and out of crimes any average Joe or Jane would see serious prison time for. And no one seemed to care or know what to do about it.

I'd had it with all the bullshit!

It seemed that everyone from mutant Klan and Nazi morons to anti-white racist black militants and irate hate-filled Muslim sects was in our face every day lately. Shouting, *Kill the evil white man! Kill the damn blacks! Kill the Jews! Kill the...* Well, you can fill in the blank. 'Kill them all!' is what all too many people only understand. Everyone at each others' throats. All the problems, all the pain, all the lies – because all the time the implication too often seemed that violence was the only solution to the problems we faced.

As a nation. As individuals.

It's in the news every single day.

It made me so sick.

You see, I understand violence.

That's why it sickens me.

Yeah, me, Vic Powers, killer and louse, and a real bad guy. Some say too dangerous to let live. Them that tried to alter that reality are no longer with us. Yeah, so I'm a bad one. Sometimes. But I'm not an evil one.

And there's a big difference.

I admit it. I've committed homicide. I believe in homicide. Sometimes it's the only way to fight the true Evil. Or to fix something that's gotten way out of hand and need's to be fixed real bad.

You see, I know Evil too. Evil never gives up. It never goes away. Evil is hungry. Always hungry. Insatiable. It never stops.

See, I don't believe that Good can ever triumph over Evil like a lot of the fools do. I've seen too much not to know how things really work. Evil is just too strong, too incredibly relentless. In any kind of fair fight between Good and Evil, Evil will always win. Evil is tougher, stronger, Evil knows all the dirty tricks and uses them to devastating effect. Good is not single-minded or persistent. When Good guys win they pack it in and go home. The war's over for them. Good guys don't understand that while a battle may end, the war never ends. The war is never over. Evil never quits.

Let's say you put up Bad against Evil. Now, that's a different story. That's where I come in. Bad will use Evil's ways against itself. Like I do. Like I use homicide. I'm not afraid of taking care of any scumbag who deserves it either. I believe in homicide. So I'll kill, but only those that deserve itx – and there's a lot deserving, believe me. But I'll never cross over. Never kill an innocent. Never.

I wondered who I was kidding. I'm telling myself this stuff and it ain't exactly true. I crossed over. Once. Killed an innocent person. It was horrible. I'm not proud to say it. It damn near destroyed me and it's something I'll have remorse over and be ashamed of until the day I die. And I deserved every bit of pain I got from it and every bit of pain I gave myself from it too. I ain't complaining, but it happened. I'll never do it again. I'll never crossover again. I'll be real careful.

But I still believe in homicide. That's the way I am.

And even with all this stuff in my head, all this pain and rage and fire eating away at me, I still wanted to have a life. Like, a normal life. Sorta. Like what could pass as normal for me, Vic Powers. Something like my old partner Larry had made for himself so many years ago when we'd been on the job together. It seemed like another life now. Looking back. So far away. So long ago. But I had wanted that once. That road Larry had marked out to me back then – he'd made it all seem so clear and attainable, living a wholesome life, having a good loving woman at your side, raising children, loving them, building a home together. Something for the future. Larry had shown me the way. And I wanted to follow his lead, his excellent example. At least, I'd wanted to follow it as best I could. At least I wanted to try.

But it was not for me.

And besides, it didn't seem like the country would let me. Things just kept getting in my way.

It was weird. I'd just walked into this situation, and now it was left up to me – Vic Powers, of all people – to uphold the middle ground of tolerance and sanity against violent extremes full of lunatics who were dangerous, hateful killers. I'd fallen into a world headed for the dumpster at supersonic speed, and even though I held all the pieces naturally at the time I had no idea of any of what was really going on.

All I knew was that things had been going down in America the last few years, a lot of stuff really scared me. Some things I had been involved in. Some things I had seen. Some I had heard about. It got me nervous. Now it seemed I was the one who might have to set some things right.

And that was the scariest thought of all to me.

Had we sunk that low?

★

It started out as a missing person case. Evolved into a runaway. Then went to hell from there on. There was this couple and they had a daughter. She was twenty-something years old. Blonde, cute, and probably hot and horny. Looking for thrills or action or something. Maybe just to get away? To run? Freedom? Safety? I'd find out.

I was called over to the Rauch apartment. Swanky place on West Street. They gave me photos of their daughter.

I said, 'I'll need info about all her friends, her hangout places, stuff like that, so I can find her.'

The father told me, 'You don't need that.'

The mother said, 'It's not that Lori is missing, Mr Powers. Not exactly. You see, we *know* where she is. That's the problem.'

'You'll have to explain that to me. On the phone you said it was a simple missing person case.'

'It is, Mr Powers. Lori is missing, but it's simple because we know where she is.'

I said, 'Okay, maybe we should try again. What exactly is the problem if you know where Lori is?'

'It's because of where she is. That's what bothers Morris and me so much,' Mrs Rauch said. She looked over to her husband nervously and he sighed, got up and walked away. He looked sad, beaten down, a defeated man. There were tears in the wife's eyes as she watched him.

As he walked off he said, 'I wish I could kill them. I wish I could kill them all with my bare hands, but violence is never a solution to our problems, Mr Powers. I believe that. I have to.'

I laughed. 'Violence is never a solution to our problems? Just look around you, every damn minute of every damn day in this stinking world violence is being used to solve problems.'

There was silence while Morris looked at me and then left the room.

His wife sat across from me and sighed deeply. 'It s just so hard to talk about it.'

'I know,' I lied.

'You know, I married Morris after Bill, my husband, died. That was almost four years ago.'

I didn't say anything, I just watched her wring her hands like an old mop, shaking them and then her head, like it was all so terrible, trying to summon up the courage to tell me something unbelievable.

I said softly, 'Go on, Mrs Rauch, it's best to tell it, get it all out.'

She sighed, said, 'Morris is Jewish.'

I smiled, 'I sorta figured that.'

She nodded. 'You don't know what it's been like for us, Mr Powers. My family is old Catholic and I was raised strict Catholic. Morris is Jewish and a very good man, but not a particularly religious one. He'd lost family in the Holocaust, so while he is naturally cynical toward God and religion, he does have a very strong Jewish identity. Culturally. Do you know what I mean?'

I nodded. I think I knew what she meant.

'Anyway,' she continued, 'Morris and I have known each other for a long time, a very long time. Long ago, when we were young, we were... but we could never, never think of marriage in those days. Things were so different then. There was the family situation. My father. Morris' mother. It was so impossible. You understand?'

I nodded. A lot of stuff was different in the old days, 20-30 years ago, maybe even 5-10 years ago in some places, with some people. Lotta changes. Some for the better, some for the worse. Stupid bigotry that kept lovers apart was some of that Evil.

I figured it was just the 'Shit Quotient' making itself known again. Somehow it always stayed the same in the world – things change, times change, sometimes a real lot of changes – but the Shit Quotient always remains at the same level. The Shit Quotient is the one constant in an ever- changing world. Some people are treated like hell, screwed over, killed, but somewhere else others have it all sweet and easy. Then the world tilts and things change. The Shit Quotient kicks in and those people get beat up, robbed, raped, hurt, killed. It's always the same. It's just that it's not always the same people. Or the same type of people. Or people from the same country. Jews, Armenians, American Indians, Colonial settlers, Slavs, Bosnians, Mayans, white Dominicans, the black Haitians under the Ton-Ton, the Khmer Rouge piling up of fellow Cambodian's, Iraqi poison gas... it never ends. I figured the Shit Quotient was kicking in again in America.

I sighed, looked over at Mrs Rauch – I just knew she was about to tell me some sadsack crap that I did not want to hear, that I did not want to know about, and that I was sure would make me angry and sick and probably want to do something seriously bad to stop.

I also knew that she didn't feel right talking about it. She had pride. She was ashamed.

I said, 'It's all right, get it out. Tell me the whole story, Mrs Rauch.'

She sighed, 'It's so terrible, Mr Powers, so... so...'

She didn't know how to describe it. I knew. 'Evil?' I offered.

She looked into my eyes then for the first time, staring, and I knew and she knew. She finally said, 'Yes. That's the word for it, Mr Powers. Evil.'

I felt the nape hairs on my neck tingle, then nodded, waiting for her to begin.

'I wasn't watching. You always have to watch, Mr Powers. If you don't watch, it... Evil, will spring up on you. I know now, it's always there. waiting. I'm sure of it. Now. It happened like that with Morris and me, we didn't realize about Lori, how serious things had become, until it was too late. My God!'

'Realize what, Mrs Rauch?'

She was flustered, beginning to cry. I watched the tears stream down her face. I didn't try to comfort her. Her sobs grew louder and terrible to hear. It was like she'd lost her daughter, like she'd lost her to death, killed, murdered, but of course it wasn't anything like that at all. Lori wasn't physically dead at all, as far as I could tell. No, that wasn't it. It was far worse. It was a deeper and darker loss. Lori was not dead, but she was just as dead as if she were dead, and in some ways she was deader than any of the dead. The one thing in Mrs. Rauch's life she had loved had turned out rotten, and now the Evil had Lori within its grasp and was beginning to squeeze.

I knew Morris would come back eventually. He looked a mess now. I could see the pain in his face, the sorrow in his eyes. I'd seen cheerier faces in old photos of Nazi concentration camp victims. It was scary. It haunted me. His gaze was deep, his eyes like tombstones, with ovens in them, and skeletons crying out in pain and rage. Forever.

I had to shake my head to clear my mind.

I looked away from Morris and his pain, I knew all about that stuff. There was something else there in his eyes that made me want to look though. It was the man's deep love for his wife and his longing to ease her own pain. It made him come out of himself, to step outside of his own terrible distress, to comfort his wife, to hold her, to tell her how much he loved her.

I didn't say anything. I didn't have to. I got the picture all right when Morris handed me the photo. The photo that showed Lori, all pale and blonde and blue-eyed, young and shiny, with that lovely smile of hers. She was a pretty girl, pretty special. She was dressed in a white shirt, starched insignia on the collars, right armband boldly proclaiming something that disgusted all sane people, a silver death's head in the center of her black field cap, smiling. Anticipating. Hungry. Her black boots shined to a glow, the gun in her hand cocked and apparently ready to be fired, the man next to her holding a large framed photograph of Adolph Hitler in one hand, and a Nazi swastika flag in the other. Lori and the man with her in the photo were smiling. Likely thinking some pure Aryan-type thoughts.

Morris Rauch handed me the photograph.

I took it, put it away in my pocket.

'This filth… I… I… oh, my God! Why, after all these years, and all we have been through?'

'I'll find her and I'll bring her back.'

Morris Rauch looked up at me then, 'I don't even know if I want her back, Mr Powers.'

I said, 'Look, she's fallen in with evil people, but...' and I was gonna give the, 'but she's still your daughter' spiel. But, of course, she wasn't – his daughter, that is.

'Bad companions, Mr Powers? Is that what you think this is? It's a bit deeper than that. These are Nazis, Mr Powers, not some group of rambunctious kids.'

I nodded. But I knew things weren't always that simple, either. There had to be more to this than met the eye. As it would turn out, there was.

★

It's a funny thing about being twisted. The right amount of pressure and the wrong ideas can sure bring out amazing things in some people. I remember years ago when the KKK had been very active against Jews in Alabama, the Feds eventually found that the guy responsible for all the pain and problems down there against the Jews, the local KKK Grand Dragon, had actually been born a Jew.

Then there was Wayne Williams, a successful young black man from Atlanta, and a serial murderer of 29 of Atlanta's black children. He figured that he could improve the black race by killing off all the poor and uneducated black children. There's a man could've won a lifetime membership in the KKK.

Twisted.

I didn't even want to think about where Vic Powers fit in all that but I could sure understand it. Anger and hatred is a deadly mix. I feel the anger. But, none of the hate – except hate for haters. I do hate the haters.

And I sure do understand anger.

★

When I got back to my car I sat there a while and studied the photo. It was from a few years ago. Thing was, if Lori Rauch had run off to join the local Fourth Reich Nazi and Klan gang, it might take a bit of work to get her out of there. Especially since she was, apparently, a part of the problem now. I knew something else too, the guy in the photo with Lori, was Arthur Burk. He was trouble. He had been a young Aryan skinhead who'd since gone legit (sort of) and was sporting a more rational political line. Hey, Communists use the cover of the left and liberals all the time, so why not the other way around? David Duke was just one former American Nazi who came to my mind. Farakann is another Nazi, only he comes in a different color.

Burk didn't wear Nazi uniforms any longer. He'd gone legit long ago like David Duke, but he was the same swine he always was. Aiming now to be a legit pol. I'd heard of him. He was dangerous. He had four things that made him dangerous: He was serious, he was smart, he had a lot of money backing him from somewhere, and he had heavy connections. Favors owed. He was also a good-looking ladies' man and could be a very charming fellow when it suited his purpose. And he was something else. He was not as racist as he let on. He was just an opportunist who was into death and destruction for its own sake. And to use people. And death. And now, apparently, Lori. All for his own ends.

He was also a man with a plan.

I asked around, from the local riff-raff and some people I knew in some pretty unsavory organizations, radical offshoots of the old Jewish Defense League, some right-wing loonies, leftovers of the old Communist Workers Party. I found out some amazing things. I was surprised by it all. There seemed to be a lot of stuff going on in the hate underground lately. Things were a hop, skip, and a jump more extreme than the merely radical underground that most people are aware of; the 'talkers'. The hate underground is something else. The hate underground was making ready for war. The problem with them is that they re not just 'talkers', a lot of them are 'doers'. Timothy McVeign? Silent, but a doer. You get my drift? From what I found out something big was in the works and they were just waiting for the word.

★

I didn't really want to get involved in all that crap now. All I wanted to do was find Lori and bring her home. Maybe slap some sense into her on the ride back? Maybe not. I didn't know what I could do or say to make her come back. Not home, but to reality. Snow her photos of death camp survivors? Play on her empathy? If she had any? If she really was in with these people she'd spout the line, it was all made up, some Jewish conspiracy, and she'd just laugh it all off. And that would drive me nuts and then I'd knock her block off. Her mind and soul may have fallen so deeply into the dark pit of hatred that I could never really save her. It's damn deep and dark in there. Like a black hole. No light escapes once its fallen within. Neither does anything else. Maybe even Lori.

The Fourth Reich Klan skinheads had places all over the country. Safe houses and club houses and such. Rat-trap bars and hole-in-the-wall skell joints. Most of the members and hangers-on didn't amount to much – a bunch of two-bit losers, the kind of kids, and later on adults, who always blame someone else for their own miserable problems. Never realizing that we make our own hell. But once in a while the group would latch on to a real hardcore bad guy with balls. One that was either too stupid or too full of hate to back down. A doer. An action-oriented type of guy. The kind they'd send up the line, up through the network, one who could be useful for bigger things. It was a kind of upward mobility program for hate mongers.

It was like that in the Fourth Reich Klan skinheads. It was also like that in the elite Fruit of Islam killers; among the leadership of the Bloods (who were national now); the old Born to Kill (BTK) making a comeback; the Black Liberation Army, still full of hate and out to kill white cops; the Chicago El Ricans who had worked for the government of Libya; the Yahwahs, whose 'charming' organization originated as a rape gang; the old hardcore KKK that wanted revenge; the enforcement arm of the Latin Kings who wanted respect; the old Ghost Shadows now in the Tongs of every Chinatown across the nation and in the trade big-time; the Crips, who worked with Hell's Angels; the radical Jewish Kanane-hai, loaded and ready to fight; Aryan Nations and the Eoleim City leaders wanting to spill blood; the old Mafia and the new drug Mafia out to take their turf back; the Russian Mafia; vicious and violent Colombian and Nigerian gangs; wicked Jamaican posses; and all the various Arab and anti-American terrorist cells that were sitting and planning and waiting patiently. There were Chinese Triads and Japanese Yakuza here in cities doing their work; international drug cartel guys; rich arms merchants always ready to bring in a shipment for a good cause; South African racists with no place left to go; rightwing anti-abortion nuts and leftwing neo-hippy environmental Uni-bomber type thugs; and animal rights crazies who'd kill you for wearing leather shoes or a wool scarf in the winter. And a lot more who were even more crazier like the NAMBLA and pedophile gangs.

It was always the same shit. Since Garfield, since McKinley, since Kennedy and Oswald, and King with James Earl Ray. Find the real crazies and then use them to deal out more pain, deal out more death and destruction, all for the glorious cause or to 'save' America.

Bullshit! All that ever happens is that a lot of innocent people, usually women and children, end up getting hurt or killed – people that aren't involved in any of this crap in any way and have no idea what the hell is really going on. Like in Oklahoma City, they're the ones that are always hurt or killed. Average citizens just trying to live their lives, earn a living, feed their kids, put a roof over their heads – blown up or murdered. Or politicians, killed for what? Words? Ideas? Talk? I know, I don't like politicians, or lawyers either, but that's a different matter.

All I knew was that Lori was deep into this kind of shit. It all made me so damn sick. So damn angry.

From what I'd been able to find out, Arthur Burk's organization owned some country club in the New Jersey boon docks where Lori was supposed to be working. I found out that her job was head of security for the Fourth

Reich Klan skinheads. That kinda blew me the wrong way to hear that. That's a leadership role. That means serious ideological commitment. I knew it sure as hell would make a hard job that much tougher. And it could get me killed a lot easier and quicker than I thought might be possible.

There was supposed to be some kind of big meeting at this country club in a few days. Lori was supposedly there early with a few of her goons to check out the place and prepare it. I figured I'd sneak in, grab her, then be out before I got caught. Or killed. At least, I hoped so. I'd gotten into better protected places, after all.

So I drove on out to the Jersey boonies Tuesday night. Decided I'd sneak onto the grounds after midnight, then lay low until I could find Lori when she came back Wednesday morning. Getting into the grounds was no problem. I caught a big break because the dogs were all kennelled out by the barn. It was dark and quiet. A guard was here and there but nothing serious right now, it was still too early for the big Friday night meeting. That would be when security really got serious.

I eventually made it to the clubhouse without being spotted. It was a huge building with a large central meeting area. I didn't see anyone. I headed down into the basement to hide out until dawn. Later I'd scout the area and try to get to Lori. At least that was the master plan. Not one of my better plans to be sure. Especially once I discovered that I was hiding out in the middle of a basement full of high explosives. The whole damn place was loaded with crates of weapons, as well as C-4, dynamite and other ordnance, even grenades and bombs. It looked like the place was stuffed to the rafters with every damn kind of weapon and device invented by man to kill as many other men as possible. Being down there with all those explosives made me glad that I had quit smoking years ago, but I could've sure used a good stiff drink just then all the same.

★

Wednesday came and went and no Lori. I tried to be cool, stay hidden. Things were still quiet outside but once in a while one of the Nazi goons would come downstairs and get a weapon or a box of shells. Then I'd hide and hope he wouldn't find me. Once I heard two guys at the foot of the stairs talking about the big meeting.

'We'll bring the fuckin' country right to its knees!' one of them said.

'And set it right again! The way we want it to be,' the other replied.

'Freakin' right, brother! To its knees! Bleeding all the way down. Burk will rip America a brand new asshole!'

They laughed then and went away. It didn't sound encouraging. Something big was up. But what? I let it pass for the moment.

I just couldn't figure it. I couldn't see how a bunch of freaks and geek Nazi morons could ever bring America to its knees. First off, there weren't nowhere enough of them. Secondly they weren't really organised, they didn't take orders or have direction, they were lazy misfits and losers. Except for a very few like Arthur Burk, they really were just a bunch of overweight hateful losers. But then I thought about now the original Nazi movement had begun so long ago in Germany. I thought about Hitler and his brownshirts – they were originally just a bunch of crude beerhall assholes, and they'd damn near destroyed the world once. Not to mention killing tens of millions of people. And now I wasn't so sure about anything anymore. I began to feel a chill down there sitting alone in that Nazi cache basement full of explosives... and it didn't have anything to do with the cool seventy degree summer temperature outside. It was a chill about the future, about my country.

So Wednesday came and went. Uneventful. By Thursday morning it was a different story. Now things were really hopping. I heard big trucks and a lot of voices, frenzied activity in the hall above me and all around the grounds. The dogs were let loose now, being led around the grounds by armed handlers wearing your traditional Nazi brownshirt uniform complete with Swastika armbands. Kinda made me feel like I'd fallen into some bizarre World War II movie. But this was no damn movie, this was the stinking end of 1997 and there was no big John Wayne or Audie Murphy out there to save my miserable ass if I fucked up on this one.

All the time I hid out I was looking for Lori, but the words of those two goons from the day before went around and around in my head. I decided that I might need some insurance, some serious insurance, so I set to work, found some wires, a miniature electronic detonator, rigged the whole damn mess and then slipped the small duct tape wrapped package into the pocket of my green jacket. It was too hot to wear the damn thing in the summer heat, so I carried it as I left the basement, as I moved up into the big hall above.

It was Thursday night and it was dark and quiet, but I didn't let that fool me. There were enemies all over the place. All around me. No, I wasn't paranoid. I was being common sensical. Imagine that – me, Vic Powers, and common sense. I smiled. The world can sometimes become so very weird.

I saw that the main floor of the huge hall was loaded with people talking and shouting and cursing and threats filled the air. It sounded hot. Explosive. It was so loud in the room but it was all muffled and fuzzy outside, where I was, in the outer hall. The huge dark wood doors were closed shut, tighter than a crack whore's heart. In front of those door's, amazingly, instead of finding armed guards, I saw a tripod display stand with a large sign on it that said: *'Welcome Sales Reps To The National Conference!'*

I didn't know what the hell to make of that. It sure didn't seem like Nazis to put on a sales conference, but I let it pass for the moment. It was strange though, and I began to wonder if I'd done some Rip Van Winkle scene when suddenly the outside door opened wide and I saw Lori Rauch enter with a squad of stormtrooper goons following behind her.

I froze for a moment. Stunned. She looked my way. I gave her a Nazi salute, then opened the two big doors and entered the assembly room as fast as I could. My heart was in my mouth and my nerves were frazzled to the limit as I waited for Lori and her goon squad to come in after me and pound my head into the floor. But they didn't. They didn't have to. I'd walked right into a huge chamber full of every kind of Nazi, skinhead, neo-Nazi, race conscious Aryan thug and Klan monster in the country. They seemed to all be there, having some kind of big secret meeting, dozens of them were seated around this huge circular table. I shuddered. There were so many of them. Just my dumb luck, it looked like they'd moved up their meeting by one day and I'd fallen right into it.

Then I heard the voice, and my name.

'Well, well, if it isn't Vic Powers.'

It was a male voice, rough, hard, deadly.

I grimaced. I looked to where the voice was coming from and saw Arthur Burk, older now, and meaner, stand up and come toward me. Along with him came a dozen of the biggest and nastiest looking white guys I'd ever seen this side of the WWF. They were all armed. I was wishing that I was also, though in that company it would not have done me the least bit of good.

Burk was older, I remembered him now, and he had filled out from the way he'd looked years ago when he'd been a lanky skinhead and half-assed crim. Larry and I had busted him a decade or more back when I'd been on the cops. Burk had been penny-ante back then, but he did have brains and balls. He went away and came back meaner and worse than ever. Prison – the 'University of Crime' – had never turned out a more hardcore nor devoted graduate.

I could see it in his face. Now it was his revenge time.

'You remember me, I see,' Burk told me, smiling nastily as his cold eyes bore down into my own blank orbs. It must have been like looking in a mirror for him, and he soon turned away. His goons grabbed me, frisked me, then held me. Hard and fast. I didn't see any sense in starting a fight just then with over a dozen Nazi killers so I opted for conversation with the Fuhrer junior instead.

'Yeah,' I said. 'I remember you, and you remember me.'

'You sent me away.'

'It wasn't long enough, apparently.'

He laughed. Saw me look around, said, 'Oh, you mean all this? This is nothing. Nothing. Tomorrow, Mr Powers, that is the day that will go down in history.'

He saw that I didn't know what he was talking about. He liked that. It made him feel like a big man. Powerful.

Important. I guess he was, for the moment. Until I got to him, that is. But I put that on hold, too, now. I didn't particularly care about all this stuff, my mind was working overtime figuring on just what the hell I was going to do to get my ass out of this mess. I was not encouraged by the way things seemed to be going at the moment.

Burk continued, 'I know all about you coming here, trying to rescue my Lori, so you can bring her back to that old Jew stepfather and her whore mother – that bitch of a race traitor.'

'Now you sound like a real Nazi.'

He slapped my face, back and forth. 'Listen to me!' he barked.

'I'm listening!' I shouted back at him.

He smiled. 'That's better. Of course you realize that when you go to the underground for information your very inquiry becomes information that can also be sold on the same market. Your asking about Lori? Me? Our little group? The very people you are asking let us know who has been doing the asking. And why. It's basic shit, Powers.'

I nodded. 'I know how things work, but it got me here to Lori. To you. Didn't it?'

'And you'll die for it. Like all race traitors will.'

I got a bit offended. 'So now you're calling me a race traitor?'

'Whites who go against white supremacy. Whites who are traitors to their race, who oppose our goals, are traitors to their race. Just like you, Powers.'

I laughed at that. 'I'm no race traitor.'

'You're white, aren't you?' Burk sneered.

'I'm white, but that's just skin color. My *race*, asshole, my fucking *race* is not *white* – it's *human*! That's what binds us all together. That's the only 'racism' I believe in.

It's you and your kind, in whatever color you come in, that are the true race traitors – traitors to the one race we are all a part of. The only race that's important. The *human* race.'

Burk laughed. 'Nice speech, Powers.'

'I thought you might like it.'

He smacked me in the face. 'I don't, but that doesn't matter. After tomorrow this will all be sorted out. There'll be a new America. One where "blood in the face" will rule, where all whites will stand together against the mud people.'

'I don't think so, asshole,' I said.

'A lot of Americans are listening to us now.'

'Yeah, and a lot of people would tell you how good shit tastes if it came in a different flavor, but it's still just shit!' I barked.

Arthur Burk smiled. It got me nervous. He wasn't angry, he was confident. He said, 'Take him out and kill him!'

The goons dragged me off and I heard guns cocked, rounds loaded into chambers, bolts pulled back. The army was getting ready for action. On me.

Then... 'Wait!' Burk suddenly ordered. He came over to me, looking me up and down carefully. 'You really don't understand what this is all about, do you? Well, I'm going to give you a wonderful opportunity, Powers. I'm going to keep you alive just a bit longer so you can see what I am talking about. I want you to see my plan for America's future.'

I didn't say a word.

Burk added, with laughter, 'You know, Powers, you're a fool. Always were. You should join us. I'm white, you're white. We're all white here. And I know you don't like niggers. Ain't I right, Powers?'

I didn't say anything.

He insisted that I answer. He slapped my face back and forth, asking the question again and again.

'You don't like niggers! I know it, Powers!'

I glared at him and finally growled, 'I don't like niggers, but I like black people. There is a difference, and I know the difference. And I don't like white niggers either, asshole!'

Burk grew red.

I waited for what I figured was on the way.

Then he just laughed. 'That doesn't matter any more, Powers. Nothing matters any more after tomorrow. You see, my problems aren't with the niggers, or even the queers... or the damn Jews and the ZOG. My problems are more focused. My problems are with the whites that have sold out their race, their children, and their blood. They're the ones I'm after. They're all cowards, and they'll bend if I put enough pressure on them – like if I kill a few – which I am all set to do. They either climb on board with me and my program or they'll drown in the mud. And eventually, Powers – and you know it – they'll all come to me! Eventually. There will be no alternative after tomorrow.'

I didn't know what the hell to say. So I said nothing. I sweated bullets as they dragged me away.

They chained me to a wall in a back room of one of the numerous outbuildings on the country club grounds. I think it was a storage room of the damn pro shop.

★

Lori Rauch came to see me about an hour later. She was dressed in her best Nazi-bitch uniform and shiny black boots. She left her goons outside, but she still held a gun on me. It didn't matter at that point because there wasn't much I could do about anything.

'So you are the man my mother hired?'

'Your mother and father love you very much. They want you to come home.'

'Liar! And don't ever say that that old Jew is my father. He is my *step*father. He is a Jew and I hate him!'

Well, I saw where this was going. I just laughed at her. It really was quite funny to my warped sense of humor. My laughing shocked her, not at all what she expected.

'Don't laugh!'

Which just made me laugh at her all the more.

'Why are you laughing at me?' she demanded.

I couldn't help it, 'I was just thinking about twisted people.'

She slapped me. Hard.

I just laughed harder, almost hysterical now.

I saw her finger twitch on the trigger of the gun in her hand. She slapped me again.

I just couldn't stop laughing.

'Stop laughing at me!' she screamed.

Then she kicked me in the gut. I doubled over. It hurt, she had good aim, but I just kept on laughing. I don't think I could have stopped even had I wanted to just then.

'Fucking son of a bitch! I'll kill you!' and she lowered her weapon at me and meant it.

Between laughing I was able to utter, 'Well, then you'll never know why I'm laughing at you, will you, Lori?' And that just made me laugh all the harder.

She stopped, and lowered her weapon away from me. I don't know how it happened, but I stopped laughing then.

She looked at me like I was a mad man.

Which I'm sure that at that moment, I was.

I took a deep breath. 'It really is funny. I mean, if you have any sense of humor, Lori, especially a macabre sense of humor like I do, you'll just love this. I'm sure even you will find it hysterically funny.'

'*What?*' she shouted.

'About you. About Morris Rauch. I hate to break it to you, Lori, but Morris isn't your stepfather... he's your *real* father.'

She was stunned for a second, her face grew red with rage and then she shouted, 'Liar! Bloody liar!'

I shrugged and laughed.

Then I got another slap in the face, this time with the pistol barrel. It was her best hit on me yet.

'Pig!' she cried.

'It's true,' I said, with a smaller laugh this time – I didn't want any of my loose teeth to fall out as I talked; that last slap had opened up my cheek. 'And the best part of it all,' I laughed, 'is that this makes you Jewish! Not officially through Halachic Law, but it's almost the same. Which I think is a hell of a funny irony, just as long as your Nazi friends don't find out.'

'Fucking liar!' she screamed.

I smiled 'It's no lie, Lori.' Now I had to talk fast and I knew it. 'I have proof. Your mother and Morris were lovers many years back. They were lovers but could never marry because religious and ethnic barriers were impossible to overcome back then with their families. But, Lori, they were in love and they still are, and your mother had a daughter by Morris, and it was you. And then, when Morris went off to fight in Vietnam, your mother met Bill – the man you *believe* is your father. But Morris is your real father. And I have proof...'

But I didn't get to say any more because I got a steel shod boot in the face that knocked me down, and she stormed out so fast it was like a blur from a tornado.

★

Time passed. I tried to mend my wounds and pride as best I could. Took a hell of a beating from that girl, worse than what Burk had done to me. Those damn rings on Lori's fingers had done a nasty job on my face and head, not to mention that gun barrel upside my skull. To say nothing of her Nazi jack boots slamming into my gut and groin. But all that was the least of my problems. I had to figure a way to get out of here and I didn't see any way I could break these chains. And I didn't want to think about what that meant for my future prospects, severely limited as they apparently were.

I dozed off, and was in my thirteenth nightmare when the door to the storage room groaned open and Lori came back inside. Quietly. She was alone.

She wasn't dressed in Nazi crap this time. She didn't say anything. She just looked down at me. Kinda weird. Confused. It scared me.

I took a long look at her and, of course, I said, 'You guessed all along. Just didn't want to admit it to yourself. Didn't you, Lori?'

She didn't say anything. She didn't have to say anything.

I knew all about being twisted. Things her mother had told me. Secrets. How Bill had not been the best of husbands. How he was a mean kind of stepfather, a miserable lazy bastard, a no-good bum, but Lori's mom didn't have much recourse back then.

Yet Lori never needed for anything. She always had the clothes, the toys, the best things she needed growing up. A bit spoiled. All those checks from 'the insurance man' she'd remembered had made it possible for her to have nice clothes and go to the best school. It had paid for her college – even though 'she'd dropped out after the first few months. Morris Rauch had loved his daughter, and even after so many years apart, he still sent money to Lori's mother to help take care of her.

I said, 'You know in your heart I'm not lying.'

She didn't reply. She was shocked. Almost frozen. 'He would beat me, Mr Powers. Bill. Bill hurt me, told me I was no good. He would make me cry and... and I thought he was my real father and that I was bad and that he didn't love me. I thought... I was no good. That it was all my fault. I believed all his lies.'

'I know, but Bill was not your father. Morris is your father. He's a different man, a good man. And you have that goodness from him in you – if you allow it to come out. If you let it overcome the hate.'

She stared at me silently.

'And you know something? He loves you very much.'

There were tears now and she tried to hide them. It was soon impossible to stem the tide. She nodded, began crying, letting it all out.

I said, 'He helped raise you, from a distance, the only way he was allowed to. He didn't have to do it, he could nave walked away, but he loved his daughter. It was hard in those days, a Jewish man, an Irish Catholic woman, with their strict families. It was very difficult, but they're together now. Your mother and Morris love each other and they both love you very much.'

She was quiet.

I said, 'He's Jewish.'

I saw her cringe a bit.

'And that makes you Jewish, too. Not legally, according to their religious law, but morally. You're a Jew too, Lori.'

She stared at me like I'd called her the worst name you could call a person. Then she sighed and just nodded, resigned to it all.

I smiled at her. 'It's not a disease.'

'You said you had proof.'

My mind jumped back to what I'd told her earlier. 'Yeah. Papers.'

'Where?'

'In my jacket pocket.'

'What jacket?'

'I was holding a green jacket when you saw me in the foyer outside of the main room yesterday. The papers are in that jacket. I hung it on the rack with all the other jackets out in the foyer.'

She thought about that for a moment. She said, 'You're in bad trouble.'

The fucking understatement of the year, but I said, 'I need you to help me. We both have to get away from here.'

She hadn't thought that far ahead yet. She might help me, but she wasn't thinking of herself. If she did help me escape she'd better damn well think of herself and escape too, before Burk and her friends found out.

★

Lori left me alone. I didn't know what to make of her. Just what the hell was going on in that twisted head of hers. A mind which I had just helped to twist a few more considerable turns tighter.

Time went by and things started heating up outside. I could near most of it. There was a lot of noise and activity on the grounds of the country club. And it wasn't golfers pairing up to do a quick nine holes either.

I could make out some things through a slit in the wooden wall behind me and it didn't sound encouraging. Guards and dogs prowled every foot of the grounds now, and there was a lot of commotion and military-style movement. Then late in the morning limousines began coming into the compound and soon after that, helicopters began landing on the flat hill behind the main hall and I knew that there was serious shit brewing.

This wasn't just a meeting of a bunch of the local Nazi / Aryan / Klan groups I'd seen Thursday night with Burk. This was something more. Bigger. Much bigger. Something much more serious and dangerous. Maybe even something that might bring America to its knees? I felt a horrible chill run through me. I knew that I had to find out just what the hell was going on.

Lori came back a few hours later. She was dressed back in her Nazi-bitch best but I could tell that while her body was in that uniform, her heart wasn't any longer. Her heart just wasn't in it.

She said, 'It's too dangerous now. They're all here, from all over, but maybe it might be the best time, too.'

I didn't know what she was talking about. I didn't care either, because I brightened when I saw her pull out a couple of keys and watched with relief as she undid the shackles and chains that bound me.

She said, 'Keep them on, make it look like you're still a prisoner. I'll call the guards and we'll take them out, get their weapons, and get out of here.'

It was going fast, that was good, but I still had to find out. 'What's going on here, Lori? Who are all the people that have been coming here all day?'

She stopped. 'We can't talk about it now, it's much too dangerous.'

'I know, but I have to know what's going on,' I said.

'A meeting. It's like... Burk somehow got it all worked out... it's amazing... all the groups... all kinds... the hardcore, the leaders, the Klan, Crips, Bloods, BTK, BLA, FOI, Yahwahs, Mafia, Hezzbolah and Hammas, terrorist cells, Asian Tongs and Triads, Jamaican Posses, old guard 60s Commie terrorists, The Black Barons, Aryan Nation, contigents from Elonim City, others... so many!'

'In other words, this psycho creep has gathered together the leaders of every fucking hate group, criminal enterprise and underground anti-American terrorist cell in the United States?' I asked, stunned.

'Yeah,' she said, 'pretty amazing, huh?'

Now I really shuddered. 'For what purpose?'

Lori looked at me with that 'We really gotta get outta here' look, but I just said, 'Come on, Lori! What are they planning?'

She shrugged. 'To, you know, work together. Arthur Burk has figured some way to get to them, to make all the leaders agree to work together.'

I swallowed hard. 'To do what?'

She looked at me. Incredulous. 'Work together.'

'To do what, Lori?' I repeated.

'What the hell do you think? To take over! To break down the country! Right now they're parcelling out areas of control, spheres of influence Arthur likes to call them, certain cities and certain states will go to each group. To do with as they please.'

I shivered. It was actually happening.

Arthur Burk and leaders from a hundred violent hate groups and crime organizations were ready to join forces to make war and cut up my country into their own private fiefdoms. It was something that could never be done by one group alone, but if united, even for a little while, operating all at once, coordinating their actions, then they could make the country scream. Bleed. Maybe even fall. The resulting mess would have everyone at each other's throats, then they would pick up the pieces.

'Now come *on*,' Lori insisted. 'We have to get away.'

'We have to stop it, Lori. Have to find a way to stop them.'

'Are you crazy? Do you know who you're dealing with?'

'That's exactly the reason why they have to be stopped.' I said.

'Yeah, call the cops!' She smiled, 'You know how many of them are here? Cops, I mean?'

I nodded.

'We have to get out of here first,' Lori said. She was scared now, and with good reason – my words were making her nervous. So was I. She told me to get ready, then she called in the two guard's stationed outside.

The door opened and two Aryan biker types with Chinese Red Army AK47s entered. Lori was on them in a moment and before I could do anything she had them both down and out. She passed me one of the AK47s and took the other. Then she quickly gagged and tied up the two guards.

Afterwards I said to Lori, 'My jacket? Is it still…?'

'I never went to check the papers. I guess I knew all along you were telling me the truth, and…'

'Forget about that. Where's the jacket?'

'I don't know, I guess it's where you left it.'

'I've got to see what's going on here, and I've got to get that jacket back!'

'Vic, you're crazy! Leave the damn jacket! Let's just get out of here!'

'No, you don't understand.' I put down the AK47, picked up the chains wrapping them around me so that it looked like I was a bound prisoner again. 'You're going to get me into that main hall. I want to see what's going on in there. First hand. And if what's going on there is what I think it is, I want that jacket and what's in it real bad.'

She didn't get me, but that was okay. She took me at gunpoint from the outbuilding, across the compound loaded with people, over to the steps of the main hall.

The compound area was flooded with lights, vehicles, men, women, growling pit bulls, all types of creeps all over the place and each one heavily loaded down with weapons of all kinds. There were six guards at the entrance hall. They wore full Totenkoff Death's Head SS regalia. They looked it. Killers. Ready. Just waiting for the word.

Lori walked me through them with a 'Heil Hitler' and a Nazi salute, then on into the inner foyer, turning down assistance from the guards to handle her prisoner. She was still security chief and had proven her prowess to these men on numerous occasions, just as she had proven it to me by dispatching the two guards at my cell so recently.

Once in the foyer there were two more guards standing in front of the large oak doors that lead into the huge main room. My destination. Lori sent these two guards away on some pretext and for the moment the two of us were alone.

'We won't nave much time,' she said. 'They'll be back soon.'

Then I saw my green jacket. It was just where I had left it on a hook on the coat rack with a hundred other coats and jackets. I picked it up, quickly checked the pocket for my little toy.

It was still there.

I moved over to the huge oak doors of the main hall. There was a small slit between the two doors and I could just barely get a glimpse into the room. What I saw there sent a chill down my back that I'll never forget. All around a huge table sat the leaders of every hate group and crime organization, terrorist cell and drug gang in the country. All colors, all creeds, all ideologies, all types... all of them! Together! I recognized a few of them from the TV news. There must have been a hundred leaders, and behind them were their lackeys, bodyguards, flags and emblems; everything from Nazi Swastika flags to flags of Hezzballan, Aryan Nation, Fruit of Islam, Black Liberation Army, Yahwahs, Crips, La Cosa Nostra, Colombian Cartel families, Mexican drug Lord Generalismo's, and a hundred others. A United Nations of hate. One leader for each group or organization, a nest of the worst vipers and parasitical maggots of hatred this country has ever produced. Extreme right wing, extreme left wing, extreme center middle-class back-to-the-1950s authoritarian assholes. And all of them armed to the teeth with weapons.

Arthur Burk rose to speak, a blood red swastika flag draped behind him, the various leaders quiet, but each one looking to him now. Expectantly.

He said, 'We are not friends, but we do share common goals. Let us always keep that in mind and we shall see those goals accomplished.'

There were nods of approval all round.

'We all hate America for our own reasons and we seek to carve out a place here for our own identity and destiny from the ashes of this repressive, corrupt, and weak dying nation. If there is something else we can all agree on here tonight, it is that we all want to make America bleed!'

There were cheers. I almost burst a blood vessel listening to it. Knowing what it meant. All the innocents these maniacs would murder, the women, the children, but none of that mattered to these monsters.

Burk continued, emboldened by the support, 'Now we all know what we have to do, each of our groups will begin action at the pre-arranged and agreed upon time. According to schedule. The plan cannot fail. The government cannot stand up to all of us, everywhere, at the same time. Imagine, what they are up against, not just *one* Oklahoma City, but *one hundred*! They will not even understand the enormity of what has happened until it is too late. And by then, our various groups will have consolidated control in our respective areas, to begin the carving of America that we shall remake into our own image. It is time. The time for violence is now! Violence is the only solution!'

I'd seen enough. 'We have to get away from here fast!'

She didn't argue, she'd been trying like hell to get me to leave since we left the storage shack where I'd been imprisoned.

I pressed the button on the tiny electronic timing device in my jacket pocket. The detonator was armed and running. We had thirty minutes and then half the wilderness of the state of New Jersey was going to explode into an inferno of thunder and flames and wholesale death. Or so I hoped.

On the way out across the compound Lori and I passed the soldiers and bodyguards of many of the groups present: black and white racists, crime orgs, gangs, Commie-America-hating-traitors, right wing mutants, religious nuts with guns, dreadlocked freaks with Cuban weapons, NAMBLA scum, killers for hire from the IRA, human bombs from Hammas, crooked FBI and ATF weasels, shitbag moron losers and low-lifes, all openly boasting about how they were going to kill all the people they didn't like. Get back at the ones they wanted to get back at. Get back at the blacks. Get back at the whites. Get back at the Jews. Jews who wanted to get back at Arabs. Who were getting back at them. Islam guys who were going to put women back in Purdah, after they killed all the Jews and burned all the churches... It never ended. Fantasies. Or would it be worse? Reality? Reality that was just a few hours away from beginning? Some talked of how they were going to make all the blacks slaves again, others of how they were going to drive the 'white devils' into the sea, reopen the ovens for the Jews, wipe out the 'mud people', or the 'ice people', destroy all the gays, anyone they hated enough to want to hurt – when the people they really hated the most were themselves. And it made me so sick to see and hear it all, so much hatred, so useless, from so many sides, from every race, every conceivable ideology, all ethnic backgrounds, each ready to destroy the country that had given them so much. The country I loved.

The country I loved. The country I also knew that was very sick. The country I knew that had problems. But a country that was still the best there ever was, if people would only cool down and give things a chance. But that wasn't in the cards for these monsters. They lived on hate, and planned to go on a spree of murder and genocide the likes of which America had never seen before. Each hate group, each crim gang, each posse, each drug lord carving up a piece of the American pie to become their own private territory. Their 'sphere of influence' as Arthur Burk had called it, and God help the innocent people unlucky enough to be the 'wrong' people caught in the sights of their guns.

With Lori pushing me onward we were able to reach one of the gates at the rear of the country club grounds. Thanks to Lori, we quickly got the jump on the few unwitting guards there and then headed over the fence and into the pitch black New Jersey wilderness.

The explosion shook the ground like an earthquake, sending shock waves all around us, with a huge fireball hundreds of feet into the night sky. It was an incredible sight, and lit the Jersey sky for miles. Immediately afterwards there were many smaller explosions, and soon fires grew all around the central compound.

I looked at Lori and she looked at me and I said, 'Arthur Burk was right about one thing – violence is the only solution – for people like him.'

Lori nodded and ripped off the swastika armband, throwing it down into the New Jersey mud. 'Let's get out of here, Vic. I want to go home, I miss my Mom, and I have a lot to talk about – with my *real* father.'

I nodded. We kept on moving.

★

The TV was on in the background in the Rauch apartment but no one was watching it. Lori was hugging her mother and the two of them were crying.

When Morris Rauch came into the room and saw his daughter I could see the conflict etched in his old face, anger fighting love, sadness and disgust, so many emotions, but the love in him was winning out. It always did with good men like him. He said, 'Lori, I'm glad you've come home.'

Then Lori and her mother went over to Morris and the three hugged so tight and for so long I thought that they'd break their bones or something and the mother just said, 'Now we're a real family.'

★

I was sitting alone watching the TV news later on when Lori's mother came into the room. They'd all been gone a long time in one of the back rooms having a private talk. I sat down watching a rerun of Bonanza. Hoss had found a girlfriend and...

'Lori and Morris are talking. They have a lot to talk about.'

'I imagine so,' I said.

Lori's mother smiled at me. 'We shouldn't have kept the truth from her, but Bill, he was such a rotten bastard and so anti-Semitic, he poisoned her mind... I thought we were doing a good thing by hiding the truth, but now I know it was the wrong thing...'

I nodded. 'It's over now. It's all for the best.' I thought of Burk and those scumbags all dead, and said, 'It really did turn out for the best.'

'Lori is so sorry,' her mother told me.

I said, 'That's a start.'

She nodded quietly. Thoughtful.

The TV flicked with bright light. It got our attention. The news was on now and the lead story was being shouted in our faces. The TV newsman saying, '...and a terrible explosion at this prestigious New Jersey country club... early indications seem to point to a gas pipeline that burst and was somehow ignited... a national sales conference was underway this weekend...'

Lori's mother was shocked by the news. She didn't know. I hadn't told her. And I was sure Lori hadn't told her either. 'So much violence in the news these days, Mr Powers...' she said with a helpless sigh.

'Yeah,' I said.

The TV newsman continued, 'Many bodies have been pulled from the raging fires... Some weapons were recovered... Preliminary investigations indicate... it seems to have been billed as some kind of sales conference, but... anyway, the amount of destruction out here is so devastating that we may never know what really happened.'

And Lori's mother said, 'My God, such a terrible explosion, Mr Powers. So many people dead!'

'Ah, yeah, too bad.'

She looked at me curiously. 'Seems strange to me to have weapons at a sales conference, though. I wonder what they were selling? Weapons, I guess?'

'Hate,' I said.

'Hate, Mr Powers?'

'They were selling hate, Mrs Rauch,' I said. And I don't think she understood and I didn't feel like explaining it to her. Maybe Lori would tell her one day, but I was too damn sick of it all to talk about it just then.

'They were selling... hate?' she continued. I could see her stretching to understand something that she knew I was purposefully not making clear to her. And that I wasn't going to make clear to her. I'd not bring up Lori. I left it at that. I smiled, said, 'Yeah, they were selling hate, but no one's gonna be buying now. They're all dead.'

'I don't understand, Mr Powers,' she said.

And I said, 'I'm sure you don't, Mrs Rauch. You and your husband are good people. Good people usually don't understand the lengths to which Evil will go. A fellow recently told me he thought that violence was the only solution to the problems we have in America. But the truth is, violence is never any kind of solution at all…' I smiled, then added, '…except for people like him.'

★

I was sitting home alone. Thinking about my city, my state, my country. Things weren't all that great in the good old USA these days but maybe they weren't that bad either. There are problems, but they're workable. I took a deep breath, let it out slow. It's kinda like that. Breathing. Breathing room. It makes things better. Maybe if everyone gave everyone else a chance to breathe, or at least if we tried – made an honest effort – things could be a little bit better. And sometimes just a little bit better can mean a whole lot better.

I was thinking how things were already a lot better in a country without Arthur Burk or any of his ilk left alive in it. You see, America was one hell of a better place already.

★

Of course, it wasn't over. Months had passed but these things are never over. They're never done, especially when you think they're done. They have a life all their own. They just go on, pre-programmed since childhood, passing from one person to the next, like some damn virus. Worse than AIDS, like a bubonic plague of hate.

I got the call from a flatfoot oldtimer dick that ran the Seventy-First. He said, 'Powers?'

'Yeah?'

'McCready here, remember me?'

'Slow Joe?'

'Don't call me that. I wanna see you. Now. Here. 241 West Street.'

I felt that old chill creeping up on me as my nape hair stood on end. 'What's up?'

'You did some work for the Rauchs a while back?'

'Yes?'

'Get over here. I'm sending a prowl car for you. I want you here. Now.'

'What the hell is up?'

'Powers, ah, I don't know. We got a deuce here.'

I knew what that meant. Shit! 'Who?'

'White male, mid sixties, white female mid fifties.'

'What about the kid?' I asked.

'What kid?'

I said, 'Forget about sending the car, I'll be right over.'

★

McCready met me at the door. I saw them taking out Morris and Mrs Rauch. I never did remember her first name.

'Double murder? Suicide? What?' I asked.

'You tell me,' McCready insisted.

'I don't know, I did some missing person work for them a few months back. Found their daughter, brought her home. No big deal,' I lied.

'We don't know, it looks like a domestic. A bad domestic. The wife and husband fought. Looks like the husband beat her pretty bad, she may have went for his gun, they fought, the gun went off. The husband kills the wife, then turns the gun on himself. Puts one through his temple.'

I nodded, 'Domestic shit.'

'Yeah,' he replied. 'I guess I don't need you here right now. It looks pretty cut and dried.'

'Yeah,' I said. 'Pretty straight forward if you ask me. Guy goes off on his wife.'

'Happens all the time, Powers,' McCready laughed and he winked at me. 'Tempted to go off on my old lady a few times myself. That woman can bitch a man to hell!'

I asked him if I could leave and he told me to get the hell out.

I was out on the street five blocks away before I shouted, 'Fucking bullshit!' No way Morris killed his wife! No way they fought! She was the love of his life! No way this was any kind of domestic shit.

This was murder! I'd been played for a fool.

This was Lori. God damn her!

★

She was at my place when I got there. Waiting for me. She knew. She was smart. Tying up loose ends.

'Sit down,' she said, motioning me to my sofa with her gun trained on me meaningfully.

I remembered, she knew how to use it.

I sat.

'You did it?' I asked. I don't know why. I knew she did, but I just had to ask. Maybe there was an explanation. A reason. Something.

'Yeah,' she admitted. That was all she said.

'Did they have to die?' I asked.

She smiled, her eyes wide, crazy, 'They all have to die, Mr Powers. And so do you.'

'You tricked me,' I said.

'I'm very good,' she said with some pride. 'Arthur Burk was a fool. But useful, up to a point, until he tried to take over. Well, now he's out of my way and I can still go forward with the plan. My plan, Mr Powers. Delayed a year or so, but all the more potent for that delay when placed into action.

I shook my head. What a fucking mess.

She laughed. 'We're a lot alike, Mr Powers, and I would truly like to speak to you at length, but I don't have a lot of time right now, and you have to die.'

'You don't have to kill me!'

She laughed again, then said, 'Vic, I do like you, but you're such a dickhead.'

Then she got up and came over to me. Always letting me know that the gun was there, ready. But she came in close, then closer still, until we were touching. She still held the gun on me, this time pressing the barrel hard against my head, while her lips sought out mine.

She was some piece of work.

She smiled and I almost wet my pants, then she kissed me, and so help me I grabbed for her throat and just squeezed. She didn't react, just bit my lip, drawing blood.

As I squeezed harder, she bit down harder, all the time her tongue reaching down deep into my mouth.

The taste of blood was everywhere.

I was terrified, expecting her to pull the trigger any moment and blow the top of my head away, but it never happened.

Instead I kissed her back, loving her perfect lips, holding her to me tightly with my left hand, as I tried my best to strangle her to death with my right.

I squeezed hard, cutting off her breathing, feeling her go cold, blue, scared, like she was getting ready to die.

She still did not pull the trigger of the gun she had to my head.

I never knew why.

She died in my arms.

We never said a word to each other.

I guess that's the way it had to be.

I didn't care.

It was the right thing to do.

You see…

I really do believe…

…in homicide.

Sometimes violence is the only solution.

New titles from The Do-Not Press:

Stewart Home: C*nt
1 899344 45 4 – B-format paperback original, £7.50
David Kelso is a writer who claims to be so lacking in imagination that his fiction isn't fiction at all. He returns from a faked death to complete a trilogy that necessitates him having repeat sex with the first thousand women he ever slept with. But then he starts to lose the plot – literally... Stewart Home's brilliant new novel is abrasive and darkly witty; essential reading for psychopaths, sociopaths and anyone else interested in the ins-and-outs of the book trade.
'Home is reconfiguring books as explosive elements – pages so stuffed with ideas that they might go off in your hands.' – Ben Slater, The Independent

Andy Soutter: DN Angels
1 899344 46 2 – B-format paperback original, £7.50
Theo Riddle leaves home and hits the road, looking for love and money. Sheltering in a derelict boathouse on a Devon estuary, he first encounters a strange, passionate woman and then an art dealer heading for the Mediterranean in a stolen yacht. A dangerous adventure; an intriguing collection of psychopaths, hustlers and philosophers. But who is in control? Theo or his new-found accomplice – the cosmic gypsy who claims to have his best interests at heart but who appears to have a sinister agenda of her own?

Carol Anne Davis: Safe as Houses Bloodlines
1 899344 47 0 – B-format paperback original, £7.50
Second psychological thriller from the author of Shrouded. Women are disappearing from the streets of Edinburgh and only one man knows their fate.
'Carol Anne Davis writes with dangerous authority about the deadly everyday. Her work is dark in ways that Ruth Rendell and Minette Waters can only dream of. This is our world, skewed and skewered, revealed in its true sanguinary colours.
You've got to read her.' – IAN RANKIN

Hellbent on Homicide by Gary Lovisi Bloodlines
ISBN 1 899344 18 7 – C-format paperback original, £7
"This isn't a first novel, this is a book written by a craftsman who learned his business from the masters, and in HELLBENT ON HOMICIDE, that education rings loud and long." –Eugene Izzi
1962, a sweet, innocent time in America... after McCarthy, before Vietnam. A time of peace and trust, when girls hitch-hiked without a care. But for an ice-hearted killer, a time of easy pickings. "A wonderful throwback to the glory days of hardboiled American crime fiction. In my considered literary judgement, if you pass up HELLBENT ON HOMICIDE, you're a stone chump." –Andrew Vachss
Brooklyn-based Gary Lovisi's powerhouse début novel is a major contribution to the hardboiled school, a roller-coaster of sex, violence and suspense, evocative of past masters like Jim Thompson, Carroll John Daly and Ross Macdonald.

Also available from The Do-Not Press: RECENT TITLES

Ken Bruen: A WHITE ARREST Bloodlines
1 899344 41 1 – B-format paperback original, £6.50
Galway-born Ken Bruen's most accomplished and darkest crime noir novel to date is a police-procedural, but this is no well-ordered 57th Precinct romp. Centred around the corrupt and seedy worlds of Detective Sergeant Brant and Chief Inspector Roberts, A White Arrest concerns itself with the search for The Umpire, a cricket-obsessed serial killer that is wiping out the England team. And to add insult to injury a group of vigilantes appear to to doing the police's job for them by stringing up drug-dealers… and the police like it even less than the victims. This first novel in an original and thought provoking new series from the author of whom Books in Ireland said: "If Martin Amis was writing crime novels, this is what he would hope to write."

Mark Sanderson: AUDACIOUS PERVERSION Bloodlines
1 899344 32 2 – B-format paperback original, £6.50
Martin Rudrum, good-looking, young media-mover, has a massive chip on his shoulder. A chip so large it leads him to commit a series of murders in which the medium very much becomes the message. A fast-moving and intelligent thriller, described by one leading Channel 4 TV producer as "Barbara Pym meets Bret Easton Ellis".

Jerry Sykes (ed): MEAN TIME Bloodlines
1 899344 40 3 – B-format paperback original, £6.50
Sixteen original and thought-provoking stories for the Millennium from some of the finest crime writers from USA and Britain, including **Ian Rankin** (current holder of the Crime Writers' Association Gold Dagger for Best Novel) **Ed Gorman, John Harvey, Lauren Henderson, Colin Bateman, Nicholas Blincoe, Paul Charles, Dennis Lehane, Maxim Jakubowski** and **John Foster**.

Maxim Jakubowski: THE STATE OF MONTANA
1 899344 43 8 half-C-format paperback original £5
Despite the title, as the novels opening line proclaims: 'Montana had never been to Montana". An unusual and erotic portrait of a woman from the "King of the erotic thriller" (Crime Time magazine).

Miles Gibson: KINGDOM SWANN
1 899344 34 9 – B-format paperback, £6.50
Kingdom Swann, Victorian master of the epic nude painting turns to photography and finds himself recording the erotic fantasies of a generation through the eye of the camera. A disgraceful tale of murky morals and unbridled matrons in a world of Suffragettes, flying machines and the shadow of war.
"Gibson has few equals among his contemporaries" —Time Out
"Gibson writes with a nervous versatility that is often very funny and never lacks a life of its own, speaking the language of our times as convincingly as aerosol graffiti" —The Guardian

Miles Gibson: VINEGAR SOUP
1 899344 33 0 – B-format paperback, £6.50
Gilbert Firestone, fat and fifty, works in the kitchen of the Hercules Café and dreams of travel and adventure. When his wife drowns in a pan of soup he abandons the kitchen and takes his family to start a new life in a jungle hotel in Africa. But rain, pygmies and crazy chickens start to turn his dreams into nightmares. And then the enormous Charlotte arrives with her brothel on wheels. An epic romance of true love, travel and food…
"I was tremendously cheered to find a book as original and refreshing as this one. Required reading…" —The Literary Review

Paul Charles: FOUNTAIN OF SORROW Bloodlines
1 899344 38 1 – demy 8vo casebound, £15.00
1 899344 39 X – B-format paperback original, £6.50
Third in the increasingly popular Detective Inspector Christy Kennedy mystery series, set in the fashionable Camden Town and Primrose Hill area of north London. Two men are killed in bizarre circumstances; is there a connection between their deaths and if so, what is it? It's up to DI Kennedy and his team to discover the truth and stop to a dangerous killer. The suspects are many and varied: a traditional jobbing criminal, a successful rock group manager, and the mysterious Miss Black Lipstick, to name but three. As BBC Radio's Talking Music programme avowed: "If you enjoy Morse, you'll enjoy Kennedy."

Tooth & Nail by John B Spencer Bloodlines
ISBN 1 899344 31 4 – C-format paperback original, £7
The long-awaited new noir thriller from the author of Perhaps She'll Die. A dark, Rackmanesque tale of avarice and malice-aforethought from one of Britain's most exciting and accomplished writers. "Spencer offers yet another demonstration that our crime writers can hold their own with the best of their American counterparts when it comes to snappy dialogue and criminal energy. Recommended." – Time Out

Perhaps She'll Die! by John B Spencer Bloodlines
ISBN 1 899344 14 4 – C-format paperback original, £5.99
Giles could never say 'no' to a woman… any woman. But when he tangled with Celeste, he made a mistake… A bad mistake.
Celeste was married to Harry, and Harry walked a dark side of the street that Giles – with his comfortable lifestyle and fashionable media job – could only imagine in his worst nightmares. And when Harry got involved in nightmares, people had a habit of getting hurt. Set against the boom and gloom of eighties Britain, Perhaps She'll Die! is classic noir with a centre as hard as toughened diamond.

The Hackman Blues by Ken Bruen Bloodlines
ISBN 1899344 22 5 — C-format paperback original, £7
"If Martin Amis was writing crime novels, this is what he would hope to write."
— Books in Ireland
A job of pure simplicity. Find a white girl in Brixton. Piece of cake. What I should have done is doubled my medication and lit a candle to St Jude — maybe a lot of candles."
Add to the mixture a lethal ex-con, an Irish builder obsessed with Gene Hackman, the biggest funeral Brixton has ever seen, and what you get is the Blues like they've never been sung before. Ken Bruen's powerful second novel is a gritty and grainy mix of crime noir and Urban Blues that greets you like a mugger stays with you like a razor-scar.

Smalltime by Jerry Raine Bloodlines
ISBN 1 899344 13 6 — C-format paperback original, £5.99
Smalltime is a taut, psychological crime thriller, set among the seedy world of petty criminals and no-hopers. In this remarkable début, Jerry Raine shows just how easily curiosity can turn into fear amid the horrors, despair and despondency of life lived a little too near the edge.
"The first British contemporary crime novel featuring an underclass which no one wants. Absolutely authentic and quite possibly important."— Philip Oakes, Literary Review.

That Angel Look by Mike Ripley Bloodlines
    "The outrageous, rip-roarious Mr Ripley is an abiding delight…" — Colin Dexter
1 899344 23 3 — C-format paperback original, £8
A chance encounter (in a pub, of course) lands street-wise, cab-driving Angel the ideal job as an all-purpose assistant to a trio of young and very sexy fashion designers.
But things are nowhere near as straightforward as they should be and it soon becomes apparent that no-one is telling the truth — least of all Angel!

Fresh Blood edited by Mike Ripley & Maxim Jakubowski Bloodlines
ISBN 1 899344 03 9 — C-format paperback original, £6.99
Featuring the cream of the British New Wave of crime writers including John Harvey, Mark Timlin, Chaz Brenchley, Russell James, Stella Duffy, Ian Rankin, Nicholas Blincoe, Joe Canzius, Denise Danks, John B Spencer, Graeme Gordon, and a previously unpublished extract from the late Derek Raymond.

Fresh Blood II edited by Mike Ripley & Maxim Jakubowski Bloodlines
ISBN 1 899 344 20 9 — C-format paperback original, £8.
Follow-up to the highly-acclaimed original volume, featuring short stories from John Baker, Christopher Brookmyre, Ken Bruen, Carol Anne Davis, Christine Green, Lauren Henderson, Charles Higson, Maxim Jakubowski, Phil Lovesey, Mike Ripley, Iain Sinclair, John Tilsley, John Williams, and RD Wingfield (Inspector Frost)

The Do-Not Press
Fiercely Independent Publishing

Keep in touch with what's happening at the cutting edge of independent British publishing.

Join The Do-Not Press Information Service and receive advance information of all our new titles, as well as news of events and launches in your area, and the occasional free gift and special offer.

Simply send your name and address to:
The Do-Not Press (Dept. BIB)
PO Box 4215
London
SE23 2QD
or email us: thedonotpress@zoo.co.uk

There is no obligation to purchase and no salesman will call.

Visit our regularly-updated web site:

http://www.thedonotpress.co.uk

Mail Order

All our titles are available from good bookshops, or (in case of difficulty) direct from The Do-Not Press at the address above. There is no charge for post and packing.
(NB: A postman may call.)

Hector Malot

Sans famille

☆

Préface de
Richard Roudaut

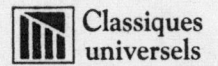

Classiques
universels

© L'Aventurine, Paris, 2000
ISBN 2-84595-038-1

Préface

Le succès considérable qu'obtint ce roman dès sa parution en 1878 trouve encore cent vingt ans plus tard un écho bien légitime. Pourquoi? Mais parce qu'il évoque des situations, des drames, et aussi des joies qui peuvent sans trop de risques être qualifiés d'intemporels.

Certes, le langage a un peu vieilli, mais pas au point d'être un obstacle. Le monde aussi a changé. Mais en changeant, il n'a pas supprimé les situations odieuses, l'exploitation des enfants, l'indifférence vis-à-vis des malheurs d'autrui, la routine peureuse et l'aveuglement volontaire qui sont responsables de tant de maux. Il n'a pas non plus complètement tué l'espoir, et c'est au fond ce qui importe le plus.

Il est heureux que de tels livres existent pour témoigner de la réalité des choses dont on ne prend jamais conscience assez tôt. C'est avec raison que la République, pendant de nombreuses années, favorisa la réimpression de *Sans famille* et sa diffusion dans les écoles : on aurait pu faire de bien plus mauvais choix.

Hector Malot, l'auteur, n'en était pas à son coup d'essai. Né en 1830 en Normandie, il était venu à Paris poursuivre des études de droit; à l'instar de Jules Verne, son contemporain, il se lança dans les métiers d'écrivain et de journaliste. Son premier roman, *Les Amants,* parut en 1859 et obtint un vif succès, ce qui lui donna l'idée d'écrire ultérieurement une suite très morale, *Les Époux,* suivie elle-même des *Enfants.* Jusqu'en 1896 – il mourut en 1907 – Hector Malot ne publia pas moins de quarante romans presque tous hantés par le thème de la famille; citons au hasard *Les Batailles du mariage, Un Mariage sous le Second Empire* et, bien sûr, *Sans famille,* qui eut une suite moins connue, *En famille.*

Trois éléments clés ont concouru au succès des œuvres de Malot : la composition, jamais ennuyeuse; l'imagination, qui aide le lecteur à bien visualiser les scènes décrites ; et surtout l'émotion, où l'on sent une réelle sympathie pour les personnages. On ne peut pas dire qu'il s'agisse d'un écrivain « à thèse » : il est très éloigné du naturalisme de Zola, par exemple. Ce n'est pas non plus un tribun enflammé par une cause quelconque ; pas de déclaration virulente, pas d'implication politique évidente. Ainsi, il ne s'est aliéné aucun public. Il s'est contenté de raconter et de décrire, avec beaucoup de réalisme mais sans forcer le trait.

Sans famille, c'est l'histoire de l'un de ces enfants que l'on appelait encore à l'époque « enfant trouvé ». L'expression a disparu, après avoir été longtemps officielle ; un hôpital de Paris en portait le nom. Le phénomène des enfants abandonnés, en général pour cause de misère, ne date pas d'hier ; leur sort était dans l'ensemble assez misérable. La plupart mouraient très vite ; les autres menaient une vie ardue. Il est difficile, de nos jours, d'imaginer quel poids de mépris et de superstition pouvait s'attacher à l'existence de ceux n'ayant aucune famille avouable... Vouloir faire son chemin dans l'existence avec un mauvais jeu au départ, c'était pratiquement tenter l'impossible. Ce n'est pas exagérer que de dire que ces enfants étaient considérés comme des objets. C'est d'ailleurs de cette façon qu'est traité Rémi, le héros du livre, dès les premières pages. Ayant été recueilli par une brave mais très pauvre femme, la mère Barberin, il est littéralement vendu par le compagnon de celle-ci, qui a besoin d'argent. À quel prix ? Quarante francs. Deux louis... ce n'était même pas le prix d'une place de diligence pour aller de Paris à Lyon. L'acquéreur n'est pas un mauvais homme : c'est une sorte de baladin itinérant italien d'un certain âge, *il Signor Vitalis*. Celui-ci ne se déplace pas seul : il y a le singe Joli-Cœur, affublé d'un costume de général anglais (!) fait à ses mesures, et trois chiens : l'intelligent caniche blanc Capitano, dit Capi ; Zerbino, le chien noir, pour les rôles « mondains » ; et Dolce, le suiveur. Tout ce petit monde se met en route, armé de son seul courage. Et commence une odyssée qui n'est pas sans rappeler *Le Capitaine Fracasse* de Théophile Gautier.

Le long périple entrepris par nos amis est d'ailleurs l'occasion, pour Hector Malot, de nous livrer une description de la France. Mine de rien, celle-ci s'éloigne beaucoup des clichés officiels et est, à ce titre, une source d'informations non négligeable sur la société de la seconde moitié du XIXe siècle. De village en village, nos baladins à deux et quatre pattes entreprennent de séduire par leurs talents d'artistes et de musiciens ; Rémi apprend sur le tas. Harpe, fifre, violon... tout cela plaît. Après tout, dans la légende grecque, Orphée arrive bien à séduire les fauves avec sa musique... Mais les côtés plaisants de cette existence sont moins fréquents que les côtés noirs : la faim, le froid, la pluie, la boue, et souvent aussi la haine, voilà leur lot quasi quotidien. D'autant plus que, partis à peu près du centre de la France, ils commencent leur périple par les abords du Massif Central, région plutôt désolée : n'oublions pas que c'est la misère qui a poussé pendant des siècles les Auvergnats à venir à pied jusqu'à Paris pour y travailler ! À Toulouse, les ennuis sérieux commencent : l'application obtuse de règlements conduit Vitalis en prison ; quant aux chiens, ils sont contraints de mettre une muselière ! Rémi, à peu près dépourvu d'argent – il ne met pas ses chaussures pour les économiser – se retrouve seul responsable de tout son petit monde animal. Le « hasard » intervient alors dans la rencontre d'une aimable dame anglaise et de son jeune fils. Les deux enfants se prennent d'amitié. Mme Milligan, c'est le nom de la dame, se déplace en bateau privé sur le canal du Midi. Quelques jours de bonheur pour Rémi ; puis Vitalis vient le reprendre à Sète, et l'heureuse parenthèse semble se refermer... Le séjour en prison a fait réfléchir le vieil Italien, qui se sent vieux et éprouve peut-être le besoin de se confier ; il conte donc son histoire à Rémi, étonné d'apprendre qu'il est en compagnie de celui qui fut « le plus fameux chanteur d'Italie ».

Et le périple reprend. Mais, au cours d'un hiver terrible, où abonde la neige et hurlent les loups, Vitalis meurt. Après quelques péripéties, Rémi arrive à Paris et rentre au service d'un maraîcher du XIIIe arrondissement, quand celui-ci, fraîchement annexé par la capitale, était encore assez champêtre. Rémi découvre Paris, qui le stupéfie ; il découvre aussi, c'est de son âge, Lise, la fille muette du jardinier. Est-ce donc la perspective de retrouver un foyer ? non, car le roman tournerait court ! La grêle, fléau de tout temps redouté, s'en mêle ; le maraîcher est ruiné en quelques minutes. Le père est conduit en prison pour dettes ; toute la petite famille est dispersée dans les provinces ; et Rémi reprend sa harpe et la route en compagnie du chien Capi. Ici commence la deuxième partie de l'ouvrage ; c'est une montée, en un savant crescendo, vers le coup de théâtre final. On y découvre au passage la très dure vie des mineurs ; la solidarité, mais aussi l'âpreté des pauvres ; les vertus de l'association. Rémi rencontre un petit Italien, Mattis, qui est déjà un virtuose du violon. Se produisant ensemble, ils parviennent à mettre de côté un peu d'argent ; quel bonheur pour Rémi que le jour où il peut enfin offrir une vache à la mère Barberin en compensation de la pauvre Roussette dont elle avait dû se défaire, dans les premières pages du roman ! À partir de là, les événements s'accélèrent, et les révélations se multiplient. Elles conduiront Rémi jusqu'à Londres, pour y avoir la certitude que sa mère n'est autre – mais vous l'aviez sans doute déjà deviné – que cette dame anglaise rencontrée sur le canal du Midi. Dans la plus pure tradition du XVIIIe siècle finissant, Malot déploie la panoplie habituelle des signes de reconnaissance, linge de prix, circonstances obliques... qui dénouent les fils de l'histoire. Nous vous laissons le soin de les découvrir par vous-mêmes ; il y a bien sûr une « fin heureuse », semblable au bouquet final d'un feu d'artifice... Richesse, amour, sympathie, reconnaissance, aucune de ces fusées merveilleuses ne manque au tableau !

On l'a dit plus haut, le roman obtint un succès considérable à sa parution en 1878. Cette époque était-elle particulièrement sensible ou émotive ? elle était surtout troublée par de grands débats de politique intérieure et extérieure. Mac-Mahon, président monarchiste d'une République pas très assurée, était sur sa fin, et avec lui l'ordre moral né de la terrible défaite de 1870. Il nous léguera un chantier long de quarante ans : le Sacré Cœur de Montmartre. Cette année-là se tient à Paris une Exposition Universelle ; un peu oubliée, car le seul monument qu'elle laissa fut totalement transformé en 1937 (le Palais de Chaillot). Dans le domaine artistique, l'impressionnisme pointe le bout de son nez ; les plus grands noms de cette tendance produisent leurs premiers chefs-d'œuvre. La poésie et la musique – Mallarmé, Fauré... – se mettent au diapason de cette école. La vie des humbles – c'est-à-dire la majorité des gens – est tout aussi difficile qu'avant, et le premier mouvement socialiste français est sur le point de naître. À l'étranger, se tient à Berlin un congrès qui pèse encore sur le monde actuel, car il redécoupe la planète en fonction des intérêts des puissances coloniales. Voilà dans quelles circonstances fut publié *Sans famille*. Il ne fait pas de doute qu'il existait en France un courant assez fort de sympathie envers les situations difficiles, notamment celles des femmes et des enfants. Dès la Restauration, d'ailleurs, quelques penseurs avaient attiré l'attention sur les conditions épouvantables de l'existence des plus défavorisés. Nul doute que *Sans famille*, mettant sans agressivité le doigt sur quelques réalités, aussi déplaisantes fussent-elles, a contribué à une prise de conscience dont les effets se manifesteront à long terme. Toutes proportions gardées, c'est un peu l'équivalent français du roman américain de Harriett Beecher-Stowe, *La Case de l'oncle Tom*.

Nous pensons que ce livre est toujours d'actualité ; dans beaucoup de pays du monde, on trouve de nos jours des situations et des odyssées d'enfants comparables à celles de Rémi, sans qu'il y ait pour cela de « fin heureuse ».

Richard ROUDAUT

À Lucie Malot

Pendant que j'ai écrit ce livre, j'ai constamment pensé à toi, mon enfant, et ton nom m'est venu à chaque instant sur les lèvres. – Lucie sentira-t-elle cela ? – Lucie prendra-t-elle intérêt à cela ? – Lucie, toujours. Ton nom, prononcé si souvent, doit donc être inscrit en tête de ces pages : je ne sais la fortune qui leur est réservée, mais quelle qu'elle soit, elles m'auront donné des plaisirs qui valent tous les succès – la satisfaction de penser que tu peux les lire –, la joie de te les offrir.

Première partie

☆

I

Au village

Je suis un enfant trouvé.

Mais, jusqu'à huit ans, j'ai cru que, comme tous les autres enfants, j'avais une mère, car, lorsque je pleurais, il y avait une femme qui me serrait si doucement dans ses bras en me berçant, que mes larmes s'arrêtaient de couler.

Jamais je ne me couchais dans mon lit sans qu'une femme vînt m'embrasser, et, quand le vent de décembre collait la neige contre les vitres blanchies, elle me prenait les pieds entre ses deux mains et elle restait à me les réchauffer en me chantant une chanson, dont je retrouve encore dans ma mémoire l'air et quelques paroles.

Quand je gardais notre vache le long des chemins herbus ou dans les brandes, et que j'étais surpris par une pluie d'orage, elle accourait au-devant de moi et me forçait à m'abriter sous son jupon de laine soigneusement ramené par elle sur ma tête et sur mes épaules.

Enfin, quand j'avais une querelle avec un de mes camarades, elle me faisait conter mes chagrins, et presque toujours elle trouvait de bonnes paroles pour me consoler ou me donner raison.

Par tout cela et par bien d'autres choses encore, par la façon dont elle me parlait, par la façon dont elle me regardait, par ses caresses, par la douceur qu'elle mettait dans ses gronderies, je croyais qu'elle était ma mère.

Voici comment j'appris qu'elle n'était que ma nourrice.

Mon village, ou, pour parler plus justement, le village où j'ai été élevé, car je n'ai pas eu de village à moi, pas de lieu de naissance, pas plus que je n'ai eu de père et de mère, le village enfin où j'ai passé mon enfance se nomme Chavanon ; c'est l'un des plus pauvres du Centre de la France.

Cette pauvreté, il la doit non à l'apathie ou à la paresse de ses habitants, mais à sa situation même dans une contrée peu fertile. Le sol n'a pas de profondeur, et pour produire de bonnes récoltes il lui faudrait des engrais ou des amendements qui manquent dans le pays. Aussi ne rencontre-t-on (ou tout au moins ne rencontrait-on à l'époque dont je parle) que peu de champs cultivés, tandis qu'on voit partout de vastes étendues de brandes dans lesquelles ne croissent que des bruyères et des genêts. Là où les brandes cessent, les landes commencent ; et sur ces landes élevées les vents âpres rabougrissent les maigres bouquets d'arbres qui dressent çà et là leurs branches tordues et tourmentées.

Pour trouver de beaux arbres, il faut abandonner les hauteurs et descendre dans les plis du terrain, sur les bords des rivières, où, dans d'étroites prairies, poussent de grands châtaigniers et des chênes vigoureux.

C'est dans un de ces replis de terrain, sur les bords d'un ruisseau qui va perdre ses eaux rapides dans un des affluents de la Loire, que se dresse la maison où j'ai passé mes premières années.

Jusqu'à huit ans, je n'avais jamais vu d'homme dans cette maison ; cependant ma mère n'était pas veuve, mais son mari, qui était tailleur de pierre, comme un grand nombre d'autres ouvriers de la contrée, travaillait à Paris, et il n'était pas revenu au pays depuis que j'étais en âge de voir ou de comprendre ce qui m'entourait. De temps en temps seulement, il envoyait de ses nouvelles par un de ses camarades qui rentrait au village.

« Mère Barberin, votre homme va bien ; il m'a chargé de vous dire que l'ouvrage marche fort, et de vous remettre l'argent que voilà ; voulez-vous compter ? »

Et c'était tout. Mère Barberin se contentait de ces nouvelles : son homme était en bonne santé ; l'ouvrage donnait ; il gagnait sa vie.

De ce que Barberin était resté si longtemps à Paris, il ne faut pas croire qu'il était en mauvaise amitié avec sa femme. La question de désaccord n'était pour rien dans cette absence. Il demeurait à Paris parce que le travail l'y retenait ; voilà tout.

Quand il serait vieux, il reviendrait vivre près de sa vieille femme, et avec l'argent qu'ils auraient amassé ils seraient à l'abri de la misère pour le temps où l'âge leur aurait enlevé la force et la santé.

Un jour de novembre, comme le soir tombait, un homme, que je ne connaissais pas, s'arrêta devant notre barrière. J'étais sur le seuil de la maison occupé à casser une bourrée. Sans pousser la barrière, mais en levant sa tête par-dessus en me regardant, l'homme me demanda si ce n'était pas là que demeurait la mère Barberin.

Je lui dis d'entrer.

Il poussa la barrière qui cria dans sa hart, et à pas lents il s'avança vers la maison.

Jamais je n'avais vu un homme aussi crotté ; des plaques de boue, les unes encore humides, les autres déjà sèches, le couvraient des pieds à la tête, et à le regarder on comprenait que depuis longtemps il marchait dans les mauvais chemins.

Au bruit de nos voix, mère Barberin accourut et, au moment où il franchissait notre seuil, elle se trouva face à face avec lui.

— J'apporte des nouvelles de Paris, dit-il.

C'étaient là des paroles bien simples et qui déjà plus d'une fois avaient frappé nos oreilles ; mais le ton avec lequel elles furent prononcées ne ressemblait en rien à celui qui autrefois accompagnait les mots : « Votre homme va bien, l'ouvrage marche. »

— Ah ! mon Dieu ! s'écria mère Barberin en joignant les mains, un malheur est arrivé à Jérôme !

— Eh bien, oui, mais il ne faut pas vous rendre malade de peur ; votre homme a été blessé, voilà la vérité ; seulement il n'est pas mort. Pourtant il sera peut-être estropié. Pour le moment il est à l'hôpital. J'ai été son voisin de lit, et, comme je rentrais au pays, il m'a demandé de vous dire la chose en passant. Je ne peux pas m'arrêter, car j'ai encore trois lieues à faire, et la nuit vient vite.

Mère Barberin, qui voulait en savoir plus long, pria l'homme de rester à souper ; les routes étaient mauvaises ; on parlait de loups qui s'étaient montrés dans les bois ; il repartirait le lendemain matin.

Il s'assit dans le coin de la cheminée et, tout en mangeant, il nous raconta comment le malheur était arrivé : Barberin avait été à moitié écrasé par des échafaudages qui s'étaient abattus, et comme on avait prouvé qu'il ne devait pas se trouver à la place où il avait été blessé, l'entrepreneur refusait de lui payer aucune indemnité.

— Pas de chance, le pauvre Barberin, dit-il, pas de chance ; il y a des malins qui auraient trouvé là-dedans un moyen pour se faire faire des rentes, mais votre homme n'aura rien.

Et, tout en séchant les jambes de son pantalon qui devenaient raides sous leur enduit de boue durcie, il répétait ce mot : « pas de chance », avec une peine sincère, qui montrait que, pour lui, il se fût fait volontiers estropier dans l'espérance de gagner ainsi de bonnes rentes.

— Pourtant, dit-il en terminant son récit, je lui ai donné le conseil de faire un procès à l'entrepreneur.

— Un procès, cela coûte gros.

— Oui, mais quand on le gagne !

Mère Barberin aurait voulu aller à Paris, mais c'était une terrible affaire qu'un voyage si long et si coûteux.

Le lendemain matin, nous descendîmes au village pour consulter le curé. Celui-ci ne voulut pas la laisser partir sans savoir avant si elle pouvait être utile à son mari. Il écrivit à l'aumônier de l'hôpital où Barberin était soigné, et, quelques jours après, il reçut une réponse, disant que mère Barberin ne devait pas se mettre en route, mais qu'elle devait envoyer une certaine somme d'argent à son mari, parce que celui-ci allait faire un procès à l'entrepreneur chez lequel il avait été blessé.

Les journées, les semaines s'écoulèrent, et de temps en temps il arriva des lettres qui toutes demandaient de nouveaux envois d'argent ; la dernière, plus pressante que les autres, disait que, s'il n'y avait plus d'argent, il fallait vendre la vache pour s'en procurer.

Ceux-là seuls qui ont vécu à la campagne avec les paysans savent ce qu'il y a de détresses et de douleurs dans ces trois mots : « vendre la vache ».

Pour le naturaliste, la vache est un animal ruminant ; pour le promeneur, c'est une bête qui fait bien dans le paysage lorsqu'elle lève au-dessus des herbes son mufle noir humide de rosée ; pour l'enfant des villes, c'est la source du café au lait et du fromage à la crème ; mais pour le paysan, c'est bien plus et mieux encore. Si pauvre qu'il puisse être et si nombreuse que soit sa famille, il est assuré de ne pas souffrir de la faim tant qu'il a une vache dans son étable. Avec une longe ou même avec une simple hart nouée autour des cornes, un enfant promène la vache le long des chemins herbus, là où la pâture n'appartient à personne, et le soir la famille entière a du beurre dans sa soupe et du lait pour mouiller ses pommes de terre ; le père, la mère, les enfants, les grands comme les petits, tout le monde vit de la vache.

Nous vivions si bien de la nôtre, mère Barberin et moi, que jusqu'à ce moment je n'avais presque jamais mangé de viande. Mais ce n'était pas seulement notre nourrice qu'elle était, c'était encore notre camarade, notre amie, car il ne faut pas s'imaginer que la vache est une bête stupide, c'est au contraire un animal plein d'intelligence et de qualités morales d'autant plus développées qu'on les aura cultivées par l'éducation. Nous caressions la nôtre, nous lui parlions, elle nous comprenait, et de son côté, avec ses grands yeux ronds pleins de douceur, elle savait très bien nous faire entendre ce qu'elle voulait ou ce qu'elle ressentait.

Enfin nous l'aimions et elle nous aimait, ce qui est tout dire.

Pourtant il fallut s'en séparer, car c'était seulement par « la vente de la vache » qu'on pouvait satisfaire Barberin.

Il vint un marchand à la maison et, après avoir bien examiné la Roussette, après l'avoir longuement palpée en secouant la tête d'un air mécontent, après avoir dit et répété cent fois qu'elle ne lui convenait pas du tout, que c'était une vache de pauvres gens qu'il ne pourrait pas revendre, qu'elle n'avait pas de lait, qu'elle faisait du mauvais beurre, il avait fini par dire qu'il voulait bien la prendre, mais seulement par bonté d'âme et pour obliger mère Barberin qui était une brave femme.

La pauvre Roussette, comme si elle comprenait ce qui se passait, avait refusé de sortir de son étable et elle s'était mise à meugler.

— Passe derrière et chasse-la, m'avait dit le marchand en me tendant le fouet qu'il portait passé autour de son cou.

— Pour ça non, avait dit mère Barberin.

Et, prenant la vache par la longe, elle lui avait parlé doucement.

« Allons, ma belle, viens, viens. »

Et Roussette n'avait plus résisté ; arrivée sur la route, le marchand l'avait attachée derrière sa voiture, et il avait bien fallu qu'elle suivît le cheval.

Nous étions rentrés dans la maison. Mais longtemps encore nous avions entendu ses beuglements.

Plus de lait, plus de beurre. Le matin un morceau de pain ; le soir des pommes de terre au sel.

Le mardi gras arriva justement peu de temps après la vente de Roussette ; l'année précédente, pour le mardi gras, mère Barberin m'avait fait un régal avec des crêpes et des beignets ; et j'en avais tant mangé, tant mangé, qu'elle en avait été tout heureuse.

Mais alors nous avions Roussette, qui nous avait donné le lait pour délayer la pâte et le beurre pour mettre dans la poêle.

Plus de Roussette, plus de lait, plus de beurre, plus de mardi gras ; c'était ce que je m'étais dit tristement.

Mais mère Barberin m'avait fait une surprise ; bien qu'elle ne fût pas emprunteuse, elle avait demandé une tasse de lait à l'une de nos voisines, un morceau de beurre à une autre, et, quand j'étais rentré, vers midi, je l'avais trouvée en train de verser de la farine dans un grand poêlon en terre.

— Tiens ! de la farine, dis-je en m'approchant d'elle.

— Mais oui, fit-elle en souriant, c'est bien de la farine, mon petit Rémi, de la belle farine de blé ; tiens, vois comme elle fleure bon.

Si j'avais osé, j'aurais demandé à quoi devait servir cette farine ; mais, précisément parce que j'avais grande envie de le savoir, je n'osais pas en parler. Et puis d'un autre côté je ne voulais pas dire que je savais que nous étions au mardi gras, pour ne pas faire de la peine à mère Barberin.

— Qu'est-ce qu'on fait avec de la farine ? dit-elle me regardant.

— Du pain.

— Et puis encore ?

— De la bouillie.

— Et puis encore ?

— Dame... Je ne sais pas.

— Si, tu sais bien. Mais, comme tu es un bon petit garçon, tu n'oses pas le dire. Tu sais que c'est aujourd'hui mardi gras, le jour des crêpes et des beignets. Mais, comme tu sais aussi que nous n'avons ni beurre, ni lait, tu n'oses pas en parler. C'est vrai ça ?

— Oh ! mère Barberin.

— Comme d'avance j'avais deviné tout cela, je me suis arrangée pour que mardi gras ne te fasse pas vilaine figure. Regarde dans la huche.

Le couvercle levé, et il le fut vivement, j'aperçus le lait, le beurre, des œufs et trois pommes.

— Donne-moi les œufs, me dit-elle, et, pendant que je les casse, pèle les pommes.

Pendant que je coupais les pommes en tranches, elle cassa les œufs dans la farine et se mit à battre le tout, en versant dessus, de temps en temps, une cuillerée de lait.

Quand la pâte fut délayée, mère Barberin posa la terrine sur les cendres chaudes, et il n'y eut plus qu'à attendre le soir, car c'était à notre souper que nous devions manger les crêpes et les beignets.

Pour être franc, je dois avouer que la journée me parut longue et que plus d'une fois j'allai soulever le linge qui recouvrait la terrine.

— Tu vas faire prendre froid à la pâte, disait mère Barberin, et elle lèvera mal.

Mais elle levait bien et de place en place se montraient des renflements, des sortes de bouillons qui venaient crever à la surface. De toute la pâte en fermentation se dégageait une bonne odeur d'œufs et de lait.

— Casse de la bourrée, me disait-elle ; il nous faut un bon feu clair, sans fumée.

Enfin, la chandelle fut allumée.

— Mets du bois au feu ! me dit-elle.

Il ne fut pas nécessaire de me répéter deux fois cette parole que j'attendais avec tant d'impatience. Bientôt une grande flamme monta dans la cheminée, et sa lueur vacillante emplit la cuisine.

Alors mère Barberin décrocha de la muraille la poêle à frire et la posa au-dessus de la flamme.

— Donne-moi le beurre.

Elle en prit, au bout de son couteau, un morceau gros comme une petite noix, et le mit dans la poêle, où il fondit en grésillant.

Ah ! c'était vraiment une bonne odeur qui chatouillait d'autant plus agréablement notre palais que depuis longtemps nous ne l'avions pas respirée.

C'était aussi une joyeuse musique que celle produite par les grésillements et les sifflements du beurre.

Cependant, si attentif que je fusse à cette musique, il me sembla entendre un bruit de pas dans la cour.

Qui pouvait venir nous déranger à cette heure ? Une voisine sans doute, pour nous demander du feu.

Mais je ne m'arrêtai pas à cette idée, car mère Barberin, qui avait plongé la cuiller à pot dans la terrine, venait de faire couler dans la poêle une nappe de pâte blanche, et ce n'était pas le moment de se laisser aller aux distractions.

Un bâton heurta le seuil, puis aussitôt la porte s'ouvrit brusquement.

— Qui est là ? demanda mère Barberin sans se retourner.

Un homme était entré, et la flamme qui l'avait éclairé en plein m'avait montré qu'il était vêtu d'une blouse blanche et qu'il tenait à la main un gros bâton.

— On fait donc la fête ici ? Ne vous gênez pas, dit-il d'un ton rude.

— Ah ! mon Dieu ! s'écria mère Barberin en posant vivement sa poêle à terre, c'est toi, Jérôme ?

Puis me prenant par le bras elle me poussa vers l'homme qui s'était arrêté sur le seuil :

— C'est ton père.

II

Un père nourricier

Je m'étais approché pour l'embrasser à mon tour, mais du bout de son bâton il m'arrêta :

— Qu'est-ce que c'est que celui-là ?
— C'est Rémi.
— Tu m'avais dit...
— Eh bien, oui, mais... ce n'était pas vrai, parce que...
— Ah ! pas vrai, pas vrai.

Il fit quelques pas vers moi son bâton levé, et instinctivement je reculai.

Qu'avais-je fait ? De quoi étais-je coupable ? Pourquoi cet accueil lorsque j'allais à lui pour l'embrasser ?

Je n'eus pas le temps d'examiner ces diverses questions qui se pressaient dans mon esprit troublé.

— Je vois que vous faisiez mardi gras, dit-il ; ça se trouve bien, car j'ai une solide faim. Qu'est-ce que tu as pour souper ?
— Je faisais des crêpes.
— Je vois bien ; mais ce n'est pas des crêpes que tu vas donner à manger à un homme qui a dix lieues dans les jambes.
— C'est que je n'ai rien ; nous ne t'attendions pas.
— Comment, rien ; rien à souper ?

Il regarda autour de lui.

— Voilà du beurre.

Il leva les yeux au plafond à l'endroit où l'on accrochait le lard autrefois ; mais depuis longtemps le crochet était vide, et à la poutre pendaient seulement maintenant quelques glanes d'ail et d'oignon.

— Voilà de l'oignon, dit-il en faisant tomber une glane avec son bâton ; quatre ou cinq oignons, un morceau de beurre, et nous aurons une bonne soupe. Retire ta crêpe et fricasse-nous les oignons dans la poêle.

Retirer la crêpe de la poêle ! mère Barberin ne répliqua rien. Au contraire elle s'empressa de faire ce que son homme demandait, tandis que celui-ci s'asseyait sur le banc qui était dans le coin de la cheminée.

Je n'avais pas osé quitter la place où le bâton m'avait amené, et, appuyé contre la table, je le regardais.

C'était un homme d'une cinquantaine d'années environ, au visage rude, à l'air dur ; il portait la tête inclinée sur l'épaule droite par suite de la blessure qu'il avait reçue, et cette difformité contribuait à rendre son aspect peu rassurant.

Mère Barberin avait replacé la poêle sur le feu.

— Est-ce que c'est avec ce petit morceau de beurre que tu vas nous faire la soupe ? dit-il.

Alors, prenant lui-même l'assiette où se trouvait le beurre, il fit tomber la motte entière dans la poêle.

Plus de beurre, dès lors plus de crêpes.

En tout autre moment, il est certain que j'aurais été profondément touché par cette catastrophe ; mais je ne pensais plus aux crêpes, ni aux beignets, et l'idée qui occupait mon esprit, c'était que cet homme qui paraissait si dur était mon père.

« Mon père, mon père ! » C'était là le mot que je me répétais machinalement.

Je ne m'étais jamais demandé d'une façon bien précise ce que c'était qu'un père, et vaguement, d'instinct, j'avais cru que c'était une mère à grosse voix ; mais en regardant celui qui me tombait du ciel, je me sentis pris d'un effroi douloureux.

J'avais voulu l'embrasser, il m'avait repoussé du bout de son bâton, pourquoi ? Mère Barberin ne me repoussait jamais lorsque j'allais l'embrasser ; bien au contraire, elle me prenait dans ses bras et me serrait contre elle.

— Au lieu de rester immobile comme si tu étais gelé, me dit-il, mets les assiettes sur la table.

Je me hâtai d'obéir. La soupe était faite. Mère Barberin la servit dans les assiettes.

Alors, quittant le coin de la cheminée, il vint s'asseoir à table et commença à manger, s'arrêtant seulement de temps en temps pour me regarder.

J'étais si troublé, si inquiet, que je ne pouvais manger, et je le regardais aussi, mais à la dérobée, baissant les yeux quand je rencontrais les siens.

— Est-ce qu'il ne mange pas plus que ça d'ordinaire ? dit-il tout à coup en tendant vers moi sa cuiller.

— Ah ! si, il mange bien.

— Tant pis ! si encore il ne mangeait pas !

Naturellement, je n'avais pas envie de parler, et mère Barberin n'était pas plus que moi disposée à la conversation ; elle allait et venait autour de la table, attentive à servir son mari.

— Alors tu n'as pas faim ? me dit-il.

— Non.

— Eh bien, va te coucher, et tâche de dormir tout de suite ; sinon, je me fâche.

Mère Barberin me lança un coup d'œil qui me disait d'obéir sans répliquer. Mais cette recommandation était inutile, je ne pensais pas à me révolter.

Comme cela se rencontre dans un grand nombre de maisons de paysans, notre cuisine était en même temps notre chambre à coucher. Auprès de la cheminée tout ce qui servait au manger, la table, la huche, le buffet ; à l'autre bout les meubles propres au coucher ; dans un angle le lit de mère Barberin, dans le coin opposé le mien, qui se trouvait dans une sorte d'armoire entourée d'un lambrequin en toile rouge.

Je me dépêchai de me déshabiller et de me coucher. Mais dormir était une autre affaire.

On ne dort pas par ordre ; on dort parce qu'on a sommeil et qu'on est tranquille.

Or je n'avais pas sommeil et n'étais pas tranquille.

Terriblement tourmenté au contraire, et de plus très malheureux.

Comment, cet homme était mon père ! Alors pourquoi me traitait-il si durement ?

Le nez collé contre la muraille, je faisais effort pour chasser ces idées et m'endormir comme il me l'avait ordonné ; mais c'était impossible. Le sommeil ne venait pas ; je ne m'étais jamais senti si bien éveillé.

Au bout d'un certain temps, je ne saurais dire combien, j'entendis qu'on s'approchait de mon lit.

Au pas lent, traînant et lourd, je reconnus tout de suite que ce n'était pas mère Barberin.

Un souffle chaud effleura mes cheveux.

— Dors-tu ? demanda une voix étouffée.

Je n'eus garde de répondre, car les terribles mots : « Je me fâche », retentissaient encore à mon oreille.

— Il dort, dit mère Barberin ; aussitôt couché, aussitôt endormi, c'est son habitude ; tu peux parler sans craindre qu'il t'entende.

Sans doute, j'aurais dû dire que je ne dormais pas, mais je n'osais point ; on m'avait commandé de dormir, je ne dormais pas, j'étais en faute.

— Ton procès, où en est-il ? demanda mère Barberin.

— Perdu ! Les juges ont décidé que j'étais en faute de me trouver sous les échafaudages et que l'entrepreneur ne me devait rien.

Là-dessus il donna un coup de poing sur la table et se mit à jurer sans dire aucune parole sensée.

— Le procès perdu, reprit-il bientôt ; notre argent perdu, estropié, la misère ; voilà ! Et comme si ce n'était pas assez, en rentrant ici je trouve un enfant. M'expliqueras-tu pourquoi tu n'as pas fait comme je t'avais dit de faire ?

— Parce que je n'ai pas pu.

— Tu n'as pas pu le porter aux Enfants trouvés ?

— On n'abandonne pas comme ça un enfant qu'on a nourri de son lait et qu'on aime.

— Ce n'était pas ton enfant.

— Enfin je voulais faire ce que tu demandais, mais voilà précisément qu'il est tombé malade.

— Malade ?

— Oui, malade ; ce n'était pas le moment, n'est-ce pas, de le porter à l'hospice pour le tuer ?

— Et quand il a été guéri ?

— C'est qu'il n'a pas été guéri tout de suite. Après cette maladie en est venue une autre : il toussait, le pauvre petit, à vous fendre le cœur. C'est comme ça que notre petit Nicolas est mort ; il me semblait que, si je portais celui-là à la ville, il mourrait aussi.

— Mais après ?

— Le temps avait marché. Puisque j'avais attendu jusque-là, je pouvais bien attendre encore.

— Quel âge a-t-il présentement ?

— Huit ans.

— Eh bien ! il ira à huit ans où il aurait dû aller autrefois, et ça ne lui sera pas plus agréable ; voilà ce qu'il y aura gagné.

— Ah ! Jérôme, tu ne feras pas ça.

— Je ne ferai pas ça! Et qui m'en empêchera? Crois-tu que nous pouvons le garder toujours?

Il y eut un moment de silence et je pus respirer; l'émotion me serrait à la gorge au point de m'étouffer.

Bientôt mère Barberin reprit :

— Ah! comme Paris t'a changé! tu n'aurais pas parlé comme ça avant d'aller à Paris.

— Peut-être. Mais ce qu'il y a de sûr, c'est que, si Paris m'a changé, il m'a aussi estropié. Comment gagner sa vie maintenant, la tienne, la mienne? nous n'avons plus d'argent. La vache est vendue. Faut-il que, quand nous n'avons pas de quoi manger, nous nourrissions un enfant qui n'est pas le nôtre?

— C'est le mien.

— Ce n'est pas plus le tien que le mien. Ce n'est pas un enfant de paysan. Je le regardais pendant le souper : c'est délicat, c'est maigre, pas de bras, pas de jambes.

— C'est le plus joli enfant du pays.

— Joli, je ne dis pas. Mais solide! Est-ce que c'est sa gentillesse qui lui donnera à manger? Est-ce qu'on est un travailleur avec des épaules comme les siennes? On est un enfant de la ville, et les enfants des villes, il ne nous en faut pas ici.

— Je te dis que c'est un brave enfant, et il a de l'esprit comme un chat, et avec cela bon cœur. Il travaillera pour nous.

— En attendant, il faudra que nous travaillions pour lui, et moi je ne peux plus travailler.

— Et si ses parents le réclament, qu'est-ce que tu diras?

— Ses parents! Est-ce qu'il a des parents? S'il en avait, ils l'auraient cherché, et, depuis huit ans, trouvé bien sûr. Ah! j'ai fait une fameuse sottise de croire qu'il avait des parents qui le réclameraient un jour, et nous paieraient notre peine pour l'avoir élevé. Je n'ai été qu'un nigaud, qu'un imbécile. Parce qu'il était enveloppé dans de beaux langes avec des dentelles, cela ne voulait pas dire que ses parents le chercheraient. Ils sont peut-être morts, d'ailleurs.

— Et s'ils ne le sont pas? Si un jour ils viennent nous le demander? J'ai dans l'idée qu'ils viendront.

— Que les femmes sont donc obstinées!

— Enfin, s'ils viennent?

— Eh bien! nous les enverrons à l'hospice. Mais assez causé. Tout cela m'ennuie. Demain je le conduirai au maire. Ce soir, je vais aller dire bonjour à François. Dans une heure je reviendrai.

La porte s'ouvrit et se referma. Il était parti.

Alors, me redressant vivement, je me mis à appeler mère Barberin.

— Ah! maman.

Elle accourut près de mon lit :

— Est-ce que tu me laisseras aller à l'hospice?

— Non, mon petit Rémi, non.

Et elle m'embrassa tendrement en me serrant dans ses bras.

Cette caresse me rendit le courage, et mes larmes s'arrêtèrent de couler.

— Tu ne dormais donc pas? me demanda-t-elle doucement.

— Ce n'est pas ma faute.

— Je ne te gronde pas; alors tu as entendu tout ce qu'a dit Jérôme?

— Oui, tu n'es pas ma maman; mais lui n'est pas mon père.

Je ne prononçai pas ces quelques mots sur le même ton, car, si j'étais désolé d'apprendre qu'elle n'était pas ma mère, j'étais heureux, presque fier de savoir que lui n'était pas mon père. De là une contradiction dans mes sentiments qui se traduisit dans ma voix.

Mais mère Barberin ne parut pas y prendre attention.

— J'aurais peut-être dû, dit-elle, te faire connaître la vérité; mais tu étais si bien mon enfant, que je ne pouvais pas te dire, sans raison, que je n'étais pas ta vraie mère! Ta mère, pauvre petit, tu l'as entendu, on ne la connaît pas. Est-elle vivante, ne l'est-elle plus? On n'en sait rien. Un matin, à Paris, comme Jérôme allait à son travail et qu'il passait dans une rue qu'on appelle l'avenue de Breteuil, qui est large et plantée d'arbres, il entendit les cris d'un enfant. Ils semblaient partir de l'embrasure d'une porte d'un jardin. C'était au mois de février; il faisait petit jour. Il s'approcha de la porte et aperçut un enfant couché sur le seuil. Comme il regardait autour de lui pour appeler quelqu'un, il vit un homme sortir de derrière un gros arbre et se sauver. Sans doute cet homme s'était caché là pour voir si l'on trouverait l'enfant qu'il avait lui-même placé dans l'embrasure de la porte. Voilà Jérôme bien embarrassé, car l'enfant criait de toutes ses forces, comme s'il avait compris qu'un secours lui était arrivé, et qu'il ne fallait pas le laisser échapper. Pendant que Jérôme réfléchissait à ce qu'il devait faire, il fut rejoint par d'autres ouvriers, et l'on décida qu'il fallait porter l'enfant chez le commissaire de police. Il ne cessait pas de crier. Sans doute il souffrait du froid. Mais, comme dans le bureau du commissaire il faisait très chaud, et que les cris continuaient, on pensa qu'il souffrait de la faim, et l'on alla chercher une voisine qui voudrait bien lui donner le sein. Il se jeta dessus. Il était véritablement affamé. Alors on le déshabilla devant le feu. C'était un beau garçon de cinq ou six mois, rose, gros, gras, superbe ; les langes et les linges dans lesquels il était enveloppé disaient clairement qu'il appartenait à des parents riches. C'était donc un enfant qu'on avait volé et ensuite abandonné. Ce fut au moins ce que le commissaire expliqua. Qu'allait-on en faire ? Après avoir écrit tout ce que Jérôme savait, et aussi la description de l'enfant avec celle de ses langes qui n'étaient pas marqués, le commissaire dit qu'il allait l'envoyer à l'hospice des Enfants trouvés, si personne, parmi tous ceux qui étaient là, ne voulait s'en charger ; c'était un bel enfant, sain, solide, qui ne serait pas difficile à élever ; ses parents, qui bien sûr allaient le chercher, récompenseraient généreusement ceux qui en auraient pris soin. Là-dessus, Jérôme s'avança et dit qu'il voulait bien s'en charger ; on le lui donna. J'avais justement un enfant du même âge ; mais ce n'était pas pour moi une affaire d'en nourrir deux. Ce fut ainsi que je devins ta mère.

— Oh ! maman.

— Au bout de trois mois, je perdis mon enfant, et alors je m'attachai à toi davantage. J'oubliai que tu n'étais pas vraiment notre fils. Malheureusement Jérôme ne l'oublia pas, lui, et, voyant au bout de trois ans que tes parents ne t'avaient pas cherché, au moins qu'ils ne t'avaient pas trouvé, il voulut te mettre à l'hospice. Tu as entendu pourquoi je ne lui ai pas obéi.

— Oh ! pas à l'hospice, m'écriai-je en me cramponnant à elle ; mère Barberin, pas à l'hospice, je t'en prie !

— Non, mon enfant, tu n'iras pas. J'arrangerai cela. Jérôme n'est pas un méchant homme, tu verras ; c'est le chagrin, c'est la peur du besoin, qui l'ont monté. Nous travaillerons, tu travailleras aussi.

— Oui, tout ce que tu voudras. Mais pas l'hospice.

— Tu n'iras pas, mais à une condition, c'est que tu vas tout de suite dormir. Il ne faut pas, quand il rentrera, qu'il te trouve éveillé.

Et, après m'avoir embrassé, elle me tourna le nez contre la muraille. J'aurais voulu m'endormir, mais j'avais été trop rudement ébranlé, trop profondément ému pour trouver à volonté le calme et le sommeil.

Ainsi, mère Barberin, si bonne, si douce pour moi, n'était pas ma vraie mère ! mais alors qu'était donc une vraie mère ? Meilleure, plus douce encore ? Oh ! non, ce n'était pas possible.

Mais ce que je comprenais, ce que je sentais parfaitement, c'est qu'un père eût été moins dur que Barberin, et ne m'eût pas regardé avec ces yeux froids, le bâton levé.

Il voulait m'envoyer à l'hospice ; mère Barberin pourrait-elle l'en empêcher ? Qu'était-ce que l'hospice ?

Il y avait au village deux enfants qu'on appelait « les enfants de l'hospice » ; ils avaient une plaque de plomb au cou avec un numéro ; ils étaient mal habillés et sales ; on se moquait d'eux ; on les battait. Les autres enfants avaient la méchanceté de les poursuivre souvent comme on poursuit un chien perdu pour s'amuser, et aussi parce qu'un chien perdu n'a personne pour le défendre.

Ah ! je ne voulais pas être comme ces enfants ; je ne voulais pas avoir un numéro au cou, je ne voulais pas qu'on courût après moi en criant : « À l'hospice ! à l'hospice ! »

Cette pensée seule me donnait froid et me faisait claquer les dents.

Et je ne dormais pas. Et Barberin allait rentrer.

Heureusement il ne revint pas aussitôt qu'il avait dit, et le sommeil arriva pour moi avant lui.

III

La troupe du signor Vitalis

Sans doute je dormis toute la nuit sous l'impression du chagrin et de la crainte, car le lendemain matin en m'éveillant mon premier mouvement fut de tâter mon lit et de regarder autour de moi, pour être certain qu'on ne m'avait pas emporté.

Pendant toute la matinée, Barberin ne me dit rien, et je commençai à croire que le projet de m'envoyer à l'hospice était abandonné. Sans doute mère Barberin avait parlé ; elle l'avait décidé à me garder.

Mais, comme midi sonnait, Barberin me dit de mettre ma casquette et de le suivre.

Effrayé, je tournai les yeux vers mère Barberin pour implorer son secours. Mais, à la dérobée, elle me fit un signe qui disait que je devais obéir ; en même temps un mouvement de sa main me rassura : il n'y avait rien à craindre.

Alors, sans répliquer, je me mis en route derrière Barberin.

La distance est longue de notre maison au village ; il y en a bien pour une heure de marche. Cette heure s'écoula sans qu'il m'adressât une seule fois la parole. Il marchait devant, doucement, en clopinant, sans que sa tête fît un seul mouvement, et de temps en temps il se retournait tout d'une pièce pour voir si je le suivais.

Où me conduisait-il ?

Cette question m'inquiétait, malgré le signe rassurant que m'avait fait mère Barberin, et, pour me soustraire à un danger que je pressentais sans le connaître, je pensais à me sauver.

Dans ce but, je tâchais de rester en arrière ; quand je serais assez loin, je me jetterais dans le fossé, et il ne pourrait pas me rejoindre.

Tout d'abord, il se contenta de me dire de marcher sur ses talons ; mais bientôt il devina sans doute mon intention et me prit par le poignet.

Je n'avais plus qu'à le suivre, ce que je fis.

Ce fut ainsi que nous entrâmes dans le village, et tout le monde sur notre passage se retourna pour nous voir passer, car j'avais l'air d'un chien hargneux qu'on mène en laisse.

Comme nous passions devant le café, un homme qui se trouvait sur le seuil appela Barberin et l'engagea à entrer.

Celui-ci, me prenant par l'oreille, me fit passer devant lui, et, quand nous fûmes entrés, il referma la porte.

Je me sentis soulagé ; le café ne me paraissait pas un endroit dangereux ; et puis d'un autre côté c'était le café, et il y avait longtemps que j'avais envie de franchir sa porte.

Le café, le café de l'auberge Notre-Dame ! qu'est-ce que cela pouvait bien être ?

Combien de fois m'étais-je posé cette question !

J'avais vu des gens sortir du café la figure enluminée et les jambes flageolantes ; en passant devant sa porte, j'avais souvent entendu des cris et des chansons qui faisaient trembler les vitres.

Que faisait-on là-dedans ? Que se passait-il derrière ses rideaux rouges ?

J'allais donc le savoir.

Tandis que Barberin se plaçait à une table avec le maître du café qui l'avait engagé à entrer, j'allai m'asseoir près de la cheminée et regardai autour de moi.

Dans le coin opposé à celui que j'occupais, se trouvait un grand vieillard à barbe blanche, qui portait un costume bizarre et tel que je n'en avais jamais vu.

Sur ses cheveux, qui tombaient en longues mèches sur ses épaules, était posé un haut chapeau de feutre gris orné de plumes vertes et rouges. Une peau de mouton, dont la laine était en dedans, le serrait à la taille. Cette peau n'avait pas de manches, et, par deux trous ouverts aux épaules, sortaient les bras vêtus d'une étoffe de velours qui autrefois avait dû être bleue. De grandes guêtres en laine lui montaient jusqu'aux genoux, et elles étaient serrées par des rubans rouges qui s'entrecroisaient plusieurs fois autour des jambes.

Il se tenait allongé sur sa chaise, le menton appuyé dans sa main droite ; son coude reposait sur son genou ployé.

Jamais je n'avais vu une personne vivante dans une attitude si calme ; il ressemblait à l'un des saints en bois de notre église.

Auprès de lui trois chiens, tassés sous sa chaise, se chauffaient sans remuer : un caniche blanc, un barbet noir, et une petite chienne grise à la mine futée et douce ; le caniche était coiffé d'un vieux bonnet de police retenu sous son menton par une lanière de cuir.

Pendant que je regardais le vieillard avec une curiosité étonnée, Barberin et le maître du café causaient à demi-voix, et j'entendais qu'il était question de moi.

Barberin racontait qu'il était venu au village pour me conduire au maire, afin que celui-ci demandât aux hospices de lui payer une pension pour me garder.

C'était donc là ce que mère Barberin avait pu obtenir de son mari, et je compris tout de suite que, si Barberin trouvait avantage à me garder près de lui, je n'avais plus rien à craindre.

Le vieillard, sans en avoir l'air, écoutait aussi ce qui se disait ; tout à coup il étendit la main droite vers moi et, s'adressant à Barberin :

— C'est cet enfant-là qui vous gêne ? dit-il avec un accent étranger.

— Lui-même.

— Et vous croyez que l'administration des hospices de votre département va vous payer des mois de nourrice ?

— Dame ! puisqu'il n'a pas de parents et qu'il est à ma charge, il faut bien que quelqu'un paie pour lui ; c'est juste, il me semble.

— Je ne dis pas non ; mais croyez-vous que tout ce qui est juste peut toujours se faire ?

— Pour ça non.

— Eh bien, je crois bien que vous n'obtiendrez jamais la pension que vous demandez.

— Alors, il ira à l'hospice ; il n'y a pas de loi qui me force à le garder dans ma maison, si je n'en veux pas.

— Vous avez consenti autrefois à le recevoir, c'était prendre l'engagement de le garder.

— Eh bien, je ne le garderai pas, et, quand je devrais le mettre dans la rue, je m'en débarrasserai.

— Il y aurait peut-être un moyen de vous en débarrasser tout de suite, dit le vieillard après un moment de réflexion, et même de gagner à cela quelque chose.

— Si vous me donnez ce moyen-là, je vous paie une bouteille et de bon cœur encore.

— Commandez la bouteille, et votre affaire est faite.

— Sûrement ?

— Sûrement.

Le vieillard, quittant sa chaise, vint s'asseoir vis-à-vis de Barberin. Chose étrange, au moment où il se leva, sa peau de mouton fut soulevée par un mouvement que je ne m'expliquai pas ; c'était à croire qu'il avait un chien dans le bras gauche.

Qu'allait-il dire ? Qu'allait-il se passer ?

Je l'avais suivi des yeux avec une émotion cruelle.

— Ce que vous voulez, n'est-ce pas, dit-il, c'est que cet enfant ne mange pas plus longtemps votre pain ; ou bien, s'il continue à le manger, c'est qu'on vous le paie ?

— Juste ; parce que...

— Oh ! le motif, vous savez, ça ne me regarde pas, je n'ai donc pas besoin de le connaître ; il me suffit de savoir que vous ne voulez plus de l'enfant ; s'il en est ainsi, donnez-le-moi, je m'en charge.

— Vous le donner !

— Dame ! ne voulez-vous pas vous en débarrasser ?

— Vous donner un enfant comme celui-là, un si bel enfant, car il est bel enfant, regardez-le.

— Je l'ai regardé.

— Rémi ! viens ici.

Je m'approchai de la table en tremblant.

— Allons, n'aie pas peur, petit, dit le vieillard.

— Regardez, continua Barberin.

— Je ne dis pas que c'est un vilain enfant. Si c'était un vilain enfant, je n'en voudrais pas ; les monstres, ce n'est pas mon affaire.

— Ah ! si c'était un monstre à deux têtes, ou seulement un nain...

— Vous ne parleriez pas de l'envoyer à l'hospice. Vous savez qu'un monstre a de la valeur et qu'on peut en tirer profit, soit en le louant, soit en l'exploitant soi-même. Mais celui-là n'est ni nain ni monstre ; bâti comme tout le monde, il n'est bon à rien.

— Il est bon pour travailler.

— Il est bien faible.

— Lui faible, allons donc ! il est fort comme un homme et solide et sain ; tenez, voyez ses jambes, en avez-vous jamais vu de plus droites ?

Barberin releva mon pantalon.

— Trop minces, dit le vieillard.

— Et ses bras ? continua Barberin.

— Les bras sont comme les jambes ; ça peut aller ; mais ça ne résisterait pas à la fatigue et à la misère.

— Lui ne pas résister ; mais tâtez donc, voyez, tâtez vous-même.

Le vieillard passa sa main décharnée sur mes jambes en les palpant, secouant la tête et faisant la moue.

J'avais déjà assisté à une scène semblable quand le marchand était venu pour acheter notre vache. Lui aussi l'avait tâtée et palpée. Lui aussi avait secoué la tête et fait la moue : ce n'était pas une bonne vache, il lui serait impossible de la revendre, et cependant il l'avait achetée, puis emmenée.

Le vieillard allait-il m'acheter et m'emmener ? ah ! mère Barberin, mère Barberin !

Malheureusement elle n'était pas là pour me défendre.

Si j'avais osé, j'aurais dit que la veille Barberin m'avait précisément reproché d'être délicat et de n'avoir ni bras ni jambes ; mais je compris que cette interruption ne servirait à rien qu'à m'attirer une bourrade, et je me tus.

— C'est un enfant comme il y en a beaucoup, dit le vieillard, voilà la vérité, mais un enfant des villes ; aussi est-il bien certain qu'il ne sera jamais bon à rien pour le travail de la terre ; mettez-le un peu devant la charrue à piquer les bœufs, vous verrez combien il durera.

— Dix ans.

— Pas un mois.

— Mais voyez-le donc.

— Voyez-le vous-même.

J'étais au bout de la table entre Barberin et le vieillard, poussé par l'un, repoussé par l'autre.

— Enfin, dit le vieillard, tel qu'il est, je le prends. Seulement, bien entendu, je ne vous l'achète pas, je vous le loue. Je vous en donne vingt francs par an.

— Vingt francs !

— C'est un bon prix et je paie d'avance ; vous touchez quatre belles pièces de cent sous et vous êtes débarrassé de l'enfant.

— Mais, si je le garde, l'hospice me paiera plus de dix francs par mois.

— Mettez-en sept, mettez-en huit, je connais les prix, et encore faudra-t-il que vous le nourrissiez.

— Il travaillera.

— Si vous le sentiez capable de travailler, vous ne voudriez pas le renvoyer. Ce n'est pas pour l'argent de leur pension qu'on prend les enfants de l'hospice, c'est pour leur travail ; on en fait des domestiques qui paient et ne sont pas payés. Encore un coup, si celui-là était en état de vous rendre des services, vous le garderiez.

— En tout cas, j'aurais toujours les dix francs.

— Et si l'hospice, au lieu de vous le laisser, le donne à un autre, vous n'aurez rien du tout ; tandis qu'avec moi pas de chance à courir : toute votre peine consiste à allonger la main.

Il fouilla dans sa poche et en tira une bourse de cuir dans laquelle il prit quatre pièces d'argent qu'il étala sur la table en les faisant sonner.

— Pensez donc, s'écria Barberin, que cet enfant aura des parents un jour ou l'autre !

— Qu'importe ?

— Il y aura du profit pour ceux qui l'auront élevé ; si je n'avais pas compté là-dessus, je ne m'en serais jamais chargé.

Ce mot de Barberin : « Si je n'avais pas compté sur ses parents, je ne me serais jamais chargé de lui », me fit le détester un peu plus encore. Quel méchant homme !

— Et c'est parce que vous ne comptez plus sur ses parents, dit le vieillard, que vous le mettez à la porte. Enfin, à qui s'adresseront-ils, ces parents, si jamais ils paraissaient ? à vous, n'est-ce pas, et non à moi qu'ils ne connaissent pas ?

— Et si c'est vous qui les retrouvez ?

— Alors convenons que, s'il a des parents un jour, nous partagerons le profit, et je mets trente francs.

— Mettez-en quarante.

— Non ; pour les services qu'il me rendra, ce n'est pas possible.

— Et quels services voulez-vous qu'il vous rende ? Pour de bonnes jambes, il a de bonnes jambes ; pour de bons bras, il a de bons bras ; je m'en tiens à ce que j'ai dit, mais enfin à quoi le trouvez-vous propre ?

Le vieillard regarda Barberin d'un air narquois, et, vidant son verre à petits coups :

— À me tenir compagnie, dit-il ; je me fais vieux et le soir quelquefois, après une journée de fatigue, quand le temps est mauvais, j'ai des idées tristes ; il me distraira.

— Il est sûr que pour cela les jambes seront assez solides.

— Mais pas trop, car il faudra danser, et puis sauter, et puis marcher, et puis, après avoir marché, sauter encore ; enfin il prendra place dans la troupe du signor Vitalis.

— Et où est-elle, votre troupe ?

— Le signor Vitalis, c'est moi, comme vous devez vous en douter ; la troupe, je vais vous la montrer, puisque vous désirez faire sa connaissance.

Disant cela, il ouvrit sa peau de mouton et prit dans sa main un animal étrange qu'il tenait sous son bras gauche serré contre sa poitrine.

C'était cet animal qui plusieurs fois avait fait soulever la peau de mouton ; mais ce n'était pas un petit chien comme je l'avais pensé.

Quelle pouvait être cette bête ?

Était-ce même une bête ?

Je ne trouvais pas de nom à donner à cette créature bizarre que je voyais pour la première fois, et que je regardais avec stupéfaction.

Elle était vêtue d'une blouse rouge bordée d'un galon doré ; mais les bras et les jambes étaient nus, car c'étaient bien des bras et des jambes qu'elle avait et non des pattes ; seulement ces bras et ces jambes étaient couverts d'une peau noire, et non blanche ou carnée.

Noire aussi était la tête, grosse à peu près comme mon poing fermé ; la face était large et courte, le nez était retroussé avec des narines écartées, les lèvres étaient jaunes ; mais ce qui plus que tout le reste me frappa, ce furent deux yeux très rapprochés l'un de l'autre, d'une mobilité extrême, brillants comme des miroirs.

— Ah ! le vilain singe ! s'écria Barberin.

Ce mot me tira de ma stupéfaction, car, si je n'avais jamais vu des singes, j'en avais au moins entendu parler ; ce n'était donc pas un enfant noir que j'avais devant moi, c'était un singe.

— Voici le premier sujet de ma troupe, dit Vitalis, c'est M. Joli-Cœur. Joli-Cœur, mon ami, saluez la société.

Joli-Cœur porta sa main fermée à ses lèvres et nous envoya à tous un baiser.

— Maintenant, continua Vitalis étendant sa main vers le caniche blanc, à un autre ; le signor Capi va avoir l'honneur de présenter ses amis à l'estimable société ici présente.

À ce commandement le caniche, qui jusque-là n'avait pas fait le plus petit mouvement, se leva vivement et, se dressant sur ses pattes de derrière, il croisa ses deux pattes de devant sur sa poitrine, puis il salua son maître si bas que son bonnet de police toucha le sol.

Ce devoir de politesse accompli, il se tourna vers ses camarades, et d'une patte, tandis qu'il tenait toujours l'autre sur sa poitrine, il leur fit signe d'approcher.

Les deux chiens, qui avaient les yeux attachés sur leur camarade, se dressèrent aussitôt, et, se donnant chacun une patte de devant, comme on se donne la main dans le monde, ils firent gravement six pas en avant, puis après trois pas en arrière, et saluèrent la société.

— Celui que j'appelle Capi, continua Vitalis, autrement dit *Capitano* en italien, est le chef des chiens; c'est lui qui, comme le plus intelligent, transmet mes ordres. Ce jeune élégant à poil noir est le signor Zerbino, ce qui signifie le galant, nom qu'il mérite à tous les égards. Quant à cette jeune personne à l'air modeste, c'est la signora Dolce, une charmante Anglaise qui n'a pas volé son nom de douce. C'est avec ces sujets remarquables à des titres différents que j'ai l'avantage de parcourir le monde en gagnant ma vie plus ou moins bien, suivant les hasards de la bonne ou de la mauvaise fortune. Capi!

Le caniche croisa les pattes.

— Capi, venez ici, mon ami, et soyez assez aimable, je vous prie – ce sont des personnages bien élevés à qui je parle toujours poliment –, soyez assez aimable pour dire à ce jeune garçon, qui vous regarde avec des yeux ronds comme des billes, quelle heure il est.

Capi décroisa les pattes, s'approcha de son maître, écarta la peau de mouton, fouilla dans la poche du gilet, en tira une grosse montre en argent, regarda le cadran et jappa deux fois distinctement; puis après ces deux jappements bien accentués, d'une voix forte et nette, il en poussa trois autres plus faibles.

Il était en effet deux heures et trois quarts.

— C'est bien, dit Vitalis, je vous remercie, signor Capi; et, maintenant, je vous prie d'inviter la signora Dolce à nous faire le plaisir de danser un peu à la corde.

Capi fouilla aussitôt dans la poche de la veste de son maître et en tira une corde. Il fit un signe à Zerbino, et celui-ci alla vivement lui faire vis-à-vis. Alors Capi lui jeta un bout de la corde, et tous deux se mirent gravement à la faire tourner.

Quand le mouvement fut régulier, Dolce s'élança dans le cercle et sauta légèrement en tenant ses beaux yeux tendres sur les yeux de son maître.

— Vous voyez, dit celui-ci, que mes élèves sont intelligents ; mais l'intelligence ne s'apprécie à toute sa valeur que par la comparaison. Voilà pourquoi j'engage ce garçon dans ma troupe ; il fera le rôle d'une bête, et l'esprit de mes élèves n'en sera que mieux apprécié.

— Oh ! pour faire la bête… interrompit Barberin.

— Il faut avoir de l'esprit, continua Vitalis, et je crois que ce garçon n'en manquera pas quand il aura pris quelques leçons. Au reste, nous verrons bien. Et pour commencer nous allons en avoir tout de suite une preuve. S'il est intelligent, il comprendra qu'avec le signor Vitalis on a la chance de se promener, de parcourir la France et dix autres pays, de mener une vie libre au lieu de rester derrière des bœufs, à marcher tous les jours dans le même champ, du matin au soir, tandis que, s'il n'est pas intelligent, il pleurera, il criera, et, comme le signor Vitalis n'aime pas les enfants méchants, il ne l'emmènera pas avec lui. Alors l'enfant méchant ira à l'hospice où il faut travailler dur et manger peu.

J'étais assez intelligent pour comprendre ces paroles ; mais de la compréhension à l'exécution, il y avait une terrible distance à franchir.

Assurément les élèves du signor Vitalis étaient bien drôles, bien amusants, et ce devait être bien amusant aussi de se promener toujours ; mais, pour les suivre et se promener avec eux, il fallait quitter mère Barberin.

Il est vrai que, si je refusais, je ne resterais peut-être pas avec mère Barberin ; on m'enverrait à l'hospice.

Comme je demeurais troublé, les larmes dans les yeux, Vitalis me frappa doucement du bout du doigt sur la joue.

— Allons, dit-il, l'enfant comprend, puisqu'il ne crie pas ; la raison entrera dans cette petite tête, et demain…

— Oh ! monsieur, m'écriai-je, laissez-moi à maman Barberin, je vous en prie !

Mais avant d'en avoir dit davantage je fus interrompu par un formidable aboiement de Capi.

En même temps le chien s'élança vers la table sur laquelle Joli-Cœur était resté assis.

Celui-ci, profitant d'un moment où tout le monde était tourné vers moi, avait doucement pris le verre de son maître, qui était plein de vin, et il était en train de le vider. Mais Capi, qui faisait bonne garde, avait vu cette friponnerie du singe, et, en fidèle serviteur qu'il était, il avait voulu l'empêcher.

— Monsieur Joli-Cœur, dit Vitalis d'une voix sévère, vous

êtes un gourmand et un fripon; allez vous mettre là-bas, dans le coin, le nez tourné contre la muraille, et vous, Zerbino, montez la garde devant lui; s'il bouge, donnez-lui une bonne claque. Quant à vous, monsieur Capi, vous êtes un bon chien; tendez-moi la patte, que je vous la serre.

Tandis que le singe obéissait en poussant des petits cris étouffés, le chien, heureux, fier, tendait la patte à son maître.

— Maintenant, continua Vitalis, revenons à nos affaires. Je vous donne donc trente francs.

— Non, quarante.

Une discussion s'engagea, mais bientôt Vitalis l'interrompit :

— Cet enfant doit s'ennuyer ici, dit-il; qu'il aille donc se promener dans la cour de l'auberge et s'amuser.

En même temps il fit un signe à Barberin.

— Oui, c'est cela, dit celui-ci, va dans la cour, mais n'en bouge pas avant que je t'appelle, ou sinon je me fâche.

Je n'avais qu'à obéir, ce que je fis.

J'allai donc dans la cour, mais je n'avais pas le cœur à m'amuser. Je m'assis sur une pierre et restai à réfléchir.

C'était mon sort qui se décidait en ce moment même. Quel allait-il être? Le froid et l'angoisse me faisaient grelotter.

La discussion entre Vitalis et Barberin dura longtemps, car il s'écoula plus d'une heure avant que celui-ci vînt dans la cour.

Enfin je le vis paraître; il était seul. Venait-il me chercher pour me remettre aux mains de Vitalis?

— Allons, me dit-il, en route pour la maison.

La maison! Je ne quitterais donc pas mère Barberin?

J'aurais voulu l'interroger, mais je n'osai pas, car il paraissait de fort mauvaise humeur.

La route se fit silencieusement.

Mais, environ dix minutes avant d'arriver, Barberin, qui marchait devant, s'arrêta :

— Tu sais, me dit-il en me prenant rudement par l'oreille, que, si tu racontes un seul mot de ce que tu as entendu aujourd'hui, tu le paieras cher; ainsi, attention!

IV

La maison maternelle

— Eh bien ! demanda mère Barberin quand nous rentrâmes, qu'a dit le maire ?

— Nous ne l'avons pas vu.

— Comment ! vous ne l'avez pas vu ?

— Non, j'ai rencontré des amis au café Notre-Dame et, quand nous sommes sortis, il était trop tard ; nous y retournerons demain.

Ainsi Barberin avait bien décidément renoncé à son marché avec l'homme aux chiens.

En route je m'étais plus d'une fois demandé s'il n'y avait pas une ruse dans ce retour à la maison ; mais ces derniers mots chassèrent les doutes qui s'agitaient confusément dans mon esprit troublé. Puisque nous devions retourner le lendemain au village pour voir le maire, il était certain que Barberin n'avait pas accepté les propositions de Vitalis.

Cependant, malgré ses menaces, j'aurais parlé de mes doutes à mère Barberin, si j'avais pu me trouver seul un instant avec elle ; mais de toute la soirée Barberin ne quitta pas la maison, et je me couchai sans avoir pu trouver l'occasion que j'attendais.

Je m'endormis en me disant que ce serait pour le lendemain.

Mais, le lendemain, quand je me levai, je n'aperçus point mère Barberin.

— Maman ?

— Elle est au village, elle ne reviendra qu'après midi.

Sans savoir pourquoi, cette absence m'inquiéta. Elle n'avait pas dit la veille qu'elle irait au village. Comment n'avait-elle pas attendu pour nous accompagner, puisque nous devions y aller après midi ? Serait-elle revenue quand nous partirions ?

Une crainte vague me serra le cœur ; sans me rendre compte du danger qui me menaçait, j'eus cependant le pressentiment d'un danger.

Barberin me regardait d'un air étrange, peu fait pour me rassurer.

Voulant échapper à ce regard, je m'en allai dans le jardin.

Ce jardin, qui n'était pas grand, avait pour nous une valeur considérable, car c'était lui qui nous nourrissait, nous fournissant, à l'exception du blé, à peu près tout ce que nous mangions : pommes de terre, fèves, choux, carottes, navets. Aussi n'y trouvait-on pas de terrain perdu. Cependant mère Barberin m'en avait donné un petit coin dans lequel j'avais réuni une infinité de plantes, d'herbes, de mousses arrachées le matin à la lisière des bois ou le long des haies pendant que je gardais notre vache, et replantées l'après-midi dans mon jardin, pêle-mêle, au hasard, les unes à côté des autres.

Assurément ce n'était point un beau jardin avec des allées bien sablées et des plates-bandes divisées au cordeau, pleines de fleurs rares ; ceux qui passaient dans le chemin ne s'arrêtaient point pour le regarder par-dessus la haie d'épine tondue au ciseau, mais tel qu'il était il avait ce mérite et ce charme de m'appartenir. Il était ma chose, mon bien, mon ouvrage ; je l'arrangeais comme je voulais, selon ma fantaisie de l'heure présente, et, quand j'en parlais, ce qui m'arrivait vingt fois par jour, je disais « mon jardin ».

C'était pendant l'été précédent que j'avais récolté et planté ma collection, c'était donc au printemps qu'elle devait sortir de terre, les espèces précoces sans même attendre la fin de l'hiver, les autres successivement.

De là ma curiosité, en ce moment vivement excitée.

Déjà les jonquilles montraient leurs boutons, dont la pointe jaunissait ; les lilas de terre poussaient leurs petites hampes pointillées de violet, et du centre des feuilles ridées des primevères sortaient des bourgeons qui semblaient prêts à s'épanouir.

Comment tout cela fleurirait-il ?

C'était ce que je venais voir tous les jours avec curiosité.

Mais il y avait une autre partie de mon jardin que j'étudiais avec un sentiment plus vif que la curiosité, c'est-à-dire avec une sorte d'anxiété.

Dans cette partie de jardin, j'avais planté un légume qu'on m'avait donné et qui était presque inconnu dans notre village – des topinambours. On m'avait dit qu'il produisait des tubercules bien meilleurs que ceux des pommes de terre, car ils avaient le goût de l'artichaut, du navet et plusieurs autres légumes encore. Ces belles promesses m'avaient inspiré l'idée d'une surprise à faire à mère Barberin. Je ne lui disais rien de ce cadeau, je plantais mes tubercules dans mon jardin ; quand ils poussaient des tiges, je lui laissais croire que c'étaient des fleurs ; puis, un beau jour, quand le moment de la maturité était arrivé, je profitais de l'absence de mère Barberin pour arracher mes topinambours, je les faisais cuire moi-même ; comment ? je ne savais pas trop, mais mon imagination ne s'inquiétait pas d'un aussi petit détail, et, quand mère Barberin rentrait pour souper, je lui servais mon plat.

Qui était bien étonnée ? mère Barberin.

Qui était bien contente ? encore mère Barberin.

Car nous avions un nouveau mets pour remplacer nos éternelles pommes de terre, et mère Barberin n'avait plus autant à souffrir de la vente de la pauvre Roussette.

Et l'inventeur de ce nouveau mets, c'était moi, moi Rémi : j'étais donc utile dans la maison.

Avec un pareil projet dans la tête, on comprend combien je devais être attentif à la levée de mes topinambours ; tous les jours je venais regarder le coin dans lequel je les avais plantés, et il semblait à mon impatience qu'ils ne pousseraient jamais.

J'étais à deux genoux sur la terre, appuyé sur mes mains, le nez baissé dans mes topinambours, quand j'entendis crier mon nom d'une voix impatiente. C'était Barberin qui m'appelait.

Que me voulait-il ?

Je me hâtai de rentrer à la maison.

Quelle ne fut pas ma surprise d'apercevoir devant la cheminée Vitalis et ses chiens !

Instantanément je compris ce que Barberin voulait de moi.

Vitalis venait me chercher, et c'était pour que mère Barberin ne pût pas me défendre que, le matin, Barberin l'avait envoyée au village.

Sentant bien que je n'avais ni secours ni pitié à attendre de Barberin, je courus à Vitalis :

— Oh ! monsieur, m'écriai-je, je vous en prie, ne m'emmenez pas.

Et j'éclatai en sanglots.

— Allons, mon garçon, me dit-il assez doucement, tu ne seras pas malheureux avec moi ; je ne bats point les enfants, et puis tu auras la compagnie de mes élèves qui sont très amusants. Qu'as-tu à regretter ?

— Mère Barberin ! mère Barberin !

— En tout cas, tu ne resteras pas ici, dit Barberin en me prenant rudement par l'oreille ; Monsieur ou l'hospice, choisis !

— Non ! mère Barberin !

— Ah ! tu m'ennuies à la fin, s'écria Barberin, qui se mit dans une terrible colère ; s'il faut te chasser d'ici à coups de bâton, c'est ce que je vas faire.

— Cet enfant regrette sa mère Barberin, dit Vitalis ; il ne faut pas le battre pour cela ; il a du cœur, c'est bon signe.

— Si vous le plaignez, il va hurler plus fort.

— Maintenant, aux affaires.

Disant cela, Vitalis étala sur la table huit pièces de cinq francs, que Barberin, en un tour de main, fit disparaître dans sa poche.

— Où est le paquet ? demanda Vitalis.

— Le voilà, répondit Barberin en montrant un mouchoir en cotonnade bleue noué par les quatre coins.

Vitalis défit ces nœuds et regarda ce que renfermait le mouchoir ; il s'y trouvait deux de mes chemises et un pantalon de toile.

— Ce n'est pas de cela que nous étions convenus, dit Vitalis ; vous deviez me donner ses affaires et je ne trouve là que des guenilles.

— Il n'en a pas d'autres.

— Si j'interrogeais l'enfant, je suis sûr qu'il dirait que ce n'est pas vrai. Mais je ne veux pas disputer là-dessus. Je n'ai pas le temps. Il faut se mettre en route. Allons, mon petit. Comment se nomme-t-il ?

— Rémi.

— Allons, Rémi, prends ton paquet, et passe devant Capi ; en avant, marche !

Je tendis les mains vers lui, puis vers Barberin ; mais tous deux détournèrent la tête, et je sentis que Vitalis me prenait par le poignet.

Il fallut marcher.

Ah ! la pauvre maison, il me sembla, quand j'en franchis le seuil, que j'y laissais un morceau de ma peau.

Vivement je regardai autour de moi, mes yeux obscurcis par les larmes ne virent personne à qui demander secours : personne sur la route, personne dans les prés d'alentour.

Je me mis à appeler :

— Maman ! mère Barberin !

Mais personne ne répondit à ma voix, qui s'éteignit dans un sanglot.

Il fallut suivre Vitalis, qui ne m'avait pas lâché le poignet.

— Bon voyage ! cria Barberin.

Et il rentra dans la maison.

Hélas ! c'était fini.

— Allons, Rémi, marchons, mon enfant, dit Vitalis.

Et sa main tira mon bras.

Alors je me mis à marcher près de lui. Heureusement il ne pressa point son pas, et même je crois bien qu'il le régla sur le mien.

Le chemin que nous suivions s'élevait en lacet le long de la montagne, et, à chaque détour, j'apercevais la maison de mère Barberin qui diminuait, diminuait. Bien souvent j'avais parcouru ce chemin et je savais que, quand nous serions à son dernier détour, j'apercevrais la maison encore une fois, puis qu'aussitôt que nous aurions fait quelques pas sur le plateau, ce serait fini ; plus rien ; devant moi l'inconnu ; derrière moi la maison où j'avais vécu jusqu'à ce jour si heureux, et que sans doute je ne reverrais jamais.

Heureusement la montée était longue ; cependant, à force de marcher, nous arrivâmes au haut.

Vitalis ne m'avait pas lâché le poignet.

— Voulez-vous me laisser reposer un peu ? lui dis-je.

— Volontiers, mon garçon.

Et, pour la première fois, il desserra la main.

Mais, en même temps, je vis son regard se diriger vers Capi, et faire un signe que celui-ci comprit.

Aussitôt, comme un chien de berger, Capi abandonna la tête de la troupe et vint se placer derrière moi.

Cette manœuvre acheva de me faire comprendre ce que le signe m'avait déjà indiqué : Capi était mon gardien ; si je faisais un mouvement pour me sauver, il devait me sauter aux jambes.

J'allai m'asseoir sur le parapet gazonné, et Capi me suivit de près.

Assis sur le parapet, je cherchai de mes yeux obscurcis par les larmes la maison de mère Barberin.

Au-dessous de nous descendait le vallon que nous venions de remonter, coupé de prés et de bois, puis tout au bas se dressait isolée la maison maternelle, celle où j'avais été élevé.

Elle était d'autant plus facile à trouver au milieu des arbres, qu'en ce moment même une petite colonne de fumée jaune sortait de sa cheminée, et, montant droit dans l'air tranquille, s'élevait jusqu'à nous.

Soit illusion du souvenir, soit réalité, cette fumée m'apportait l'odeur des feuilles de chêne qui avaient séché autour des branches des bourrées avec lesquelles nous avions fait du feu pendant tout l'hiver ; il me sembla que j'étais encore au coin du foyer, sur mon petit banc, les pieds dans les cendres, quand le vent s'engouffrant dans la cheminée nous rabattait la fumée au visage.

Malgré la distance et la hauteur à laquelle nous nous trouvions, les choses avaient conservé leurs formes nettes, distinctes, diminuées, rapetissées seulement.

Sur le fumier, notre poule, la dernière qui restât, allait deçà et delà, mais elle n'avait plus sa grosseur ordinaire, et, si je ne l'avais pas bien connue, je l'aurais prise pour un petit pigeon. Au bout de la maison je voyais le poirier au tronc crochu que pendant si longtemps j'avais transformé en cheval. Puis, à côté du ruisseau qui traçait une ligne blanche dans l'herbe verte, je devinais le canal de dérivation que j'avais eu tant de peine à creuser pour qu'il allât mettre en mouvement une roue de moulin, fabriquée de mes mains, laquelle roue, hélas ! n'avait jamais pu tourner malgré tout le travail qu'elle m'avait coûté.

Tout était là à sa place ordinaire, et ma brouette, et ma charrue faite d'une branche torse, et la niche dans laquelle j'élevais des lapins quand nous avions des lapins, et mon jardin, mon cher jardin.

Qui les verrait fleurir, mes pauvres fleurs ? Qui les arrangerait, mes topinambours ? Barberin sans doute, le méchant Barberin.

Encore un pas sur la route, et à jamais tout cela disparaissait.

Tout à coup, dans le chemin qui du village monte à la maison, j'aperçus au loin une coiffe blanche. Elle disparut derrière un groupe d'arbres ; puis elle reparut bientôt.

La distance était telle que je ne distinguais que la blancheur de la coiffe, qui, comme un papillon printanier aux couleurs pâles, voltigeait entre les branches.

Mais il y a des moments où le cœur voit mieux et plus loin que les yeux les plus perçants : je reconnus mère Barberin ; c'était elle ; j'en étais certain ; je sentais que c'était elle.

— Eh bien ? demanda Vitalis, nous mettons-nous en route ?
— Oh ! monsieur, je vous en prie...

— C'est donc faux ce qu'on disait, tu n'as pas de jambes ; pour si peu, déjà fatigué ; cela ne nous promet pas de bonnes journées.

Mais je ne répondis pas, je regardais.

C'était mère Barberin ; c'était sa coiffe, c'était son jupon bleu, c'était elle.

Elle marchait à grands pas, comme si elle avait hâte de rentrer à la maison.

Arrivée devant notre barrière, elle la poussa et entra dans la cour qu'elle traversa rapidement.

Aussitôt je me levai debout sur le parapet, sans penser à Capi qui sauta près de moi.

Mère Barberin ne resta pas longtemps dans la maison. Elle ressortit et se mit à courir deçà et delà, dans la cour, les bras étendus.

Elle me cherchait.

Je me penchai en avant, et de toutes mes forces je me mis à crier :

— Maman ! maman !

Mais ma voix ne pouvait ni descendre, ni dominer le murmure du ruisseau, elle se perdit dans l'air.

— Qu'as-tu donc ? demanda Vitalis, deviens-tu fou ?

Sans répondre, je restai les yeux attachés sur mère Barberin ; mais elle ne me savait pas si près d'elle et elle ne pensa pas à lever la tête.

Elle avait traversé la cour et, revenue sur le chemin, elle regardait de tous côtés.

Je criai plus fort, mais, comme la première fois, inutilement.

Alors Vitalis, soupçonnant la vérité, monta aussi sur le parapet.

Il ne lui fallut pas longtemps pour apercevoir la coiffe blanche.

— Pauvre petit ! dit-il à mi-voix.

— Oh ! je vous en prie, m'écriai-je encouragé par ces mots de compassion, laissez-moi retourner.

Mais il me prit par le poignet et me fit descendre sur la route.

— Puisque tu es reposé, dit-il, en marche, mon garçon.

Je voulus me dégager, mais il me tenait solidement.

— Capi, dit-il, Zerbino !

Et les deux chiens m'entourèrent : Capi derrière, Zerbino devant.

Il fallut suivre Vitalis.

Au bout de quelques pas, je tournai la tête.

Nous avions dépassé la crête de la montagne et je ne vis plus ni notre vallée, ni notre maison. Tout au loin seulement des collines bleuâtres semblaient remonter jusqu'au ciel ; mes yeux se perdirent dans des espaces sans bornes.

V

En route

Pour acheter les enfants quarante francs, il n'en résulte pas nécessairement qu'on soit un ogre et qu'on fasse provision de chair fraîche afin de la manger.

Vitalis ne voulait pas me manger, et, par une exception rare chez les acheteurs d'enfants, ce n'était pas un méchant homme.

J'en eus bientôt la preuve.

C'était sur la crête même de la montagne qui sépare le bassin de la Loire de celui de la Dordogne qu'il m'avait repris le poignet, et, presque aussitôt, nous avions commencé à descendre sur le versant exposé au midi.

Après avoir marché environ un quart d'heure, il m'abandonna le bras.

— Maintenant, dit-il, chemine doucement près de moi ; mais n'oublie pas que, si tu voulais te sauver, Capi et Zerbino t'auraient bien vite rejoint ; ils ont les dents pointues.

Me sauver, je sentais que c'était maintenant impossible et que par suite il était inutile de le tenter.

Je poussai un soupir.

— Tu as le cœur gros, continua Vitalis, je comprends cela et ne t'en veux pas. Tu peux pleurer librement, si tu en as envie. Seulement tâche de sentir que ce n'est pas pour ton malheur que je t'emmène. Que serais-tu devenu ? Tu aurais été très probablement à l'hospice. Les gens qui t'ont élevé ne sont pas tes père et mère. Ta maman, comme tu dis, a été bonne pour toi et tu l'aimes, tu es désolé de la quitter, tout cela c'est bien ; mais fais réflexion qu'elle n'aurait pas pu te garder malgré son mari. Ce mari, de son côté, n'est peut-être pas aussi dur que tu le crois. Il n'a pas de quoi vivre, il est estropié, il ne peut plus travailler, et il calcule qu'il ne peut pas se laisser mourir de faim pour te nourrir. Comprends aujourd'hui, mon garçon, que la vie est trop souvent une bataille dans laquelle on ne fait pas ce qu'on veut.

Sans doute c'étaient là des paroles de sagesse, ou tout au moins d'expérience. Mais il y avait un fait qui, en ce moment, criait plus fort que toutes les paroles – la séparation.

Je ne verrais plus celle qui m'avait élevé, qui m'avait caressé, celle que j'aimais – ma mère.

Et cette pensée me serrait à la gorge, m'étouffait.

Cependant je marchais près de Vitalis, cherchant à me répéter ce qu'il venait de me dire.

Sans doute, tout cela était vrai; Barberin n'était pas mon père, il n'y avait pas de raisons qui l'obligeassent à souffrir la misère pour moi. Il avait bien voulu me recueillir et m'élever; si maintenant il me renvoyait, c'était parce qu'il ne pouvait plus me garder. Ce n'était pas de la présente journée que je devais me souvenir en pensant à lui, mais des années passées dans sa maison.

— Réfléchis à ce que je t'ai dit, petit, répétait de temps en temps Vitalis, tu ne seras pas trop malheureux avec moi.

Après avoir descendu une pente assez rapide, nous étions arrivés sur une vaste lande qui s'étendait plate et monotone à perte de vue. Pas de maisons, pas d'arbres. Un plateau couvert de bruyères rousses, avec çà et là de grandes nappes de genêts rabougris qui ondoyaient sous le souffle du vent.

— Tu vois, me dit Vitalis étendant la main sur la lande, qu'il serait inutile de chercher à te sauver, tu serais tout de suite repris par Capi et Zerbino.

Me sauver! Je n'y pensais plus. Où aller d'ailleurs? Chez qui?

Après tout, ce grand et beau vieillard à barbe blanche n'était peut-être pas aussi terrible que je l'avais cru d'abord; et s'il était mon maître, peut-être ne serait-il pas un maître impitoyable.

Longtemps nous cheminâmes au milieu de tristes solitudes, ne quittant les landes que pour trouver des champs de brandes, et n'apercevant tout autour de nous, aussi loin que le regard s'étendait, que quelques collines arrondies aux sommets stériles.

Je m'étais fait une tout autre idée des voyages, et quand parfois, dans mes rêveries enfantines, j'avais quitté mon village, ç'avait été pour de belles contrées qui ne ressemblaient en rien à celle que la réalité me montrait.

C'était la première fois que je faisais une pareille marche d'une seule traite et sans me reposer.

Mon maître avançait d'un grand pas régulier, portant Joli-Cœur sur son épaule ou sur son sac, et autour de lui les chiens trottinaient sans s'écarter.

De temps en temps Vitalis leur disait un mot d'amitié, tantôt en français, tantôt dans une langue que je ne connaissais pas. Ni lui ni eux ne paraissaient penser à la fatigue. Mais il n'en était pas de même pour moi. J'étais épuisé. La lassitude physique, s'ajoutant au trouble moral, m'avait mis à bout de forces.

Je traînais les jambes et j'avais la plus grande peine à suivre mon maître. Cependant je n'osais pas demander à m'arrêter.

— Ce sont tes sabots qui te fatiguent, me dit-il ; à Ussel je t'achèterai des souliers.

Ce mot me rendit le courage.

En effet, des souliers avaient toujours été ce que j'avais le plus ardemment désiré. Le fils du maire et aussi le fils de l'aubergiste avaient des souliers, de sorte que le dimanche, quand ils arrivaient à la messe, ils glissaient sans bruit sur les dalles sonores, tandis que nous autres paysans, avec nos sabots, nous faisions un tapage assourdissant.

— Ussel, c'est encore loin ?

— Voilà un cri du cœur, dit Vitalis en riant ; tu as donc bien envie d'avoir des souliers, mon garçon ? Eh bien ! je t'en promets avec des clous dessous. Et je te promets aussi une culotte de velours, une veste et un chapeau. Cela va sécher tes larmes, j'espère, et te donner des jambes pour faire les six lieues qui nous restent.

Des souliers avec des clous dessous ! Je fus ébloui. C'était déjà une chose prodigieuse pour moi que ces souliers, mais, quand j'entendis parler de clous, j'oubliai mon chagrin.

Non, bien certainement, mon maître n'était pas un méchant homme.

Est-ce qu'un méchant se serait aperçu que mes sabots me fatiguaient ?

Des souliers, des souliers à clous ! une culotte de velours ! une veste ! un chapeau !

Ah ! si mère Barberin me voyait, comme elle serait contente, comme elle serait fière de moi !

Quel malheur qu'Ussel fût encore si loin !

Malgré les souliers et la culotte de velours qui étaient au bout des six lieues qui nous restaient à faire, il me sembla que je ne pourrais pas marcher si loin.

Heureusement le temps vint à mon aide.

Le ciel, qui avait été bleu depuis notre départ, s'emplit peu à peu de nuages gris, et bientôt il se mit à tomber une pluie fine qui ne cessa plus.

Avec sa peau de mouton, Vitalis était assez bien protégé, et il pouvait abriter Joli-Cœur, qui, à la première goutte de pluie, était promptement rentré dans sa cachette. Mais les chiens et moi, qui n'avions rien pour nous couvrir, nous n'avions pas tardé à être mouillés jusqu'à la peau ; encore les chiens pouvaient-ils de temps en temps se secouer, tandis que, ce moyen naturel n'étant pas fait pour moi, je devais marcher sous un poids qui m'écrasait et me glaçait.

— T'enrhumes-tu facilement ? me demanda mon maître.

— Je ne sais pas ; je ne me rappelle pas avoir été jamais enrhumé.

— Bien cela, bien ; décidément il y a du bon en toi. Mais je ne veux pas t'exposer inutilement, nous n'irons pas plus loin aujourd'hui. Voilà un village là-bas, nous y coucherons.

Mais il n'y avait pas d'auberge dans ce village, et personne ne voulut recevoir une sorte de mendiant qui traînait avec lui un enfant et trois chiens aussi crottés les uns que les autres.

— On ne loge pas ici, nous disait-on.

Et l'on nous fermait la porte au nez. Nous allions d'une maison à l'autre, sans qu'aucune s'ouvrît.

Faudrait-il donc faire encore, et sans repos, les quatre lieues qui nous séparaient d'Ussel ? La nuit arrivait, la pluie nous glaçait, et pour moi je sentais mes jambes raides comme des barres de bois.

Ah ! la maison de mère Barberin !

Enfin un paysan plus charitable que ses voisins voulut bien nous ouvrir la porte d'une grange. Mais, avant de nous laisser entrer, il nous imposa la condition de ne pas avoir de lumière.

— Donnez-moi vos allumettes, dit-il à Vitalis ; je vous les rendrai demain, quand vous partirez.

Au moins nous avions un toit pour nous abriter et la pluie ne nous tombait plus sur le corps.

Vitalis était un homme de précaution qui ne se mettait pas en route sans provisions. Dans le sac de soldat qu'il portait sur ses épaules se trouvait une grosse miche de pain qu'il partagea en quatre morceaux.

Alors je vis pour la première fois comment il maintenait l'obéissance et la discipline dans sa troupe.

Pendant que nous errions de porte en porte, cherchant notre gîte, Zerbino était entré dans une maison, et il en était ressorti aussitôt rapidement, portant une croûte dans sa gueule. Vitalis n'avait dit qu'un mot :

— À ce soir, Zerbino.

Je ne pensais plus à ce vol, quand je vis, au moment où notre maître coupait la miche, Zerbino prendre une mine basse.

Nous étions assis sur deux bottes de fougère, Vitalis et moi, à côté l'un de l'autre, Joli-Cœur entre nous deux ; les trois chiens étaient alignés devant nous, Capi et Dolce les yeux attachés sur ceux de leur maître, Zerbino le nez incliné en avant, les oreilles rasées.

— Que le voleur sorte des rangs, dit Vitalis d'une voix de commandement, et qu'il aille dans un coin ; il se couchera sans souper.

Aussitôt Zerbino quitta sa place et, marchant en rampant, il alla se cacher dans le coin que la main de son maître lui avait indiqué. Il se fourra tout entier sous un amas de fougère, et nous ne le vîmes plus ; mais nous l'entendions souffler plaintivement avec des petits cris étouffés.

Cette exécution accomplie, Vitalis me tendit mon pain, et, tout en mangeant le sien, il partagea par petites bouchées, entre Joli-Cœur, Capi et Dolce, les morceaux qui leur étaient destinés.

Pendant les derniers mois que j'avais vécu auprès de mère Barberin, je n'avais certes pas été gâté ; cependant le changement me parut rude.

Ah ! comme la soupe chaude, que mère Barberin nous faisait tous les soirs, m'eût paru bonne, même sans beurre !

Comme le coin du feu m'eût été agréable ! comme je me serais glissé avec bonheur dans mes draps, en remontant les couvertures jusqu'à mon nez !

Mais, hélas ! il ne pouvait être question ni de draps, ni de couvertures, et nous devions nous trouver encore bien heureux d'avoir un lit de fougère.

Brisé par la fatigue, les pieds écorchés par mes sabots, je tremblais de froid dans mes vêtements mouillés.

La nuit était venue tout à fait, mais je ne pensais pas à dormir.

— Tes dents claquent, dit Vitalis, tu as froid ?

— Un peu.

Je l'entendis ouvrir son sac.

— Je n'ai pas une garde-robe bien montée, dit-il, mais voici une chemise sèche et un gilet dans lesquels tu pourras t'envelopper après avoir défait tes vêtements mouillés ; puis tu t'enfonceras sous la fougère, tu ne tarderas pas à te réchauffer et à t'endormir.

Cependant, je ne me réchauffai pas aussi vite que Vitalis le croyait ; longtemps je me tournai et me retournai sur mon lit de fougère, trop endolori, trop malheureux pour pouvoir m'en dormir.

Est-ce qu'il en serait maintenant tous les jours ainsi ? marcher sans repos sous la pluie, coucher dans une grange, trembler de froid, n'avoir pour souper qu'un morceau de pain sec, personne pour me plaindre, personne à aimer, plus de mère Barberin !

Comme je réfléchissais tristement, le cœur gros et les yeux pleins de larmes, je sentis un souffle tiède me passer sur le visage.

J'étendis la main en avant et je rencontrai le poil laineux de Capi.

Il s'était doucement approché de moi, s'avançant avec précaution sur la fougère, et il me sentait ; il reniflait doucement ; son haleine me courait sur la figure et dans les cheveux.

Que voulait-il ?

Il se coucha bientôt sur la fougère, tout près de moi, et délicatement il se mit à me lécher la main.

Tout ému de cette caresse, je me soulevai à demi et l'embrassai sur son nez froid.

Il poussa un petit cri étouffé, puis, vivement, il mit sa patte dans ma main et ne bougea plus.

Alors j'oubliai fatigue et chagrins ; ma gorge contractée se desserra, je respirai, je n'étais plus seul : j'avais un ami.

VI

Mes débuts

Le lendemain nous nous mîmes en route de bonne heure. Plus de pluie ; un ciel bleu, et, grâce au vent sec qui avait soufflé pendant la nuit, peu de boue. Les oiseaux chantaient joyeusement dans les buissons du chemin, et les chiens gambadaient autour de nous. De temps en temps, Capi se dressait sur ses pattes de derrière, et il me lançait au visage deux ou trois aboiements dont je comprenais très bien la signification.

— Du courage, du courage ! disaient-ils.

Car c'était un chien fort intelligent, qui savait tout comprendre et toujours se faire comprendre. Bien souvent j'ai entendu dire qu'il ne lui manquait que la parole. Mais je n'ai jamais pensé ainsi. Dans sa queue seule il y avait plus d'esprit et d'éloquence que dans la langue ou dans les yeux de bien des gens. En tout cas la parole n'a jamais été utile entre lui et moi ; du premier jour nous nous sommes tout de suite compris.

N'étant jamais sorti de mon village, j'étais curieux de voir une ville.

Mais je dois avouer qu'Ussel ne m'éblouit point. Ses vieilles maisons à tourelles, qui font sans doute le bonheur des archéologues, me laissèrent tout à fait indifférent.

Il est vrai de dire que, dans ces maisons, ce que je cherchais, ce n'était point le pittoresque.

Une idée emplissait ma tête et obscurcissait mes yeux, ou tout au moins ne leur permettait de voir qu'une seule chose : une boutique de cordonnier.

Mes souliers, les souliers promis de Vitalis, l'heure était venue de les chausser.

Où était la bienheureuse boutique qui allait me les fournir ?

C'était cette boutique que je cherchais ; le reste, tourelles, ogives, colonnes, n'avait aucun intérêt pour moi.

Aussi le seul souvenir qui me reste d'Ussel est-il celui d'une boutique sombre et enfumée située auprès des halles. Il y avait en étalage devant sa devanture de vieux fusils, un habit galonné sur les coutures avec des épaulettes en argent, beaucoup de lampes, et dans des corbeilles de la ferraille, surtout des cadenas et des clefs rouillées.

Il fallait descendre trois marches pour entrer, et alors on se trouvait dans une grande salle, où la lumière du soleil n'avait assurément jamais pénétré depuis que le toit avait été posé sur la maison.

Comment une aussi belle chose que des souliers pouvait-elle se vendre dans un endroit aussi affreux !

Cependant Vitalis savait ce qu'il faisait en venant dans cette boutique, et bientôt j'eus le bonheur de chausser mes pieds dans des souliers ferrés qui pesaient bien dix fois le poids de mes sabots.

La générosité de mon maître ne s'arrêta pas là ; après les souliers, il m'acheta une veste de velours bleu, un pantalon de laine et un chapeau de feutre ; enfin tout ce qu'il m'avait promis.

Du velours pour moi, qui n'avais jamais porté que de la toile ; des souliers ; un chapeau quand je n'avais eu que mes cheveux pour coiffure ; décidément c'était le meilleur homme du monde, le plus généreux et le plus riche.

Il est vrai que le velours était froissé, il est vrai que la laine était râpée ; il est vrai qu'il était fort difficile de savoir quelle avait été la couleur primitive du feutre, tant il avait reçu de pluie et de poussière ; mais, ébloui par tant de splendeurs, j'étais insensible aux imperfections qui se cachaient sous leur éclat.

J'avais hâte de revêtir ces beaux habits ; mais, avant de me les donner, Vitalis leur fit subir une transformation qui me jeta dans un étonnement douloureux.

En rentrant à l'auberge, il prit des ciseaux dans son sac et coupa les deux jambes de mon pantalon à la hauteur des genoux.

Comme je le regardais avec des yeux effarés :

— Ceci est à seule fin, me dit-il, que tu ne ressembles pas à tout le monde. Nous sommes en France, je t'habille en Italien ;

si nous allons en Italie, ce qui est possible, je t'habillerai en Français.

Cette explication ne faisant pas cesser mon étonnement, il continua :

— Que sommes-nous ? Des artistes, n'est-ce pas ? des comédiens qui par leur seul aspect doivent provoquer la curiosité. Crois-tu que, si nous allions tantôt sur la place publique habillés comme des bourgeois ou des paysans, nous forcerions les gens à nous regarder et à s'arrêter autour de nous ? Non, n'est-ce pas ? Apprends donc que dans la vie le paraître est quelquefois indispensable ; cela est fâcheux, mais nous n'y pouvons rien.

Voilà comment, de Français que j'étais le matin, je devins Italien avant le soir.

Mon pantalon s'arrêtant au genou, Vitalis attacha mes bas avec des cordons rouges croisés tout le long de la jambe ; sur mon feutre il croisa aussi d'autres rubans, et il l'orna d'un bouquet de fleurs en laine.

Je ne sais pas ce que d'autres auraient pu penser de moi, mais, pour être sincère, je dois déclarer que je me trouvai superbe, et cela devait être, car mon ami Capi, après m'avoir longuement contemplé, me tendit la patte d'un air satisfait.

L'approbation que Capi donnait à ma transformation me fut d'autant plus agréable que, pendant que j'endossais mes nouveaux vêtements, Joli-Cœur s'était campé devant moi et avait imité mes mouvements en les exagérant. Ma toilette terminée, il s'était posé les mains sur les hanches et, renversant sa tête en arrière, il s'était mis à rire en poussant des petits cris moqueurs.

J'ai entendu dire que c'était une question scientifique intéressante de savoir si les singes riaient. Je pense que ceux qui se sont posé cette question sont des savants en chambre, qui n'ont jamais pris la peine d'étudier les singes. Pour moi qui, pendant longtemps, ai vécu dans l'intimité de Joli-Cœur, je puis affirmer qu'il riait et souvent même d'une façon qui me mortifiait. Sans doute son rire n'était pas exactement semblable à celui de l'homme. Mais enfin, lorsqu'un sentiment quelconque provoquait sa gaieté, on voyait les coins de sa bouche se tirer en arrière ; ses paupières se plissaient, ses mâchoires remuaient rapidement, et ses yeux noirs semblaient lancer des flammes comme de petits charbons sur lesquels on aurait soufflé.

Au reste, je fus bientôt à même d'observer en lui ces signes caractéristiques du rire dans des conditions assez pénibles pour mon amour-propre.

— Maintenant que voilà ta toilette terminée, me dit Vitalis quand je me fus coiffé de mon chapeau, nous allons nous mettre au travail, afin de donner demain, jour de marché, une grande représentation dans laquelle tu débuteras.

Je demandai ce que c'était que débuter, et Vitalis m'expliqua que c'était paraître pour la première fois devant le public en jouant la comédie.

— Nous donnerons demain notre première représentation, dit-il, et tu y figureras. Il faut donc que je te fasse répéter le rôle que je te destine.

Mes yeux étonnés lui dirent que je ne le comprenais pas.

— J'entends par rôle ce que tu auras à faire dans cette représentation. Si je t'ai emmené avec moi, ce n'est pas précisément pour te procurer le plaisir de la promenade. Je ne suis pas assez riche pour cela. C'est pour que tu travailles. Et ton travail consistera à jouer la comédie avec mes chiens et Joli-Cœur.

— Mais je ne sais pas jouer la comédie ! m'écriai-je effrayé.

— C'est justement pour cela que je dois te l'apprendre. Tu penses bien que ce n'est pas naturellement que Capi marche si gracieusement sur ses deux pattes de derrière, pas plus que ce n'est pour son plaisir que Dolce danse à la corde. Capi a appris à se tenir debout sur ses pattes, et Dolce a appris aussi à danser à la corde ; ils ont même dû travailler beaucoup et longtemps pour acquérir ces talents, ainsi que ceux qui les rendent d'habiles comédiens. Eh bien ! toi aussi, tu dois travailler pour apprendre les différents rôles que tu joueras avec eux. Mettons-nous donc à l'ouvrage.

J'avais à cette époque des idées tout à fait primitives sur le travail. Je croyais que pour travailler il fallait bêcher la terre, ou fendre un arbre, ou tailler la pierre, et n'imaginais point autre chose.

— La pièce que nous allons représenter, continua Vitalis, a pour titre *Le Domestique de M. Joli-Cœur* ou *Le plus bête des deux n'est pas celui qu'on pense*. Voici le sujet : M. Joli-Cœur a eu jusqu'à ce jour un domestique dont il est très content, c'est Capi. Mais Capi devient vieux ; et, d'un autre côté, M. Joli-Cœur veut un nouveau domestique. Capi se charge de lui en procurer un. Mais ce ne sera pas un chien qu'il se donnera pour successeur, ce sera un jeune garçon, un paysan nommé Rémi.

— Comme moi ?

— Non, pas comme toi, mais toi-même. Tu arrives de ton village pour entrer au service de Joli-Cœur.

— Les singes n'ont pas de domestiques.
— Dans les comédies ils en ont. Tu arrives donc, et M. Joli-Cœur trouve que tu as l'air d'un imbécile.
— Ce n'est pas amusant, cela.
— Qu'est-ce que cela te fait, puisque c'est pour rire? D'ailleurs, figure-toi que tu arrives véritablement chez un monsieur pour être domestique et qu'on te dit, par exemple, de mettre la table. Précisément en voici une qui doit servir dans notre représentation. Avance et dispose le couvert.

Sur cette table, il y avait des assiettes, un verre, un couteau, une fourchette et du linge blanc.

Comment devait-on arranger tout cela?

Comme je me posais ces questions et restais les bras tendus, penché en avant, la bouche ouverte, ne sachant par où commencer, mon maître battit des mains en riant aux éclats.

— Bravo, dit-il, bravo! c'est parfait. Ton jeu de physionomie est excellent. Le garçon que j'avais avant toi prenait une mine futée et son air disait clairement : « Vous allez voir comme je fais bien la bête »; tu ne dis rien, toi, tu es, ta naïveté est admirable.

— Je ne sais pas ce que je dois faire.
— Et c'est par là précisément que tu es excellent. Demain, dans quelques jours tu sauras à merveille ce que tu devras faire. C'est alors qu'il faudra te rappeler l'embarras que tu éprouves présentement, et feindre ce que tu ne sentiras plus. Si tu peux retrouver ce jeu de physionomie et cette attitude, je te prédis le plus beau succès. Qu'est ton personnage dans ma comédie? celui d'un jeune paysan qui n'a rien vu et qui ne sait rien; il arrive chez un singe et il se trouve plus ignorant et plus maladroit que ce singe; de là mon sous-titre : « Le plus bête des deux n'est pas celui qu'on pense. » Plus bête que Joli-Cœur, voilà ton rôle; pour le jouer dans la perfection, tu n'aurais qu'à rester ce que tu es en ce moment; mais, comme cela est impossible, tu devras te rappeler ce que tu as été et devenir par effort d'art ce que tu ne seras plus naturellement.

Le Domestique de M. Joli-Cœur n'était pas une grande comédie, et sa représentation ne prenait pas plus de vingt minutes. Mais notre répétition dura près de trois heures, Vitalis nous faisant recommencer deux fois, quatre fois, dix fois la même chose, aux chiens comme à moi.

Ceux-ci, en effet, avaient oublié certaines parties de leur rôle, et il fallait les leur apprendre de nouveau.

Je fus alors bien surpris de voir la patience et la douceur de notre maître. Ce n'était point ainsi qu'on traitait les bêtes dans mon village, où les jurons et les coups étaient les seuls procédés d'éducation qu'on employât à leur égard.

Pour lui, tant que se prolongea cette longue répétition, il ne se fâcha pas une seule fois ; pas une seule fois il ne jura.

— Allons, recommençons, disait-il sévèrement, quand ce qu'il avait demandé n'était pas réussi ; c'est mal, Capi ; vous ne faites pas attention, Joli-Cœur, vous serez grondé.

Et c'était tout ; mais cependant c'était assez.

— Eh bien, me dit-il, quand la répétition fut terminée, crois-tu que tu t'habitueras à jouer la comédie ?

— Je ne sais pas.

— Cela t'ennuie-t-il ?

— Non, cela m'amuse.

— Alors tout ira bien ; tu as de l'intelligence et, ce qui est plus précieux encore peut-être, de l'attention ; avec de l'attention et de la docilité, on arrive à tout. Vois mes chiens et compare-les à Joli-Cœur. Joli-Cœur a peut-être plus de vivacité et d'intelligence, mais il n'a pas de docilité. Il apprend facilement ce qu'on lui enseigne, mais il l'oublie aussitôt. D'ailleurs ce n'est jamais avec plaisir qu'il fait ce qu'on lui demande ; volontiers il se révolterait, et toujours il est contrariant. Cela tient à sa nature, et voilà pourquoi je ne me fâche pas contre lui : le singe n'a pas, comme le chien, la conscience du devoir, et par là il lui est très inférieur. Comprends-tu cela ?

— Il me semble.

— Sois donc attentif, mon garçon ; sois docile ; fais de ton mieux ce que tu dois faire. Dans la vie, tout est là !

Causant ainsi, je m'enhardis à lui dire que ce qui m'avait le plus étonné dans cette répétition, ç'avait été l'inaltérable patience dont il avait fait preuve, aussi bien avec Joli-Cœur et les chiens qu'avec moi.

Il se mit alors à sourire doucement :

— On voit bien, me dit-il, que tu n'as vécu jusqu'à ce jour qu'avec des paysans durs aux bêtes et qui croient qu'on doit conduire celles-ci le bâton toujours levé.

— Maman Barberin était très douce pour notre vache la Roussette, lui dis-je.

— Elle avait raison, reprit-il. Tu me donnes une bonne idée de maman Barberin ; c'est qu'elle savait ce que les gens de campagne ignorent trop souvent, qu'on obtient peu de chose par la brutalité, tandis qu'on obtient beaucoup, pour ne pas dire tout, par la douceur. Pour moi, c'est en ne me fâchant jamais contre mes bêtes que j'ai fait d'elles ce qu'elles sont. Si je les avais battues, elles seraient craintives, et la crainte paralyse l'intelligence. Au reste, en me laissant aller à la colère avec elles, je ne serais pas moi-même ce que je suis, et je n'aurais pas acquis cette patience à toute épreuve qui m'a gagné ta confiance. C'est que qui instruit les autres s'instruit soi-même. Mes chiens m'ont donné autant de leçons qu'ils en ont reçu de moi. J'ai développé leur intelligence, ils m'ont formé le caractère.

Ce que j'entendais me parut si étrange, que je me mis à rire.

— Tu trouves cela bien bizarre, n'est-ce pas, qu'un chien puisse donner des leçons à un homme ? Et cependant rien n'est plus vrai. Réfléchis un peu. Admets-tu qu'un chien subisse l'influence de son maître ?

— Oh ! bien sûr.

— Alors tu vas comprendre que le maître est obligé de veiller sur lui-même quand il entreprend l'éducation d'un chien. Ainsi suppose un moment qu'en instruisant Capi je me sois abandonné à l'emportement et à la colère. Qu'aura fait Capi ? il aura pris l'habitude de la colère et de l'emportement, c'est-à-dire qu'en se modelant sur mon exemple il se sera corrompu. Le chien est presque toujours le miroir de son maître, et qui voit l'un voit l'autre. Montre-moi ton chien, je dirai qui tu es. Le brigand a pour chien un gredin ; le voleur, un voleur ; le paysan sans intelligence, un chien grossier ; l'homme poli et affable, un chien aimable.

Mes camarades, les chiens et le singe, avaient sur moi le grand avantage d'être habitués à paraître en public, de sorte qu'ils virent arriver le lendemain sans crainte. Pour eux il s'agissait de faire ce qu'ils avaient déjà fait cent fois, mille fois peut-être.

Mais pour moi, je n'avais pas leur tranquille assurance. Que dirait Vitalis, si je jouais mal mon rôle ? Que diraient nos spectateurs ? Cette préoccupation troubla mon sommeil et, quand je m'endormis, je vis en rêve des gens qui se tenaient les côtes à force de rire, tant ils se moquaient de moi.

Aussi mon émotion était-elle vive, lorsque, le lendemain, nous quittâmes notre auberge pour nous rendre sur la place, où devait avoir lieu notre représentation.

Vitalis ouvrait la marche, la tête haute, la poitrine cambrée, et il marquait le pas des deux bras et des pieds en jouant une valse sur un fifre en métal. Derrière lui venait Capi, sur le dos duquel se prélassait M. Joli-Cœur, en costume de général anglais, habit et pantalon rouges galonnés d'or, avec un chapeau à claque surmonté d'un large plumet. Puis, à une distance respectueuse, s'avançaient sur une même ligne Zerbino et Dolce. Enfin je formais la queue du cortège, qui, grâce à l'espacement indiqué par notre maître, tenait une certaine place dans la rue.

Mais ce qui, mieux encore que la pompe de notre défilé, provoquait l'attention, c'étaient les sons perçants du fifre qui allaient jusqu'au fond des maisons éveiller la curiosité des habitants d'Ussel. On accourait sur les portes pour nous voir passer ; les rideaux de toutes les fenêtres se soulevaient rapidement.

Quelques enfants s'étaient mis à nous suivre ; des paysans ébahis s'étaient joints à eux, et, quand nous étions arrivés sur la place, nous avions derrière nous et autour de nous un véritable cortège.

Notre salle de spectacle fut bien vite dressée ; elle consistait en une corde attachée à quatre arbres, de manière à former un carré long, au milieu duquel nous nous plaçâmes.

La première partie de la représentation consista en différents tours exécutés par les chiens ; mais ce que furent ces tours, je ne saurais le dire, occupé que j'étais à me répéter mon rôle et troublé par l'inquiétude.

Tout ce que je me rappelle, c'est que Vitalis avait abandonné son fifre et l'avait remplacé par un violon au moyen duquel il accompagnait les exercices des chiens, tantôt avec des airs de danse, tantôt avec une musique douce et tendre.

La foule s'était rapidement amassée contre nos cordes, et, quand je regardais autour de moi, machinalement bien plus qu'avec une intention déterminée, je voyais une infinité de prunelles qui, toutes fixées sur nous, semblaient projeter des rayons.

La première pièce terminée, Capi prit une sébile entre ses dents et, marchant sur ses pattes de derrière, commença à faire le tour « de l'honorable société ». Lorsque les sous ne tombaient pas dans la sébile, il s'arrêtait et, plaçant celle-ci dans l'intérieur du cercle hors la portée des mains, il posait ses deux pattes de devant sur le spectateur récalcitrant, poussait deux ou trois aboiements, et frappait des petits coups sur la poche qu'il voulait ouvrir.

Alors dans le public c'étaient des cris, des propos joyeux et des railleries.

— Il est malin, le caniche, il connaît ceux qui ont le gousset garni.

— Allons, la main à la poche !
— Il donnera !
— Il ne donnera pas !
— L'héritage de votre oncle vous le rendra.

Et les sous étaient finalement arrachés des profondeurs où ils se cachaient.

Pendant ce temps, Vitalis, sans dire un mot, mais ne quittant pas la sébile des yeux, jouait des airs joyeux sur son violon qu'il levait et qu'il baissait selon la mesure.

Bientôt Capi revint auprès de son maître, portant fièrement la sébile pleine.

C'était à Joli-Cœur et à moi à entrer en scène.

— Mesdames et messieurs, dit Vitalis en gesticulant d'une main avec son archet et de l'autre avec son violon, nous allons continuer le spectacle par une charmante comédie intitulée : *Le Domestique de M. Joli-Cœur*, ou *Le plus bête des deux n'est pas celui qu'on pense*. Un homme comme moi ne s'abaisse pas à faire d'avance l'éloge de ses pièces et de ses acteurs ; je ne vous dis donc qu'une chose : écarquillez les yeux, ouvrez les oreilles et préparez vos mains pour applaudir.

Ce qu'il appelait « une charmante comédie » était en réalité une pantomime, c'est-à-dire une pièce jouée avec des gestes et non avec des paroles. Et cela devait être ainsi, par cette bonne raison que deux des principaux acteurs, Joli-Cœur et Capi, ne savaient pas parler, et que le troisième (qui était moi-même) aurait été parfaitement incapable de dire deux mots.

Cependant, pour rendre le jeu des comédiens plus facilement compréhensible, Vitalis l'accompagnait de quelques paroles qui préparaient les situations de la pièce et les expliquaient.

Ce fut ainsi que, jouant en sourdine un air guerrier, il annonça l'entrée de M. Joli-Cœur, général anglais qui avait gagné ses grades et sa fortune dans les guerres des Indes. Jusqu'à ce jour, M. Joli-Cœur n'avait eu pour domestique que le seul Capi, mais il voulait se faire servir désormais par un homme, ses moyens lui permettant ce luxe : les bêtes avaient été assez longtemps les esclaves des hommes, il était temps que cela changeât.

En attendant que ce domestique arrivât, le général Joli-Cœur se promenait en long et en large, et fumait son cigare. Il fallait voir comme il lançait sa fumée au nez du public !

Il s'impatientait, le général, et il commençait à rouler de gros yeux comme quelqu'un qui va se mettre en colère ; il se mordait les lèvres et frappait la terre du pied.

Au troisième coup de pied, je devais entrer en scène, amené par Capi.

Si j'avais oublié mon rôle, le chien me l'aurait rappelé. Au moment voulu, il me tendit la patte et m'introduisit auprès du général.

Celui-ci, en m'apercevant, leva les deux bras d'un air désolé. Eh quoi! c'était là le domestique qu'on lui présentait? Puis il vint me regarder sous le nez et tourner autour de moi en haussant les épaules. Sa mine fut si drolatique que tout le monde éclata de rire : on avait compris qu'il me prenait pour un parfait imbécile, et c'était aussi le sentiment des spectateurs.

La pièce était, bien entendu, bâtie pour montrer cette imbécillité sous toutes les faces; dans chaque scène je devais faire quelque balourdise nouvelle, tandis que Joli-Cœur, au contraire, devait trouver une occasion pour développer son intelligence et son adresse.

Après m'avoir examiné longuement, le général, pris de pitié, me faisait servir à déjeuner.

— Le général croit que, quand ce garçon aura mangé, il sera moins bête, disait Vitalis; nous allons voir cela.

Et je m'asseyais devant une petite table sur laquelle le couvert était mis, une serviette posée sur mon assiette.

Que faire de cette serviette?

Capi m'indiquait que je devais m'en servir. Mais comment?

Après avoir bien cherché, je fis le geste de me moucher dedans.

Là-dessus le général se tordit de rire, et Capi tomba les quatre pattes en l'air renversé par ma stupidité.

Voyant que je me trompais, je contemplais de nouveau la serviette, me demandant comment l'employer.

Enfin une idée m'arriva; je roulai la serviette et m'en fis une cravate.

Nouveaux rires du général, nouvelle chute de Capi. Et ainsi de suite jusqu'au moment où le général exaspéré m'arracha de ma chaise, s'assit à ma place et mangea le déjeuner qui m'était destiné.

Ah! il savait se servir d'une serviette, le général. Avec quelle grâce il la passa dans une boutonnière de son uniforme et l'étala sur ses genoux! Avec quelle élégance il cassa son pain et vida son verre!

Mais où ses belles manières produisirent un effet irrésistible, ce fut lorsque, le déjeuner terminé, il demanda un cure-dent et le passa rapidement entre ses dents.

Alors les applaudissements éclatèrent de tous les côtés, et la représentation s'acheva dans un triomphe.

Comme le singe était intelligent ! comme le domestique était bête !

En revenant à notre auberge, Vitalis me fit ce compliment, et j'étais si bien comédien, que je fus fier de cet éloge.

VII

J'apprends à lire

C'étaient assurément des comédiens du plus grand talent, que ceux qui composaient la troupe du signor Vitalis – je parle des chiens et du singe –, mais ce talent n'était pas très varié.

Lorsqu'ils avaient donné trois ou quatre représentations, on connaissait tout leur répertoire ; ils ne pouvaient plus que se répéter.

De là résultait la nécessité de ne pas rester longtemps dans une même ville.

Trois jours après notre arrivée à Ussel, il fallut donc se remettre en route.

Où allions-nous ? Je m'étais assez enhardi avec mon maître pour me permettre cette question.

— Tu connais le pays ? me répondit-il en me regardant
— Non.
— Alors pourquoi me demandes-tu où nous allons ?
— Pour savoir.
— Savoir quoi ?

Je restai interloqué, regardant, sans trouver un mot, la route blanche qui s'allongeait devant nous au fond d'un vallon boisé.

— Si je te dis, continua-t-il, que nous allons à Aurillac pour nous diriger ensuite sur Bordeaux et de Bordeaux sur les Pyrénées, qu'est-ce que cela t'apprendra ?

— Mais vous, vous connaissez donc le pays ?
— Je n'y suis jamais venu.
— Et pourtant vous savez où nous allons ?

Il me regarda encore longuement comme s'il cherchait quelque chose en moi.

— Tu ne sais pas lire, n'est-ce pas ? me dit-il

— Non.

— Sais-tu ce que c'est qu'un livre ?

— Oui ; on emporte les livres à la messe pour dire ses prières quand on ne récite pas son chapelet ; j'en ai vu, des livres, et des beaux, avec des images dedans et du cuir tout autour.

— Bon ; alors tu comprends qu'on peut mettre des prières dans un livre ?

— Oui.

— On peut y mettre autre chose encore. Quand tu récites ton chapelet, tu récites des mots que ta mère t'a mis dans l'oreille, et qui de ton oreille ont été s'entasser dans ton esprit pour revenir ensuite au bout de ta langue et sur tes lèvres quand tu les appelles. Eh bien, ceux qui disent leurs prières avec des livres ne tirent point les mots dont se composent ces prières de leur mémoire, mais ils les prennent avec leurs yeux dans les livres où ils ont été mis, c'est-à-dire qu'ils lisent.

— J'ai vu lire, dis-je tout glorieux, comme une personne qui n'est point une bête, et qui sait parfaitement ce dont on lui parle.

— Ce qu'on fait pour les prières, on le fait pour tout. Dans un livre que je vais te montrer quand nous nous reposerons, nous trouverons les noms et l'histoire des pays que nous traversons. Des hommes qui ont habité ou parcouru ces pays ont mis dans mon livre ce qu'ils avaient vu ou appris ; si bien que je n'ai qu'à ouvrir ce livre et à le lire pour connaître ces pays ; je les vois comme si je les regardais avec mes propres yeux ; j'apprends leur histoire comme si on me la racontait.

J'avais été élevé comme un véritable sauvage qui n'a aucune idée de la vie civilisée. Ces paroles furent pour moi une sorte de révélation, confuse d'abord, mais qui peu à peu s'éclaircit. Il est vrai cependant qu'on m'avait envoyé à l'école. Mais ce n'avait été que pour un mois. Et, pendant ce mois, on ne m'avait pas mis un livre entre les mains, on ne m'avait parlé ni de lecture, ni d'écriture, on ne m'avait donné aucune leçon de quelque genre que ce fût.

Il ne faut pas conclure de ce qui se passe actuellement dans les écoles, que ce que je dis là est impossible. À l'époque dont je parle, il y avait un grand nombre de communes en France qui n'avaient pas d'écoles, et parmi celles qui existaient il s'en trouvait qui étaient dirigées par des maîtres qui, pour une raison ou pour une autre, parce qu'ils ne savaient rien, ou bien parce qu'ils avaient autre chose à faire, ne donnaient aucun enseignement aux enfants qu'on leur confiait. Ils gardaient les enfants, croyant que c'était le principal.

C'était là le cas du maître d'école de notre village. Savait-il quelque chose? c'est possible, et je ne veux pas porter contre lui une accusation d'ignorance. Mais la vérité est que, pendant le temps que je restai chez lui, il ne nous donna pas la plus petite leçon ni à mes camarades, ni à moi. Étant de son véritable métier sabotier, c'était à ses sabots qu'il travaillait, et, du matin au soir, on le voyait faire voler autour de lui les copeaux de hêtre et de noyer. Jamais il ne nous adressait la parole, si ce n'est pour nous parler de nos parents, ou bien du froid, ou bien de la pluie; mais de lecture, de calcul, jamais un mot. Pour cela il s'en remettait à sa fille, qui était chargée de le remplacer et de nous faire la classe. Mais, comme celle-ci de son véritable métier était couturière, elle faisait comme son père, et, tandis qu'il manœuvrait sa plane ou sa cuiller, elle poussait vivement son aiguille.

Il fallait bien vivre, et, comme nous étions douze élèves payant chacun cinquante centimes par mois, ce n'était pas six francs qui pouvaient nourrir deux personnes pendant trente jours; les sabots et la couture complétaient ce que l'école ne pouvait pas fournir. On n'a de tout que pour son argent. Je n'avais donc absolument rien appris à l'école, pas même mes lettres.

— C'est difficile de lire? demandai-je à Vitalis après avoir marché assez longtemps en réfléchissant.

— C'est difficile pour ceux qui ont la tête dure, et plus difficile encore pour ceux qui ont mauvaise volonté As-tu la tête dure?

— Je ne sais pas, mais il me semble que, si vous vouliez m'apprendre à lire, je n'aurais pas mauvaise volonté.

— Eh bien, nous verrons; nous avons du temps devant nous.

Du temps devant nous! Pourquoi ne pas commencer aussitôt? Je ne savais pas combien il est difficile d'apprendre à lire, et je m'imaginais que tout de suite j'allais ouvrir un livre et voir ce qu'il y avait dedans.

Le lendemain, comme nous cheminions, je vis mon maître se baisser et ramasser sur la route un bout de planche à moitié recouvert par la poussière

— Voilà le livre dans lequel tu vas apprendre à lire, me dit-il
Un livre, cette planche ! Je le regardai pour voir s'il ne se moquait pas de moi. Puis, comme je le trouvai sérieux, je regardai attentivement sa trouvaille.

C'était bien une planche, rien qu'une planche de bois de hêtre, longue comme le bras, large comme les deux mains, bien polie ; il ne se trouvait dessus aucune inscription, aucun dessin.

Comment lire sur cette planche, et quoi lire ?

— Ton esprit travaille, me dit Vitalis en riant.

— Vous voulez vous moquer de moi ?

— Jamais, mon garçon ; la moquerie peut avoir du bon pour réformer un caractère vicieux, mais, lorsqu'elle s'adresse à l'ignorance, elle est une marque de sottise chez celui qui l'emploie. Attends que nous soyons arrivés à ce bouquet d'arbres qui est là-bas ; nous nous y reposerons, et tu verras comment je peux t'enseigner la lecture avec ce morceau de bois.

Nous arrivâmes rapidement à ce bouquet d'arbres et, nos sacs mis à terre, nous nous assîmes sur le gazon qui commençait à reverdir et dans lequel des pâquerettes se montraient çà et là. Joli-Cœur, débarrassé de sa chaîne, s'élança sur un des arbres en secouant les branches les unes après les autres, comme pour en faire tomber des noix, tandis que les chiens, plus tranquilles et surtout plus fatigués, se couchaient en rond autour de nous.

Alors Vitalis, tirant son couteau de sa poche, essaya de détacher de la planche une petite lame de bois aussi mince que possible. Ayant réussi, il polit cette lame sur ses deux faces, dans toute sa longueur, puis, cela fait, il la coupa en petits carrés, de sorte qu'elle lui donna une douzaine de petits morceaux plats d'égale grandeur.

Je ne le quittais pas des yeux, mais j'avoue que, malgré ma tension d'esprit, je ne comprenais pas du tout comment avec ces petits morceaux de bois il voulait faire un livre, car enfin, si ignorant que je fusse, je savais qu'un livre se composait d'un certain nombre de feuilles de papier sur lesquelles étaient tracés des signes noirs. Où étaient les feuilles de papier ? Où étaient les signes noirs ?

— Sur chacun de ces petits morceaux de bois, me dit-il, je creuserai demain, avec la pointe de mon couteau, une lettre de l'alphabet. Tu apprendras ainsi la forme des lettres, et, quand tu les sauras bien sans te tromper, de manière à les reconnaître rapidement à première vue, tu les réuniras les unes au bout des autres de manière à former des mots. Quand tu pourras ainsi former les mots que je te dirai, tu seras en état de lire dans un livre.

Bientôt j'eus mes poches pleines d'une collection de petits morceaux de bois, et je ne tardai pas à connaître les lettres de l'alphabet ; mais, pour savoir lire, ce fut une autre affaire, les choses n'allèrent pas si vite, et il arriva même un moment où je regrettai d'avoir voulu apprendre à lire.

Je dois dire cependant, pour être juste envers moi-même, que ce ne fut pas la paresse qui m'inspira ce regret, ce fut l'amour-propre.

En m'apprenant les lettres de l'alphabet, Vitalis avait pensé qu'il pourrait les apprendre en même temps à Capi ; puisque le chien avait bien su se mettre les chiffres des heures dans la tête, pourquoi ne s'y mettrait-il pas les lettres?

Et nous avions pris nos leçons en commun ; j'étais devenu le camarade de classe de Capi, ou le chien était devenu le mien, comme on voudra. Bien entendu, Capi ne devait pas épeler les lettres qu'il voyait, puisqu'il n'avait pas la parole ; mais, lorsque nos morceaux de bois étaient étalés sur l'herbe, il devait avec sa patte tirer les lettres que notre maître nommait.

Tout d'abord j'avais fait des progrès plus rapides que lui, mais, si j'avais l'intelligence plus prompte, il avait par contre la mémoire plus sûre : une chose bien apprise était pour lui une chose sue pour toujours ; il ne l'oubliait plus, et, comme il n'avait pas de distractions, il n'hésitait ou ne se trompait jamais.

Alors, quand je me trouvais en faute, notre maître ne manquait jamais de dire :

— Capi saura lire avant Rémi.

Et le chien, comprenant sans doute, remuait la queue d'un air de triomphe.

— Plus bête qu'une bête, c'est bon dans la comédie, disait encore Vitalis, mais dans la réalité c'est honteux.

Cela me piqua si bien, que je m'appliquai de tout cœur, et, tandis que le pauvre chien en restait à écrire son nom, en triant les quatre lettres qui le composent parmi toutes les lettres de l'alphabet, j'arrivai enfin à lire dans un livre.

— Maintenant que tu sais lire l'écriture, me dit Vitalis, veux-tu apprendre à lire la musique?

— Est-ce que, quand je saurai la musique, je pourrai chanter comme vous?

Vitalis chantait quelquefois, et sans qu'il s'en doutât c'était une fête pour moi de l'écouter.

— Tu voudrais donc chanter comme moi ?

— Oh ! pas comme vous, je sais bien que cela n'est pas possible, mais enfin chanter.

— Tu as du plaisir à m'entendre chanter ?

— Le plus grand plaisir qu'on puisse éprouver ; le rossignol chante bien, mais il me semble que vous chantez bien mieux encore. Et puis ce n'est pas du tout la même chose ; quand vous chantez, vous faites de moi ce que vous voulez, j'ai envie de pleurer ou bien j'ai envie de rire, et puis je vais vous dire une chose qui va peut-être vous paraître bête : quand vous chantez un air doux ou triste, cela me ramène auprès de mère Barberin, c'est à elle que je pense, c'est elle que je vois dans notre maison ; et pourtant je ne comprends pas les paroles que vous prononcez, puisqu'elles sont italiennes.

Je lui parlais en le regardant, il me sembla voir ses yeux se mouiller ; alors je m'arrêtai et lui demandai si je le peinais de parler ainsi.

— Non, mon enfant, me dit-il d'une voix émue, tu ne me peines pas, bien au contraire, tu me rappelles ma jeunesse, mon beau temps ; sois tranquille, je t'apprendrai à chanter, et, comme tu as du cœur, toi aussi tu feras pleurer et tu seras applaudi, tu verras...

Il s'arrêta tout à coup, et je crus comprendre qu'il ne voulait point se laisser aller sur ce sujet. Mais les raisons qui le retenaient, je ne les devinai point. Ce fut plus tard seulement que je les ai connues, beaucoup plus tard, et dans des circonstances douloureuses, terribles pour moi, que je raconterai lorsqu'elles se présenteront au cours de mon récit.

Dès le lendemain, mon maître fit pour la musique ce qu'il avait déjà fait pour la lecture, c'est-à-dire qu'il recommença à tailler des petits carrés de bois, qu'il grava avec la pointe de son couteau.

Mais cette fois son travail fut plus considérable, car les divers signes nécessaires à la notation de la musique offrent des combinaisons plus compliquées que l'alphabet.

Afin d'alléger mes poches, il utilisa les deux faces de ses carrés de bois, et, après les avoir rayées toutes deux de cinq lignes qui représentaient la portée, il inscrivit sur une face la clé de *sol* et sur l'autre la clé de *fa*. Puis, quand il eut tout préparé, les leçons commencèrent, et j'avoue qu'elles ne furent pas moins dures que ne l'avaient été celles de lecture. Plus d'une fois Vitalis, si patient avec ses chiens, s'exaspéra contre moi.

— Avec une bête, s'écriait-il, on se contient parce qu'on sait que c'est une bête, mais toi tu me feras mourir !

Et alors, levant les mains au ciel dans un mouvement théâtral, il les laissait tomber tout à coup sur ses cuisses où elles claquaient fortement. Joli-Cœur, qui prenait plaisir à répéter tout ce qu'il trouvait drôle, avait copié ce geste, et, comme il assistait presque toujours à mes leçons, j'avais le dépit, lorsque j'hésitais, de le voir lever les bras au ciel et laisser tomber ses mains sur ses cuisses en les faisant claquer.

— Joli-Cœur lui-même se moque de toi ! s'écriait Vitalis.

Si j'avais osé, j'aurais répliqué qu'il se moquait autant du maître que de l'élève, mais le respect autant qu'une certaine crainte vague arrêtèrent toujours heureusement cette repartie ; je me contentai de me la dire tout bas, quand Joli-Cœur faisait claquer ses mains avec une mauvaise grimace, et cela me rendait jusqu'à un certain point la mortification moins pénible.

Enfin les premiers pas furent franchis avec plus ou moins de peine, et j'eus la satisfaction de solfier un air écrit par Vitalis sur une feuille de papier.

Ce jour-là il ne fit pas claquer ses mains, mais il me donna deux bonnes petites tapes amicales sur chaque joue, en déclarant que, si je continuais ainsi, je deviendrais certainement un grand chanteur.

Bien entendu, ces études ne se firent pas en un jour, et, pendant des semaines, pendant des mois, mes poches furent constamment remplies de mes petits morceaux de bois.

D'ailleurs, mon travail n'était pas régulier comme celui d'un enfant qui suit les classes d'une école, et c'était seulement à ses moments perdus que mon maître pouvait me donner mes leçons.

Il fallait chaque jour accomplir notre parcours, qui était plus ou moins long, selon que les villages étaient plus ou moins éloignés les uns des autres ; il fallait donner nos représentations partout où nous avions chance de ramasser une recette ; il fallait faire répéter les rôles aux chiens et à M. Joli-Cœur ; il fallait préparer nous-mêmes notre déjeuner ou notre dîner, et c'était seulement après tout cela qu'il était question de lecture ou de musique, le plus souvent dans une halte, au pied d'un arbre, ou bien sur un tas de cailloux, le gazon ou la route servant de table pour étaler mes morceaux de bois.

Cette éducation ne ressemblait guère à celle que reçoivent tant d'enfants, qui n'ont qu'à travailler, et qui se plaignent pourtant de n'avoir pas le temps de faire les devoirs qu'on leur donne. Mais il faut bien dire qu'il y a quelque chose de plus important encore que le temps qu'on emploie au travail, c'est l'application qu'on y apporte ; ce n'est pas l'heure que nous passons sur notre leçon qui met cette leçon dans notre mémoire, c'est la volonté d'apprendre.

Par bonheur, j'étais capable de tendre ma volonté sans me laisser trop souvent entraîner par les distractions qui nous entouraient. Qu'aurais-je appris, si je n'avais pu travailler que dans une chambre, les oreilles bouchées avec mes deux mains, les yeux collés sur un livre comme certains écoliers ? Rien, car nous n'avions pas de chambre pour nous enfermer, et, en marchant le long des grandes routes, je devais regarder au bout de mes pieds, sous peine de me laisser souvent choir sur le nez.

Enfin j'appris quelque chose, et en même temps j'appris aussi à faire de longues marches qui ne me furent pas moins utiles que les leçons de Vitalis. J'étais un enfant assez chétif quand je vivais avec mère Barberin, et la façon dont on avait parlé de moi le prouve bien ; « un enfant de la ville », avait dit Barberin, « avec des jambes et des bras trop minces », avait dit Vitalis ; auprès de mon maître et vivant de sa vie en plein air, à la dure, mes jambes et mes bras se fortifièrent, mes poumons se développèrent, ma peau se cuirassa, et je devins capable de supporter, sans en souffrir, le froid comme le chaud, le soleil comme la pluie, la peine, les privations, les fatigues.

Et ce me fut un grand bonheur que cet apprentissage ; il me mit à même de résister aux coups qui plus d'une fois devaient s'abattre sur moi, durs et écrasants, pendant ma jeunesse.

VIII

Par monts et par vaux

Nous avions parcouru une partie du midi de la France : l'Auvergne, le Velay, le Vivarais, le Quercy, le Rouergue, les Cévennes, le Languedoc. Notre façon de voyager était des plus simples : nous allions droit devant nous, au hasard, et, quand nous trouvions un village qui de loin ne nous paraissait pas trop misérable, nous nous préparions pour faire une entrée triomphale. Je faisais la toilette des chiens, coiffant Dolce, habillant Zerbino, mettant un emplâtre sur l'œil de Capi pour qu'il pût jouer le rôle d'un vieux grognard ; enfin je forçais Joli-Cœur à endosser son habit de général. Mais c'était là la partie la plus difficile de ma tâche, car le singe, qui savait très bien que cette toilette était le prélude d'un travail pour lui, se défendait tant qu'il pouvait, et inventait les tours les plus drôles pour m'empêcher de l'habiller. Alors j'appelais Capi à mon aide, et par sa vigilance, par son instinct et sa finesse, il arrivait presque toujours à déjouer les malices du singe.

La troupe en grande tenue, Vitalis prenait son fifre, et, nous mettant en bel ordre, nous défilions par le village.

Si le nombre des curieux que nous entraînions derrière nous était suffisant, nous donnions une représentation ; si, au contraire, il était trop faible pour faire espérer une recette, nous continuions notre marche. Dans les villes seulement nous restions plusieurs jours, et alors, le matin, j'avais la liberté d'aller me promener où je voulais. Je prenais Capi avec moi – Capi, simple chien, bien entendu, sans son costume de théâtre, et nous flânions par les rues.

Vitalis, qui d'ordinaire me tenait étroitement près de lui, pour cela me mettait volontiers la bride sur le cou.

— Puisque le hasard, me disait-il, te fait parcourir la France à un âge où les enfants sont généralement à l'école ou au collège, ouvre les yeux, regarde et apprends. Quand tu seras embarrassé, quand tu verras quelque chose que tu ne comprendras pas, si tu as des questions à me faire, adresse-les-moi sans peur. Peut-être ne pourrai-je pas toujours te répondre, car je n'ai pas la prétention de tout connaître, mais peut-être aussi me sera-t-il possible de satisfaire parfois ta curiosité. Je n'ai pas toujours été directeur d'une troupe d'animaux savants, et j'ai appris autre chose que ce qui m'est en ce moment utile pour « présenter Capi ou M. Joli-Cœur devant l'honorable société ».

— Quoi donc ?

— Nous causerons de cela plus tard. Pour le moment sache seulement qu'un montreur de chiens peut avoir occupé une certaine position dans le monde. En même temps, comprends aussi que, si en ce moment tu es sur la marche la plus basse de l'escalier de la vie, tu peux, si tu le veux, arriver peu à peu à une plus haute. Cela dépend des circonstances pour un peu, et pour beaucoup de toi. Écoute mes leçons, écoute mes conseils, enfant, et plus tard, quand tu seras grand, tu penseras, je l'espère, avec émotion, avec reconnaissance, au pauvre musicien qui t'a fait si grande peur quand il t'a enlevé à ta mère nourrice ; j'ai dans l'idée que notre rencontre te sera heureuse.

Quelle avait pu être cette position dont mon maître parlait assez souvent avec une retenue qu'il s'imposait ? Cette question excitait ma curiosité et faisait travailler mon esprit. S'il avait été sur une marche haute de l'escalier de la vie, comme il disait, pourquoi était-il maintenant sur une marche basse ? Il prétendait que je pouvais m'élever, si je le voulais, moi qui n'étais rien, qui ne savais rien, qui étais sans famille, qui n'avais personne pour m'aider. Alors pourquoi lui-même était-il descendu ?

Après avoir quitté les montagnes de l'Auvergne, nous étions arrivés dans les *Causses* du Quercy. On appelle ainsi de grandes plaines inégalement ondulées, où l'on ne rencontre guère que des terrains incultes et de maigres taillis. Aucun pays n'est plus triste, plus pauvre. Et ce qui accentue encore cette impression que le voyageur reçoit en le traversant, c'est que presque nulle part il n'aperçoit des eaux. Point de rivières, point de ruisseaux, point d'étangs. Çà et là des lits pierreux de torrents, mais vides. Les eaux se sont engouffrées dans des précipices et elles ont disparu sous la terre, pour aller sourdre plus loin et former des rivières ou des fontaines.

Au milieu de cette plaine, brûlée par la sécheresse au moment où nous la traversâmes, se trouve un gros village qui a nom la Bastide-Murat ; nous y passâmes la nuit dans la grange d'une auberge.

— C'est ici, me dit Vitalis en causant le soir avant de nous coucher, c'est ici, dans ce pays, et probablement dans cette auberge, qu'est né un homme qui a fait tuer des milliers de soldats et qui, ayant commencé la vie par être garçon d'écurie, est devenu prince et roi : il s'appelait Murat ; on en a fait un héros et l'on a donné son nom à ce village. Je l'ai connu, et bien souvent je me suis entretenu avec lui.

Malgré moi une interruption m'échappa.

— Quand il était garçon d'écurie ?

— Non, répondit Vitalis en riant, quand il était roi. C'est la première fois que je viens à la Bastide, et c'est à Naples que je l'ai connu, au milieu de sa cour.

— Vous avez connu un roi ?

Il est à croire que le ton de mon exclamation fut fort drôle, car le rire de mon maître éclata de nouveau et se prolongea longtemps.

Nous étions assis sur un banc devant l'écurie, le dos appuyé contre la muraille qui gardait la chaleur du jour. Dans un grand sycomore qui nous couvrait de son feuillage, des cigales chantaient leur chanson monotone. Devant nous, par-dessus le toit des maisons, la pleine lune, qui venait de se lever, montait doucement au ciel. Cette soirée était pour nous d'autant plus douce que la journée avait été brûlante.

— Veux-tu dormir ? me demanda Vitalis, ou bien veux-tu que je te conte l'histoire du roi Murat ?

— Oh ! l'histoire du roi ; je vous en prie.

Alors il me raconta tout au long cette histoire, et, pendant plusieurs heures, nous restâmes sur notre banc ; lui, parlant, moi, les yeux attachés sur son visage, que la lune éclairait de sa pâle lumière. Eh quoi, tout cela était possible ; non seulement possible, mais encore vrai !

Je n'avais eu jusqu'alors aucune idée de ce qu'était l'histoire. Qui m'en eût parlé ? Pas mère Barberin, à coup sûr ; elle ne savait même pas ce que c'était. Elle était née à Chavanon, et elle devait y mourir. Son esprit n'avait jamais été plus loin que ses yeux. Et pour ses yeux l'univers tenait dans le pays qu'enfermait l'horizon qui se développait du haut du mont Audouze.

Mon maître avait vu tant de choses !

Qu'était donc mon maître, au temps de sa jeunesse ? Et comment était-il devenu ce que je le voyais au temps de sa vieillesse ?

Il y avait là, on en conviendra, de quoi faire travailler une imagination enfantine, éveillée, alerte et curieuse de merveilleux.

IX

Je rencontre un géant
chaussé de bottes de sept lieues

En quittant le sol desséché des *causses* et des *garrigues,* je me trouve, par le souvenir, dans une vallée toujours fraîche et verte, celle de la Dordogne, que nous descendons à petites journées, car la richesse du pays fait celle des habitants, et nos représentations sont nombreuses ; les sous tombent assez facilement dans la sébile de Capi.

Un pont aérien, léger, comme s'il était soutenu dans le brouillard par des fils de la Vierge, s'élève au-dessus d'une large rivière qui roule doucement ses eaux paresseuses – c'est le pont de Cubzac, et la rivière est la Dordogne.

Une ville en ruine avec des fossés, des grottes, des tours, et, au milieu des murailles croulantes d'un cloître, des cigales qui chantent dans les arbustes accrochés çà et là, – c'est Saint-Émilion.

Mais tout cela se brouille confusément dans ma mémoire, tandis que bientôt se présente un spectacle qui la frappe assez fortement pour qu'elle garde l'empreinte qu'elle en a alors reçue et se le représente aujourd'hui avec tout son relief.

Nous avions couché dans un village assez misérable, et nous en étions partis le matin, au jour naissant. Longtemps nous avions marché sur une route poudreuse, lorsque tout à coup nos regards, jusque-là enfermés dans un chemin que bordaient des vignes, s'étendirent librement sur un espace immense, comme si un rideau, touché par une baguette magique, s'était subitement abaissé devant nous.

Une large rivière s'arrondissait doucement autour de la colline sur laquelle nous venions d'arriver ; et, au-delà de cette rivière, les toits et les clochers d'une grande ville s'éparpillaient jusqu'à la courbe indécise de l'horizon. Que de maisons ! que de cheminées ! Quelques-unes plus hautes et plus étroites, élancées comme des colonnes, vomissaient des tourbillons de fumée noire qui, s'envolant au caprice de la brise, formait au-dessus de la ville un nuage de vapeur sombre. Sur la rivière, au milieu de son cours et le long d'une ligne de quais, se tassaient de nombreux navires qui, comme les arbres d'une forêt, emmêlaient les uns dans les autres leurs mâtures, leurs cordages, leurs voiles, leurs drapeaux multicolores qui flottaient au vent. On entendait des ronflements sourds, des bruits de ferraille et de chaudronnerie, des coups de marteaux et par-dessus tout le tapage produit par le roulement de nombreuses voitures qu'on voyait courir çà et là sur les quais.

— C'est Bordeaux, me dit Vitalis.

Pour un enfant élevé comme moi, qui n'avait vu jusque-là que les pauvres villages de la Creuse, ou les quelques petites villes que le hasard de la route nous avait fait rencontrer, c'était féerique.

Sans que j'eusse réfléchi, mes pieds s'arrêtèrent, je restai immobile, regardant devant moi, au loin, auprès, tout à l'entour.

Mais bientôt mes yeux se fixèrent sur un point : la rivière et les navires qui la couvraient. En effet, il se produisait là un mouvement confus qui m'intéressait d'autant plus fortement que je n'y comprenais absolument rien.

Des navires, leurs voiles déployées, descendaient la rivière légèrement inclinés sur un côté, d'autres la remontaient ; il y en avait qui restaient immobiles comme des îles, et il y en avait aussi qui tournaient sur eux-mêmes sans qu'on vît ce qui les faisait tourner ; enfin il y en avait encore qui, sans mâture, sans voilure, mais avec une cheminée qui déroulait dans le ciel des tourbillons de fumée, se mouvaient rapidement, allant en tous sens et laissant derrière eux, sur l'eau jaunâtre, des sillons d'écume blanche.

— C'est l'heure de la marée, me dit Vitalis, répondant, sans que je l'eusse interrogé, à mon étonnement ; il y a des navires qui arrivent de la pleine mer, après de longs voyages : ce sont ceux dont la peinture est salie et qui sont comme rouillés ; il y en a d'autres qui quittent le port ; ceux que tu vois, au milieu de la rivière, tourner sur eux-mêmes, évitent sur leurs ancres de manière à présenter leur proue au flot montant. Ceux qui courent enveloppés dans des nuages de fumée sont des remorqueurs.

Que de mots étranges pour moi ! que d'idées nouvelles !

Lorsque nous arrivâmes au pont qui fait communiquer la Bastide avec Bordeaux, Vitalis n'avait pas eu le temps de répondre à la centième partie des questions que je voulais lui adresser.

Jusque-là nous n'avions jamais fait long séjour dans les villes qui s'étaient trouvées sur notre passage, car les nécessités de notre spectacle nous obligeaient à changer chaque jour le lieu de nos représentations, afin d'avoir un public nouveau. Avec des comédiens tels que ceux qui composaient « la troupe de l'illustre signor Vitalis », le répertoire ne pouvait pas en effet être bien varié, et, quand nous avions joué *Le Domestique de M. Joli-Cœur*, *La Mort du général*, *Le Triomphe du juste*, *Le Malade purgé* et trois ou quatre autres pièces, c'était fini, nos acteurs avaient donné tout ce qu'ils pouvaient ; il fallait ailleurs recommencer *Le Malade purgé* ou *Le Triomphe du juste* devant des spectateurs qui n'eussent pas vu ces pièces.

Mais Bordeaux est une grande ville, où le public se renouvelle facilement, et en changeant de quartier nous pouvions donner jusqu'à trois et quatre représentations par jour, sans qu'on nous criât, comme cela nous était arrivé à Cahors :

— C'est donc toujours la même chose ?

De Bordeaux, nous devions aller à Pau. Notre itinéraire nous fit traverser ce grand désert qui, des portes de Bordeaux, s'étend jusqu'aux Pyrénées et qu'on appelle les Landes.

Bien que je ne fusse plus tout à fait le jeune souriceau dont parle la fable et qui trouve dans tout ce qu'il voit un sujet d'étonnement, d'admiration ou d'épouvante, je tombai, dès le commencement de ce voyage, dans une erreur qui fit bien rire mon maître et me valut ses railleries jusqu'à notre arrivée à Pau.

Nous avions quitté Bordeaux depuis sept ou huit jours et, après avoir tout d'abord suivi les bords de la Garonne, nous avions abandonné la rivière à Langon et nous avions pris la route de Mont-de-Marsan, qui s'enfonce à travers les terres. Plus de vignes, plus de prairies, plus de vergers, mais des bois de pins et des bruyères. Bientôt les maisons devinrent plus rares, plus misérables. Puis nous nous trouvâmes au milieu d'une immense plaine qui s'étendait devant nous à perte de vue, avec de légères ondulations. Pas de cultures, pas de bois, la terre grise au loin, et, tout auprès de nous, le long de la route recouverte d'une mousse veloutée, des bruyères desséchées et des genêts rabougris.

— Nous voici dans les Landes, dit Vitalis ; nous avons vingt ou vingt-cinq lieues à faire au milieu de ce désert. Mets ton courage dans tes jambes.

C'était non seulement dans les jambes qu'il fallait le mettre, mais dans la tête et le cœur, car, à marcher sur cette route qui semblait ne devoir finir jamais, on se sentait envahi par une insurmontable tristesse.

Depuis cette époque, j'ai fait plusieurs voyages en mer, et toujours, lorsque j'ai été au milieu de l'Océan sans aucune voile en vue, j'ai retrouvé en moi ce sentiment de mélancolie indéfinissable qui me saisit dans ces solitudes.

Comme sur l'Océan, nos yeux couraient jusqu'à l'horizon noyé dans les vapeurs de l'automne, sans apercevoir rien que la plaine grise qui s'étendait devant nous plate et monotone.

Nous marchions. Et lorsque nous regardions machinalement autour de nous, c'était à croire que nous avions piétiné sur place sans avancer, car le spectacle était toujours le même : toujours des bruyères, toujours des genêts, toujours des mousses ; puis des fougères, dont les feuilles souples et mobiles ondulaient sous la pression du vent, se creusant, se redressant, se mouvant comme des vagues.

À de longs intervalles seulement nous traversions des bois de petite étendue ; mais ces bois n'égayaient pas le paysage comme cela se produit ordinairement. Ils étaient plantés de pins dont les branches étaient coupées jusqu'à la cime. Le long de leur tronc on avait fait des entailles profondes, et par ces cicatrices rouges s'écoulait leur résine en larmes blanches cristallisées. Quand le vent passait par rafales dans leurs ramures, il produisait une musique si plaintive qu'on croyait entendre la voix même de ces pauvres arbres mutilés qui se plaignaient de leurs blessures.

Vitalis m'avait dit que nous arriverions le soir à un village où nous pourrions coucher.

Mais le soir approchait, et nous n'apercevions rien qui nous signalât le voisinage de ce village : ni champs cultivés, ni animaux pâturant dans la lande, ni au loin une colonne de fumée qui nous aurait annoncé une maison.

J'étais fatigué de la route parcourue depuis le matin, et encore plus abattu par une sorte de lassitude générale. Ce bienheureux village ne surgirait-il donc jamais au bout de cette route interminable ?

J'avais beau ouvrir les yeux et regarder au loin, je n'apercevais rien que la lande, et toujours la lande dont les buissons se brouillaient de plus en plus dans l'obscurité qui s'épaississait.

L'espérance d'arriver bientôt nous avait fait hâter le pas, et mon maître lui-même, malgré son habitude des longues marches, se sentait fatigué. Il voulut s'arrêter et se reposer un moment sur le bord de la route.

Mais, au lieu de m'asseoir près de lui, je voulus gravir un petit monticule planté de genêts qui se trouvait à une courte distance du chemin, pour voir si de là je n'apercevrais pas quelque lumière dans la plaine.

J'appelai Capi pour qu'il vînt avec moi ; mais Capi, lui aussi, était fatigué, et il avait fait la sourde oreille, ce qui était sa tactique habituelle avec moi lorsqu'il ne lui plaisait pas de m'obéir.

— As-tu peur ? demanda Vitalis.

Ce mot me décida à ne pas insister, et je partis seul pour mon exploration ; je voulais d'autant moins m'exposer aux plaisanteries de mon maître que je ne me sentais pas la moindre frayeur.

Cependant la nuit était venue, sans lune, mais avec des étoiles scintillantes qui éclairaient le ciel et versaient leur lumière dans l'air chargé de légères vapeurs que le regard traversait.

Tout en marchant et en jetant les yeux à droite et à gauche, je remarquai que ce crépuscule vaporeux donnait aux choses des formes étranges. Il fallait faire un raisonnement pour reconnaître les buissons, les bouquets de genêts et surtout les quelques petits arbres qui çà et là dressaient leurs troncs tordus et leurs branches contournées ; de loin ces buissons, ces genêts et ces arbres ressemblaient à des êtres vivants appartenant à un monde fantastique.

Cela était bizarre, et il semblait qu'avec l'ombre la lande s'était transfigurée comme si elle s'était peuplée d'apparitions mystérieuses.

L'idée me vint, je ne sais comment, qu'un autre à ma place aurait peut-être été effrayé par ces apparitions ; cela était possible, après tout, puisque Vitalis m'avait demandé si j'avais peur ; cependant, en m'interrogeant, je ne trouvai pas en moi cette frayeur.

À mesure que je gravissais la pente du monticule, les genêts devenaient plus forts, les bruyères et les fougères plus hautes ;

leur cime dépassait souvent ma tête, et parfois j'étais obligé de me glisser sous leur couvert.

Cependant je ne tardai pas à atteindre le sommet de ce petit tertre. Mais j'eus beau ouvrir les yeux, je n'aperçus pas la moindre lumière. Mes regards se perdaient dans l'obscurité : rien que des formes indécises, des ombres étranges, des genêts qui semblaient tendre leurs branches vers moi comme de longs bras flexibles, des buissons qui dansaient.

Ne voyant rien qui m'annonçât le voisinage d'une maison, j'écoutai pour tâcher de percevoir un bruit quelconque, le meuglement d'une vache, l'aboiement d'un chien.

Après être resté un moment l'oreille tendue, ne respirant pas pour mieux entendre, un frisson me fit tressaillir, le silence de la lande m'avait effaré ; j'avais peur. De quoi ? Je n'en savais rien. Du silence sans doute, de la solitude et de la nuit. En tout cas, je me sentais comme sous le coup d'un danger.

À ce moment même, regardant autour de moi avec angoisse, j'aperçus au loin une grande ombre se mouvoir rapidement au-dessus des genêts, et en même temps j'entendis comme un bruissement de branches qu'on frôlait.

J'essayai de me dire que c'était la peur qui m'abusait, et que ce que je prenais pour une ombre était sans doute un arbre, que tout d'abord je n'avais pas aperçu.

Mais ce bruit, quel était-il ? Il ne faisait pas un souffle de vent.

Les branches, si légères qu'elles soient, ne se meuvent pas seules, il faut que la brise les agite, ou bien que quelqu'un les remue.

Quelqu'un ? Mais non, ce ne pouvait pas être un homme, ce grand corps noir qui venait sur moi ; un animal que je ne connaissais pas plutôt, un oiseau de nuit gigantesque, ou bien une immense araignée à quatre pattes dont les membres grêles se découpaient au-dessus des buissons et des fougères sur la pâleur du ciel.

Ce qu'il y avait de certain, c'est que cette bête, montée sur des jambes d'une longueur démesurée, s'avançait de mon côté par des bonds précipités.

Assurément elle m'avait vu, et c'était sur moi qu'elle accourait.

Cette pensée me fit retrouver mes jambes, et, tournant sur moi-même, je me précipitai dans la descente pour rejoindre Vitalis.

Mais, chose étrange ! j'allai moins vite en dévalant que je n'avais été en montant ; je me jetais dans les touffes de genêts et de bruyères, me heurtant, m'accrochant, j'étais à chaque pas arrêté.

En me dépêtrant d'un buisson, je glissai un regard en arrière ; la bête s'était rapprochée, elle arrivait sur moi.

Heureusement la lande n'était plus embarrassée de broussailles, je pus courir plus vite à travers les herbes.

Mais, si vite que j'allasse, la bête allait encore plus vite que moi ; je n'avais plus besoin de me retourner, je la sentais sur mon dos.

Je ne respirais plus, étouffé que j'étais par l'angoisse et par ma course folle ; je fis cependant un dernier effort et vins tomber aux pieds de mon maître, tandis que les trois chiens, qui s'étaient brusquement levés, aboyaient à pleine voix.

Je ne pus dire que deux mots que je répétai machinalement :

— La bête, la bête !

Au milieu des vociférations des chiens, j'entendis tout à coup un grand éclat de rire. En même temps mon maître, me posant la main sur l'épaule, m'obligea à me retourner.

— La bête, c'est toujours toi, disait-il en riant ; regarde donc un peu, si tu l'oses.

Son rire, plus encore que ses paroles, m'avait rappelé à la raison ; j'osai ouvrir les yeux et suivre la direction de sa main.

L'apparition qui m'avait affolé s'était arrêtée, elle se tenait immobile sur la route.

J'eus encore, je l'avoue, un premier mouvement de répulsion et d'effroi ; mais je n'étais plus au milieu de la lande, Vitalis était là, les chiens m'entouraient, je ne subissais plus l'influence troublante de la solitude et du silence.

Je m'enhardis et je fixai sur elle des yeux plus fermes.

Était-ce une bête ? Était-ce un homme ?

De l'homme, elle avait le corps, la tête et les bras.

De la bête, une peau velue qui la couvrait entièrement, et deux longues pattes maigres de cinq ou six pieds de haut sur lesquelles elle restait posée.

Bien que la nuit se fût épaissie, je distinguais ces détails, car cette grande ombre se dessinait en noir, comme une silhouette, sur le ciel, où de nombreuses étoiles versaient une pâle lumière.

Je serais probablement resté longtemps indécis à tourner et retourner ma question, si mon maître n'avait adressé la parole à mon apparition.

« Pourriez-vous me dire si nous sommes éloignés d'un village ? » demanda-t-il.

C'était donc un homme, puisqu'on lui parlait?

Mais pour toute réponse je n'entendis qu'un rire sec semblable au cri d'un oiseau.

C'était donc un animal?

Cependant mon maître continua ses questions, ce qui me parut tout à fait déraisonnable, car chacun sait que, si les animaux comprennent quelquefois ce que nous leur disons, ils ne peuvent pas nous répondre.

Quel ne fut pas mon étonnement lorsque cet animal dit qu'il n'y avait pas de maisons aux environs, mais seulement une bergerie, où il nous proposa de nous conduire!

Puisqu'il parlait, comment avait-il des pattes?

Si j'avais osé, je me serais approché de lui, pour voir comment étaient faites ces pattes; mais, bien qu'il ne parût pas méchant, je n'eus pas ce courage, et, ayant ramassé mon sac, je suivis mon maître sans rien dire.

— Vois-tu maintenant ce qui t'a fait si grande peur? me demanda-t-il en marchant.

— Oui, mais je ne sais pas ce que c'est : il y a donc des géants dans ce pays-ci?

— Oui, quand ils sont montés sur des échasses.

Et il m'expliqua comment les Landais, pour traverser leurs terres sablonneuses ou marécageuses et ne pas enfoncer dedans jusqu'aux hanches, se servaient de deux longs bâtons garnis d'un étrier, auxquels ils attachaient leurs pieds.

« Et voilà comment ils deviennent des géants avec des bottes de sept lieues pour les enfants peureux. »

X

Devant la justice

De Pau il m'est resté un souvenir agréable ; dans cette ville, le vent ne souffle presque jamais. Et, comme nous y restâmes pendant l'hiver, passant nos journées dans les rues, sur les places publiques et sur les promenades, on comprend que je dus être sensible à un avantage de ce genre.

Ce ne fut pourtant pas cette raison qui, contrairement à nos habitudes, détermina ce long séjour en un même endroit, mais une autre très légitimement toute-puissante auprès de mon maître – je veux dire l'abondance de nos recettes.

En effet, pendant tout l'hiver, nous eûmes un public d'enfants qui ne se fatigua point de notre répertoire et ne nous cria jamais : « C'est donc toujours la même chose ! »

C'étaient, pour le plus grand nombre, des enfants anglais : de gros garçons avec des chairs roses et de jolies petites filles avec des grands yeux doux, presque aussi beaux que ceux de Dolce. Ce fut alors que j'appris à connaître les *Albert,* les *Huntley* et autres pâtisseries sèches, dont, avant de sortir, ils avaient soin de bourrer leurs poches, pour les distribuer généreusement entre Joli-Cœur, les chiens et moi.

Quand le printemps s'annonça par de chaudes journées, notre public commença à devenir moins nombreux, et, après la représentation, plus d'une fois des enfants vinrent donner des poignées de main à Joli-Cœur et à Capi. C'étaient leurs adieux qu'ils faisaient ; le lendemain nous ne devions plus les revoir.

Bientôt nous nous trouvâmes seuls sur les places publiques, et il fallut songer à abandonner, nous aussi, les promenades de la Basse-Plante et du Parc.

Un matin nous nous mîmes en route, et nous ne tardâmes pas à perdre de vue les tours de Gaston Phœbus et de Montauset.

Nous avions repris notre vie errante, à l'aventure, par les grands chemins.

Pendant longtemps, je ne sais combien de jours, combien de semaines, nous allâmes devant nous, suivant des vallées, escaladant des collines, laissant toujours à notre droite les cimes bleuâtres des Pyrénées, semblables à des entassements de nuages.

Puis, un soir, nous arrivâmes dans une grande ville, située au bord d'une rivière, au milieu d'une plaine fertile. Les maisons, fort laides pour la plupart, étaient construites en briques rouges ; les rues étaient pavées de petits cailloux pointus, durs aux pieds des voyageurs qui avaient fait une dizaine de lieues dans leur journée.

Mon maître me dit que nous étions à Toulouse et que nous y resterions longtemps.

Comme à l'ordinaire, notre premier soin, le lendemain, fut de chercher des endroits propices à nos représentations.

Nous en trouvâmes un grand nombre, car les promenades ne manquent pas à Toulouse, surtout dans la partie de la ville qui avoisine le Jardin des Plantes ; il y a là une belle pelouse ombragée de grands arbres, sur laquelle viennent déboucher plusieurs boulevards qu'on appelle des allées. Ce fut dans une de ces allées que nous nous installâmes, et dès nos premières représentations nous eûmes un public nombreux.

Par malheur, l'homme de police qui avait la garde de cette allée vit cette installation avec déplaisir, et, soit qu'il n'aimât pas les chiens, soit que nous fussions une cause de dérangement dans son service, soit toute autre raison, il voulut nous faire abandonner notre place.

Peut-être, dans notre position, eût-il été sage de céder à cette tracasserie, car la lutte entre de pauvres saltimbanques tels que nous et des gens de police n'était pas à armes égales ; mais, par suite d'une disposition d'esprit qui n'était pas ordinaire à mon maître, presque toujours très patient, il n'en jugea pas ainsi.

Bien qu'il ne fût qu'un montreur de chiens savants pauvre et vieux – au moins présentement –, il avait de la fierté ; de plus, il avait ce qu'il appelait le sentiment de son droit, c'est-à-dire, ainsi qu'il me l'expliqua, la conviction qu'il devait être protégé tant qu'il ne ferait rien de contraire aux lois ou règlements de police.

Il refusa donc d'obéir à l'agent lorsque celui-ci voulut nous expulser de notre allée.

Lorsque mon maître ne voulait pas se laisser emporter par la colère, il avait pour habitude d'exagérer sa politesse italienne : c'était à croire alors, en entendant ses façons de s'exprimer, qu'il s'adressait à des personnages considérables.

— Le très honorable représentant de l'autorité, dit-il en répondant chapeau bas à l'agent de police, peut-il me montrer un règlement émanant de ladite autorité, par lequel il serait interdit à d'infimes baladins tels que nous d'exercer leur chétive industrie sur cette place publique ?

L'agent répondit qu'il n'y avait pas à discuter mais à obéir.

— Assurément, répliqua Vitalis, et c'est bien ainsi que je l'entends ; aussi je vous promets de me conformer à vos ordres aussitôt que vous m'aurez fait savoir en vertu de quels règlements vous les donnez.

Ce jour-là, l'agent de police nous tourna le dos, tandis que mon maître, le chapeau à la main, le bras arrondi et la taille courbée, l'accompagnait avec un respect affecté.

Mais il revint le lendemain, et, franchissant les cordes qui formaient l'enceinte de notre théâtre, il se jeta au beau milieu de notre représentation.

— Il faut museler vos chiens, dit-il durement à Vitalis.

— Museler mes chiens !

— Il y a un règlement de police ; vous devez le connaître.

Nous étions en train de jouer *Le Malade purgé,* et, comme c'était la première représentation de cette comédie à Toulouse, notre public était plein d'attention.

L'intervention de l'agent provoqua des murmures et des réclamations.

— N'interrompez pas !

— Laissez finir la représentation.

Mais d'un geste Vitalis réclama et obtint le silence.

Alors, ôtant son feutre dont les plumes balayèrent le sable, tant son salut fut profond, il s'approcha de l'agent en faisant trois grandes révérences.

— Le très respectable représentant de l'autorité n'a-t-il pas dit que je devais museler mes comédiens ? demanda-t-il.

— Oui, muselez vos chiens, et plus vite que ça.

— Museler Capi, Zerbino, Dolce! s'écria Vitalis s'adressant bien plus au public qu'à l'agent, mais Votre Seigneurie n'y pense pas! Comment le savant médecin Capi, connu de l'univers entier, pourra-t-il administrer ses médicaments à son malade, si celui-ci porte au bout de son nez une muselière? C'est par la bouche, signor, permettez-moi de vous le faire remarquer, que la médecine doit être prise pour opérer son effet. Le docteur Capi ne se serait jamais permis de lui indiquer une autre direction devant ce public distingué.

Sur ce mot, il y eut une explosion de fous rires.

Il était clair qu'on approuvait Vitalis; on se moquait de l'agent, et surtout on s'amusait des grimaces de Joli-Cœur, qui, s'étant placé derrière « le représentant de l'autorité », faisait des grimaces dans le dos de celui-ci, croisant ses bras comme lui, se campant le poing sur la hanche et rejetant sa tête en arrière avec des mines et des contorsions tout à fait réjouissantes.

Agacé par le discours de Vitalis, exaspéré par les rires du public, l'agent de police, qui n'avait pas l'air d'un homme patient, tourna brusquement sur ses talons.

Mais alors il aperçut le singe qui se tenait le poing sur la hanche dans l'attitude d'un matamore; durant quelques secondes l'homme et la bête restèrent en face l'un de l'autre, se regardant comme s'il s'agissait de savoir lequel des deux baisserait les yeux le premier.

Les rires qui éclatèrent encore, irrésistibles et bruyants, mirent fin à cette scène.

— Si demain vos chiens ne sont pas muselés, s'écria l'agent en nous menaçant du poing, je vous fais un procès; je ne vous dis que cela.

— À demain, signor, dit Vitalis, à demain.

Et, tandis que l'agent s'éloignait à grands pas, Vitalis resta courbé en deux dans une attitude respectueuse; puis, la représentation continua.

Je croyais que mon maître allait acheter des muselières pour nos chiens, mais il n'en fit rien, et la soirée s'écoula même sans qu'il parlât de sa querelle avec l'homme de police.

Alors je m'enhardis à lui en parler moi-même.

— Si vous voulez que Capi ne brise pas demain sa muselière pendant la représentation, lui dis-je, il me semble qu'il serait bon de la lui mettre un peu à l'avance. En le surveillant, on pourrait peut-être l'y habituer.

— Tu crois donc que je vais leur mettre une carcasse de fer ?
— Dame ! il me semble que l'agent est disposé à vous tourmenter.
— Sois tranquille, je m'arrangerai demain pour que l'agent ne puisse pas me faire un procès, et en même temps pour que mes élèves ne soient pas trop malheureux. D'un autre côté, il est bon aussi que le public s'amuse un peu. Cet agent nous procurera plus d'une bonne recette ; il jouera, sans s'en douter, un rôle comique dans la pièce que je lui prépare ; cela donnera de la variété à notre répertoire et n'ira pas plus loin qu'il ne faut. Pour cela, tu te rendras tout seul demain à notre place avec Joli-Cœur ; tu tendras les cordes, tu joueras quelques morceaux de harpe, et, quand tu auras autour de toi un public suffisant et que l'agent sera arrivé, je ferai mon entrée avec les chiens. C'est alors que la comédie commencera.

Je n'avais pas bonne idée de tout cela.

Il ne me plaisait guère de m'en aller seul ainsi préparer notre représentation ; mais je commençais à connaître mon maître et à savoir quand je pouvais lui résister ; or, il était évident que dans les circonstances présentes je n'avais aucune chance de lui faire abandonner l'idée de la petite scène sur laquelle il comptait : je me décidai donc à obéir.

Le lendemain je m'en allai à notre place ordinaire, et je tendis mes cordes. J'avais à peine joué quelques mesures, qu'on accourut de tous côtés, et qu'on s'entassa dans l'enceinte que je venais de tracer.

En ces derniers temps, surtout pendant notre séjour à Pau, mon maître m'avait fait travailler la harpe, et je commençais à ne pas trop mal jouer quelques morceaux qu'il m'avait appris. Il y avait entre autres une *canzonetta* napolitaine que je chantais en m'accompagnant et qui me valait toujours des applaudissements.

J'étais déjà artiste par plus d'un côté, et par conséquent disposé à croire, quand notre troupe avait du succès, que c'était à mon talent que ce succès était dû ; cependant, ce jour-là, j'eus le bon sens de comprendre que ce n'était point pour entendre ma *canzonetta* qu'on se pressait ainsi dans nos cordes.

Ceux qui avaient assisté la veille à la scène de l'agent de police étaient revenus, et ils avaient amené avec eux des amis. On aime peu les gens de police à Toulouse, et l'on était curieux de voir comment le vieil Italien se tirerait d'affaire. Bien que Vitalis n'eût pas prononcé d'autres mots que : « À demain, signor », il avait été compris par tout le monde que ce rendez-vous donné et accepté était l'annonce d'une grande représentation, dans laquelle on trouverait des occasions de rire et de s'amuser aux dépens de l'agent maladroit et maussade.

De là l'empressement du public.

Aussi, en me voyant seul avec Joli-Cœur, plus d'un spectateur inquiet m'interrompait-il pour me demander si « l'Italien » ne viendrait pas.

« Il va arriver bientôt. »

Et je continuai ma *canzonetta*.

Ce ne fut pas mon maître qui arriva, ce fut l'agent de police. Joli-Cœur l'aperçut le premier, et aussitôt, se campant la main sur la hanche et rejetant sa tête en arrière, il se mit à se promener autour de moi en long et en large, raide, cambré, avec une prestance ridicule.

Le public partit d'un éclat de rire et applaudit à plusieurs reprises.

L'agent fut déconcerté et il me lança des yeux furieux.

Bien entendu, cela redoubla l'hilarité du public.

J'avais moi-même envie de rire, mais d'un autre côté je n'étais guère rassuré. Comment tout cela allait-il finir ? Quand Vitalis était là, il répondait à l'agent. Mais j'étais seul, et, je l'avoue, je ne savais comment je m'en tirerais, si l'agent m'interpellait.

La figure de l'agent n'était pas faite pour me donner bonne espérance ; il était vraiment furieux, exaspéré par la colère.

Il allait de long en large devant mes cordes et, quand il passait près de moi, il avait une façon de me regarder par-dessus son épaule qui me faisait craindre une mauvaise fin.

Joli-Cœur, qui ne comprenait pas la gravité de la situation, s'amusait de l'attitude de l'agent. Il se promenait, lui aussi, le long de ma corde, mais en dedans, tandis que l'agent se promenait en dehors, et en passant devant moi il me regardait à son tour par-dessus son épaule avec une mine si drôle, que les rires du public redoublaient.

Ne voulant point pousser à bout l'exaspération de l'agent, j'appelai Joli-Cœur ; mais celui-ci n'était point en disposition d'obéissance, ce jeu l'amusait, il continua sa promenade en courant, et m'échappait lorsque je voulais le prendre.

Je ne sais comment cela se fit, mais l'agent, que la colère aveuglait sans doute, s'imagina que j'excitais le singe, et vivement il enjamba la corde.

En deux enjambées il fut sur moi, et je me sentis à moitié renversé par un soufflet.

Quand je me remis sur mes jambes et rouvris les yeux, Vitalis, survenu je ne sais comment, était placé entre moi et l'agent qu'il tenait par le poignet.

— Je vous défends de frapper cet enfant, dit-il ; ce que vous avez fait est une lâcheté.

L'agent voulut dégager sa main, mais Vitalis serra la sienne.

Et, pendant quelques secondes, les deux hommes se regardèrent en face, les yeux dans les yeux.

L'agent était fou de colère.

Mon maître était magnifique de noblesse ; il tenait haute sa belle tête encadrée de cheveux blancs et son visage exprimait l'indignation et le commandement.

Il me sembla que, devant cette attitude, l'agent allait rentrer sous terre, mais il n'en fut rien : d'un mouvement vigoureux, il dégagea sa main, empoigna mon maître par le collet et le poussa devant lui avec brutalité.

Vitalis, indigné, se redressa, et, levant son bras droit, il en frappa fortement le poignet de l'agent pour se dégager.

— Que voulez-vous donc de nous ? demanda Vitalis.

— Je veux vous arrêter ; suivez-moi au poste.

— Pour arriver à vos fins, il n'était pas nécessaire de frapper cet enfant, répondit Vitalis.

— Pas de paroles, suivez-moi !

Vitalis avait retrouvé tout son sang-froid ; il ne répliqua pas, mais, se tournant vers moi :

— Rentre à l'auberge, me dit-il, restes-y avec les chiens, je te ferai parvenir des nouvelles.

Il n'en put dire davantage, l'agent l'entraîna.

Ainsi finit cette représentation, que mon maître avait voulu faire amusante et qui finit si tristement.

Le premier mouvement des chiens avait été de suivre leur maître ; mais Vitalis leur ordonna de rester près de moi, et, habitués à obéir, ils revinrent sur leurs pas. Je m'aperçus alors qu'ils étaient muselés, mais, au lieu d'avoir le nez pris dans une carcasse en fer ou dans un filet, ils portaient tout simplement une faveur en soie nouée avec des bouffettes autour de leur museau ; pour Capi, qui était à poil blanc, la faveur était rouge ; pour Zerbino, qui était noir, blanche ; pour Dolce, qui était grise, bleue. C'étaient des muselières de théâtre.

Le public s'était rapidement dispersé ; quelques personnes

seulement avaient gardé leurs places, discutant sur ce qui venait de se passer.

— Le vieux a eu raison.

— Il a eu tort.

— Pourquoi l'agent a-t-il frappé l'enfant, qui ne lui avait rien dit ni rien fait ?

— Mauvaise affaire ; le vieux ne s'en tirera pas sans prison, si l'agent constate la rébellion.

Je rentrai à l'auberge fort affligé et très inquiet.

Je n'étais plus au temps où Vitalis m'inspirait de l'effroi. À vrai dire, ce temps n'avait duré que quelques heures. Assez rapidement, je m'étais attaché à lui d'une affection sincère, et cette affection avait été en grandissant chaque jour. Nous vivions de la même vie, toujours ensemble du matin au soir, et souvent du soir au matin, quand, pour notre coucher, nous partagions la même botte de paille. Un père n'a pas plus de soins pour son enfant qu'il en avait pour moi. Il m'avait appris à lire, à chanter, à écrire, à compter. Dans nos longues marches, il avait toujours employé le temps à me donner des leçons tantôt sur une chose, tantôt sur une autre, selon que les circonstances ou le hasard lui suggéraient ces leçons. Dans les journées de grand froid, il avait partagé avec moi ses couvertures ; par les fortes chaleurs, il m'avait toujours aidé à porter la part de bagages et d'objets dont j'étais chargé. À table, ou plus justement, dans nos repas, car nous ne mangions pas souvent à table, il ne me laissait jamais le mauvais morceau, se réservant le meilleur ; au contraire, il nous partageait également le bon et le mauvais. Quelquefois, il est vrai qu'il me tirait les oreilles et m'allongeait une taloche ; mais il n'y avait pas, dans ces petites corrections, de quoi me faire oublier ses soins, ses bonnes paroles et tous les témoignages de tendresse qu'il m'avait donnés depuis que nous étions ensemble. Il m'aimait et je l'aimais.

Cette séparation m'atteignit donc douloureusement.

Quand nous reverrions-nous ?

On avait parlé de prison. Combien de temps pouvait durer cet emprisonnement ?

Qu'allais-je faire pendant ce temps ? Comment vivre ? De quoi ?

Mon maître avait l'habitude de porter sa fortune sur lui, et, avant de se laisser entraîner par l'agent de police, il n'avait pas eu le temps de me donner de l'argent.

Je n'avais que quelques sous dans ma poche ; seraient-ils suffisants pour nous nourrir tous, Joli-Cœur, les chiens et moi ?

Je passai ainsi deux journées dans l'angoisse, n'osant pas sortir de la cour de l'auberge, m'occupant de Joli-Cœur et des chiens, qui, tous, se montraient inquiets et chagrins.

Enfin, le troisième jour, un homme m'apporta une lettre de Vitalis.

Par cette lettre, mon maître me disait qu'on le gardait en prison pour le faire passer en police correctionnelle le samedi suivant, sous la prévention de résistance à un agent de l'autorité, et de *voies de fait* sur la personne de celui-ci.

« En me laissant emporter par la colère, ajoutait-il, j'ai fait une lourde faute qui pourra me coûter cher. Viens à l'audience; tu y trouveras une leçon. »

Puis il ajoutait des conseils pour ma conduite; il terminait en m'embrassant et me recommandant de faire pour lui une caresse à Capi, à Joli-Cœur, à Dolce et à Zerbino.

Pendant que je lisais cette lettre, Capi, entre mes jambes, tenait son nez dessus, la flairant, reniflant, et les mouvements de sa queue me disaient que, bien certainement, il reconnaissait, par l'odorat, que ce papier avait passé par les mains de son maître; depuis trois jours, c'était la première fois qu'il manifestait de l'animation et de la joie.

Ayant pris des renseignements, on me dit que l'audience de la police correctionnelle commençait à dix heures. À neuf heures, le samedi, j'allai m'adosser contre la porte et, le premier, je pénétrai dans la salle. Peu à peu, la salle s'emplit, je reconnus plusieurs personnes qui avaient assisté à la scène avec l'agent de police.

Je ne savais pas ce que c'était que les tribunaux et la justice, mais d'instinct j'en avais une peur horrible; il me semblait que, bien qu'il s'agît de mon maître et non de moi, j'étais en danger. J'allai me blottir derrière un gros poêle et, m'enfonçant contre la muraille, je me fis aussi petit que possible.

Ce ne fut pas mon maître qu'on jugea le premier, mais des gens qui avaient volé, qui s'étaient battus, qui, tous, se disaient innocents, et qui, tous, furent condamnés. Enfin, Vitalis vint s'asseoir entre deux gendarmes sur le banc où tous ces gens l'avaient précédé.

Ce qui se dit tout d'abord, ce qu'on lui demanda, ce qu'il répondit, je n'en sais rien; j'étais trop ému pour entendre, ou tout au moins pour comprendre. D'ailleurs, je ne pensais pas à écouter, je regardais. Je regardais mon maître qui se tenait debout, ses grands cheveux blancs rejetés en arrière, dans l'attitude d'un homme honteux et peiné; je regardais le juge qui l'interrogeait.

— Ainsi, dit celui-ci, vous reconnaissez avoir porté des coups à l'agent qui vous arrêtait?

— Non des coups, monsieur le président, mais un coup, et pour me dégager de son étreinte; lorsque j'arrivai sur la place où devait avoir lieu notre représentation, je vis l'agent donner un soufflet à l'enfant qui m'accompagnait.

— Cet enfant n'est pas à vous?

— Non, monsieur le président, mais je l'aime comme s'il était mon fils. Lorsque je le vis frapper, je me laissai entraîner par la colère, je saisis vivement la main de l'agent et l'empêchai de frapper de nouveau.

— Vous avez vous-même frappé l'agent?

— C'est-à-dire que, lorsque celui-ci me mit la main au collet, j'oubliai quel était l'homme qui se jetait sur moi, ou plutôt je ne vis en lui qu'un homme au lieu de voir un agent, et un mouvement instinctif, involontaire, m'a emporté.

— À votre âge, on ne se laisse pas emporter.

— On ne devrait pas se laisser emporter; malheureusement on ne fait pas toujours ce qu'on doit, je le sens aujourd'hui.

— Nous allons entendre l'agent.

Celui-ci raconta les faits tels qu'ils s'étaient passés, mais en insistant plus sur la façon dont on s'était moqué de sa personne, de sa voix, de ses gestes, que sur le coup qu'il avait reçu.

Pendant cette déposition, Vitalis, au lieu d'écouter avec attention, regardait de tous côtés dans la salle. Je compris qu'il me cherchait. Alors, je me décidai à quitter mon abri, et, me faufilant au milieu des curieux, j'arrivai au premier rang.

Il m'aperçut, et sa figure attristée s'éclaira; je sentis qu'il était heureux de me voir, et, malgré moi, mes yeux s'emplirent de larmes.

— C'est tout ce que vous avez à dire pour votre défense? demanda enfin le président.

— Pour moi, je n'aurais rien à ajouter, mais, pour l'enfant que j'aime tendrement et qui va rester seul, pour lui, je réclame l'indulgence du tribunal, et le prie de nous tenir séparés le moins longtemps possible.

Je croyais qu'on allait mettre mon maître en liberté. Mais il n'en fut rien.

Un autre magistrat parla pendant quelques minutes; puis le président, d'une voix grave, dit que le nommé Vitalis, convaincu d'injures et de voies de fait envers un agent de la force publique, était condamné à deux mois de prison et à cent francs d'amende.

Deux mois de prison !

À travers mes larmes, je vis la porte par laquelle Vitalis était entré se rouvrir ; celui-ci suivit un gendarme, puis la porte se referma.

Deux mois de séparation !

Où aller ?

XI

En bateau

Quand je rentrai à l'auberge, le cœur gros, les yeux rouges, je trouvai sous la porte de la cour l'aubergiste qui me regarda longuement.

J'allais passer pour rejoindre les chiens, quand il m'arrêta.

— Eh bien, me dit-il, ton maître ?
— Il est condamné.
— À combien ?
— À deux mois de prison.
— Et à combien d'amende ?
— Cent francs.
— Deux mois, cent francs, répéta-t-il à trois ou quatre reprises.

Je voulus continuer mon chemin ; de nouveau il m'arrêta.

— Et qu'est-ce que tu veux faire pendant ces deux mois ?
— Je ne sais pas, monsieur.
— Ah ! tu ne sais pas. Tu as de l'argent pour vivre et pour nourrir tes bêtes, je pense ?
— Non, monsieur.
— Alors tu comptes sur moi pour vous loger ?
— Oh ! non, monsieur, je ne compte sur personne.

Rien n'était plus vrai, je ne comptais sur personne.

— Eh bien ! mon garçon, continua l'aubergiste, tu as raison, ton maître me doit déjà trop d'argent, je ne peux pas te faire crédit pendant deux mois sans savoir si au bout du compte je serai payé ; il faut t'en aller d'ici.

— M'en aller ! mais où voulez-vous que j'aille, monsieur ?

— Ça, ce n'est pas mon affaire : je ne suis pas ton père, je ne suis pas non plus ton maître. Pourquoi veux-tu que je te garde ?

Je restai un moment abasourdi. Que dire ? Cet homme avait raison. Pourquoi m'aurait-il gardé chez lui ? Je ne lui étais rien qu'un embarras et une charge.

— Allons, mon garçon, prends tes chiens et ton singe, puis file ; tu me laisseras, bien entendu, le sac de ton maître. Quand il sortira de prison il viendra le chercher, et alors nous réglerons notre compte.

Ce mot me suggéra une idée, et je crus avoir trouvé le moyen de rester dans cette auberge.

— Puisque vous êtes certain de faire régler votre compte à ce moment, gardez-moi jusque-là, et vous ajouterez ma dépense à celle de mon maître.

— Vraiment, mon garçon ? Ton maître pourra bien me payer quelques journées, mais deux mois, c'est une autre affaire.

— Je mangerai aussi peu que vous voudrez.

— Et tes bêtes ? Non, vois-tu, il faut t'en aller ! Tu trouveras bien à travailler et à gagner ta vie dans les villages.

— Mais, monsieur, où voulez-vous que mon maître me trouve en sortant de prison ? C'est ici qu'il viendra me chercher.

— Tu n'auras qu'à revenir ce jour-là ; d'ici là, va faire une promenade de deux mois dans les environs, dans les villes d'eaux. À Bagnères, à Cauterets, à Luz, il y a de l'argent à gagner.

— Et si mon maître m'écrit ?

— Je te garderai sa lettre.

— Mais, si je ne lui réponds pas ?

— Ah ! tu m'ennuies à la fin. Je t'ai dit de t'en aller ; il faut sortir d'ici, et plus vite que ça ! Je te donne cinq minutes pour partir ; si je te retrouve quand je vais revenir dans la cour, tu auras affaire à moi.

Je sentis bien que toute insistance était inutile. Comme le disait l'aubergiste, « il fallait sortir d'ici ».

J'entrai à l'écurie, et, après avoir détaché les chiens et Joli-Cœur, après avoir bouclé mon sac et passé sur mon épaule la bretelle de ma harpe, je sortis de l'auberge.

L'aubergiste était sur sa porte pour me surveiller.

— S'il vient une lettre, me cria-t-il, je te la conserverai !

J'avais hâte de sortir de la ville, car mes chiens n'étaient pas muselés. Que répondre, si je rencontrais un agent de police ?

Que je n'avais pas d'argent pour leur acheter des muselières ? C'était la vérité, car, tout compte fait, je n'avais que onze sous dans ma poche, et ce n'était pas suffisant pour une pareille acquisition. Ne m'arrêterait-il pas à mon tour ? Mon maître en prison, moi aussi, que deviendraient les chiens et Joli-Cœur ? J'étais devenu directeur de troupe, chef de famille, moi, l'enfant sans famille, et je sentais ma responsabilité.

Tout en marchant rapidement, les chiens levaient la tête vers moi et me regardaient d'un air qui n'avait pas besoin de paroles pour être compris : ils avaient faim.

Joli-Cœur, que je portais juché sur mon sac, me tirait de temps en temps l'oreille pour m'obliger à tourner la tête vers lui ; alors il se brossait le ventre par un geste qui n'était pas moins expressif que le regard des chiens.

Moi aussi j'aurais bien, comme eux, parlé de ma faim, car je n'avais pas déjeuné plus qu'eux tous ; mais à quoi bon ?

Mes onze sous ne pouvaient pas nous donner à déjeuner et à dîner ; nous devions tous nous contenter d'un seul repas, qui, fait au milieu de la journée, nous tiendrait lieu des deux.

L'auberge où nous avions logé et d'où nous venions d'être chassés se trouvant dans le faubourg Saint-Michel sur la route de Montpellier, c'était naturellement cette route que j'avais suivie.

Dans ma hâte de fuir une ville où je pouvais rencontrer des agents de police, je n'avais pas le temps de me demander où les routes conduisaient ; ce que je désirais, c'était qu'elles m'éloignassent de Toulouse, le reste m'importait peu. Je n'avais pas intérêt à aller dans un pays plutôt qu'un autre ; partout on nous demanderait de l'argent pour manger et pour nous loger. Encore la question du logement était-elle de beaucoup la moins importante ; nous étions dans la saison chaude, et nous pouvions coucher à la belle étoile à l'abri d'un buisson ou d'un mur.

Mais manger ?

Je crois bien que nous marchâmes près de deux heures sans que j'osasse m'arrêter, et cependant les chiens me faisaient des yeux de plus en plus suppliants, tandis que Joli-Cœur me tirait l'oreille et se brossait le ventre de plus en plus fort.

Enfin je me crus assez loin de Toulouse pour n'avoir rien à craindre, ou tout au moins pour dire que je musellerais mes chiens le lendemain, si on me demandait de le faire, et j'entrai dans la première boutique de boulanger que je trouvai.

Je demandai qu'on me servît une livre et demie de pain.

— Vous prendrez bien un pain de deux livres, me dit la boulangère ; avec votre ménagerie ce n'est pas trop ; il faut bien les nourrir, ces pauvres bêtes !

Sans doute ce n'était pas trop pour ma ménagerie qu'un pain de deux livres, car, sans compter Joli-Cœur, qui ne mangeait pas de gros morceaux, cela ne nous donnait qu'une demi-livre pour chacun de nous, mais c'était trop pour ma bourse.

Le pain était alors à cinq sous la livre, et, si j'en prenais deux livres, elles me coûteraient dix sous, de sorte que sur mes onze sous il ne m'en resterait qu'un seul.

Or, je ne trouvais pas prudent de me laisser entraîner à une aussi grande prodigalité avant d'avoir mon lendemain assuré. En n'achetant qu'une livre et demie de pain qui me coûtait sept sous et trois centimes, il me restait pour le lendemain trois sous et deux centimes, c'est-à-dire assez pour ne pas mourir de faim et attendre une occasion de gagner quelque argent.

J'eus vite fait ce calcul et je dis à la boulangère, d'un air que je tâchai de rendre assuré, que j'avais bien assez d'une livre et demie de pain et que je la priais de ne pas m'en couper davantage.

— C'est bon, c'est bon, répondit-elle.

Et, autour d'un beau pain de six livres que nous aurions bien certainement mangé tout entier, elle me coupa la quantité que je demandais et la mit dans la balance, à laquelle elle donna un petit coup.

— C'est un peu fort, dit-elle, cela sera pour les deux centimes.

Et elle fit tomber mes huit sous dans son tiroir.

J'ai vu des gens repousser les centimes qu'on leur rendait, disant qu'ils n'en sauraient que faire ; moi, je n'aurais pas repoussé ceux qui m'étaient dus ; cependant je n'osai pas les réclamer et sortis sans rien dire, avec mon pain étroitement serré sous mon bras.

Les chiens, joyeux, sautaient autour de moi, et Joli-Cœur me tirait les cheveux en poussant des petits cris.

Nous n'allâmes pas bien loin.

Au premier arbre qui se trouva sur la route, je posai ma harpe contre son tronc et m'allongeai sur l'herbe ; les chiens s'assirent en face de moi, Capi au milieu, Dolce d'un côté, Zerbino de l'autre ; quant à Joli-Cœur, qui n'était pas fatigué, il resta debout pour être tout prêt à voler les morceaux qui lui conviendraient.

C'était une affaire délicate que le découpage de ma miche ; j'en fis cinq parts aussi égales que possible, et, pour qu'il n'y eût pas de pain gaspillé, je les distribuai en petites tranches ; chacun avait son morceau à son tour, comme si nous avions mangé à la gamelle.

Joli-Cœur, qui avait besoin de moins de nourriture que nous, se trouva le mieux partagé, et il n'eut plus faim alors que nous étions encore affamés. Sur sa part je pris trois morceaux que je serrai dans mon sac pour les donner aux chiens plus tard ; puis, comme il en restait encore quatre, nous en eûmes chacun un ; ce fut à la fois notre plat de supplément et notre dessert.

Bien que ce festin n'eût rien de ceux qui provoquent aux discours, le moment me parut venu d'adresser quelques paroles à mes camarades. Je me considérais naturellement comme leur chef, mais je ne me croyais pas assez au-dessus d'eux pour être dispensé de leur faire part des circonstances graves dans lesquelles nous nous trouvions.

Capi avait sans doute deviné mon intention, car il tenait collés sur les miens ses grands yeux intelligents et affectueux.

— Oui, mon ami Capi, dis-je, oui, mes amis Dolce, Zerbino et Joli-Cœur, oui, mes chers camarades, j'ai une mauvaise nouvelle à vous annoncer : notre maître est éloigné de nous pour deux mois.

— Ouah ! cria Capi.

— Cela est bien triste pour lui d'abord, et aussi pour nous. C'était lui qui nous faisait vivre, et en son absence nous allons nous trouver dans une terrible situation. Nous n'avons pas d'argent.

Sur ce mot, qu'il connaissait parfaitement, Capi se dressa sur ses pattes de derrière et se mit à marcher en rond comme s'il faisait la quête dans les « rangs de l'honorable société ».

— Tu veux que nous donnions des représentations, continuai-je, c'est assurément un bon conseil, mais ferons-nous recette ? Tout est là. Si nous ne réussissons pas, je vous préviens que nous n'avons que trois sous pour toute fortune. Il faudra donc se serrer le ventre. Les choses étant ainsi, j'ose espérer que vous comprendrez la gravité des circonstances, et qu'au lieu de me jouer de mauvais tours vous mettrez votre intelligence au service de la société. Je vous demande de l'obéissance, de la sobriété et du courage. Serrons nos rangs, et comptez sur moi comme je compte sur vous-mêmes.

Je n'ose pas affirmer que mes camarades comprirent toutes

les beautés de mon discours improvisé, mais certainement ils en sentirent les idées générales. Ils savaient par l'absence de notre maître qu'il se passait quelque chose de grave, et ils attendaient de moi une explication. S'ils ne comprirent pas tout ce que je leur dis, ils furent au moins satisfaits de mon procédé à leur égard, et ils me prouvèrent leur contentement par leur attention.

Quand je dis leur attention, je parle des chiens seulement, car, pour Joli-Cœur, il lui était impossible de tenir son esprit longtemps fixé sur un même sujet. Pendant la première partie de mon discours, il m'avait écouté avec les marques du plus vif intérêt ; mais, au bout d'une vingtaine de mots, il s'était élancé sur l'arbre qui nous couvrait de son feuillage, et il s'amusait maintenant à se balancer en sautant de branche en branche. Si Capi m'avait fait une pareille injure, j'en aurais certes été blessé, mais de Joli-Cœur rien ne m'étonnait. Ce n'était qu'un étourdi, une cervelle creuse ; et puis, après tout, il était bien naturel qu'il eût envie de s'amuser un peu.

J'avoue que j'en aurais fait volontiers autant et que comme lui je me serais balancé avec plaisir ; mais l'importance et la dignité de mes fonctions ne me permettaient plus de semblables distractions.

Après quelques instants de repos, je donnai le signal du départ ; il nous fallait gagner notre coucher, en tout cas notre déjeuner du lendemain, si, comme cela était probable, nous faisions l'économie de coucher en plein air.

Au bout d'une heure de marche à peu près, nous arrivâmes en vue d'un village qui me parut propre à la réalisation de mon dessein.

De loin il s'annonçait comme assez misérable, et la recette ne pouvait être par conséquent que bien chétive, mais il n'y avait pas là de quoi me décourager ; je n'étais pas exigeant sur le chiffre de la recette, et je me disais que, plus le village était petit, moins nous avions de chance de rencontrer des agents de police.

Je fis donc la toilette de mes comédiens, et, en aussi bel ordre que possible, nous entrâmes dans ce village ; malheureusement le fifre de Vitalis nous manquait et aussi sa prestance qui, comme celle d'un tambour-major, attirait toujours les regards. Je n'avais pas comme lui l'avantage d'une grande taille et d'une tête expressive ; bien petite au contraire était ma taille, bien mince, et sur mon visage devait se montrer plus d'inquiétude que d'assurance.

Tout en marchant je regardais à droite et à gauche pour voir l'effet que nous produisions ; il était médiocre, on levait la tête, puis on la rebaissait, personne ne nous suivait.

Arrivés sur une petite place au milieu de laquelle se trouvait une fontaine ombragée par des platanes, je pris ma harpe et commençai à jouer une valse. La musique était gaie, mes doigts étaient légers, mais mon cœur était chagrin, et il me semblait que je portais sur mes épaules un poids bien lourd.

Je dis à Zerbino et à Dolce de valser ; ils m'obéirent aussitôt et se mirent à tourner en mesure.

Mais personne ne se dérangea pour venir nous regarder, et cependant sur le seuil des portes je voyais des femmes qui tricotaient ou qui causaient.

Je continuai de jouer ; Zerbino et Dolce continuèrent de valser.

Peut-être quelqu'un se déciderait-il à s'approcher de nous ; s'il venait une personne, il en viendrait une seconde, puis dix, puis vingt autres.

Mais j'avais beau jouer, Zerbino et Dolce avaient beau tourner, les gens restaient chez eux ; ils ne regardaient même plus de notre côté.

C'était à désespérer.

Cependant je ne désespérais pas et jouais avec plus de force, faisant sonner les cordes de ma harpe à les casser.

Tout à coup un petit enfant, si petit qu'il s'essayait, je crois bien, à ses premiers pas, quitta le seuil de sa maison et se dirigea vers nous.

Sa mère allait le suivre sans doute, puis, après la mère, arriverait une amie, nous aurions notre public, et nous aurions ensuite une recette.

Je jouai moins fort pour ne pas effrayer l'enfant et pour l'attirer plutôt.

Les mains dressées, se balançant sur ses hanches, il s'avança doucement.

Il venait, il arrivait ; encore quelques pas, et il était près de nous.

La mère leva la tête, surprise sans doute et inquiète de ne pas le sentir près d'elle.

Elle l'aperçut aussitôt. Mais alors, au lieu de courir après lui comme je l'avais espéré, elle se contenta de l'appeler, et l'enfant docile retourna près d'elle.

Peut-être ces gens n'aimaient-ils pas la danse. Après tout, c'était possible.

Je commandai à Zerbino et à Dolce de se coucher et me mis à chanter ma *canzonetta*; et jamais bien certainement je ne m'y appliquai avec plus de zèle :

> Fenesta vascia e patrona crudele,
> Quanta sospire m'aje fatto jettare.

J'entamais la deuxième strophe quand je vis un homme vêtu d'une veste et coiffé d'un feutre se diriger vers nous.

Enfin !

Je chantai avec plus d'entraînement.

— Holà ! cria-t-il, que fais-tu ici, mauvais garnement ?

Je m'interrompis, stupéfié par cette interpellation, et restai à le regarder venir vers moi, bouche ouverte.

— Eh bien, répondras-tu ? dit-il.

— Vous voyez, monsieur, je chante.

— As-tu une permission pour chanter sur la place de notre commune ?

— Non, monsieur.

— Alors va-t'en, si tu ne veux pas que je te fasse un procès.

— Mais, monsieur.

— Appelle-moi monsieur le garde champêtre, et tourne les talons, mauvais mendiant !

Un garde champêtre ! Je savais par l'exemple de mon maître ce qu'il en coûtait de vouloir se révolter contre les sergents de ville et les gardes champêtres.

Je ne me fis pas répéter cet ordre deux fois ; je tournai sur mes talons comme il m'avait ordonné, et rapidement je repris le chemin par lequel j'étais venu.

Mendiant ! cela n'était pas juste cependant. Je n'avais pas mendié : j'avais chanté, j'avais dansé, ce qui était ma manière de travailler ; quel mal avais-je fait ?

En cinq minutes je sortis de cette commune peu hospitalière, mais bien gardée.

Mes chiens me suivaient la tête basse et la mine attristée, comprenant assurément qu'il venait de nous arriver une mauvaise aventure.

Capi, de temps en temps, me dépassait et, se tournant vers moi, il me regardait curieusement avec ses yeux intelligents. Tout autre à sa place m'eût interrogé ; mais Capi était un chien trop bien élevé, trop bien discipliné pour se permettre une question indiscrète ; il se contentait seulement de manifester sa curiosité, et je voyais ses mâchoires trembler, agitées par l'effort qu'il faisait pour retenir ses aboiements.

Lorsque nous fûmes assez éloignés pour n'avoir plus à craindre la brutale arrivée du garde champêtre, je fis un signe de la main, et immédiatement les trois chiens formèrent le cercle autour de moi, Capi au milieu, immobile, les yeux sur les miens.

Le moment était venu de leur donner l'explication qu'ils attendaient.

— Comme nous n'avons pas de permission pour jouer, dis-je, on nous renvoie.

— Et alors ? demanda Capi d'un coup de tête.

— Alors nous allons coucher à la belle étoile, n'importe où, sans souper.

Au mot souper, il y eut un grognement général.

Je montrai mes trois sous.

— Vous savez que c'est tout ce qui nous reste ; si nous dépensons nos trois sous ce soir, nous n'aurons rien pour déjeuner demain ; or, comme nous avons mangé aujourd'hui, je trouve qu'il est sage de penser au lendemain.

Et je remis mes trois sous dans ma poche.

Capi et Dolce baissèrent la tête avec résignation ; mais Zerbino, qui n'avait pas toujours bon caractère et qui de plus était gourmand, continua de gronder.

Après l'avoir regardé sévèrement sans pouvoir le faire taire, je me tournai vers Capi :

— Explique à Zerbino, lui dis-je, ce qu'il paraît ne pas vouloir comprendre ; il faut nous priver d'un second repas aujourd'hui, si nous voulons en faire un seul demain.

Aussitôt Capi donna un coup de patte à son camarade, et une discussion parut s'engager entre eux.

Qu'on ne trouve pas le mot « discussion » impropre parce qu'il est appliqué à deux bêtes. Il est bien certain, en effet, que les bêtes ont un langage particulier à chaque espèce. Si vous avez habité une maison aux corniches ou aux fenêtres de laquelle les hirondelles suspendent leurs nids, vous êtes assurément convaincu que ces oiseaux ne sifflent pas simplement un petit air de musique, alors qu'au jour naissant elles jacassent si vivement entre elles ; ce sont de vrais discours qu'elles tiennent, des affaires sérieuses qu'elles agitent, ou des paroles de tendresse qu'elles échangent. Et les fourmis d'une même tribu, lorsqu'elles se rencontrent dans un sentier et se frottent antennes contre antennes, que croyez-vous qu'elles fassent, si vous n'admettez pas qu'elles se communiquent ce qui les intéresse ? Quant aux chiens, non seulement ils savent parler, mais encore ils savent lire : voyez-les le nez en l'air, ou bien la tête basse flairant le sol, sentant les cailloux et les buissons ; tout à coup ils s'arrêtent devant une touffe d'herbes ou une muraille et ils restent là un moment ; nous ne voyons rien sur cette muraille, tandis que le chien y lit toutes sortes de choses curieuses, écrites dans un caractère mystérieux que nous ne voyons même pas.

Ce que Capi dit à Zerbino, je ne l'entendis pas, car, si les chiens comprennent le langage des hommes, les hommes ne comprennent pas le langage des chiens ; je vis seulement que Zerbino refusait d'entendre raison et qu'il insistait pour dépenser immédiatement les trois sous ; il fallut que Capi se fâchât, et ce fut seulement quand il eut montré ses crocs que Zerbino, qui n'était pas très brave, se résigna au silence.

La question du souper étant ainsi réglée, il ne restait plus que celle du coucher.

Heureusement le temps était beau, la journée était chaude, et coucher à la belle étoile en cette saison n'était pas bien grave ; il fallait s'installer seulement de manière à échapper aux loups, s'il y en avait dans le pays, et, ce qui me paraissait beaucoup plus dangereux, aux gardes champêtres, les hommes étant encore plus à craindre pour nous.

Il n'y avait donc qu'à marcher droit devant soi sur la route blanche jusqu'à la rencontre d'un gîte.

Ce que nous fîmes.

La route s'allongea, les kilomètres succédèrent aux kilomètres, et les dernières lueurs roses du soleil couchant avaient disparu du ciel que nous n'avions pas encore trouvé de gîte.

Il fallait, tant bien que mal, se décider.

Quand je me décidai à nous arrêter pour passer la nuit, nous étions dans un bois que coupaient çà et là des espaces dénudés au milieu desquels se dressaient des blocs de granit. L'endroit était bien triste, bien désert, mais nous n'avions pas mieux à choisir, et je pensai qu'au milieu de ces blocs de granit nous pourrions trouver un abri contre la fraîcheur de la nuit. Je dis nous, en parlant de Joli-Cœur et de moi, car, pour les chiens, je n'étais pas en peine d'eux ; il n'y avait pas à craindre qu'ils gagnassent la fièvre à coucher dehors. Mais, pour moi, je devais être soigneux, car j'avais conscience de ma responsabilité. Que deviendrait ma troupe, si je tombais malade ? que deviendrais-je moi-même, si j'avais Joli-Cœur à soigner ?

Quittant la route, nous nous engageâmes au milieu des pierres, et bientôt j'aperçus un énorme bloc de granit planté de travers de manière à former une sorte de cavité à sa base et un toit à son sommet. Dans cette cavité les vents avaient amoncelé un lit épais d'aiguilles de pin desséchées. Nous ne pouvions mieux trouver : un matelas pour nous étendre, une toiture pour nous abriter ; il ne nous manquait qu'un morceau de pain pour souper ; mais il fallait tâcher de ne pas penser à cela ; d'ailleurs le proverbe n'a-t-il pas dit : « Qui dort dîne » ?

Avant de dormir, j'expliquai à Capi que je comptais sur lui pour nous garder, et la bonne bête, au lieu de venir avec nous se coucher sur les aiguilles de pin, resta en dehors de notre abri, postée en sentinelle. Je pouvais être tranquille, je savais que personne ne nous approcherait sans que j'en fusse prévenu.

Cependant, bien que rassuré sur ce point, je ne m'endormis pas aussitôt que je fus étendu sur les aiguilles de pin, Joli-Cœur enveloppé près de moi dans ma veste, Zerbino et Dolce couchés en rond à mes pieds, mon inquiétude étant plus grande encore que ma fatigue.

La journée, cette première journée de voyage, avait été mauvaise ; que serait celle du lendemain ? J'avais faim, j'avais soif, et il ne me restait que trois sous. J'avais beau les manier machinalement dans ma poche, ils n'augmentaient pas : un, deux, trois, je m'arrêtais toujours à ce chiffre.

Comment nourrir ma troupe, comment me nourrir moi-même, si je ne trouvais pas le lendemain et les jours suivants à donner des représentations ? Des muselières, une permission pour chanter, où voulait-on que j'en eusse ? Faudrait-il donc tous mourir de faim au coin d'un bois, sous un buisson ?

Et, tout en agitant ces tristes questions, je regardais les étoiles qui brillaient au-dessus de ma tête dans le ciel sombre. Il ne faisait pas un souffle de vent. Partout le silence, pas un bruissement de feuilles, pas un cri d'oiseau, pas un roulement de voiture sur la route ; aussi loin que ma vue pouvait s'étendre dans les profondeurs bleuâtres, le vide. Comme nous étions seuls, abandonnés !

Je sentis mes yeux s'emplir de larmes, puis tout à coup je me mis à pleurer : pauvre mère Barberin ! pauvre Vitalis !

Je m'étais couché sur le ventre, et je pleurais dans mes deux mains sans pouvoir m'arrêter quand je sentis un souffle tiède passer dans mes cheveux ; vivement je me retournai, et une grande langue douce et chaude se colla sur mon visage. C'était Capi, qui m'avait entendu pleurer et qui venait me consoler, comme il était déjà venu à mon secours lors de ma première nuit de voyage.

Je le pris par le cou à deux bras et j'embrassai son museau humide ; alors il poussa deux ou trois gémissements étouffés, et il me sembla qu'il pleurait avec moi.

Quand je me réveillai, il faisait grand jour, et Capi, assis devant moi, me regardait ; les oiseaux sifflaient dans le feuillage ; au loin, tout au loin, une cloche sonnait l'*angelus* ; le soleil, déjà haut dans le ciel, lançait des rayons chauds et réconfortants, aussi bien pour le cœur que pour le corps.

Notre toilette matinale fut bien vite faite, et nous nous mîmes en route, nous dirigeant du côté d'où venaient les tintements de la cloche ; là était un village, là sans doute était un boulanger ; quand on s'est couché sans dîner et sans souper, la faim parle de bonne heure.

Mon parti était pris : je dépenserais mes trois sous, et après nous verrions.

En arrivant dans le village, je n'eus pas besoin de demander où était la boulangerie ; notre nez nous guida sûrement vers elle ; j'eus l'odorat presque aussi fin que celui de mes chiens pour sentir de loin la bonne odeur du pain chaud.

Trois sous de pain quand il coûte cinq sous la livre ne nous donnèrent à chacun qu'un bien petit morceau, et notre déjeuner fut rapidement terminé.

Le moment était donc venu de voir, c'est-à-dire d'aviser aux moyens de faire une recette dans la journée. Pour cela je me mis à parcourir le village en cherchant la place la plus favorable à une représentation, et aussi en examinant la physionomie des gens pour tâcher de deviner s'ils nous seraient amis ou ennemis.

Mon intention n'était pas de donner immédiatement cette représentation, car l'heure n'était pas convenable, mais d'étudier le pays, de faire choix du meilleur emplacement, et de revenir dans le milieu de la journée, sur cet emplacement, tenter la chance.

J'étais absorbé par cette idée, quand tout à coup j'entendis crier derrière moi ; je me retournai vivement et je vis arriver Zerbino poursuivi par une vieille femme. Il ne me fallut pas longtemps pour comprendre ce qui provoquait cette poursuite et ces cris : profitant de ma distraction, Zerbino m'avait abandonné, et il était entré dans une maison où il avait volé un morceau de viande qu'il emportait dans sa gueule.

— Au voleur! criait la vieille femme, arrêtez-le, arrêtez-les tous!

En entendant ces derniers mots, me sentant coupable, ou tout au moins responsable de la faute de mon chien, je me mis à courir aussi : Que répondre, si la vieille femme me demandait le prix du morceau de viande volé? Comment le payer? Une fois arrêtés, ne nous garderait-on pas?

Me voyant fuir, Capi et Dolce ne restèrent pas en arrière, et je les sentis sur mes talons, tandis que Joli-Cœur que je portais sur mon épaule m'empoignait par le cou pour ne pas tomber.

Il n'y avait guère à craindre qu'on nous attrapât en nous rejoignant, mais on pouvait nous arrêter au passage, et justement il me sembla que telle était l'intention de deux ou trois personnes qui barraient la route. Heureusement une ruelle transversale venait déboucher sur la route avant ce groupe d'adversaires. Je me jetai dedans accompagné des chiens, et, toujours courant à toutes jambes, nous fûmes bientôt en pleine campagne. Je m'arrêtai lorsque la respiration commença à me manquer; c'est-à-dire après avoir fait au moins deux kilomètres. Alors je me retournai, osant regarder en arrière; personne ne nous suivait; Capi et Dolce étaient toujours sur mes talons, Zerbino arrivait tout au loin, s'étant arrêté sans doute pour manger son morceau de viande.

Je l'appelai; mais Zerbino, qui savait qu'il avait mérité une sévère correction, s'arrêta, puis, au lieu de venir à moi, il se sauva.

C'était poussé par la faim que Zerbino avait volé ce morceau de viande. Mais je ne pouvais pas accepter cette raison comme une excuse. Il y avait vol. Il fallait que le coupable fût puni, ou bien c'en était fait de la discipline dans ma troupe; au prochain village, Dolce imiterait son camarade, et Capi lui-même finirait par succomber à la tentation.

Je devais donc administrer une correction publique à Zerbino. Mais pour cela il fallait qu'il voulût bien comparaître devant moi, et ce n'était pas chose facile que de le décider.

J'eus recours à Capi.

— Va me chercher Zerbino.

Et il partit aussitôt pour accomplir la mission que je lui confiais. Cependant il me sembla qu'il acceptait ce rôle avec moins de zèle que de coutume, et dans le regard qu'il me jeta avant de partir je crus voir qu'il se ferait plus volontiers l'avocat de Zerbino que mon gendarme.

Je n'avais plus qu'à attendre le retour de Capi et de son prisonnier, ce qui pouvait être assez long, car Zerbino, très probablement, ne se laisserait pas ramener tout de suite. Mais il n'y avait rien de bien désagréable pour moi dans cette attente. J'étais assez loin du village pour n'avoir guère à craindre qu'on me poursuivît. Et d'un autre côté, j'étais assez fatigué de ma course pour désirer me reposer un moment. D'ailleurs à quoi bon me presser, puisque je ne savais pas où aller et que je n'avais rien à faire ?

Justement l'endroit où je m'étais arrêté était fait à souhait pour l'attente et le repos. Sans savoir où j'allais dans ma course folle, j'étais arrivé sur les bords du canal du Midi, et, après avoir traversé des campagnes poussiéreuses depuis mon départ de Toulouse, je me trouvais dans un pays vert et frais : des eaux, des arbres, de l'herbe, une petite source coulant à travers les fentes d'un rocher tapissé de plantes qui tombaient en cascades fleuries suivant le cours de l'eau ; c'était charmant, et j'étais là à merveille pour attendre le retour des chiens.

Une heure s'écoula sans que je les visse revenir ni l'un ni l'autre, et je commençais à m'inquiéter, quand Capi reparut seul, la tête basse.

— Où est Zerbino ?

Capi se coucha dans une attitude craintive ; alors, en le regardant, je m'aperçus qu'une de ses oreilles était ensanglantée.

Je n'eus pas besoin d'explication pour comprendre ce qui s'était passé : Zerbino s'était révolté contre la gendarmerie, il avait fait résistance, et Capi, qui peut-être n'obéissait qu'à regret à un ordre qu'il considérait comme bien sévère, s'était laissé battre.

Fallait-il le gronder et le corriger aussi ? Je n'en eus pas le courage, je n'étais pas en disposition de peiner les autres, étant déjà bien assez affligé de mon propre chagrin.

L'expédition de Capi n'ayant pas réussi, il ne me restait qu'une ressource, qui était d'attendre que Zerbino voulût bien revenir ; je le connaissais, après un premier mouvement de révolte, il se résignerait à subir sa punition, et je le verrais apparaître repentant.

Je m'étendis sous un arbre, tenant Joli-Cœur attaché, de peur qu'il ne lui prît fantaisie de rejoindre Zerbino ; Capi et Dolce s'étaient couchés à mes pieds.

Le temps s'écoula, Zerbino ne parut pas ; insensiblement le sommeil me prit et je m'endormis.

Quand je m'éveillai le soleil était au-dessus de ma tête, et les heures avaient marché. Mais je n'avais plus besoin du soleil pour me dire qu'il était tard, mon estomac me criait qu'il y avait longtemps que j'avais mangé mon morceau de pain. De leur côté les deux chiens et Joli-Cœur me montraient aussi qu'ils avaient faim, Capi et Dolce avec des mines piteuses, Joli-Cœur avec des grimaces.

Et Zerbino n'apparaissait toujours pas.

Je l'appelai, je le sifflai ; mais tout fut inutile, il ne parut pas ; ayant bien déjeuné, il digérait tranquillement, blotti sous quelque buisson.

Ma situation devenait critique : si je m'en allais, il pouvait très bien se perdre et ne pas nous rejoindre ; si je restais, je ne trouvais pas l'occasion de gagner quelques sous et de manger.

Et précisément le besoin de manger devenait de plus en plus impérieux. Les yeux des chiens s'attachaient sur les miens désespérément, et Joli-Cœur se brossait le ventre en poussant des petits cris de colère.

Le temps s'écoulant et Zerbino ne venant pas, j'envoyai une fois encore Capi à la recherche de son camarade ; mais, au bout d'une demi-heure, il revint seul et me fit comprendre qu'il ne l'avait pas trouvé.

Que faire ?

Bien que Zerbino fût coupable et nous eût mis tous par sa faute encore dans une terrible situation, je ne pouvais pas avoir l'idée de l'abandonner. Que dirait mon maître, si je ne lui ramenais pas ses trois chiens ? Et puis, malgré tout, je l'aimais, ce coquin de Zerbino.

Je résolus donc d'attendre jusqu'au soir ; mais il était impossible de rester ainsi dans l'inaction à écouter notre estomac crier la faim, car ses cris étaient d'autant plus douloureux qu'ils étaient seuls à se faire entendre, sans aucune distraction aussi bien que sans relâche.

Il fallait inventer quelque chose qui pût nous occuper tous les quatre et nous distraire.

Si nous pouvions oublier que nous avions faim, nous aurions assurément moins faim pendant ces heures d'oubli.

Mais à quoi nous occuper ?

Comme j'examinais cette question, je me souvins que Vitalis m'avait dit qu'à la guerre, quand un régiment était fatigué par une longue marche, on faisait jouer la musique, si bien qu'en entendant des airs gais ou entraînants les soldats oubliaient leurs fatigues.

Si je jouais un air gai, peut-être oublierions-nous tous notre faim ; en tout cas, étant occupé à jouer et les chiens à danser avec Joli-Cœur, le temps passerait plus vite pour nous.

Je pris ma harpe, qui était posée contre un arbre, et, tournant le dos au canal, après avoir mis mes comédiens en position, je commençai à jouer un air de danse, puis, après, une valse.

Tout d'abord mes acteurs ne semblaient pas très disposés à la danse ; il était évident que le morceau de pain eût bien mieux fait leur affaire ; mais peu à peu ils s'animèrent, la musique produisit son effet obligé, nous oubliâmes tous le morceau de pain que nous n'avions pas et nous ne pensâmes plus, moi qu'à jouer, eux qu'à danser.

Tout à coup j'entendis une voix claire, une voix d'enfant crier : « Bravo ! » Cette voix venait de derrière moi. Je me retournai vivement.

Un bateau était arrêté sur le canal, l'avant tourné vers la rive sur laquelle je me trouvais ; les deux chevaux qui le remorquaient avaient fait halte sur la rive opposée.

C'était un singulier bateau, et tel que je n'en avais pas encore vu de pareil : il était beaucoup plus court que les péniches qui servent ordinairement à la navigation sur les canaux, et au-dessus de son pont peu élevé au-dessus de l'eau était construite une sorte de galerie vitrée. À l'avant de cette galerie se trouvait une véranda ombragée par des plantes grimpantes, dont le feuillage, accroché çà et là aux découpures du toit, retombait par places en cascades vertes ; sous cette véranda j'aperçus deux personnes : une dame jeune encore, à l'air noble et mélancolique, qui se tenait debout, et un enfant, un garçon à peu près de mon âge, qui me parut couché.

C'était cet enfant sans doute qui avait crié « bravo ».

Remis de ma surprise, car cette apparition n'avait rien d'effrayant, je soulevai mon chapeau pour remercier celui qui m'avait applaudi.

— C'est pour votre plaisir que vous jouez ? me demanda la dame, parlant avec un accent étranger.

— C'est pour faire travailler mes comédiens et aussi... pour me distraire.

L'enfant fit un signe, et la dame se pencha vers lui.

— Voulez-vous jouer encore ? me demanda la dame en relevant la tête.

Si je voulais jouer! Jouer pour un public qui m'arrivait si à propos! Je ne me fis pas prier.

— Voulez-vous une danse ou une comédie? dis-je.

— Oh! une comédie! s'écria l'enfant.

Mais la dame interrompit pour dire qu'elle préférait une danse.

— La danse, c'est trop court, s'écria l'enfant.

— Après la danse, nous pourrons, si l'honorable société le désire, représenter différents tours, tels qu'ils se font dans les cirques de Paris.

C'était une phrase de mon maître, je tâchai de la débiter comme lui avec noblesse. En réfléchissant, j'étais bien aise qu'on eût refusé la comédie, car j'aurais été assez embarrassé pour organiser la représentation, d'abord parce que Zerbino me manquait et aussi parce que je n'avais pas les costumes et les accessoires nécessaires.

Je repris donc ma harpe et je commençai à jouer une valse; aussitôt Capi entoura la taille de Dolce avec ses deux pattes, et ils se mirent à tourner en mesure. Puis Joli-Cœur dansa un pas seul. Puis successivement nous passâmes en revue tout notre répertoire. Nous ne sentions pas la fatigue. Quant à mes comédiens, ils avaient assurément compris qu'un dîner serait le paiement de leurs peines, et ils ne s'épargnaient pas plus que je ne m'épargnais moi-même.

Tout à coup, au milieu d'un de mes exercices, je vis Zerbino sortir d'un buisson, et, quand ses camarades passèrent près de lui, il se plaça effrontément au milieu d'eux et prit son rôle.

Tout en jouant et en surveillant mes comédiens, je regardais de temps en temps le jeune garçon, et, chose étrange, bien qu'il parût prendre grand plaisir à nos exercices, il ne bougeait pas; il restait couché, allongé, dans une immobilité complète, ne remuant que les deux mains pour nous applaudir.

Était-il paralysé? il semblait qu'il était attaché sur une planche.

Insensiblement le vent avait poussé le bateau contre la berge sur laquelle je me trouvais, et je voyais maintenant l'enfant comme si j'avais été sur le bateau même et près de lui : il était blond de cheveux, son visage était pâle, si pâle qu'on voyait les veines bleues de son front sous sa peau transparente; son expression était la douceur et la tristesse, avec quelque chose de maladif.

— Combien faites-vous payer les places à votre théâtre? me demanda la dame.

— On paye selon le plaisir qu'on a éprouvé.

— Alors, maman, il faut payer très cher, dit l'enfant.

Puis il ajouta quelques paroles dans une langue que je ne comprenais pas.

— Arthur voudrait voir vos acteurs de plus près, me dit la dame.

Je fis un signe à Capi qui, prenant son élan, sauta dans le bateau.

— Et les autres? cria Arthur.

Zerbino et Dolce suivirent leur camarade.

— Et le singe!

Joli-Cœur aurait facilement fait le saut, mais je n'étais jamais sûr de lui; une fois à bord, il pouvait se livrer à des plaisanteries qui n'auraient peut-être pas été du goût de la dame.

— Est-il méchant? demanda-t-elle.

— Non, madame, mais il n'est pas toujours obéissant, et j'ai peur qu'il ne se conduise pas convenablement.

— Eh bien! embarquez avec lui.

Disant cela, elle fit signe à un homme qui se tenait à l'arrière auprès du gouvernail, et aussitôt cet homme, passant à l'avant, jeta une planche sur la berge.

C'était un pont. Il me permit d'embarquer sans risquer le saut périlleux, et j'entrai dans le bateau gravement, ma harpe sur l'épaule et Joli-Cœur dans ma main.

— Le singe! le singe! s'écria Arthur.

Je m'approchai de l'enfant, et, tandis qu'il flattait et caressait Joli-Cœur, je pus l'examiner à loisir.

Chose surprenante! il était bien véritablement attaché sur une planche, comme je l'avais cru tout d'abord.

— Vous avez un père, n'est-ce pas, mon enfant? me demanda la dame.

— Oui, mais je suis seul en ce moment.

— Pour longtemps?

— Pour deux mois.

— Deux mois! Oh! mon pauvre petit! comment, seul ainsi pour si longtemps, à votre âge!

— Il le faut bien, madame!

— Votre maître vous oblige sans doute à lui rapporter une somme d'argent au bout de ces deux mois?

— Non, madame; il ne m'oblige à rien. Pourvu que je trouve à vivre avec ma troupe, cela suffit.

— Et vous avez trouvé à vivre jusqu'à ce jour?

J'hésitai avant de répondre; je n'avais jamais vu une dame qui m'inspirât un sentiment de respect comme celle qui m'interrogeait. Cependant elle me parlait avec tant de bonté, sa voix était si douce, son regard était si affable, si encourageant, que je me décidai à dire la vérité. D'ailleurs, pourquoi me taire ?

Je lui racontai donc comment j'avais dû me séparer de Vitalis, condamné à la prison pour m'avoir défendu, et comment, depuis que j'avais quitté Toulouse, je n'avais pas pu gagner un sou.

Pendant que je parlais, Arthur jouait avec les chiens ; mais cependant il écoutait et entendait ce que je disais.

— Comme vous devez tous avoir faim ! s'écria-t-il.

À ce mot, qu'ils connaissaient bien, les chiens se mirent à aboyer, et Joli-Cœur se frotta le ventre avec frénésie.

— Oh ! maman, dit Arthur.

La dame comprit cet appel ; elle dit quelques mots en langue étrangère à une femme qui montrait sa tête dans une porte entrebâillée, et presque aussitôt cette femme apporta une petite table servie.

— Asseyez-vous, mon enfant, me dit la dame.

Je ne me fis pas prier, je posai ma harpe et m'assis vivement devant la table ; les chiens se rangèrent aussitôt autour de moi, et Joli-Cœur prit place sur mon genou.

— Vos chiens mangent-ils du pain ? me demanda Arthur.

S'ils mangeaient du pain ! Je leur en donnai à chacun un morceau qu'ils dévorèrent.

— Et le singe ? dit Arthur.

Mais il n'y avait pas besoin de s'occuper de Joli-Cœur, car, tandis que je servais les chiens, il s'était emparé d'un morceau de croûte de pâté avec lequel il était en train de s'étouffer sous la table.

À mon tour, je pris une tranche de pain, et, si je ne m'étouffai pas comme Joli-Cœur, je dévorai au moins aussi gloutonnement que lui.

— Pauvre enfant ! disait la dame en emplissant mon verre.

Quant à Arthur, il ne disait rien ; mais il nous regardait, les yeux écarquillés, émerveillé assurément de notre appétit, car nous étions aussi voraces les uns que les autres, même Zerbino, qui cependant avait dû se rassasier jusqu'à un certain point avec la viande qu'il avait volée.

— Et où auriez-vous dîné ce soir, si nous ne nous étions pas rencontrés ? demanda Arthur.

— Je crois bien que nous n'aurions pas dîné.

— Et demain, où dînerez-vous ?

— Peut-être demain aurons-nous la chance de faire une bonne rencontre comme aujourd'hui.

Sans continuer de s'entretenir avec moi, Arthur se tourna vers sa mère, et une longue conversation s'engagea entre eux dans la langue étrangère que j'avais déjà entendue ; il paraissait demander une chose qu'elle n'était pas disposée à accorder ou tout au moins contre laquelle elle soulevait des objections.

Tout à coup il tourna de nouveau sa tête vers moi, car son corps ne bougeait pas.

— Voulez-vous rester avec nous ? dit-il.

Je le regardai sans répondre, tant cette question me prit à l'improviste.

— Mon fils vous demande si vous voulez rester avec nous.

— Sur ce bateau !

— Oui, sur ce bateau ; mon fils est malade, les médecins ont ordonné de le tenir attaché sur une planche, ainsi que vous le voyez. Pour qu'il ne s'ennuie pas, je le promène dans ce bateau. Vous demeurerez avec nous. Vos chiens et votre singe donneront des représentations pour Arthur, qui sera leur public. Et vous, si vous le voulez bien, mon enfant, vous nous jouerez de la harpe. Ainsi vous nous rendrez service, et nous de notre côté nous vous serons peut-être utiles. Vous n'aurez point chaque jour à trouver un public, ce qui, pour un enfant de votre âge, n'est pas toujours très facile.

En bateau ! Je n'avais jamais été en bateau, et ç'avait été mon grand désir. J'allais vivre en bateau, sur l'eau, quel bonheur !

Ce fut la première pensée qui frappa mon esprit et l'éblouit. Quel rêve !

Quelques secondes de réflexion me firent sentir tout ce qu'il y avait d'heureux pour moi dans cette proposition, et combien était généreuse celle qui me l'adressait.

Je pris la main de la dame et la baisai.

Elle parut sensible à ce témoignage de reconnaissance, et affectueusement, presque tendrement, elle me passa à plusieurs reprises la main sur le front.

— Pauvre petit ! dit-elle.

Puisqu'on me demandait de jouer de la harpe, il me sembla que je ne devais pas différer de me rendre au désir qu'on me montrait ; l'empressement était jusqu'à un certain point une manière de prouver ma bonne volonté en même temps que ma reconnaissance.

Je pris mon instrument et j'allai me placer tout à l'avant du bateau, puis je commençai à jouer.

En même temps la dame approcha de ses lèvres un petit sifflet en argent et elle en tira un son aigu.

Je cessai de jouer aussitôt, me demandant pourquoi elle sifflait ainsi : était-ce pour me dire que je jouais mal ou pour me faire taire ?

Arthur, qui voyait tout ce qui se passait autour de lui, devina mon inquiétude.

— Maman a sifflé pour que les chevaux se remettent en marche, dit-il.

En effet, le bateau, qui s'était éloigné de la berge, commençait à filer sur les eaux tranquilles du canal, entraîné par les chevaux ; l'eau clapotait contre la carène, et de chaque côté les arbres fuyaient derrière nous, éclairés par les rayons obliques du soleil couchant.

— Voulez-vous jouer ? demanda Arthur.

Et, d'un signe de tête, appelant sa mère auprès de lui, il lui prit la main et la garda dans les siennes pendant tout le temps que je jouai les divers morceaux que mon maître m'avait appris.

XII

Mon premier ami

La mère d'Arthur était anglaise, elle se nommait Mme Milligan. Elle était veuve, et je croyais qu'Arthur était son seul enfant – mais j'appris bientôt qu'elle avait eu un fils aîné, disparu dans des conditions mystérieuses. Jamais on n'avait pu retrouver ses traces. Au moment où cela était arrivé, M. Milligan était mourant, et Mme Milligan, très gravement malade, ne savait rien de ce qui se passait autour d'elle. Quand elle était revenue à la vie, son mari était mort et son fils avait disparu. Les recherches avaient été dirigées par M. James Milligan, son beau-frère. Mais il y avait cela de particulier dans ce choix, que M. James Milligan avait un intérêt opposé à celui de sa belle-sœur. En effet, son frère mort sans enfants, il devenait l'héritier de celui-ci.

Cependant M. James Milligan n'hérita point de son frère, car, sept mois après la mort de son mari, Mme Milligan mit au monde un enfant, qui était le petit Arthur.

Mais cet enfant, chétif et maladif, ne pouvait pas vivre, disaient les médecins; il devait mourir d'un moment à l'autre, et ce jour-là M. James Milligan devenait enfin l'héritier du titre et de la fortune de son frère aîné, car les lois de l'héritage ne sont pas les mêmes dans tous les pays, et, en Angleterre, elles permettent, dans certaines circonstances, que ce soit un oncle qui hérite au détriment d'une mère.

Les espérances de M. James Milligan se trouvèrent donc

retardées par la naissance de son neveu ; elles ne furent pas détruites ; il n'avait qu'à attendre.

Il attendit.

Mais les prédictions des médecins ne se réalisèrent point. Arthur resta maladif ; il ne mourut pourtant pas, ainsi qu'il avait été décidé ; les soins de sa mère le firent vivre ; c'est un miracle qui, Dieu merci ! se répète assez souvent.

Vingt fois on le crut perdu, vingt fois il fut sauvé ; successivement, quelquefois même ensemble, il avait eu toutes les maladies qui peuvent s'abattre sur les enfants.

En ces derniers temps s'était déclaré un mal terrible qu'on appelle coxalgie, et dont le siège est dans la hanche. Pour ce mal on avait ordonné les eaux sulfureuses, et Mme Milligan était venue dans les Pyrénées. Mais, après avoir essayé des eaux inutilement, on avait conseillé un autre traitement qui consistait à tenir le malade allongé, sans qu'il pût mettre le pied à terre.

C'est alors que Mme Milligan avait fait construire à Bordeaux le bateau sur lequel je m'étais embarqué.

Elle ne pouvait pas penser à laisser son fils enfermé dans une maison, il y serait mort d'ennui ou de privation d'air ; Arthur ne pouvant plus marcher, la maison qu'il habiterait devait marcher pour lui.

On avait transformé un bateau en maison flottante avec chambre, cuisine, salon et véranda. C'était dans ce salon ou sous cette véranda, selon les temps, qu'Arthur se tenait du matin au soir, avec sa mère à ses côtés, et les paysages défilaient devant lui, sans qu'il eût d'autre peine que d'ouvrir les yeux.

Ils étaient partis de Bordeaux depuis un mois, et, après avoir remonté la Garonne, ils étaient entrés dans le canal du Midi ; par ce canal, ils devaient gagner les étangs et les canaux qui longent la Méditerranée, remonter ensuite le Rhône, puis la Saône, passer de cette rivière dans la Loire jusqu'à Briare, prendre là le canal de ce nom, arriver dans la Seine et suivre le cours de ce fleuve jusqu'à Rouen, où ils s'embarqueraient sur un grand navire pour rentrer en Angleterre.

Le jour de mon arrivée, je fis seulement connaissance de la chambre que je devais occuper dans le bateau qui s'appelait le *Cygne*. Bien qu'elle fût toute petite, cette chambre, deux mètres de long sur un mètre à peu près de large, c'était la plus charmante cabine, la plus étonnante que puisse rêver une imagination enfantine.

Le mobilier qui la garnissait consistait en une seule commode ; mais cette commode ressemblait à la bouteille inépuisable des physiciens qui renferme tant de choses. Au lieu d'être fixe, la tablette supérieure était mobile, et, quand on la relevait, on trouvait sous elle un lit complet, matelas, oreiller, couverture. Bien entendu, il n'était pas très large ce lit ; cependant il était assez grand pour qu'on y fût très bien couché. Sous ce lit était un tiroir garni de tous les objets nécessaires à la toilette. Et sous ce tiroir s'en trouvait un autre divisé en plusieurs compartiments, dans lesquels on pouvait ranger le linge et les vêtements. Point de tables, point de sièges, au moins dans la forme habituelle, mais contre la cloison, du côté de la tête du lit, une planchette qui, en s'abaissant, formait table, et du côté des pieds, une autre qui formait chaise.

Un petit hublot percé dans le bordage, et qu'on pouvait fermer avec un verre rond, servait à éclairer et à aérer cette chambre.

Jamais je n'avais rien vu de si joli, ni de si propre ; tout était revêtu de boiseries en sapin verni, et sur le plancher était étendue une toile cirée à carreaux noirs et blancs.

Mais ce n'étaient pas seulement les yeux qui étaient charmés.

Quand, après m'être déshabillé, je m'étendis dans le lit, j'éprouvai un sentiment de bien-être tout nouveau pour moi ; c'était la première fois que des draps me flattaient la peau, au lieu de me la gratter. Chez mère Barberin, je couchais dans des draps de toile de chanvre raides et rugueux ; avec Vitalis, nous couchions bien souvent sans draps sur la paille ou le foin, et, quand on nous en donnait, dans les auberges, mieux aurait valu, presque toujours, une bonne litière. Comme ils étaient fins ceux dans lesquels je m'enveloppais ! comme ils étaient doux, comme ils sentaient bon ! et le matelas, comme il était plus moelleux que les aiguilles de pin sur lesquelles j'avais couché la veille ! Le silence de la nuit n'était plus inquiétant, l'ombre n'était plus peuplée, et les étoiles que je regardais par le hublot ne me disaient plus que des paroles d'encouragement et d'espérance.

Si bien couché que je fusse dans ce bon lit, je me levai dès le point du jour, car j'avais l'inquiétude de savoir comment mes comédiens avaient passé la nuit.

Je trouvai tout mon monde à la place où je l'avais installé la veille et dormant comme si ce bateau eût été leur habitation depuis plusieurs mois. À mon approche, les chiens s'éveillèrent et vinrent joyeusement me demander leur caresse du matin. Seul, Joli-Cœur, bien qu'il eût un œil à demi ouvert, ne bougea pas, mais il se mit à ronfler comme trombone.

Il n'y avait pas besoin d'un grand effort d'esprit pour comprendre ce que cela signifiait : M. Joli-Cœur, qui était la susceptibilité en personne, se fâchait avec une extrême facilité, et, une fois fâché, il boudait longtemps. Dans les circonstances présentes, il était peiné que je ne l'eusse pas emmené dans ma chambre, et il me témoignait son mécontentement par ce sommeil simulé.

Je ne pouvais pas lui expliquer les raisons qui m'avaient obligé, à mon grand regret, à le laisser sur le pont, et, comme je sentais que j'avais, du moins en apparence, des torts envers lui, je le pris dans mes bras, pour lui témoigner mes regrets par quelques caresses.

Tout d'abord il persista dans sa bouderie, mais bientôt, avec sa mobilité d'humeur, il pensa à autre chose, et par sa pantomime il m'expliqua que, si je voulais aller me promener avec lui à terre, il me pardonnerait peut-être.

Le marinier que j'avais vu la veille au gouvernail était déjà levé et il s'occupait à nettoyer le pont ; il voulut bien mettre la planche à terre, et je pus descendre dans la prairie avec ma troupe.

En jouant avec les chiens et avec Joli-Cœur, en courant, en sautant les fossés, en grimpant aux arbres, le temps passe vite ; quand nous revînmes, les chevaux étaient attelés au bateau et attachés à un peuplier sur le chemin de halage : ils n'attendaient qu'un coup de fouet pour partir.

J'embarquai vite ; quelques minutes après, l'amarre qui retenait le bateau à la rive fut larguée, le marinier prit place au gouvernail, le haleur enfourcha son cheval, la poulie dans laquelle passait la remorque grinça ; nous étions en route.

Quel plaisir que le voyage en bateau ! Les chevaux trottaient sur le chemin de halage, et, sans que nous sentissions un mouvement, nous glissions légèrement sur l'eau ; les deux rives boisées fuyaient derrière nous, et l'on n'entendait d'autre bruit que celui du remous contre la carène, dont le clapotement se mêlait à la sonnerie des grelots que les chevaux portaient à leur cou.

Nous allions, et, penché sur le bordage, je regardais les peupliers qui, les racines dans l'herbe fraîche, se dressaient fièrement, agitant dans l'air tranquille du matin leurs feuilles toujours émues ; leur longue file alignée selon la rive formait un épais rideau vert qui arrêtait les rayons obliques du soleil, et ne laissait venir à nous qu'une douce lumière tamisée par le branchage.

De place en place l'eau se montrait toute noire, comme si elle recouvrait des abîmes insondables ; ailleurs, au contraire, elle s'étalait en nappes transparentes qui laissaient voir des cailloux lustrés et des herbes veloutées.

J'étais absorbé dans ma contemplation, lorsque j'entendis prononcer mon nom derrière moi.

Je me retournai vivement : c'était Arthur qu'on apportait sur sa planche ; sa mère était près de lui.

— Vous avez bien dormi ? me demanda Arthur, mieux que dans les champs ?

Je m'approchai et répondis en cherchant des paroles polies que j'adressai à la mère tout autant qu'à l'enfant.

— Et les chiens ? dit-il.

Je les appelai, ainsi que Joli-Cœur ; ils arrivèrent en saluant et Joli-Cœur en faisant des grimaces, comme lorsqu'il prévoyait que nous allions donner une représentation.

Mais il ne fut pas question de représentation, ce matin-là.

Mme Milligan avait installé son fils à l'abri des rayons du soleil, et elle s'était placée près de lui.

— Voulez-vous emmener les chiens et le singe ? me dit-elle, nous avons à travailler.

Je fis ce qui m'était demandé, et je m'en allai avec ma troupe, tout à l'avant.

À quel travail ce pauvre petit malade était-il donc propre ?

Je vis que sa mère lui faisait répéter une leçon, dont elle suivait le texte dans un livre ouvert.

Étendu sur sa planche, Arthur répétait sans faire un mouvement.

Ou, plus justement, il essayait de répéter, car il hésitait terriblement, et ne disait pas trois mots couramment ; encore bien souvent se trompait-il.

Sa mère le reprenait avec douceur, mais en même temps avec fermeté.

— Vous ne savez pas votre fable, dit-elle.

Cela me parut étrange de l'entendre dire vous à son fils, car je ne savais pas alors que les Anglais ne se servent pas du tutoiement.

— Oh ! maman, dit-il d'une voix désolée.

— Vous faites plus de fautes aujourd'hui que vous n'en faisiez hier.

— J'ai tâché d'apprendre.

— Et vous n'avez pas appris.

— Je n'ai pas pu.
— Pourquoi ?
— Je ne sais pas... parce que je n'ai pas pu... Je suis malade.
— Vous n'êtes pas malade de la tête ; je ne consentirai jamais à ce que vous n'appreniez rien, et que, sous prétexte de maladie, vous grandissiez dans l'ignorance.

Elle me paraissait bien sévère, Mme Milligan, et cependant elle parlait sans colère et d'une voix tendre.

— Pourquoi me désolez-vous en n'apprenant pas vos leçons ?
— Je ne peux pas, maman, je vous assure que je ne peux pas.

Et Arthur se prit à pleurer.

Mais Mme Milligan ne se laissa pas ébranler par ses larmes, bien qu'elle parût touchée et même désolée, comme elle avait dit.

— J'aurais voulu vous laisser jouer ce matin avec Rémi et avec les chiens, continua-t-elle, mais vous ne jouerez que quand vous m'aurez répété votre fable sans faute.

Disant cela, elle donna le livre à Arthur et fit quelques pas, comme pour rentrer dans l'intérieur du bateau, laissant son fils couché sur sa planche.

Il pleurait à sanglots, et de ma place j'entendais sa voix entrecoupée.

Comment Mme Milligan pouvait-elle être sévère avec ce pauvre petit, qu'elle paraissait aimer si tendrement ? S'il ne pouvait pas apprendre sa leçon, ce n'était pas sa faute, c'était celle de la maladie sans doute.

Elle allait donc disparaître sans lui dire une bonne parole.

Mais elle ne disparut pas ; au lieu d'entrer dans le bateau, elle revint vers son fils.

— Voulez-vous que nous essayions de l'apprendre ensemble ? dit-elle.

— Oh ! oui, maman, ensemble.

Alors elle s'assit près de lui, et, reprenant le livre, elle commença à lire doucement la fable, qui s'appelait : *Le Loup et le Jeune Mouton* ; après elle, Arthur répétait les mots et les phrases.

Lorsqu'elle eut lu cette fable trois fois, elle donna le livre à Arthur, en lui disant d'apprendre maintenant tout seul, et elle rentra dans le bateau.

Aussitôt Arthur se mit à lire sa fable, et, de ma place où j'étais resté, je le vis remuer les lèvres.

Il était évident qu'il travaillait et qu'il s'appliquait.

Mais cette application ne dura pas longtemps ; bientôt il leva les yeux de dessus son livre, et ses lèvres remuèrent moins vite, puis tout à coup elles s'arrêtèrent complètement.

Il ne lisait plus, et ne répétait plus.

Ses yeux, qui erraient çà et là, rencontrèrent les miens.

De la main je lui fis un signe pour l'engager à revenir à sa leçon.

Il me sourit doucement comme pour me dire qu'il me remerciait de mon avertissement, et ses yeux se fixèrent de nouveau sur son livre.

Mais bientôt ils se relevèrent et allèrent d'une rive à l'autre du canal.

Comme ils ne regardaient pas de mon côté, je me levai, et, ayant ainsi provoqué son attention, je lui montrai son livre.

Il le reprit d'un air confus.

Malheureusement, deux minutes après, un martin-pêcheur, rapide comme une flèche, traversa le canal à l'avant du bateau, laissant derrière lui un rayon bleu.

Arthur souleva la tête pour le suivre.

Puis, quand la vision fut évanouie, il me regarda.

Alors m'adressant la parole :

— Je ne peux pas, dit-il, et cependant je voudrais bien.

Je m'approchai.

— Cette fable n'est pourtant pas bien difficile, lui dis-je.

— Oh! si, bien difficile, au contraire.

— Elle m'a paru très facile ; et en écoutant votre maman la lire, il me semble que je l'ai retenue.

Il se mit à sourire d'un air de doute.

— Voulez-vous que je vous la dise ?

— Pourquoi, puisque c'est impossible ?

— Mais non, ce n'est pas impossible ; voulez-vous que j'essaye ? prenez le livre.

Il reprit le livre et je commençai à réciter ; il n'eut à me reprendre que trois ou quatre fois.

— Comment, vous la savez ! s'écria-t-il.

— Pas très bien, mais maintenant je crois que je la dirais sans faute.

— Comment avez-vous fait pour l'apprendre ?

— J'ai écouté votre maman la lire, mais je l'ai écoutée avec attention, sans regarder ce qui se passait autour de nous.

Il rougit et détourna les yeux ; puis, après un court moment de honte :

— Je comprends comment vous avez écouté, dit-il, et je

tâcherai d'écouter comme vous ; mais comment avez-vous fait pour retenir tous ces mots qui se brouillent dans ma mémoire ?

Comment j'avais fait ? Je ne savais pas trop, car je n'avais pas réfléchi à cela ; cependant je tâchai de lui expliquer ce qu'il me demandait en m'en rendant compte moi-même.

— De quoi s'agit-il dans cette fable ? dis-je. D'un mouton. Je commence donc à penser à des moutons. Ensuite je pense à ce qu'ils font : « Des moutons étaient en sûreté dans leur parc. » Je vois les moutons couchés et dormant dans leur parc, puisqu'ils sont en sûreté, et, les ayant vus, je ne les oublie plus.

— Bon, dit-il, je les vois aussi : « Des moutons étaient en sûreté dans leur parc. » J'en vois des blancs et des noirs, je vois des brebis et des agneaux. Je vois même le parc ; il est fait de claies.

— Alors vous ne l'oublierez plus ?

— Oh ! non.

— Ordinairement, qui est-ce qui garde les moutons ?

— Des chiens.

— Quand ils n'ont pas besoin de garder les moutons, parce que ceux-ci sont en sûreté, que font les chiens ?

— Ils n'ont rien à faire.

— Alors ils peuvent dormir ; nous disons donc : « Les chiens dormaient. »

— C'est cela, c'est bien facile.

— N'est-ce pas que c'est très facile ? Maintenant, pensons à autre chose. Avec les chiens, qui est-ce qui garde les moutons ?

— Un berger.

— Si les moutons sont en sûreté, le berger n'a rien à faire ; à quoi peut-il employer son temps ?

— À jouer de la flûte.

— Le voyez-vous ?

— Oui.

— Où est-il ?

— À l'ombre d'un grand ormeau.

— Il est seul ?

— Non, il est avec d'autres bergers voisins.

— Alors, si vous voyez les moutons, le parc, les chiens et le berger, est-ce que vous ne pouvez pas répéter sans faute le commencement de votre fable ?

— Il me semble.

— Essayez.

En m'entendant parler ainsi et lui expliquer comment il pouvait être facile d'apprendre une leçon qui tout d'abord paraissait difficile, Arthur me regarda avec émotion et avec crainte, comme s'il n'était pas convaincu de la vérité de ce que je lui disais ; cependant, après quelques secondes d'hésitation, il se décida.

« Des moutons étaient en sûreté dans leur parc, les chiens dormaient, et le berger, à l'ombre d'un grand ormeau, jouait de la flûte avec d'autres bergers voisins. »

Alors frappant ses mains l'une contre l'autre :

— Mais je sais ! s'écria-t-il, je n'ai pas fait de faute.

— Voulez-vous apprendre le reste de la fable de la même manière ?

— Oui, avec vous je suis sûr que je vais l'apprendre. Ah ! comme maman sera contente !

Et il se mit à apprendre le reste de la fable, comme il avait appris sa première phrase.

En moins d'un quart d'heure il la sut parfaitement, et il était en train de la répéter sans faute lorsque sa mère survint derrière nous.

Tout d'abord elle se fâcha de nous voir réunis, car elle crut que nous n'étions ensemble que pour jouer ; mais Arthur ne lui laissa pas dire deux paroles.

— Je sais, s'écria-t-il, et c'est lui qui me l'a apprise.

Mme Milligan me regardait toute surprise, et elle allait sûrement m'interroger, quand Arthur se mit, sans qu'elle le lui demandât, à répéter *Le Loup et le Jeune Mouton*. Il le fit d'un air de triomphe et de joie, sans hésitation et sans faute.

Pendant ce temps, je regardais Mme Milligan. Je vis son beau visage s'éclairer d'un sourire, puis il me sembla que ses yeux se mouillèrent ; mais, comme à ce moment elle se pencha sur son fils pour l'embrasser tendrement en l'entourant de ses deux bras, je ne sais pas si elle pleurait.

— Les mots, disait Arthur, c'est bête, ça ne signifie rien, mais les choses, on les voit, et Rémi m'a fait voir le berger avec sa flûte ; quand je levais les yeux en apprenant, je ne pensais plus à ce qui m'entourait, je voyais la flûte du berger et j'entendais l'air qu'il jouait. Voulez-vous que je vous chante l'air, maman ?

Et il chanta en anglais une chanson mélancolique.

Cette fois Mme Milligan pleurait pour tout de bon, et quand elle se releva, je vis ses larmes sur les joues de son enfant. Alors elle s'approcha de moi et, me prenant la main, elle me la serra si doucement que je me sentis tout ému :

— Vous êtes un bon garçon, me dit-elle.

Si j'ai raconté tout au long ce petit incident, c'est pour faire comprendre le changement qui, à partir de ce jour-là, se fit dans ma position. La veille on m'avait pris comme montreur de bêtes pour amuser, moi, mes chiens et mon singe, un enfant malade ; mais cette leçon me sépara des chiens et du singe, je devins un camarade, presque un ami.

Il faut dire aussi, tout de suite, ce que je ne sus que plus tard, c'est que Mme Milligan était désolée de voir que son fils n'apprenait rien, ou, plus justement, ne pouvait rien apprendre. Bien qu'il fût malade, elle voulait qu'il travaillât, et précisément parce que cette maladie devait être longue, elle voulait, dès maintenant, donner à son esprit des habitudes qui lui permissent de réparer le temps perdu, le jour où la guérison serait venue.

Jusque-là, elle avait fort mal réussi. Si Arthur n'était point rétif au travail, il l'était absolument à l'attention et à l'application. Il prenait sans résistance le livre qu'on lui mettait aux mains, il ouvrait même assez volontiers ses mains pour le recevoir, mais son esprit, il ne l'ouvrait pas, et c'était mécaniquement, comme une machine, qu'il répétait tant bien que mal, et plutôt mal que bien, les mots qu'on lui faisait entrer de force dans la tête.

De là un vif chagrin chez sa mère, qui désespérait de lui.

De là aussi une vive satisfaction lorsqu'elle entendit répéter une fable apprise avec moi en une demi-heure, qu'elle-même n'avait pas pu, en plusieurs jours, lui mettre dans la mémoire.

Quand je pense maintenant aux jours passés sur ce bateau, auprès de Mme Milligan et d'Arthur, je trouve que ce sont les meilleurs de mon enfance.

Arthur s'était pris pour moi d'une ardente amitié, et, de mon côté, je me laissais aller sans réfléchir et sous l'influence de la sympathie à le regarder comme un frère : pas une querelle entre nous ; chez lui pas la moindre marque de la supériorité que lui donnait sa position, et chez moi pas le plus léger embarras ; je n'avais même pas conscience que je pouvais être embarrassé.

Cela tenait sans doute à mon âge et à mon ignorance des choses de la vie ; mais assurément cela tenait beaucoup encore à la délicatesse et à la bonté de Mme Milligan, qui bien souvent me parlait comme si j'avais été son enfant.

Et puis ce voyage en bateau était pour moi un émerveillement ; pas une heure d'ennui ou de fatigue ; du matin au soir, toutes nos heures remplies.

Depuis la construction des chemins de fer, on ne visite plus, on ne connaît même plus le canal du Midi, et cependant c'est une des curiosités de la France.

De Villefranche-de-Lauragais nous avions été à Avignonnet, et d'Avignonnet aux pierres de Naurouze où s'élève le monument érigé à la gloire de Riquet, le constructeur du canal, à l'endroit même où se trouve la ligne de faîte entre les rivières qui vont se jeter dans l'Océan et celles qui descendent à la Méditerranée.

Puis nous avions traversé Castelnaudary, la ville des moulins, Carcassonne, la cité du Moyen Âge, et par l'écluse de Fouserannes, si curieuse avec ses huit sas accolés, nous étions descendus à Béziers.

Quand le pays était intéressant, nous ne faisions que quelques lieues dans la journée ; quand au contraire il était monotone, nous allions plus vite.

C'était la route elle-même qui décidait notre marche et notre départ. Aucune des préoccupations ordinaires aux voyageurs ne nous gênait ; nous n'avions pas à faire de longues étapes pour gagner une auberge où nous serions certains de trouver à dîner et à coucher.

À heure fixe, nos repas étaient servis sous la véranda ; et, tout en mangeant, nous suivions tranquillement le spectacle mouvant des deux rives.

Quand le soleil s'abaissait, nous nous arrêtions où l'ombre nous surprenait, et nous restions là jusqu'à ce que la lumière reparût.

Toujours chez nous, dans notre maison, nous ne connaissions point les heures désœuvrées du soir, si longues et si tristes bien souvent pour le voyageur.

Ces heures du soir, tout au contraire, étaient pour nous souvent trop courtes, et le moment du coucher nous surprenait alors que nous ne pensions guère à dormir.

Le bateau arrêté, s'il faisait frais, on s'enfermait dans le salon, et, après avoir allumé un feu doux, pour chasser l'humidité ou le brouillard, qui étaient mauvais pour le malade, on apportait les lampes ; on installait Arthur devant la table ; je m'asseyais près de lui, et Mme Milligan nous montrait des livres d'images ou des vues photographiques. De même que le bateau qui nous portait avait été construit pour cette navigation spéciale, de même les livres et les vues avaient été choisis pour ce voyage. Quand nos yeux commençaient à se fatiguer, elle ouvrait un de ces livres et nous lisait les passages qui devaient nous intéresser et que nous pouvions comprendre ; ou bien, fermant livres et albums, elle nous racontait les légendes, les faits historiques se rapportant aux pays que nous venions de traverser. Elle parlait les yeux attachés sur ceux de son fils, et c'était chose touchante de voir la peine qu'elle se donnait pour n'exprimer que des idées, pour n'employer que des mots qui pussent être facilement compris.

Pour moi, quand les soirées étaient belles, j'avais aussi un rôle actif ; alors je prenais ma harpe et, descendant à terre, j'allais à une certaine distance me placer derrière un arbre qui me cachait dans son ombre, et là je chantais toutes les chansons, je jouais tous les airs que je savais. Pour Arthur, c'était un grand plaisir que d'entendre ainsi de la musique dans le calme de la nuit, sans voir celui qui la faisait ; souvent il me criait : « Encore ! » et je recommençais l'air que je venais de jouer.

C'était là une vie douce et heureuse pour un enfant qui, comme moi, n'avait quitté la chaumière de mère Barberin que pour suivre sur les grandes routes le signor Vitalis.

Quelle différence entre le plat de pommes de terre au sel de ma pauvre nourrice et les bonnes tartes aux fruits, les gelées, les crèmes, les pâtisseries de la cuisinière de Mme Milligan !

Quel contraste entre les longues marches à pied, dans la boue, sous la pluie, par un soleil de feu, derrière mon maître, et cette promenade en bateau !

Mais, pour être juste envers moi-même, je dois dire que j'étais encore plus sensible au bonheur moral que je trouvais dans cette vie nouvelle qu'aux jouissances matérielles qu'elle me donnait.

Oui, elles étaient bien bonnes, les pâtisseries de Mme Milligan ; oui, il était agréable de ne plus souffrir de la faim, du chaud ou du froid ; mais combien plus que tout cela étaient bons et agréables pour mon cœur les sentiments qui l'emplissaient !

Deux fois j'avais vu se briser ou se dénouer les liens qui m'attachaient à ceux que j'aimais : la première, lorsque j'avais été arraché d'auprès de mère Barberin ; la seconde, lorsque j'avais été séparé de Vitalis ; et ainsi deux fois je m'étais trouvé seul au monde, sans appui, sans soutien, n'ayant d'autres amis que mes bêtes.

Et voilà que, dans mon isolement et dans ma détresse, j'avais trouvé quelqu'un qui m'avait témoigné de la tendresse, et que j'avais pu aimer : une femme, une belle dame, douce, affable et tendre, un enfant de mon âge qui me traitait comme si j'avais été son frère.

Quelle joie, quel bonheur pour un cœur qui, comme le mien, avait tant besoin d'aimer !

Combien de fois, en regardant Arthur couché sur sa planche, pâle et dolent, je me prenais à envier son bonheur, moi, plein de santé et de force !

Ce n'était pas le bien-être qui l'entourait que j'enviais, ce n'étaient pas ses livres, ses jouets luxueux, ce n'était pas son bateau, c'était l'amour que sa mère lui témoignait.

Comme il devait être heureux d'être ainsi aimé, d'être ainsi embrassé dix fois, vingt fois par jour, et de pouvoir lui-même embrasser de tout son cœur cette belle dame, sa mère, dont j'osais à peine toucher la main lorsqu'elle me la tendait !

Et alors je me disais tristement que, moi, je n'aurais jamais une mère qui m'embrasserait et que j'embrasserais. Peut-être un jour je reverrais mère Barberin, et ce me serait une grande joie, mais enfin je ne pourrais plus maintenant lui dire comme autrefois : « Maman », puisqu'elle n'était pas ma mère.

Seul, je serais toujours seul !

Aussi cette pensée me faisait-elle goûter avec plus d'intensité la joie que j'éprouvais à me sentir traiter tendrement par Mme Milligan et Arthur.

Je ne devais pas me montrer trop exigeant pour ma part de bonheur en ce monde, et, puisque je n'aurais jamais ni mère, ni frère, ni famille, je devais me trouver heureux d'avoir des amis.

Je devais être heureux et en réalité je l'étais pleinement.

Cependant, si douces que me parussent ces nouvelles habitudes, il fallut bientôt les interrompre pour revenir aux anciennes.

XIII

Enfant trouvé

Le temps avait passé vite pendant ce voyage, et le moment approchait où mon maître allait sortir de prison. C'était à la fois pour moi une cause de joie et de trouble.

À mesure que nous nous éloignions de Toulouse, cette pensée m'avait de plus en plus vivement tourmenté.

C'était charmant de s'en aller ainsi en bateau, sans peine comme sans souci ; mais il faudrait revenir et faire à pied la route parcourue sur l'eau.

Ce serait moins charmant : plus de bon lit, plus de crème, plus de pâtisseries, plus de soirées autour de la table.

Et ce qui me touchait encore bien plus vivement, il faudrait me séparer d'Arthur et de Mme Milligan ; il faudrait renoncer à leur affection, les perdre comme déjà j'avais perdu mère Barberin. N'aimerais-je donc, ne serais-je donc aimé que pour être séparé brutalement de ceux près de qui je voudrais passer ma vie ? Rien ne pourrait-il les réunir ?

Je puis dire que cette préoccupation a été le seul nuage de ces journées radieuses.

Un jour enfin, je me décidai à en faire part à Mme Milligan en lui demandant combien elle croyait qu'il me faudrait de temps pour retourner à Toulouse, car je voulais me trouver devant la porte de la prison juste au moment où mon maître la franchirait.

En entendant parler de départ, Arthur poussa les hauts cris :
— Je ne veux pas que Rémi parte ! s'écria-t-il.

Je répondis que je n'étais pas libre de ma personne, que j'appartenais à mon maître, à qui mes parents m'avaient loué, et que je devais reprendre mon service auprès de lui le jour où il aurait besoin de moi.

Je parlai de mes parents sans dire qu'ils n'étaient pas réellement mes père et mère, car il aurait fallu avouer en même temps que je n'étais qu'un enfant trouvé.

— Maman, il faut retenir Rémi, continua Arthur, qui, en dehors du travail, était le maître de sa mère, et faisait d'elle tout ce qu'il voulait.

— Je serais très heureuse de garder Rémi, répondit Mme Milligan, vous l'avez pris en amitié, et moi-même j'ai pour lui beaucoup d'affection ; mais, pour le retenir près de nous, il faut la réunion de deux conditions dont ni vous ni moi ne pouvons décider. La première, c'est que Rémi veuille rester avec nous...

— Ah ! Rémi voudra bien, interrompit Arthur ; n'est-ce pas, Rémi, que vous ne voulez pas retourner à Toulouse ?

— La seconde, continua Mme Milligan sans attendre ma réponse, c'est que son maître consente à renoncer aux droits qu'il a sur lui.

— Rémi, Rémi d'abord, interrompit Arthur poursuivant son idée.

Assurément Vitalis avait été un bon maître pour moi, et je lui étais reconnaissant de ses soins aussi bien que de ses leçons ; mais il n'y avait aucune comparaison à établir entre l'existence que j'avais menée près de lui et celle que m'offrait Mme Milligan. De plus, et ce n'était pas sans remords que je me l'avouais, il n'y avait aucune comparaison à établir entre l'affection que j'éprouvais pour Vitalis et celle que m'inspiraient Mme Milligan et Arthur. Quand je pensais à cela, je me disais que c'était mal à moi de préférer à mon maître ces étrangers que je connaissais depuis si peu de temps ; mais enfin, cela était ainsi, j'aimais tendrement Mme Milligan et Arthur.

— Avant de répondre, continua Mme Milligan, Rémi doit réfléchir que ce n'est pas seulement une vie de plaisir et de promenade que je lui propose, mais encore une vie de travail ; il faudra étudier, prendre de la peine, rester penché sur les livres, suivre Arthur dans ses études ; il faut mettre cela en balance avec la liberté des grands chemins.

— Il n'y a pas de balance, dis-je, et je vous assure, madame, que je sens tout le prix de votre proposition.

— Là, voyez-vous, maman ! s'écria Arthur, Rémi veut bien.

Et il se mit à applaudir. Il était évident que je venais de le tirer d'inquiétude, car, lorsque sa mère avait parlé de travail et de livres, j'avais vu sur son visage exprimer l'anxiété. Si j'allais refuser ! et cette crainte, pour lui qui avait l'horreur des livres, avait dû être des plus vives. Mais je n'avais pas heureusement cette même crainte, et les livres, au lieu de m'épouvanter, m'attiraient. Il est vrai qu'il y avait bien peu de temps qu'on m'en avait mis entre les mains, et ceux qui y avaient passé m'avaient donné plus de plaisir que de peine. Aussi l'offre de Mme Milligan me rendait-elle très heureux, et étais-je parfaitement sincère en la remerciant de sa générosité. Si Vitalis y consentait, je pourrais ne pas abandonner le *Cygne*; je ne renoncerais pas à cette douce existence, je ne me séparerais pas d'Arthur et de sa mère.

— Maintenant, poursuivit Mme Milligan, il nous reste à obtenir le consentement de son maître ; pour cela je vais lui écrire de venir nous trouver à Cette, car nous ne pouvons pas retourner à Toulouse. Je lui enverrai ses frais de voyage, et, après lui avoir fait comprendre les raisons qui nous empêchent de prendre le chemin de fer, j'espère qu'il voudra bien se rendre à mon invitation. S'il accepte mes propositions, il ne me restera plus qu'à m'entendre avec les parents de Rémi, car eux aussi doivent être consultés.

Jusque-là tout dans cet entretien avait marché à souhait pour moi, exactement comme si une bonne fée m'avait touché de sa baguette ; mais ces derniers mots me ramenèrent durement du rêve où je planais dans la triste réalité.

Consulter mes parents !

Mais sûrement ils diraient ce que je voulais qui restât caché. La vérité éclaterait. Enfant trouvé !

Alors ce serait Arthur, ce serait peut-être Mme Milligan, qui ne voudraient pas de moi.

Je restai atterré.

Mme Milligan me regarda avec surprise et voulut me faire parler, mais je n'osai pas répondre à ses questions. Alors, croyant sans doute que c'était la pensée de la prochaine arrivée de mon maître qui me troublait ainsi, elle n'insista pas.

Heureusement cela se passait le soir, peu de temps avant l'heure du coucher ; je pus échapper bientôt aux regards curieux d'Arthur et aller m'enfermer dans ma cabine avec mes craintes et mes réflexions.

Ce fut ma première mauvaise nuit à bord du Cygne ; mais elle fut terriblement mauvaise, longue, fiévreuse.

Que faire ? Que dire ?

Je ne trouvais rien.

Et, après avoir tourné et retourné cent fois les mêmes idées, après avoir adopté les résolutions les plus contradictoires, je m'arrêtai enfin à la plus commode, mais à la moins digne, à ne rien faire et à ne rien dire. Je laisserais aller les choses et je me résignerais, si je ne pouvais mieux, à ce qui arriverait.

Peut-être Vitalis ne voudrait-il pas renoncer à moi, et dans mon cœur si combattu je ne pouvais me retenir de désirer et de craindre qu'il en fût ainsi ; dans ce cas-là, repartant avec lui, il n'y aurait pas à faire connaître la vérité.

Et tel était mon effroi de cette vérité que je croyais si horrible, que j'en vins à souhaiter ardemment que Vitalis n'acceptât pas la proposition de Mme Milligan, et que rien ne pût s'arranger entre eux à mon sujet.

Sans doute, il faudrait m'éloigner d'Arthur et de sa mère, renoncer à les revoir jamais peut-être ; mais au moins ils ne garderaient pas de moi un mauvais souvenir.

Trois jours après avoir écrit à mon maître, Mme Milligan reçut une réponse. En quelques lignes Vitalis disait qu'il aurait l'honneur de se rendre à l'invitation de Mme Milligan et qu'il arriverait à Cette le samedi suivant par le train de deux heures.

Je demandai à Mme Milligan la permission d'aller à la gare, et, prenant les chiens ainsi que Joli-Cœur avec moi, nous attendîmes l'arrivée de notre maître.

Les chiens étaient inquiets comme s'ils se doutaient de quelque chose, Joli-Cœur était indifférent, et pour moi j'étais terriblement ému. Que de combats contradictoires dans mon âme ignorante !

Je m'étais placé dans un coin de la cour de la gare, tenant mes trois chiens en laisse, et Joli-Cœur sous ma veste, et j'attendais sans trop voir ce qui se passait autour de moi.

Ce furent les chiens qui m'avertirent que le train était arrivé, et qu'ils avaient flairé notre maître. Tout à coup je me sentis entraîné en avant, et, comme je n'étais pas sur mes gardes, les chiens m'échappèrent. Ils couraient en aboyant joyeusement, et presque aussitôt je les vis sauter autour de Vitalis qui, dans son costume habituel, venait d'apparaître. Plus prompt, bien que moins souple que ses camarades, Capi s'était lancé dans les bras de son maître, tandis que Zerbino et Dolce se cramponnaient à ses jambes.

Je m'avançai à mon tour, et Vitalis, posant Capi à terre, me serra dans ses bras ; pour la première fois, il m'embrassa en me répétant à plusieurs reprises :

— *Buon dì, povero caro!*

Mon maître n'avait jamais été dur pour moi, mais n'avait jamais non plus été caressant, et je n'étais pas habitué à ces témoignages d'effusion ; cela m'attendrit, et me fit venir les larmes aux yeux, car j'étais dans des dispositions où le cœur se serre et s'ouvre vite.

Je le regardai, et je trouvai qu'il avait bien vieilli en prison ; sa taille s'était voûtée ; son visage avait pâli ; ses lèvres s'étaient décolorées.

— Eh bien ! tu me trouves changé, n'est-ce pas, mon garçon ? me dit-il ; la prison est un mauvais séjour, et l'ennui une mauvaise maladie ; mais cela va aller mieux maintenant.

Puis changeant de sujet :

— Et cette dame qui m'a écrit, dit-il, comment l'as-tu connue ?

Alors je lui racontai comment j'avais rencontré le *Cygne*, et comment depuis ce moment j'avais vécu auprès de Mme Milligan et de son fils ; ce que nous avions vu, ce que nous avions fait.

Mon récit fut d'autant plus long que j'avais peur d'arriver à la fin et d'aborder un sujet qui m'épouvantait, car jamais maintenant je ne pourrais dire à mon maître que je désirais peut-être qu'il tombât d'accord avec Mme Milligan et Arthur pour qu'ils pussent me garder.

Mais je n'eus pas cet aveu à lui faire, car, avant que mon récit fût terminé, nous arrivâmes à l'hôtel où Mme Milligan s'était logée. D'ailleurs Vitalis ne me dit rien de la lettre de Mme Milligan, et ne me parla pas des propositions qu'elle avait dû lui adresser dans cette lettre.

— Et cette dame m'attend ? dit-il, quand nous entrâmes à l'hôtel.

— Oui, je vais vous conduire à son appartement.

— C'est inutile, donne-moi le numéro et reste ici à m'attendre, avec les chiens et Joli-Cœur.

Quand mon maître avait parlé, je n'avais pas l'habitude de répliquer ou de discuter ; je voulus cependant risquer une observation, pour lui demander de l'accompagner auprès de Mme Milligan, ce qui me semblait aussi naturel que juste ; mais d'un geste il me ferma la bouche, et je lui obéis, restant à la porte de l'hôtel sur un banc, avec les chiens autour de moi. Eux aussi avaient voulu le suivre ; mais ils n'avaient pas plus résisté à son ordre de ne pas entrer que je n'y avais résisté moi-même ; Vitalis savait commander.

Pourquoi n'avait-il pas voulu que j'assistasse à son entretien avec Mme Milligan ? Ce fut ce que je me demandai, tournant cette question dans tous les sens. Je ne lui avais pas encore trouvé de réponse lorsque je le vis revenir.

— Va faire tes adieux à cette dame, me dit-il, je t'attends ici ; nous partons dans dix minutes.

J'étais très hésitant, et cependant je fus renversé par le sens qu'avait pris cette décision.

— Eh bien ! dit-il après quelques minutes d'attente, tu ne m'as donc pas compris ? Tu restes là comme une statue ; dépêchons !

Ce n'était pas son habitude de me parler durement, et depuis que j'étais avec lui il ne m'en avait jamais autant dit.

Je me levai pour obéir machinalement sans comprendre.

Mais, après avoir fait quelques pas pour monter à l'appartement de Mme Milligan :

— Vous avez donc dit..., demandai-je.

— J'ai dit que tu m'étais utile et que je t'étais moi-même utile ; par conséquent, que je n'étais pas disposé à céder les droits que j'avais sur toi ; marche et reviens.

Cela me rendit un peu de courage, car j'étais si complètement sous l'influence de mon idée fixe d'enfant trouvé, que je m'étais imaginé que, s'il fallait partir avant dix minutes, c'était parce que mon maître avait dit ce qu'il savait de ma naissance.

En entrant dans l'appartement de Mme Milligan, je trouvai Arthur en larmes et sa mère penchée sur lui pour le consoler.

— N'est-ce pas, Rémi, que vous n'allez pas partir ? s'écria Arthur.

Ce fut Mme Milligan qui répondit pour moi, en expliquant que je devais obéir.

— J'ai demandé à votre maître de vous garder près de nous, me dit-elle d'une voix qui me fit monter les larmes aux yeux, mais il ne veut pas y consentir, et rien n'a pu le décider.

— C'est un méchant homme ! s'écria Arthur.

— Non, ce n'est point un méchant homme, poursuivit Mme Milligan, vous lui êtes utile, et de plus je crois qu'il a pour vous une véritable affection. D'ailleurs, ses paroles sont celles d'un honnête homme et de quelqu'un au-dessus de sa condition. Voilà ce qu'il m'a répondu pour expliquer son refus : « J'aime cet enfant, il m'aime ; le rude apprentissage de la vie que je lui fais faire près de moi lui sera plus utile que l'état de domesticité déguisée dans lequel vous le feriez vivre malgré vous. Vous lui donneriez de l'instruction, de l'éducation, c'est vrai ; vous formeriez son esprit, c'est vrai, mais non son caractère. Il ne peut pas être votre fils, il sera le mien ; cela vaudra mieux que d'être le jouet de votre enfant malade, si doux, si aimable que paraisse être cet enfant. Moi aussi je l'instruirai. »

— Puisqu'il n'est pas le père de Rémi ! s'écria Arthur.

— Il n'est pas son père, cela est vrai, mais il est son maître, et Rémi lui appartient, puisque ses parents le lui ont donné. Il faut que pour le moment Rémi lui obéisse.

— Je ne veux pas que Rémi parte.

— Il faut cependant qu'il suive son maître ; mais j'espère que ce ne sera pas pour longtemps. Nous écrirons à ses parents, et je m'entendrai avec eux.

— Oh ! non ! m'écriai-je.

— Comment, non ?

— Oh ! non, je vous en prie !

— Il n'y a cependant que ce moyen, mon enfant.

— Je vous en prie !

Il est à peu près certain que, si Mme Milligan n'avait pas parlé de mes parents, j'aurais donné à nos adieux beaucoup plus que les dix minutes qui m'avaient été accordées par mon maître.

— C'est à Chavanon, n'est-ce pas ? continua Mme Milligan.

Sans lui répondre, je m'approchai d'Arthur et, le prenant dans mes bras, je l'embrassai à plusieurs reprises, mettant dans ces baisers toute l'amitié que je ressentais pour lui. Puis, m'arrachant à son étreinte et revenant à Mme Milligan, je me mis à genoux devant elle et lui baisai la main.

— Pauvre enfant ! dit-elle en se penchant sur moi.

Et elle m'embrassa au front.

Alors je me relevai vivement et, courant à la porte :

— Arthur, je vous aimerai toujours ! dis-je d'une voix entrecoupée par les sanglots, et vous, madame, je ne vous oublierai jamais !

— Rémi ! Rémi ! cria Arthur.

Mais je n'en entendis pas davantage ; j'étais sorti et j'avais refermé la porte.

Une minute après, j'étais auprès de mon maître.

— En route ! me dit-il.

Et nous sortîmes de Cette par la route de Frontignan.

Ce fut ainsi que je quittai mon premier ami et me trouvai lancé de nouveau dans des aventures qui m'auraient été épargnées, si, ne m'exagérant pas les conséquences d'un odieux préjugé, je ne m'étais pas laissé affoler par une sotte crainte.

XIV

Neige et loups

Il fallut de nouveau emboîter le pas derrière mon maître et, la bretelle de ma harpe tendue sur mon épaule endolorie, cheminer le long des grandes routes, par la pluie comme par le soleil, par la poussière comme par la boue.

Il fallut faire la bête sur les places publiques et rire ou pleurer pour amuser l'honorable société.

La transition fut rude, car on s'habitue vite au bien-être et au bonheur.

J'eus des dégoûts, des ennuis et des fatigues que je ne connaissais pas avant d'avoir vécu pendant deux mois de la douce vie des heureux de ce monde.

Auprès de Mme Milligan, j'avais bien des fois pensé à Vitalis ; auprès de Vitalis, mon souvenir se reportait sur Mme Milligan.

Plus d'une fois, dans nos longues marches, je restai en arrière pour penser librement à Arthur, à sa mère, au *Cygne,* et, en idée, retourner et vivre dans le passé.

Ah ! le bon temps ! Et quand le soir, couché dans une sale auberge de village, je pensais à ma cabine du *Cygne,* combien les draps de mon lit me paraissaient rugueux !

Je ne jouerais donc plus avec Arthur, je n'entendrais donc plus la voix caressante de Mme Milligan !

Heureusement, dans mon chagrin, qui était très vif et persistant, j'avais une consolation ; mon maître était beaucoup plus doux – beaucoup plus tendre même... si ce mot peut être juste, appliqué à Vitalis – qu'il ne l'avait jamais été !

De ce côté il s'était fait un grand changement dans son caractère ou tout au moins dans ses manières d'être avec moi, et cela me soutenait, cela m'empêchait de pleurer quand le souvenir d'Arthur me serrait le cœur ! Je sentais que je n'étais pas seul au monde et que, dans mon maître, il y avait plus et mieux qu'un maître.

Souvent même, si j'avais osé, je l'aurais embrassé, tant j'avais besoin d'épancher au-dehors les sentiments d'affection qui étaient en moi ; mais je n'osais pas, car Vitalis n'était pas un homme avec lequel on risquait des familiarités.

Tout d'abord, et pendant les premiers temps, ç'avait été la crainte qui m'avait tenu à distance ; maintenant c'était quelque chose de vague qui ressemblait à un sentiment de respect.

En sortant de mon village, Vitalis n'était pour moi qu'un homme comme les autres, car j'étais alors incapable de faire des distinctions ; mais mon séjour auprès de Mme Milligan m'avait jusqu'à un certain point ouvert les yeux et l'intelligence ; et, chose étrange, il me semblait, quand je regardais mon maître avec attention, que je retrouvais en lui, dans sa tenue, dans son air, dans ses manières, des points de ressemblance avec la tenue, l'air et les manières de Mme Milligan.

Alors je me disais que cela était impossible, parce que mon maître n'était qu'un montreur de bêtes, tandis que Mme Milligan était une dame.

Mais ce que me disait la réflexion n'imposait pas silence à ce que mes yeux me répétaient ; quand Vitalis le voulait, il était un monsieur tout comme Mme Milligan était une dame. La seule différence qu'il y eût entre eux tenait à ce que Mme Milligan était toujours *dame*, tandis que mon maître n'était *monsieur* que dans certaines circonstances ; mais alors il l'était si complètement, qu'il en eût imposé aux plus hardis comme aux plus insolents.

Or, comme je n'étais ni hardi, ni insolent, je subissais cette influence, et je n'osais pas m'abandonner à mes épanchements alors même qu'il les provoquait par quelques bonnes paroles.

Après être partis de Cette, nous étions restés plusieurs jours sans parler de Mme Milligan et de mon séjour sur le *Cygne* ; mais peu à peu ce sujet s'était présenté dans nos entretiens, mon maître l'abordant toujours le premier, et bientôt il ne s'était guère passé de jour sans que le nom de Mme Milligan fût prononcé.

— Tu l'aimais bien, cette dame ? me disait Vitalis ; oui, je comprends cela ; elle a été bonne, très bonne pour toi ; il ne faut penser à elle qu'avec reconnaissance.

Puis souvent il ajoutait :
— Il le fallait !
Qu'avait-il fallu ?

Tout d'abord je n'avais pas bien compris ; mais peu à peu j'en étais venu à me dire que ce qu'il avait fallu, ç'avait été de repousser la proposition de Mme Milligan de me garder près d'elle.

C'était à cela assurément que mon maître pensait quand il disait : « Il le fallait » ; et il me semblait que dans ces quelques mots il y avait comme un regret. Il aurait voulu me laisser près d'Arthur, mais cela avait été impossible.

Et au fond du cœur je lui savais gré de ce regret, bien que je ne devinasse point pourquoi il n'avait pas pu accepter les propositions de Mme Milligan, les explications qui m'avaient été répétées par celle-ci ne me paraissant pas très compréhensibles.

— Maintenant, peut-être un jour les accepterait-il.

Et c'était là pour moi un sujet de grande espérance.

— Pourquoi ne rencontrerions-nous pas le *Cygne* ?

Il devait remonter le Rhône, et nous, nous longions les rives de ce fleuve.

Aussi, tout en marchant, mes yeux se tournaient plus souvent vers l'eau que vers les collines et les plaines fertiles qui la bordent de chaque côté.

Lorsque nous arrivions dans une ville, Arles, Tarascon, Avignon, Montélimar, Valence, Tournon, Vienne, ma première visite était pour les quais et pour les ponts ; je cherchais le *Cygne*, et quand j'apercevais de loin un bateau à demi noyé dans les brumes confuses, j'attendais qu'il grandît pour voir si ce n'était pas le *Cygne*.

Mais ce n'était pas lui.

Quelquefois je m'enhardissais jusqu'à interroger les mariniers, et je leur décrivais le bateau que je cherchais ; ils ne l'avaient pas vu passer.

Maintenant que mon maître était décidé à me céder à Mme Milligan, au moins je me l'imaginais, il n'y avait plus à craindre qu'on parlât de ma naissance ou qu'on écrivît à mère Barberin. L'affaire se traiterait entre mon maître et Mme Milligan ; au moins dans mon rêve enfantin j'arrangeais ainsi les choses : Mme Milligan désirait me prendre près d'elle, mon maître consentait à renoncer à ses droits sur moi, tout était dit.

Nous restâmes plusieurs semaines à Lyon, et tout le temps que j'eus à moi, je le passai sur les quais du Rhône et de la

Saône ; je connais les ponts d'Ainay, de Tilsitt, de la Guillotière ou de l'Hôtel-Dieu, aussi bien qu'un Lyonnais de naissance.

Mais j'eus beau chercher, je ne trouvai pas le *Cygne*.

Il nous fallut quitter Lyon et nous diriger vers Dijon ; alors l'espérance de retrouver jamais Mme Milligan et Arthur commença à m'abandonner, car j'avais à Lyon étudié toutes les cartes de France que j'avais pu trouver aux étalages des bouquinistes, et je savais que le canal du Centre, que devait prendre le *Cygne* pour gagner la Loire, se détache de la Saône à Chalon.

Nous arrivâmes à Chalon et nous en repartîmes sans avoir vu le *Cygne* ; c'en était donc fait, il fallait renoncer à mon rêve.

Ce ne fut pas sans un très vif chagrin.

Justement, pour accroître mon désespoir, qui pourtant était déjà bien assez grand, le temps devint détestable ; la saison était avancée, l'hiver approchait, et les marches sous la pluie, dans la boue, devenaient de plus en plus pénibles. Quand nous arrivions le soir dans une mauvaise auberge ou dans une grange, harassés par la fatigue, mouillés jusqu'à la chemise, crottés jusqu'aux cheveux, je ne me couchais point avec des idées riantes.

Lorsque, après avoir quitté Dijon, nous traversâmes les collines de la Côte-d'Or, nous fûmes pris par un froid humide qui nous glaçait jusqu'aux os, et Joli-Cœur devint plus triste et plus maussade que moi.

Le but de mon maître était de gagner Paris au plus vite, car, à Paris seulement, nous avions chance de pouvoir donner quelques représentations pendant l'hiver ; mais, soit que l'état de sa bourse ne lui permît pas de prendre le chemin de fer, soit toute autre raison, c'était à pied que nous devions faire la route qui sépare Dijon de Paris.

Quand le temps nous le permettait, nous donnions une courte représentation dans les villes et dans les villages que nous traversions, puis, après avoir ramassé une maigre recette, nous nous remettions en route.

Jusqu'à Châtillon, les choses allèrent à peu près, quoique nous eussions toujours à souffrir du froid et de l'humidité ; mais, après avoir quitté cette ville, la pluie cessa et le vent tourna au nord.

Tout d'abord nous ne nous en plaignîmes pas, bien qu'il soit peu agréable d'avoir le vent du nord en pleine figure ; à tout prendre, mieux valait encore cette bise, si âpre qu'elle fût, que l'humidité dans laquelle nous pourrissions depuis plusieurs semaines.

Par malheur, le vent ne resta pas au sec ; le ciel s'emplit de gros nuages noirs, le soleil disparut entièrement, et tout annonça que nous aurions bientôt de la neige.

Nous pûmes cependant arriver à un gros village sans être pris par la neige ; mais l'intention de mon maître était de gagner Troyes au plus vite, parce que Troyes est une grande ville dans laquelle nous pourrions donner plusieurs représentations, si le mauvais temps nous obligeait à y séjourner.

— Couche-toi vite, me dit-il, quand nous fûmes installés dans notre auberge ; nous partirons demain matin de bonne heure ; je crains d'être surpris par la neige.

Pour lui, il ne se coucha pas aussi tôt, mais il resta au coin de l'âtre de la cheminée de la cuisine pour réchauffer Joli-Cœur qui avait beaucoup souffert du froid de la journée et qui n'avait cessé de gémir, bien que nous eussions pris soin de l'envelopper dans des couvertures.

Le lendemain matin je me levai de bonne heure comme il m'avait été commandé ; il ne faisait pas encore jour, le ciel était noir et bas, sans une étoile ; il semblait qu'un grand couvercle sombre s'était abaissé sur la terre et allait l'écraser. Quand on ouvrait la porte, un vent âpre s'engouffrait dans la cheminée et ravivait les tisons qui, la veille au soir, avaient été enfouis sous la cendre.

— À votre place, dit l'aubergiste s'adressant à mon maître, je ne partirais pas ; la neige va tomber.

— Je suis pressé, répondit Vitalis, et j'espère arriver à Troyes avant la neige.

— Trente kilomètres ne se font pas en une heure.

Nous partîmes néanmoins.

Vitalis tenait Joli-Cœur serré sous sa veste pour lui communiquer un peu de sa propre chaleur, et les chiens, joyeux de ce temps sec, couraient devant nous ; mon maître m'avait acheté à Dijon une peau de mouton, dont la laine se portait en dessous ; je m'enveloppai dedans, et la bise qui nous soufflait au visage me la colla sur le corps.

Il n'était pas agréable d'ouvrir la bouche ; nous marchâmes gardant l'un et l'autre le silence, en hâtant le pas, autant pour nous presser que pour nous réchauffer.

Bien que l'heure fût arrivée où le jour devait paraître, il ne se faisait pas d'éclaircies dans le ciel.

Enfin, du côté de l'orient, une bande blanchâtre entrouvrit les ténèbres, mais le soleil ne se montra pas. Il ne fit plus nuit, mais c'eût été une grosse exagération de dire qu'il faisait jour.

Cependant, dans la campagne, les objets étaient devenus plus distincts; la livide clarté qui rasait la terre, jaillissant du levant comme d'un immense soupirail, nous montrait des arbres dépouillés de leurs feuilles, et çà et là des haies ou des broussailles auxquelles les feuilles desséchées adhéraient encore, faisant entendre, sous l'impulsion du vent qui les secouait et les tordait, un bruissement sec.

Personne sur la route, personne dans les champs, pas un bruit de voiture, pas un coup de fouet; les seuls êtres vivants étaient les oiseaux qu'on entendait, mais qu'on ne voyait pas, car ils se tenaient abrités sous les feuilles; seules des pies sautillaient sur la route, la queue relevée, le bec en l'air, s'envolant à notre approche pour se poser en haut d'un arbre, d'où elles nous poursuivaient de leurs jacassements qui ressemblaient à des injures ou à des avertissements de mauvais augure.

Tout à coup un point blanc se montra au ciel, dans le nord; il grandit rapidement en venant sur nous, et nous entendîmes un étrange murmure de cris discordants. C'étaient des oies ou des cygnes sauvages, qui du Nord émigraient dans le Midi; ils passèrent au-dessus de nos têtes et ils étaient déjà loin qu'on voyait encore voltiger dans l'air quelques flocons de duvet, dont la blancheur se détachait sur le ciel noir.

Le pays que nous traversions était d'une tristesse lugubre qu'augmentait encore le silence; aussi loin que les regards pouvaient s'étendre dans ce jour sombre, on ne voyait que des champs dénudés, des collines arides et des bois roussis.

Le vent soufflait toujours du nord avec une légère tendance cependant à tourner à l'ouest; de ce côté de l'horizon arrivaient des nuages cuivrés, lourds et bas, qui paraissaient peser sur la cime des arbres.

Bientôt quelques flocons de neige, larges comme des papillons, nous passèrent devant les yeux; ils montaient, descendaient, tourbillonnaient sans toucher la terre.

Nous n'avions pas encore fait beaucoup de chemin, et il me paraissait impossible d'arriver à Troyes avant la neige; au reste, cela m'inquiétait peu, et je me disais même que la neige en tombant arrêterait ce vent du nord et apaiserait le froid.

Mais je ne savais pas ce que c'était qu'une tempête de neige.

Je ne tardai pas à l'apprendre, et de façon à n'oublier jamais cette leçon.

Les nuages qui venaient du nord-ouest s'étaient approchés,

et une sorte de lueur blanche éclairait le ciel de leur côté ; leurs flancs s'étaient entrouverts, c'était la neige.

Ce ne furent plus des papillons qui voltigèrent devant nous, ce fut une averse de neige qui nous enveloppa.

— Il était écrit que nous n'arriverions pas à Troyes, dit Vitalis ; il faudra nous mettre à l'abri dans la première maison que nous rencontrerons.

C'était là une bonne parole qui ne pouvait m'être que très agréable ; mais où trouverions-nous cette maison hospitalière ? Avant que la neige nous enveloppât dans sa blanche obscurité, j'avais examiné le pays aussi loin que ma vue pouvait s'étendre et je n'avais pas aperçu de maison, ni rien qui annonçât un village. Tout au contraire, nous étions sur le point d'entrer dans une forêt dont les profondeurs sombres se confondaient dans l'infini, devant nous, aussi bien que de chaque côté, sur les collines qui nous entouraient.

Il ne fallait donc pas trop compter sur cette maison promise ; mais, après tout, la neige ne continuerait peut-être pas.

Elle continua, et elle augmenta.

En peu d'instants elle avait couvert la route ou plus justement tout ce qui l'arrêtait sur la route : tas de pierres, herbes des bas-côtés, broussailles et buissons des fossés, car, poussée par le vent qui n'avait pas faibli, elle courait ras de terre pour s'entasser contre tout ce qui lui faisait obstacle.

L'ennui pour nous était d'être au nombre de ces obstacles ; lorsqu'elle nous frappait, elle glissait sur les surfaces rondes, mais, partout où se trouvait une fente, elle entrait comme une poussière et ne tardait pas à fondre.

Pour moi, je la sentais me descendre en eau froide dans le cou, et mon maître, dont la peau de mouton était soulevée pour laisser respirer Joli-Cœur, ne devait pas être mieux protégé.

Cependant nous continuions de marcher contre le vent et contre la neige sans parler ; de temps en temps nous retournions à demi la tête pour respirer.

Les chiens n'allaient plus en avant, ils marchaient sur nos talons, nous demandant un abri que nous ne pouvions leur donner.

Nous avancions lentement, avec peine, aveuglés, mouillés, glacés, et, bien que nous fussions depuis assez longtemps déjà en pleine forêt, nous ne nous trouvions nullement abrités, la route étant exposée en plein au vent.

Heureusement (est-ce bien heureusement qu'il faut dire?) ce vent qui soufflait en tourmente s'affaiblit peu à peu; mais alors la neige augmenta, et, au lieu de s'abattre en poussière, elle tomba large et compacte.

En quelques minutes la route fut couverte d'une épaisse couche de neige dans laquelle nous marchâmes sans bruit.

De temps en temps, je voyais mon maître regarder sur la gauche comme s'il cherchait quelque chose; mais on n'apercevait qu'une vaste clairière dans laquelle on avait fait une coupe au printemps précédent, et dont les jeunes baliveaux aux tiges flexibles se courbaient sous le poids de la neige.

Qu'espérait-il trouver de ce côté?

Pour moi je regardais droit devant moi, sur la route, aussi loin que mes yeux pouvaient porter, cherchant si cette forêt ne finirait pas bientôt et si nous n'apercevrions pas une maison.

Mais c'était folie de vouloir percer cette averse blanche; à quelques mètres les objets se brouillaient, et l'on ne voyait plus rien que la neige qui descendait en flocons de plus en plus serrés et nous enveloppait comme dans les mailles d'un immense filet.

La situation n'était pas gaie, car je n'ai jamais vu tomber la neige, alors même que j'étais derrière une vitre dans une chambre bien chauffée, sans éprouver un sentiment de vague tristesse, et présentement je me disais que la chambre chauffée devait être bien loin encore.

Cependant il fallait marcher et ne pas se décourager, parce que nos pieds enfonçaient de plus en plus dans la couche de neige qui nous montait aux jambes, et parce que le poids qui chargeait nos chapeaux devenait de plus en plus lourd.

Tout à coup, je vis Vitalis étendre la main dans la direction de la gauche, comme pour attirer mon attention. Je regardai, et il me sembla apercevoir confusément dans la clairière une hutte en branchages recouverte de neige.

Je ne demandai pas d'explication, comprenant que, si mon maître m'avait montré cette hutte, ce n'était pas pour que j'admirasse l'effet qu'elle produisait dans le paysage; il s'agissait de trouver le chemin qui conduisait jusqu'à elle.

C'était difficile, car la neige était déjà assez épaisse pour effacer toute trace de route ou de sentier; cependant, à l'extrémité de la clairière, à l'endroit où recommençaient les bois de haute futaie, il me sembla que le fossé de la grande route était comblé; là sans doute débouchait le chemin qui conduisait à la hutte.

C'était raisonner juste ; la neige ne céda pas sous nos pieds lorsque nous descendîmes dans le fossé, et nous ne tardâmes pas à arriver à cette hutte.

Elle était formée de fagots et de bourrées, au-dessus desquels avaient été disposés des branchages en forme de toit ; et ce toit était assez serré pour que la neige n'eût point passé à travers.

C'était un abri qui valait une maison.

Plus pressés ou plus vifs que nous, les chiens étaient entrés les premiers dans la hutte, et ils se roulaient sur le sol sec et dans la poussière en poussant des aboiements joyeux.

Notre satisfaction n'était pas moins vive que la leur ; mais nous la manifestâmes autrement qu'en nous roulant dans la poussière, ce qui cependant n'eût pas été mauvais pour nous sécher.

— Je me doutais bien, dit Vitalis, que dans cette jeune vente devait se trouver quelque part une cabane de bûcheron ; maintenant la neige peut tomber.

— Oui, qu'elle tombe ! répondis-je d'un air de défi.

Et j'allai à la porte, ou, plus justement, à l'ouverture de la hutte, car elle n'avait ni porte ni fenêtre, pour secouer ma veste et mon chapeau, de manière à ne pas mouiller l'intérieur de notre appartement.

Il était tout à fait simple, cet appartement, aussi bien dans sa construction que dans son mobilier, qui consistait en un banc de terre et en quelques grosses pierres servant de sièges. Mais ce qui, dans les circonstances où nous nous trouvions, était encore d'un plus grand prix pour nous, c'étaient cinq ou six briques posées de chant dans un coin et formant le foyer.

Du feu ! nous pouvions faire du feu.

Il est vrai qu'un foyer ne suffit pas pour faire du feu, il faut encore du bois à mettre dans le foyer.

Dans une maison comme la nôtre, le bois n'était pas difficile à trouver ; il n'y avait qu'à le prendre aux murailles et au toit, c'est-à-dire à tirer des branches de fagots et des bourrées, en ayant pour tout soin de prendre ces branches çà et là, de manière à ne pas compromettre la solidité de notre maison.

Cela fut vite fait, et une flamme claire ne tarda pas à briller en pétillant joyeusement au-dessus de notre âtre.

Ah ! le beau feu ! le bon feu !

Il est vrai qu'il ne brûlait pas sans fumée, et que celle-ci, ne montant pas dans une cheminée, se répandait dans la hutte ; mais que nous importait ? c'était de la flamme, c'était de la chaleur que nous voulions.

Pendant que, couché sur les deux mains, je soufflais le feu, les chiens s'étaient assis autour du foyer, et gravement sur leur derrière, le cou tendu, ils présentaient leur ventre mouillé et glacé au rayonnement de la flamme.

Bientôt Joli-Cœur écarta la veste de son maître, et, mettant prudemment le bout du nez dehors, il regarda où il se trouvait ; rassuré par son examen, il sauta vivement à terre, et, prenant la meilleure place devant le feu, il présenta à la flamme ses deux petites mains tremblotantes.

Nous étions assurés maintenant de ne pas mourir de froid, mais la question de la faim n'était pas résolue.

Il n'y avait dans cette cabane hospitalière ni huche à pain ni fourneau avec des casseroles chantantes.

Heureusement, notre maître était homme de précaution et d'expérience ; le matin, avant que je fusse levé, il avait fait ses provisions de route : une miche de pain et un petit morceau de fromage ; mais ce n'était pas le moment de se montrer exigeant ou difficile : aussi, quand nous vîmes apparaître la miche, y eut-il chez nous tous un vif mouvement de satisfaction.

Malheureusement les parts ne furent pas grosses, et, pour mon compte, mon espérance fut désagréablement trompée ; au lieu de la miche entière, mon maître ne nous en donna que la moitié.

— Je ne connais pas la route, dit-il en répondant à l'interrogation de mon regard, et je ne sais pas si d'ici Troyes nous trouverons une auberge où manger. De plus, je ne connais pas non plus cette forêt. Je sais seulement que ce pays est très boisé, et que d'immenses forêts se joignent les unes aux autres : les forêts de Chaource, de Rumilly, d'Othe, d'Aumont. Peut-être sommes-nous à plusieurs lieues d'une habitation. Peut-être aussi allons-nous rester bloqués longtemps dans cette cabane. Il faut garder des provisions pour notre dîner.

C'était là des raisons que je devais comprendre, en me reportant par le souvenir à notre sortie de Toulouse, après l'emprisonnement de Vitalis ; mais elles ne touchèrent point les chiens qui, voyant serrer la miche dans le sac, alors qu'ils avaient à peine mangé, tendirent la patte à leur maître, lui grattèrent les genoux, et se livrèrent à une pantomime expressive pour faire ouvrir le sac sur lequel ils dardaient leurs yeux suppliants.

Prières et caresses furent inutiles, le sac ne s'ouvrit point.

Cependant, si frugal qu'eût été ce léger repas, il nous avait réconfortés ; nous étions à l'abri, le feu nous pénétrait d'une douce chaleur; nous pouvions attendre que la neige cessât de tomber.

Rester dans cette cabane n'avait rien de bien effrayant pour moi, d'autant mieux que je n'admettais pas que nous dussions y rester bloqués longtemps, comme Vitalis l'avait dit, pour justifier son économie; la neige ne tomberait pas toujours.

Il est vrai que rien n'annonçait qu'elle dût cesser bientôt.

Par l'ouverture de notre hutte nous apercevions les flocons descendre rapides et serrés; comme il ne ventait plus, ils tombaient droit, les uns par-dessus les autres, sans interruption.

On ne voyait pas le ciel, et la clarté, au lieu de descendre d'en haut, montait d'en bas, de la nappe éblouissante qui couvrait la terre.

Les chiens avaient pris leur parti de cette halte forcée, et s'étant tous les trois installés devant le feu, celui-ci couché en rond, celui-là étalé sur le flanc, Capi le nez dans les cendres, ils dormaient.

L'idée me vint de faire comme eux; je m'étais levé de bonne heure, et il serait plus agréable de voyager dans le pays des rêves, peut-être sur le *Cygne*, que de regarder cette neige.

Je ne sais combien je dormis de temps; quand je m'éveillai la neige avait cessé de tomber, je regardai au-dehors; la couche qui s'était entassée devant notre hutte avait considérablement augmenté; s'il fallait se remettre en route, j'en aurais plus haut que les genoux.

Quelle heure était-il?

Je ne pouvais pas le demander au maître, car, en ces derniers mois, les recettes médiocres n'avaient pas remplacé l'argent que la prison et son procès lui avaient coûté, si bien qu'à Dijon, pour acheter ma peau de mouton et différents objets pour lui et pour moi, il avait dû vendre sa montre, la grosse montre en argent sur laquelle j'avais vu Capi dire l'heure, quand Vitalis m'avait engagé dans la troupe.

C'était au jour de m'apprendre ce que je ne pouvais plus demander à notre bonne grosse montre.

Mais rien au-dehors ne pouvait me répondre : en bas, sur le sol, une ligne blanche éblouissante; au-dessus et dans l'air un brouillard sombre; au ciel une lueur confuse, avec çà et là des teintes d'un jaune sale.

Rien de tout cela n'indiquait à quelle heure de la journée nous étions.

Les oreilles n'en apprenaient pas plus que les yeux, car il

s'était établi un silence absolu que ne venait troubler ni un cri d'oiseau, ni un coup de fouet, ni un roulement de voiture; jamais nuit n'avait été plus silencieuse que cette journée.

Avec cela régnait autour de nous une immobilité complète; la neige avait arrêté tout mouvement, tout pétrifié. De temps en temps seulement, après un petit bruit étouffé, à peine perceptible, on voyait une branche de sapin se balancer lourdement; sous le poids qui la chargeait, elle s'était peu à peu inclinée vers la terre, et, quand l'inclinaison avait été trop raide, la neige avait glissé jusqu'en bas; alors la branche s'était brusquement redressée, et son feuillage d'un vert-noir tranchait sur le linceul blanc qui enveloppait les autres arbres depuis la cime jusqu'aux pieds, de sorte que, lorsqu'on regardait de loin, on croyait voir un trou sombre s'ouvrir çà et là dans ce linceul.

Comme je restais dans l'embrasure de la porte, émerveillé devant ce spectacle, je m'entendis interpeller par mon maître.

— As-tu donc envie de te remettre en route? me dit-il.

— Je ne sais pas, je n'ai aucune envie; je ferai ce que vous voudrez que nous fassions.

— Eh bien, mon avis est de rester ici, où nous avons au moins un abri et du feu.

Je pensai que nous n'avions guère de pain, mais je gardai ma réflexion pour moi.

— Je crois que la neige va reprendre bientôt, poursuivit Vitalis, il ne faut pas nous exposer sur la route sans savoir à quelle distance nous sommes des habitations. La nuit ne serait pas douce au milieu de cette neige; mieux vaut encore la passer ici, au moins nous aurons les pieds secs.

La question de nourriture mise de côté, cet arrangement n'avait rien pour me déplaire; et d'ailleurs, en nous remettant en marche tout de suite, il n'était nullement certain que nous pussions, avant le soir, trouver une auberge où dîner, tandis qu'il n'était que trop évident que nous trouverions sur la route une couche de neige qui, n'ayant pas encore été foulée, serait pénible pour la marche.

Il faudrait se serrer le ventre dans notre hutte, voilà tout.

Ce fut ce qui arriva lorsque, pour notre dîner, Vitalis nous partagea entre six ce qui restait de la miche.

Hélas! qu'il en restait peu, et comme ce peu fut vite expédié, bien que nous fissions les morceaux aussi petits que possible, afin de prolonger notre repas!

Lorsque notre pauvre dîner, si chétif et si court, fut terminé, je crus que les chiens allaient recommencer leur manège du déjeuner, car il était évident qu'ils avaient encore terriblement faim. Mais il n'en fut rien, et je vis une fois de plus combien vive était leur intelligence.

Notre maître ayant remis son couteau dans la poche de son pantalon, ce qui indiquait que notre festin était fini, Capi se leva et, après avoir fait un signe de tête à ses deux camarades, il alla flairer le sac dans lequel on plaçait habituellement la nourriture. En même temps il posa délicatement la patte sur le sac pour le palper. Ce double examen le convainquit qu'il n'y avait rien à manger. Alors il revint à sa place devant le foyer, et, après avoir fait un nouveau signe de tête à Dolce et à Zerbino, il s'étala tout de son long avec un soupir de résignation :

« Il n'y a plus rien ; il est inutile de demander. »

Ce fut exprimé aussi clairement que par la parole.

Ses camarades, comprenant ce langage, s'étalèrent comme lui devant le feu, en poussant le même soupir ; mais celui de Zerbino ne fut pas résigné, car à un grand appétit Zerbino joignait une vive gourmandise, et ce sacrifice était pour lui plus douloureux que pour tout autre.

La neige avait repris depuis longtemps et elle tombait toujours avec la même persistance ; d'heure en heure on voyait la couche qu'elle formait sur le sol monter le long des jeunes cépées, dont les tiges seules émergeaient encore de la marée blanche, qui allait bientôt les engloutir.

Mais, lorsque notre dîner fut terminé, on commença à ne plus voir que confusément ce qui se passait au-dehors de la hutte, car en cette sombre journée l'obscurité était vite venue.

La nuit n'arrêta pas la chute de la neige, qui, du ciel noir, continua à descendre en gros flocons sur la terre blanche.

Puisque nous devions coucher là, le mieux était de dormir au plus vite ; je fis donc comme les chiens, et, après m'être roulé dans ma peau de mouton, qui, exposée à la flamme, avait séché durant le jour, je m'allongeai auprès du feu, la tête sur une pierre plate qui me servait d'oreiller.

— Dors, me dit Vitalis, je te réveillerai quand je voudrai dormir à mon tour, car, bien que nous n'ayons rien à craindre des bêtes ou des gens dans cette cabane, il faut que l'un de nous veille pour entretenir le feu ; nous devons prendre nos précautions contre le froid qui peut devenir âpre, si la neige cesse.

Je ne me fis pas répéter l'invitation deux fois, et je m'endormis.

Quand mon maître me réveilla, la nuit devait être déjà avancée ; au moins je me l'imaginai. La neige ne tombait plus ; notre feu brûlait toujours.

— À ton tour maintenant, me dit Vitalis, tu n'auras qu'à mettre de temps en temps du bois dans le foyer ; tu vois que je t'ai fait ta provision.

En effet, un amas de fagots était entassé à portée de la main. Mon maître, qui avait le sommeil beaucoup plus léger que moi, n'avait pas voulu que je l'éveillasse en allant tirer un morceau de bois à notre muraille, chaque fois que j'en aurais besoin, et il m'avait préparé ce tas, dans lequel il n'y avait qu'à prendre sans bruit.

C'était là sans doute une sage précaution ; mais elle n'eut pas, hélas ! les suites que Vitalis attendait.

Me voyant éveillé et prêt à prendre ma faction, il s'était allongé à son tour devant le feu, ayant Joli-Cœur contre lui, roulé dans une couverture, et bientôt sa respiration, plus haute et plus régulière, m'avait dit qu'il venait de s'endormir.

Alors je m'étais levé et doucement, sur la pointe des pieds, j'avais été jusqu'à la porte, pour voir ce qui se passait au-dehors.

La neige avait tout enseveli, les herbes, les buissons, les cépées, les arbres ; aussi loin que la vue pouvait s'étendre, ce n'était qu'une nappe inégale, mais uniformément blanche. Le ciel était parsemé d'étoiles scintillantes ; mais, si vive que fût leur clarté, c'était de la neige que montait la pâle lumière qui éclairait le paysage. Le froid avait repris et il devait geler au-dehors, car l'air qui entrait dans notre cabane était glacé. Dans le silence lugubre de la nuit, on entendait parfois des craquements qui indiquaient que la surface de la neige se congelait.

Nous avions été vraiment bien heureux de rencontrer cette cabane : que serions-nous devenus en pleine forêt, sous la neige et par ce froid ?

Si peu de bruit que j'eusse fait en marchant, j'avais éveillé les chiens, et Zerbino s'était levé pour venir avec moi à la porte. Comme il ne regardait pas avec des yeux pareils aux miens les splendeurs de cette nuit neigeuse, il s'ennuya bien vite et voulut sortir.

De la main je lui donnai l'ordre de rentrer ; quelle idée d'aller dehors par ce froid ; n'était-il pas meilleur de rester devant le feu que d'aller vagabonder ? Il obéit, mais il resta le nez tourné vers la porte, en chien obstiné qui n'abandonne pas son idée.

Je demeurai encore quelques instants à regarder la neige, car, bien que ce spectacle me remplît le cœur d'une vague tristesse, je trouvais une sorte de plaisir à le contempler; il me donnait envie de pleurer, et, quoiqu'il me fût facile de ne plus le voir, puisque je n'avais qu'à fermer les yeux ou à revenir à ma place, je ne bougeais pas.

Enfin je me rapprochai du feu, et, l'ayant chargé de trois ou quatre morceaux de bois croisés les uns par-dessus les autres, je crus que je pouvais m'asseoir sans danger sur la pierre qui m'avait servi d'oreiller.

Mon maître dormait tranquillement; les chiens et Joli-Cœur dormaient aussi, et du foyer avivé s'élevaient de belles flammes qui montaient en tourbillons jusqu'au toit, en jetant des étincelles pétillantes qui, seules, troublaient le silence.

Pendant assez longtemps je m'amusai à regarder ces étincelles; mais peu à peu la lassitude me prit et m'engourdit sans que j'en eusse conscience.

Si j'avais eu à m'occuper de ma provision de bois, je me serais levé, et, en marchant autour de la cabane, je me serais tenu éveillé; mais, en restant assis, n'ayant d'autre mouvement à faire que d'étendre la main pour mettre des branches au feu, je me laissai aller à la somnolence qui me gagnait, et, tout en me croyant sûr de me tenir éveillé, je me rendormis.

Tout à coup je fus réveillé en sursaut par un aboiement furieux.

Il faisait nuit; j'avais sans doute dormi longtemps, et le feu s'était éteint, ou tout au moins il ne donnait plus de flammes qui éclairassent la hutte.

Les aboiements continuaient : c'était la voix de Capi; mais, chose étrange, Zerbino, pas plus que Dolce, ne répondaient à leur camarade.

— Eh bien, quoi? s'écria Vitalis se réveillant aussi, que se passe-t-il?

— Je ne sais pas.

— Tu t'es endormi, et le feu s'éteint.

Capi s'était élancé vers la porte, mais n'était point sorti, et c'était de la porte qu'il aboyait.

La question que mon maître m'avait adressée, je me la posai : que se passait-il?

Aux aboiements de Capi répondirent deux ou trois hurlements plaintifs dans lesquels je reconnus la voix de Dolce. Ces hurlements venaient de derrière notre hutte, et à une assez courte distance.

J'allais sortir ; mon maître m'arrêta en me posant la main sur l'épaule.

— Mets d'abord du bois sur le feu, me commanda-t-il.

Et, pendant que j'obéissais, il prit dans le foyer un tison sur lequel il souffla pour aviver la pointe carbonisée.

Puis, au lieu de rejeter ce tison dans le foyer, lorsqu'il fut rouge, il le garda à la main.

— Allons voir, dit-il, et marche derrière moi ; en avant, Capi !

Au moment où nous allions sortir, un formidable hurlement éclata dans le silence, et Capi se rejeta dans nos jambes, effrayé.

— Ce sont des loups ; où sont Zerbino et Dolce ?

À cela je ne pouvais répondre. Sans doute les deux chiens étaient sortis pendant mon sommeil, Zerbino réalisant le caprice qu'il avait manifesté et que j'avais contrarié, Dolce suivant son camarade.

Les loups les avaient-ils emportés ? Il me semblait que l'accent de mon maître, lorsqu'il avait demandé où ils étaient, avait trahi cette crainte.

— Prends un tison, me dit-il, et allons à leur secours.

J'avais entendu raconter dans mon village d'effrayantes histoires de loups ; cependant je n'hésitai pas ; je m'armai d'un tison et suivis mon maître. Mais, lorsque nous fûmes dans la clairière, nous n'aperçûmes ni chiens, ni loups. On voyait seulement sur la neige les empreintes creusées par les deux chiens.

Nous suivîmes ces empreintes ; elles tournaient autour de la hutte ; puis, à une certaine distance, se montrait dans l'obscurité un espace où la neige avait été foulée comme si des animaux s'étaient roulés dedans.

— Cherche, cherche, Capi, disait mon maître, et en même temps il sifflait pour appeler Zerbino et Dolce.

Mais aucun aboiement ne lui répondait, aucun bruit ne troublait le silence lugubre de la forêt, et Capi, au lieu de chercher comme on le lui commandait, restait dans nos jambes, donnant des signes manifestes d'inquiétude et d'effroi, lui qui ordinairement était aussi obéissant que brave.

La réverbération de la neige ne donnait pas une clarté suffisante pour nous reconnaître dans l'obscurité et suivre les empreintes ; à une courte distance, les yeux éblouis se perdaient dans l'ombre confuse.

De nouveau, Vitalis siffla, et d'une voix forte il appela Zerbino et Dolce.

Nous écoutâmes ; le silence continua ; j'eus le cœur serré.

Pauvre Zerbino ! Pauvre Dolce !

Vitalis précisa mes craintes.

— Les loups les ont emportés, dit-il ; pourquoi les as-tu laissés sortir ?

Ah ! oui, pourquoi ? Je n'avais pas, hélas ! de réponse à donner.

— Il faut les chercher, dis-je.

Et je passai devant ; mais Vitalis m'arrêta.

— Et où vas-tu les chercher ? dit-il.

— Je ne sais pas, partout.

— Comment nous guider au milieu de l'obscurité, et dans cette neige ?

Et, de vrai, ce n'était pas chose facile ; la neige nous montait jusqu'à mi-jambe, et ce n'étaient pas nos deux tisons qui pouvaient éclairer les ténèbres.

— S'ils n'ont pas répondu à mon appel, c'est qu'ils sont... bien loin, dit-il ; et puis, il ne faut pas nous exposer à ce que les loups nous attaquent nous-mêmes ; nous n'avons rien pour nous défendre.

C'est terrible d'abandonner ainsi ces deux pauvres chiens, ces deux camarades, ces deux amis, pour moi particulièrement, puisque je me sentais responsable de leur faute ; si je n'avais pas dormi, ils ne seraient pas sortis.

Mon maître s'était dirigé vers la hutte, et je l'avais suivi, regardant derrière moi à chaque pas et m'arrêtant pour écouter ; mais je n'avais rien vu que la neige, je n'avais rien entendu que les craquements de la neige.

Dans la hutte, une surprise nouvelle nous attendait ; en notre absence, les branches que j'avais entassées sur le feu s'étaient allumées, elles flambaient, jetant leurs lueurs dans les coins les plus sombres.

Je ne vis point Joli-Cœur.

Sa couverture était restée devant le feu, mais elle était plate et le singe ne se trouvait pas dessous.

Je l'appelai ; Vitalis l'appela à son tour ; il ne se montra pas.

Qu'était-il devenu ?

Vitalis me dit qu'en s'éveillant il l'avait senti près de lui, c'était donc depuis que nous étions sortis qu'il avait disparu ?

Avait-il voulu nous suivre ?

Nous prîmes une poignée de branches enflammées, et nous sortîmes, penchés en avant, nos branches inclinées sur la neige, cherchant les traces de Joli-Cœur.

Nous n'en trouvâmes point ; il est vrai que le passage des

chiens et nos piétinements avaient brouillé les empreintes, mais pas assez, cependant, pour qu'on ne pût pas reconnaître les pieds du singe.

Il n'était donc pas sorti.

Nous rentrâmes dans la cabane pour voir s'il ne s'était pas blotti dans quelque fagot.

Notre recherche dura longtemps; dix fois nous passâmes à la même place, dans les mêmes coins; je montai sur les épaules de Vitalis pour explorer les branches qui formaient notre toit; tout fut inutile.

De temps en temps nous nous arrêtions pour l'appeler; rien, toujours rien.

Vitalis paraissait exaspéré, tandis que moi j'étais sincèrement désolé.

Pauvre Joli-Cœur!

Comme je demandais à mon maître s'il pensait que les loups avaient pu aussi l'emporter:

— Non, me dit-il, les loups n'auraient pas osé entrer dans la cabane éclairée; je crois qu'ils auront sauté sur Zerbino et sur Dolce qui étaient sortis, mais ils n'ont pas pénétré ici. Il est probable que Joli-Cœur, épouvanté, se sera caché quelque part pendant que nous étions dehors; et c'est là ce qui m'inquiète pour lui, car, par ce temps abominable, il va gagner froid, et pour lui le froid serait mortel.

— Allons, cherchons encore.

Et de nouveau nous recommençâmes nos recherches; mais elles ne furent pas plus heureuses que la première fois.

— Il faut attendre le jour, dit Vitalis.

— Quand viendra-t-il?

— Dans deux ou trois heures, je pense.

Et il s'assit devant le feu, la tête entre ses deux mains.

Je n'osai pas le troubler. Je restai immobile près de lui, ne faisant un mouvement que pour mettre des branches sur le feu. De temps en temps il se levait pour aller jusqu'à la porte; alors il regardait le ciel et se penchait pour écouter; puis il revenait prendre sa place. Il me semblait que j'aurais mieux aimé qu'il me grondât, plutôt que de le voir ainsi morne et accablé.

Les trois heures dont il avait parlé s'écoulèrent avec une lenteur exaspérante; c'était à croire que cette nuit ne finirait jamais.

Cependant les étoiles pâlirent et le ciel blanchit; c'était le matin, bientôt il ferait jour. Mais avec le jour naissant le froid augmenta; l'air qui entrait par la porte était glacé.

Si nous retrouvions Joli-Cœur, serait-il encore vivant ?

Mais quelle espérance raisonnable de le retrouver pouvions-nous avoir ?

Qui pouvait savoir si le jour n'allait pas nous ramener la neige ? Alors comment le chercher ?

Heureusement il ne la ramena pas ; le ciel, au lieu de se couvrir comme la veille, s'emplit d'une lueur rosée qui présageait le beau temps.

Aussitôt que la clarté froide du matin eut donné aux buissons et aux arbres leurs formes réelles, nous sortîmes. Vitalis s'était armé d'un fort bâton, et j'en avais pris un pareillement.

Capi ne paraissait plus être sous l'impression de frayeur qui l'avait paralysé pendant la nuit ; les yeux sur ceux de son maître, il n'attendait qu'un signe pour s'élancer en avant.

Comme nous cherchions sur la terre les empreintes de Joli-Cœur, Capi leva la tête et se mit à aboyer joyeusement ; cela signifiait que c'était en l'air qu'il fallait chercher et non à terre.

En effet, nous vîmes que la neige qui couvrait notre cabane avait été foulée çà et là, jusqu'à une grosse branche penchée sur notre toit.

Nous suivîmes des yeux cette branche, qui appartenait à un gros chêne, et, tout au haut de l'arbre, blottie dans une fourche, nous aperçûmes une petite forme de couleur sombre.

C'était Joli-Cœur, et ce qui s'était passé n'était pas difficile à deviner : effrayé par les hurlements des chiens et des loups, Joli-Cœur, au lieu de rester près du feu, s'était élancé sur le toit de notre hutte, quand nous étions sortis, et de là il avait grimpé au haut du chêne, où, se trouvant en sûreté, il était resté blotti, sans répondre à nos appels. La pauvre petite bête si frileuse devait être glacée.

Mon maître l'appela doucement, mais il ne bougea pas plus que s'il était mort.

Pendant plusieurs minutes, Vitalis répéta ses appels ; Joli-Cœur ne donna pas signe de vie.

J'avais à racheter ma négligence de la nuit.

— Si vous voulez, dis-je, je vais l'aller chercher.

— Tu vas te casser le cou.

— Il n'y a pas de danger.

Le mot n'était pas très juste : il y avait danger, au contraire, surtout il y avait difficulté ; l'arbre était gros, et de plus il était couvert de neige dans les parties de son tronc et de ses branches qui avaient été exposées au vent.

Heureusement j'avais appris de bonne heure à grim-per aux arbres, et j'avais acquis dans cet art une force remarquable. Quelques petites branches avaient poussé çà et là, le long du tronc ; elles me servirent d'échelons, et, bien que je fusse aveuglé par la neige que mes mains me faisaient tomber dans les yeux, je parvins bientôt, aidé de Vitalis, à la première fourche. Arrivé là, l'ascension devenait facile ; je n'avais plus qu'à veiller à ne pas glisser sur la neige.

Tout en montant, je parlais doucement à Joli-Cœur, qui ne bougeait pas, mais qui me regardait avec ses yeux brillants.

J'allais arriver à lui et déjà j'allongeais la main pour le prendre, lorsqu'il fit un bond et s'élança sur une autre branche.

Je le suivis sur cette branche, mais les hommes, et même les gamins, sont très inférieurs aux singes pour courir dans les arbres. Aussi est-il bien probable que je n'aurais jamais pu atteindre Joli-Cœur, si la neige n'avait pas couvert les branches ; mais, comme cette neige lui mouillait les mains et les pieds, il fut bientôt fatigué de cette poursuite. Alors, dégringolant de branche en branche, il sauta d'un bond sur les épaules de son maître et se cacha sous la veste de celui-ci.

C'était beaucoup d'avoir retrouvé Joli-Cœur, mais ce n'était pas tout ; il fallait maintenant chercher les chiens.

Nous arrivâmes en quelques pas à l'endroit où nous étions déjà venus dans la nuit, et où nous avions trouvé la neige piétinée.

Maintenant qu'il faisait jour, il nous fut facile de deviner ce qui s'était passé ; la neige gardait imprimée en creux l'histoire de la mort des chiens.

En sortant de la cabane l'un derrière l'autre, ils avaient longé les fagots, et nous suivions distinctement leurs traces pendant une vingtaine de mètres. Puis ces traces disparaissaient dans la neige bouleversée ; alors on voyait d'autres empreintes : d'un côté celles qui montraient par où les loups, en quelques bonds allongés, avaient sauté sur les chiens ; et de l'autre, celles qui disaient par où ils les avaient emportés après les avoir boulés. De traces des chiens il n'en existait plus, à l'exception d'une traînée rouge qui çà et là ensanglantait la neige.

Il n'y avait plus maintenant à poursuivre nos recherches plus loin ; les deux pauvres chiens avaient été égorgés là et emportés pour être dévorés à loisir dans quelque hallier épineux. D'ailleurs nous devions nous occuper au plus vite de réchauffer Joli-Cœur.

Nous rentrâmes dans la cabane et, tandis que Vitalis lui présentait les pieds et les mains au feu comme on fait pour les petits enfants, je chauffai bien sa couverture, et nous l'enveloppâmes dedans.

Mais ce n'était pas seulement une couverture qu'il fallait, c'était encore un bon lit bassiné, c'était surtout une boisson chaude, et nous n'avions ni l'un ni l'autre ; heureux encore d'avoir un feu.

Nous nous étions assis, mon maître et moi, autour du foyer, sans rien dire, et nous restions là, immobiles, regardant le feu brûler.

Mais il n'était pas besoin de paroles, il n'était pas besoin de regard pour exprimer ce que nous ressentions.

— Pauvre Zerbino, pauvre Dolce, pauvres amis !

C'étaient les paroles que tous deux nous murmurions chacun de notre côté, ou tout au moins les pensées de nos cœurs.

Ils avaient été nos camarades, nos compagnons de bonne et mauvaise fortune, et pour moi, pendant mes jours de détresse et de solitude, mes amis, presque mes enfants.

Et j'étais coupable de leur mort.

Car je ne pouvais m'innocenter : si j'avais fait bonne garde comme je le devais, si je ne m'étais pas endormi, ils ne seraient pas sortis, et les loups ne seraient pas venus nous attaquer dans notre cabane, ils auraient été retenus à distance, effrayés par notre feu.

J'aurais voulu que Vitalis me grondât ; j'aurais presque demandé qu'il me battît.

Mais il ne me disait rien, il ne me regardait même presque pas ; il restait la tête penchée au-dessus du foyer ; sans doute il songeait à ce que nous allions devenir sans les chiens. Comment donner nos représentations sans eux ? Comment vivre ?

XV

Monsieur Joli-Cœur

Les pronostics du jour levant s'étaient réalisés ; le soleil brillait dans un ciel sans nuages et ses pâles rayons étaient réfléchis par la neige immaculée ; la forêt, triste et livide la veille, était maintenant éblouissante d'un éclat qui aveuglait les yeux.

De temps en temps, Vitalis passait la main sous la couverture pour tâter Joli-Cœur ; mais celui-ci ne se réchauffait pas, et, lorsque je me penchais sur lui, je l'entendais grelotter.

Il devint bientôt évident que nous ne pourrions pas réchauffer ainsi son sang glacé dans ses veines.

— Il faut gagner un village, dit Vitalis en se levant, ou Joli-Cœur va mourir ici ; heureux nous serons, s'il ne meurt pas en route. Partons.

La couverture bien chauffée, Joli-Cœur fut enveloppé dedans, et mon maître le plaça sous sa veste contre sa poitrine.

Nous étions prêts à partir.

— Voilà une auberge, dit Vitalis, qui nous a fait payer cher l'hospitalité qu'elle nous a vendue.

En disant cela, sa voix tremblait.

Il sortit le premier, et je marchai dans ses pas.

Il fallut appeler Capi, qui était resté sur le seuil de la hutte, le nez tourné vers l'endroit où ses camarades avaient été surpris.

Dix minutes après être arrivés sur la grande route, nous croisâmes une voiture dont le charretier nous apprit qu'avant une heure nous trouverions un village. Cela nous donna des jambes, et cependant marcher était difficile autant que pénible, au milieu de cette neige dans laquelle j'enfonçais jusqu'à mi-corps.

De temps en temps, je demandais à Vitalis comment se trouvait Joli-Cœur, et il me répondait qu'il le sentait toujours grelotter contre lui.

Enfin, au bas d'une côte, se montrèrent les toits blancs d'un gros village ; encore un effort et nous arrivions.

Nous n'avions point pour habitude de descendre dans les meilleures auberges, celles qui, par leur apparence cossue, promettaient bon gîte et bonne table ; tout au contraire nous nous arrêtions ordinairement à l'entrée des villages ou dans les faubourgs des villes, choisissant quelque pauvre maison, d'où l'on ne nous repousserait pas, et où l'on ne viderait pas notre bourse.

Mais, cette fois, il n'en fut pas ainsi : au lieu de s'arrêter à l'entrée du village, Vitalis continua jusqu'à une auberge devant laquelle se balançait une belle enseigne dorée ; par la porte de la cuisine, grande ouverte, on voyait une table chargée de viandes, et sur un large fourneau plusieurs casseroles en cuivre rouge chantaient joyeusement, lançant au plafond de petits nuages de vapeur ; de la rue, on respirait une bonne odeur de soupe grasse qui chatouillait agréablement nos estomacs affamés.

Mon maître, ayant pris ses airs « de monsieur », entra dans la cuisine, et, le chapeau sur la tête, le cou tendu en arrière, il demanda à l'aubergiste une bonne chambre avec du feu.

Tout d'abord l'aubergiste, qui était un personnage de belle prestance, avait dédaigné de nous regarder ; mais les grands airs de mon maître lui imposèrent, et une fille de service reçut l'ordre de nous conduire.

— Vite, couche-toi, me dit Vitalis pendant que la servante allumait le feu.

Je restai un moment étonné : pourquoi me coucher ? j'aimais bien mieux me mettre à table qu'au lit.

— Allons, vite ! répéta Vitalis.

Et je n'eus qu'à obéir.

Il y avait un édredon sur le lit, Vitalis me l'appliqua jusqu'au menton.

— Tâche d'avoir chaud, me dit-il ; plus tu auras chaud, mieux cela vaudra.

Il me semblait que Joli-Cœur avait beaucoup plus que moi besoin de chaleur, car je n'avais nullement froid.

Pendant que je restais immobile sous l'édredon, pour tâcher d'avoir chaud, Vitalis, au grand étonnement de la servante, tournait et retournait le pauvre Joli-Cœur, comme s'il voulait le faire rôtir.

— As-tu chaud ? me demanda Vitalis après quelques instants.
— J'étouffe.
— C'est justement ce qu'il faut.

Et, venant à moi vivement, il mit Joli-Cœur dans mon lit, en me recommandant de le tenir bien serré contre ma poitrine.

La pauvre petite bête, qui était ordinairement si rétive lorsqu'on lui imposait quelque chose qui lui déplaisait, semblait résignée à tout. Elle se tenait collée contre moi, sans faire un mouvement ; elle n'avait plus froid, son corps était brûlant.

Mon maître était descendu à la cuisine ; bientôt il remonta portant un bol de vin chaud et sucré.

Il voulut faire boire quelques cuillerées de ce breuvage à Joli-Cœur, mais celui-ci ne put pas desserrer les dents.

Avec ses yeux brillants il nous regardait tristement, comme pour nous prier de ne pas le tourmenter.

En même temps il sortait un de ses bras du lit et nous le tendait.

Je me demandais ce que signifiait ce geste qu'il répétait à chaque instant, quand Vitalis me l'expliqua.

Avant que je fusse entré dans la troupe, Joli-Cœur avait eu une fluxion de poitrine, et on l'avait saigné au bras ; en ce moment, se sentant de nouveau malade, il nous tendait le bras pour qu'on le saignât encore et le guérît comme on l'avait guéri la première fois.

N'était-ce pas touchant ?

Non seulement Vitalis fut touché, mais encore il fut inquiété.

Il était évident que le pauvre Joli-Cœur était malade, et même il fallait qu'il se sentît bien malade pour refuser le vin sucré qu'il aimait tant.

— Bois le vin, dit Vitalis, et reste au lit, je vais aller chercher un médecin.

Il faut avouer que moi aussi j'aimais le vin sucré, et de plus j'avais une terrible faim ; je ne me fis donc pas donner cet ordre deux fois, et après avoir vidé le bol, je me replaçai sous l'édredon, où, la chaleur du vin aidant, je faillis étouffer.

Notre maître ne fut pas longtemps sorti ; bientôt il revint amenant avec lui un monsieur à lunettes d'or – le médecin.

Craignant que ce puissant personnage ne voulût pas se déranger pour un singe, Vitalis n'avait pas dit pour quel malade il l'appelait ; aussi, me voyant dans le lit, rouge comme une pivoine qui va ouvrir, le médecin vint à moi et, m'ayant posé la main sur le front :

— Congestion, dit-il.

Et il secoua la tête d'un air qui n'annonçait rien de bon.

Il était temps de le détromper, ou bien il allait peut-être me saigner.

— Ce n'est pas moi qui suis malade, dis-je.

— Comment, pas malade ? Cet enfant délire.

Sans répondre, je soulevai un peu la couverture, et, montrant Joli-Cœur qui avait posé son petit bras autour de mon cou :

— C'est lui qui est malade, dis-je.

Le médecin avait reculé de deux pas en se tournant vers Vitalis.

— Un singe ! criait-il, comment, c'est pour un singe que vous m'avez dérangé, et par un temps pareil !

Je crus qu'il allait sortir indigné.

Mais c'était un habile homme que notre maître et qui ne perdait pas facilement la tête. Poliment et avec ses grands airs il arrêta le médecin. Puis il lui expliqua la situation : comment nous avions été surpris par la neige, et comment, par la peur des loups, Joli-Cœur s'était sauvé sur un chêne où le froid l'avait glacé.

— Sans doute le malade n'était qu'un singe ; mais quel singe de génie ! et de plus un camarade, un ami pour nous ! Comment confier un comédien aussi remarquable aux soins d'un simple vétérinaire ! Tout le monde sait que les vétérinaires de village ne sont que des ânes. Tandis que tout le monde sait aussi que les médecins sont tous, à des degrés divers, des hommes de science ; si bien que, dans le moindre village, on est certain de trouver le savoir et la générosité en allant sonner à la porte du médecin. Enfin, bien que le singe ne soit qu'un animal, selon les naturalistes, il se rapproche tellement de l'homme que ses maladies sont celles de celui-ci. N'est-il pas intéressant, au point de vue de la science et de l'art, d'étudier par où ces maladies se ressemblent ou ne se ressemblent pas ?

Ce sont d'adroits flatteurs que les Italiens ; le médecin abandonna bientôt la porte pour se rapprocher du lit.

Pendant que notre maître parlait, Joli-Cœur, qui avait sans doute deviné que ce personnage à lunettes était un médecin, avait plus de dix fois sorti son petit bras, pour l'offrir à la saignée.

— Voyez comme ce singe est intelligent ; il sait que vous êtes médecin, et il vous tend le bras pour que vous tâtiez son pouls.

Cela acheva de décider le médecin.

— Au fait, dit-il, le cas est peut-être curieux.

Il était, hélas ! fort triste pour nous, et bien inquiétant : le pauvre M. Joli-Cœur était menacé d'une fluxion de poitrine.

Ce petit bras qu'il avait tendu si souvent fut pris par le médecin, et la lancette s'enfonça dans sa veine, sans qu'il poussât le plus petit gémissement. Il savait que cela devait le guérir.

Puis après la saignée vinrent les sinapismes, les cataplasmes, les potions et les tisanes. Bien entendu, je n'étais pas resté dans le lit ; j'étais devenu garde-malade sous la direction de Vitalis.

Le pauvre Joli-Cœur aimait mes soins et il me récompensait par un doux sourire ; son regard était devenu vraiment humain.

Lui, naguère si vif, si pétulant, si contrariant, toujours en mouvement pour nous jouer quelque mauvais tour, était maintenant là d'une tranquillité et d'une docilité exemplaires.

Il semblait qu'il avait besoin qu'on lui témoignât de l'amitié, demandant même celle de Capi qui tant de fois avait été sa victime.

Comme un enfant gâté, il voulait nous avoir tous auprès de lui, et, lorsque l'un de nous sortait, il se fâchait.

Sa maladie suivait la marche de toutes les fluxions de poitrine, c'est-à-dire que la toux s'était bientôt établie, le fatiguant beaucoup par les secousses qu'elle imprimait à son pauvre petit corps.

J'avais cinq sous pour toute fortune, je les employai à acheter du sucre d'orge pour Joli-Cœur.

Malheureusement, j'aggravai son mal au lieu de le soulager.

Avec l'attention qu'il apportait à tout, il ne lui fallut pas longtemps pour observer que je lui donnais un morceau de sucre d'orge toutes les fois qu'il toussait. Alors il s'empressa de profiter de cette observation, et il se mit à tousser à chaque instant, afin d'avoir plus souvent le remède qu'il aimait tant, si bien que ce remède, au lieu de le guérir, le rendit plus malade.

Quand je m'aperçus de sa ruse, je supprimai le sucre d'orge, mais il ne se découragea pas : il commençait par m'implorer de ses yeux suppliants ; puis, quand il voyait que ses prières étaient inutiles, il s'asseyait sur son séant et, courbé en deux, une main posée sur son ventre, il toussait de toutes ses forces, sa face se colorait, les veines de son front se distendaient, les larmes coulaient de ses yeux, et il finissait par suffoquer, non plus en jouant la comédie, mais pour tout de bon.

Mon maître ne m'avait jamais fait part de ses affaires, et c'était d'une façon incidente que j'avais appris qu'il avait dû vendre sa montre pour m'acheter ma peau de mouton, mais, dans les circonstances difficiles que nous traversions, il crut devoir s'écarter de cette règle.

Un matin, en revenant de déjeuner, tandis que j'étais resté auprès de Joli-Cœur que nous ne laissions pas seul, il m'apprit que l'aubergiste avait demandé le paiement de ce que nous devions, si bien qu'après ce paiement il ne lui restait plus que cinquante sous.

Que faire ?

Naturellement je ne trouvai pas de réponse à cette occasion.

Pour lui, il ne voyait qu'un moyen de sortir d'embarras, c'était de donner une représentation le soir même.

Une représentation sans Zerbino, sans Dolce, sans Joli-Cœur ! cela me paraissait impossible.

Mais nous n'étions pas dans une position à nous arrêter découragés devant une impossibilité. Il fallait à tout prix soigner Joli-Cœur et le sauver ; le médecin, les médicaments, le feu, la chambre, nous obligeaient à faire une recette immédiate d'au moins quarante francs pour payer l'aubergiste qui, voyant la couleur de notre argent, nous ouvrirait un nouveau crédit.

Quarante francs dans ce village, par ce froid, et avec les ressources dont nous disposions, quel tour de force !

Cependant mon maître, sans s'attarder aux réflexions, s'occupa activement à le réaliser.

Tandis que je gardais notre malade, il trouva une salle de spectacle dans les halles, car une représentation en plein air était impossible par le froid qu'il faisait. Il composa et colla des affiches ; il arrangea un théâtre avec quelques planches, et bravement il dépensa ses cinquante sous à acheter des chandelles qu'il coupa par le milieu, afin de doubler son éclairage.

Par la fenêtre de la chambre, je le voyais aller et venir dans la neige, passer et repasser devant notre auberge, et ce n'était pas sans angoisse que je me demandais quel serait le programme de cette représentation. Je fus bientôt fixé à ce sujet, car le tambour du village, coiffé d'un képi rouge, s'arrêta devant l'auberge et, après un magnifique roulement, donna lecture de ce programme.

Ce qu'il était, on l'imaginera facilement lorsqu'on saura que Vitalis avait prodigué les promesses les plus extravagantes : il était question « d'un artiste célèbre dans l'univers entier » – c'était Capi – et « d'un jeune chanteur qui était un prodige » –, le prodige, c'était moi.

Mais la partie la plus intéressante de ce boniment était celle qui disait qu'on ne fixait pas le prix des places et qu'on s'en rapportait à la générosité des spectateurs, qui ne paieraient qu'après avoir vu, entendu et applaudi.

Cela me parut bien hardi, car nous applaudirait-on ? Capi méritait vraiment d'être célèbre. Mais moi je n'avais pas tout à fait la conviction d'être un prodige.

En entendant le tambour, Capi avait aboyé joyeusement, et Joli-Cœur s'était à demi soulevé, quoiqu'il fût très mal en ce moment ; tous deux, je le crois bien, avaient deviné qu'il s'agissait de notre représentation.

Cette idée, qui s'était présentée à mon esprit, me fut bientôt confirmée par la pantomime de Joli-Cœur : il voulut se lever, et je dus le retenir de force ; alors il me demanda son costume de général anglais, l'habit et le pantalon rouge galonnés d'or, le chapeau à claque avec son plumet.

Il joignait les mains, il se mettait à genoux pour mieux me supplier.

Quand il vit qu'il n'obtenait rien de moi par la prière, il essaya de la colère, puis enfin des larmes.

Il était certain que nous aurions bien de la peine à le décider à renoncer à son idée de reprendre son rôle le soir, et je pensai que dans ces conditions le mieux était de lui cacher notre départ.

Malheureusement, quand Vitalis, qui ignorait ce qui s'était passé en son absence, rentra, sa première parole fut pour me dire de préparer ma harpe et tous les accessoires nécessaires à notre représentation.

À ces mots bien connus de lui, Joli-Cœur recommença ses supplications, les adressant cette fois à son maître ; il eût pu parler qu'il n'eût assurément pas mieux exprimé par le langage articulé ses désirs qu'il ne le faisait par les sons différents qu'il poussait, par les contractions de sa figure et par la mimique de tout son corps ; c'étaient de vraies larmes qui mouillaient ses joues, et c'étaient de vrais baisers ceux qu'il appliquait sur les mains de Vitalis.

— Tu veux jouer ? dit celui-ci.

— Oui, oui, cria toute la personne de Joli-Cœur.

— Mais tu es malade, pauvre petit Joli-Cœur !

— Plus malade ! cria-t-il non moins expressivement.

C'était vraiment chose touchante de voir l'ardeur que ce pauvre petit malade, qui n'avait plus que le souffle, mettait dans ses supplications, et les mines ainsi que les poses qu'il prenait pour nous décider; mais lui accorder ce qu'il demandait, c'eût été le condamner à une mort certaine.

L'heure était venue de nous rendre aux halles; j'arrangeai un bon feu dans la cheminée avec de grosses bûches qui devaient durer longtemps; j'enveloppai bien dans sa couverture le pauvre petit Joli-Cœur qui pleurait à chaudes larmes, et qui m'embrassait tant qu'il pouvait, puis nous partîmes.

En cheminant dans la neige, mon maître m'expliqua ce qu'il attendait de moi.

Il ne pouvait pas être question de nos pièces ordinaires, puisque nos principaux comédiens manquaient, mais nous devions, Capi et moi, donner tout ce que nous avions de zèle et de talent. Il s'agissait de faire une recette de quarante francs.

Quarante francs! c'était bien là le terrible.

Tout avait été préparé par Vitalis, et il ne s'agissait plus que d'allumer les chandelles; mais c'était un luxe que nous ne devions nous permettre que quand la salle serait à peu près garnie, car il fallait que notre illumination ne finît pas avant la représentation.

Pendant que nous prenions possession de notre théâtre, le tambour parcourait une dernière fois les rues du village, et nous entendions les roulements de sa caisse qui s'éloignaient ou se rapprochaient selon le caprice des rues.

Après avoir terminé la toilette de Capi et la mienne, j'allai me poster derrière un pilier pour voir l'arrivée de la compagnie.

Bientôt les roulements du tambour se rapprochèrent et j'entendis dans la rue une vague rumeur.

Elle était produite par les voix d'une vingtaine de gamins qui suivaient le tambour en marquant le pas.

Sans suspendre sa batterie, le tambour vint se placer entre deux lampions allumés à l'entrée de notre théâtre, et le public n'eut plus qu'à occuper ses places en attendant que le spectacle commençât.

Hélas! qu'il était lent à venir, et cependant, à la porte, le tambour continuait ses ra et ses fla avec une joyeuse énergie; tous les gamins du village étaient, je pense, installés; mais ce n'étaient pas les gamins qui nous feraient une recette de quarante francs; il nous fallait des gens importants à la bourse bien garnie et à la main facile à s'ouvrir. Enfin mon maître décida que nous devions commencer, bien que la salle fût loin d'être remplie; mais nous ne pouvions attendre davantage, poussés que nous étions par la terrible question des chandelles.

Ce fut à moi de paraître le premier sur le théâtre, et en m'accompagnant de ma harpe je chantai deux chansonnettes. Pour être sincère, je dois déclarer que les applaudissements que je recueillis furent assez rares.

Je n'ai jamais eu un bien grand amour-propre de comédien; mais, dans cette circonstance, la froideur du public me désola. Assurément, si je ne lui plaisais pas, il n'ouvrirait pas sa bourse. Ce n'était pas pour la gloire que je chantais, c'était pour le pauvre Joli-Cœur. Ah! comme j'aurais voulu le toucher, ce public, l'enthousiasmer, lui faire perdre la tête; mais, autant que je pouvais voir dans cette halle pleine d'ombres bizarres, il me semblait que je l'intéressais fort peu et qu'il ne m'acceptait pas comme un prodige.

Capi fut plus heureux; on l'applaudit à plusieurs reprises, et à pleines mains.

La représentation continua; grâce à Capi, elle se termina au milieu des bravos; non seulement on claquait des mains, mais encore on trépignait des pieds.

Le moment décisif était arrivé. Pendant que, sur la scène, accompagné par Vitalis, je dansais un pas espagnol, Capi, la sébile à la gueule, parcourait tous les rangs de l'assemblée. Ramasserait-il les quarante francs? c'était la question qui me serrait le cœur, tandis que je souriais au public avec mes mines les plus agréables.

J'étais à bout de souffle et je dansais toujours, car je ne devais m'arrêter que lorsque Capi serait revenu; il ne se pressait point, et, quand on ne lui donnait pas, il frappait des petits coups de patte sur la poche qui ne voulait pas s'ouvrir.

Enfin je le vis apparaître, et j'allais m'arrêter, quand Vitalis me fit signe de continuer. Je continuai et, me rapprochant de Capi, je vis que la sébile n'était pas pleine, il s'en fallait de beaucoup.

À ce moment Vitalis, qui, lui aussi, avait jugé la recette, se leva :

— Je crois pouvoir dire, sans nous flatter, que nous avons exécuté notre programme; cependant, comme nos chandelles vivent encore, je vais, si la société le désire, lui chanter quelques airs; Capi fera une nouvelle tournée, et les personnes qui n'avaient pas pu trouver l'ouverture de leur poche, à son premier passage, seront peut-être plus adroites cette fois; je les avertis de se préparer à l'avance.

Bien que Vitalis eût été mon professeur, je ne l'avais jamais entendu vraiment chanter, ou tout au moins comme il chanta ce soir-là.

Il choisit deux airs que tout le monde connaît, mais que, moi, je ne connaissais pas alors, la romance de *Joseph* : « À peine au sortir de l'enfance », et celle de *Richard Cœur de Lion* : « Ô Richard, ô mon roi ! »

Je n'étais pas à cette époque en état de juger si l'on chantait bien ou mal, avec art ou sans art ; mais ce que je puis dire, c'est le sentiment que sa façon de chanter provoqua en moi ; dans le coin de la scène où je m'étais retiré, je fondis en larmes.

À travers le brouillard qui obscurcissait mes yeux, je vis une jeune dame qui occupait le premier banc applaudir de toutes ses forces. Je l'avais déjà remarquée, car ce n'était point une paysanne, comme celles qui composaient le public : c'était une vraie dame, jeune, belle et que, à son manteau de fourrure, j'avais jugée être la plus riche du village ; elle avait près d'elle un enfant qui, lui aussi, avait beaucoup applaudi Capi ; son fils sans doute, car il avait une grande ressemblance avec elle.

Après la première romance, Capi avait recommencé sa quête, et j'avais vu avec surprise que la belle dame n'avait rien mis dans la sébile.

Quand mon maître eut achevé l'air de *Richard*, elle me fit un signe de main, et je m'approchai d'elle.

— Je voudrais parler à votre maître, me dit-elle.

Cela m'étonna un peu que cette belle dame voulût parler à mon maître. Elle aurait mieux fait, selon moi, de mettre son offrande dans la sébile ; cependant j'allai transmettre ce désir ainsi exprimé à Vitalis, et, pendant ce temps, Capi revint près de nous. La seconde quête avait été encore moins productive que la première.

— Que me veut cette dame ? demanda Vitalis.

— Vous parler.

— Je n'ai rien à lui dire.

— Elle n'a rien donné à Capi ; elle veut peut-être lui donner maintenant.

— Alors, c'est à Capi d'aller à elle et non à moi.

Cependant il se décida, mais en prenant Capi avec lui.

Je les suivis.

Pendant ce temps un domestique, portant une lanterne et une couverture, était venu se placer près de la dame et de l'enfant.

Vitalis s'était approché et avait salué, mais froidement.

— Pardonnez-moi de vous avoir dérangé, dit la dame, mais j'ai voulu vous féliciter.

Vitalis s'inclina sans répliquer un seul mot.

— Je suis musicienne, continua la dame, c'est vous dire combien je suis sensible à un grand talent comme le vôtre.

Un grand talent chez mon maître, chez Vitalis, le chanteur des rues, le montreur de bêtes ! je restai stupéfait.

— Il n'y a pas de talent chez un vieux bonhomme tel que moi, dit Vitalis.

— Ne croyez pas que je sois poussée par une curiosité indiscrète, dit la dame.

— Mais je serais tout prêt à satisfaire cette curiosité ; vous avez été surprise, n'est-ce pas, d'entendre chanter à peu près un montreur de chiens ?

— Émerveillée.

— C'est bien simple cependant ; je n'ai pas toujours été ce que je suis en ce moment ; autrefois, dans ma jeunesse, il y a longtemps, j'ai été... oui, j'ai été le domestique d'un grand chanteur, et par imitation, comme un perroquet, je me suis mis à répéter quelques airs que mon maître étudiait devant moi ; voilà tout.

La dame ne répondit pas, mais elle regarda assez longuement Vitalis, qui se tenait devant elle dans une attitude embarrassée.

— Au revoir, monsieur, dit-elle en appuyant sur le mot monsieur, qu'elle prononça avec une étrange intonation ; au revoir, et encore une fois laissez-moi vous remercier de l'émotion que je viens de ressentir.

Puis, se baissant vers Capi, elle mit dans la sébile une pièce d'or.

Je croyais que Vitalis allait reconduire cette dame, mais il n'en fit rien, et, quand elle se fut éloignée de quelques pas, je l'entendis murmurer à mi-voix deux ou trois jurons italiens.

— Mais elle a donné un louis à Capi, dis-je.

Je crus qu'il allait m'allonger une taloche ; cependant il arrêta sa main levée.

— Un louis, dit-il, comme s'il sortait d'un rêve, ah ! oui, c'est vrai, pauvre Joli-Cœur, je l'oubliais, allons le rejoindre.

Notre ménage fut vite fait, et nous ne tardâmes point à rentrer à l'auberge.

Je montai l'escalier le premier et j'entrai dans la chambre en courant ; le feu n'était pas éteint, mais il ne donnait plus de flamme. J'allumai vivement une chandelle et je cherchai Joli-Cœur, surpris de ne pas l'entendre.

Il était couché sur sa couverture, tout de son long, il avait revêtu son uniforme de général, et il paraissait dormir.

Je me penchai sur lui pour lui prendre doucement la main sans le réveiller. Cette main était froide.

À ce moment, Vitalis entrait dans la chambre. Je me tournai vers lui.

— Joli-Cœur est froid !

Vitalis se pencha près de moi :

— Hélas ! dit-il, il est mort. Cela devait arriver. Vois-tu, Rémi, je n'ai peut-être pas eu raison de t'enlever à Mme Milligan. C'est à croire que je suis puni comme d'une faute. Zerbino, Dolce... Aujourd'hui Joli-Cœur. Ce n'est pas la fin.

XVI

Entrée à Paris

Nous étions encore bien éloignés de Paris.

Il fallut nous mettre en route par les chemins couverts de neige et marcher du matin au soir, contre le vent du nord qui nous soufflait au visage.

Comme elles furent tristes ces longues étapes! Vitalis tenait la tête, je venais derrière lui, et Capi marchait sur mes talons.

Nous avancions ainsi à la file, une file qui n'était pas longue, sans échanger un seul mot durant des heures, le visage bleui par la bise, les pieds mouillés, l'estomac vide; et les gens que nous croisions s'arrêtaient pour nous regarder défiler.

Évidemment des idées bizarres leur passaient par l'esprit : où donc ce grand vieillard conduisait-il cet enfant et ce chien?

Le silence m'était extrêmement douloureux; j'aurais eu besoin de parler, de m'étourdir; mais Vitalis ne me répondait que par quelques mots brefs, lorsque je lui adressais la parole, et encore sans se retourner.

Heureusement Capi était plus expansif, et souvent, en marchant, je sentais une langue humide et chaude se poser sur ma main; c'était Capi qui me léchait pour me dire :

« Tu sais, je suis là, moi, Capi, moi, ton ami. »

Et alors, je le caressais doucement sans m'arrêter.

Il paraissait aussi heureux de mon témoignage d'affection que je l'étais moi-même du sien; nous nous comprenions, nous nous aimions.

Pour moi, c'était un soutien, et pour lui, j'en suis sûr, c'en était un aussi; le cœur d'un chien n'est pas moins sensible que celui d'un enfant.

Ces caresses consolaient si bien Capi, qu'elles lui auraient fait, je crois, oublier la mort de ses camarades, si la force de l'habitude n'eût repris quelquefois le dessus ; dans ces moments-là, il s'arrêtait tout à coup sur la route pour voir venir sa troupe, comme au temps où il en était le caporal, et où il devait fréquemment la passer en revue. Mais cela ne durait que quelques secondes ; la mémoire se réveillait en lui, et, se rappelant brusquement pourquoi cette troupe ne venait pas, il nous dépassait rapidement, et regardait Vitalis en le prenant à témoin qu'il n'était pas en faute ; si Dolce, si Zerbino ne venaient pas, c'était qu'ils ne devaient plus venir. Il faisait cela avec des yeux si expressifs, si parlants, si pleins d'intelligence, que nous en avions le cœur serré.

Cela n'était pas de nature à égayer notre route, et cependant nous aurions eu bien besoin de distraction, moi au moins.

Partout sur la campagne s'étalait le blanc linceul de la neige ; point de soleil au ciel, mais un jour fauve et pâle ; point de mouvement dans les champs, point de paysans au travail ; point de hennissements de chevaux, point de beuglements de bœufs, mais seulement le croassement des corneilles qui, perchées au plus haut des branches dénudées, criaient la faim sans trouver sur la terre une place où descendre pour chercher quelques vers ; dans les villages, point de maisons ouvertes, mais le silence et la solitude ; le froid est âpre, on reste au coin de l'âtre, ou bien l'on travaille dans les étables et les granges fermées.

Et nous, sur la route raboteuse ou glissante, nous allons droit devant nous, sans nous arrêter, et sans autre repos que le sommeil de la nuit dans une écurie ou dans une bergerie ; avec un morceau de pain bien mince, pour notre repas du soir, qui est à la fois notre dîner et notre souper. Quand nous avons la bonne chance d'être envoyés à la bergerie, nous nous trouvons heureux, la chaleur des moutons nous défendra contre le froid ; et puis c'est la saison où les brebis allaitent leurs agneaux, et les bergers me permettent quelquefois de boire un peu de lait de brebis. Nous ne disons pas que nous mourons presque de faim, mais Vitalis, avec son adresse ordinaire, sait insinuer que « le petit aime beaucoup le lait de brebis, parce que, dans son enfance, il a été habitué à en boire, de sorte que ça lui rappelle son pays ». Cette fable ne réussit pas toujours. Mais c'est une bonne soirée quand elle est bien accueillie. Assurément oui, j'aime beaucoup le lait de brebis, et quand j'en ai bu je me sens, le lendemain, plus dispos et plus fort.

Les kilomètres s'ajoutèrent aux kilomètres, les étapes aux étapes ; nous approchâmes de Paris, et, quand même les bornes plantées le long de la route ne m'en auraient pas averti, je m'en serais aperçu à la circulation qui était devenue plus active, et aussi à la couleur de la neige couvrant le chemin, qui était beaucoup plus sale que dans les plaines de la Champagne.

Chose étonnante, au moins pour moi, la campagne ne me parut pas plus belle, les villages ne furent pas autres que ceux que nous avions traversés quelques jours auparavant. J'avais tant de fois entendu parler des merveilles de Paris, que je m'étais naïvement figuré que ces merveilles devaient s'annoncer au loin par quelque chose d'extraordinaire. Je ne savais pas au juste ce que je devais attendre, et n'osais pas le demander, mais enfin j'attendais des prodiges : des arbres d'or, des rues bordées de palais de marbre, et dans ces rues des habitants vêtus d'habits de soie ; cela m'eût paru tout naturel.

Si attentif que je fusse à chercher les arbres d'or, je remarquai néanmoins que les gens qui nous rencontraient ne nous regardaient plus ; sans doute ils étaient trop pressés pour cela, ou bien ils étaient peut-être habitués à des spectacles autrement douloureux que celui que nous pouvions offrir.

Cela n'était guère rassurant.

Qu'allions-nous faire à Paris et surtout dans l'état de misère où nous nous trouvions ?

C'était la question que je me posais avec anxiété et qui bien souvent occupait mon esprit pendant ces longues marches.

J'aurais bien voulu interroger Vitalis ; mais je n'osais pas, tant il se montrait sombre, et, dans ses communications, bref.

Un jour enfin il daigna prendre place à côté de moi, et à la façon dont il me regarda, je sentis que j'allais apprendre ce que j'avais tant de fois désiré connaître.

C'était un matin, nous avions couché dans une ferme, à peu de distance d'un gros village, qui, disaient les plaques bleues de la route, se nommait Boissy-Saint-Léger. Nous étions partis de bonne heure, c'est-à-dire à l'aube, et, après avoir longé les murs d'un parc et traversé dans sa longueur ce village de Boissy-Saint-Léger, nous avions, du haut d'une côte, aperçu devant nous un grand nuage de vapeurs noires qui planaient au-dessus d'une ville immense, dont on ne distinguait que quelques monuments élevés.

J'ouvrais les yeux pour tâcher de me reconnaître au milieu de cette confusion de toits, de clochers, de tours, qui se perdaient dans des brumes et dans des fumées, quand Vitalis, ralentissant le pas, vint se placer près de moi.

— Voilà donc notre vie changée, me dit-il, comme s'il continuait une conversation entamée depuis longtemps déjà ; dans quatre heures nous serons à Paris.

— Ah ! c'est Paris qui s'étend là-bas ?

— Mais sans doute.

Au moment même où Vitalis me disait que c'était Paris que nous avions devant nous, un rayon de lumière se dégagea du ciel, et j'aperçus, rapide comme un éclair, un miroitement doré.

Décidément je ne m'étais pas trompé ; j'allais trouver des arbres d'or.

Vitalis continua :

— À Paris nous allons nous séparer.

Instantanément la nuit se fit, je ne vis plus les arbres d'or.

Je tournai les yeux vers Vitalis. Lui-même me regarda, et la pâleur de mon visage, le tremblement de mes lèvres, lui dirent ce qui se passait en moi.

— Te voilà inquiet, dit-il, peiné aussi, je crois bien.

— Nous séparer ! dis-je enfin après que le premier moment du saisissement fut passé.

— Pauvre petit !

Ce mot et surtout le ton dont il fut prononcé me firent monter les larmes aux yeux ; il y avait si longtemps que je n'avais entendu une parole de sympathie !

— Ah ! vous êtes bon, m'écriai-je.

— C'est toi qui es bon, un bon garçon, un brave petit cœur. Vois-tu, il y a des moments dans la vie où l'on est disposé à reconnaître ces choses-là et à se laisser attendrir. Quand tout va bien, on suit son chemin sans trop penser à ceux qui vous accompagnent, mais quand tout va mal, quand on se sent dans une mauvaise voie, surtout quand on est vieux, c'est-à-dire sans foi dans le lendemain, on a besoin de s'appuyer sur ceux qui vous entourent et on est heureux de les trouver près de soi. Que moi je m'appuie sur toi, cela te paraît étonnant, n'est-ce pas vrai ? Et pourtant cela est ainsi. Et rien que par cela que tu as les yeux humides en m'écoutant, je me sens soulagé. Car moi aussi, mon petit Rémi, j'ai de la peine.

C'est seulement plus tard, quand j'ai eu quelqu'un à aimer, que j'ai senti et éprouvé la justesse de ces paroles.

— Le malheur est, continua Vitalis, qu'il faille toujours se séparer précisément à l'heure où l'on voudrait au contraire se rapprocher.

— Mais, dis-je timidement, vous ne voulez pas m'abandonner dans Paris ?

— Non, certes ; je ne veux pas t'abandonner, crois-le bien. Que ferais-tu à Paris, tout seul, pauvre garçon ? Et puis, je n'ai pas le droit de t'abandonner, dis-toi bien cela. Le jour où je n'ai pas voulu te remettre aux soins de cette brave dame qui voulait se charger de toi et t'élever comme son fils, j'ai contracté l'obligation de t'élever moi-même de mon mieux. Par malheur, les circonstances me sont contraires. Je ne puis rien pour toi en ce moment, et voilà pourquoi je pense à nous séparer, non pour toujours, mais pour quelques mois, afin que nous puissions vivre chacun de notre côté pendant les derniers mois de la mauvaise saison. Nous allons arriver à Paris dans quelques heures. Que veux-tu que nous y fassions avec une troupe réduite au seul Capi ?

En entendant prononcer son nom, le chien vint se camper devant nous, et, ayant porté la main à son oreille pour faire le salut militaire, il la posa sur son cœur comme s'il voulait nous dire que nous pouvions compter sur son dévouement.

Dans la situation où nous nous trouvions, cela ne calma pas notre émotion.

Vitalis s'arrêta un moment pour lui passer la main sur la tête.

— Toi aussi, dit-il, tu es un brave chien ; mais on ne vit pas de bonté dans le monde ; il en faut pour le bonheur de ceux qui nous entourent, mais il faut aussi autre chose, et cela nous ne l'avons point. Que veux-tu que nous fassions avec le seul Capi ? Tu comprends bien, n'est-ce pas, que nous ne pouvons pas maintenant donner des représentations ?

— Il est vrai.

— Les gamins se moqueraient de nous, nous jetteraient des trognons de pommes, et nous ne ferions pas vingt sous de recette par jour ; veux-tu que nous vivions tous les trois avec vingt sous qui, par les journées de pluie, de neige ou de grand froid, se réduiront à rien ?

— Mais ma harpe ?

— Si j'avais deux enfants comme toi, cela irait peut-être, mais un vieux comme moi avec un enfant de ton âge, c'est une mauvaise affaire. Je ne suis pas encore assez vieux. Si j'étais plus cassé, ou bien si j'étais aveugle… Mais par malheur je suis ce que je suis, c'est-à-dire non en état d'inspirer la pitié, et à Paris, pour émouvoir la compassion des gens pressés qui vont à leurs affaires, il vaudrait peut-être mieux avoir un aspect lamentable ; encore faut-il n'avoir pas honte de faire appel à la charité publique, et cela, je ne le pourrais jamais. Il nous faut autre chose. Voici donc à quoi j'ai pensé, et ce que j'ai décidé. Je te donnerai jusqu'à la fin de l'hiver à un *padrone* qui t'enrôlera avec d'autres enfants pour jouer de la harpe.

En parlant de ma harpe, ce n'était pas à une pareille conclusion que j'avais songé.

Vitalis ne me laissa pas le temps d'interrompre.

— Pour moi, dit-il en poursuivant, je donnerai des leçons de harpe, de *piva*, de violon, aux enfants italiens qui travaillent dans les rues de Paris. Je suis connu dans Paris où je suis resté plusieurs fois, et d'où je venais quand je suis arrivé dans ton village ; je n'ai qu'à demander des leçons pour en trouver plus que je n'en puis donner. Nous vivrons, mais chacun de notre côté. Puis, en même temps que je donnerai mes leçons, je m'occuperai à instruire deux chiens pour remplacer Zerbino et Dolce. Je pousserai leur éducation, et au printemps nous pourrons nous remettre en route tous les deux, mon petit Rémi, pour ne plus nous quitter, car la fortune n'est pas toujours mauvaise à ceux qui ont le courage de lutter. C'est justement du courage que je te demande en ce moment, et aussi de la résignation. Plus tard, les choses iront mieux ; ce n'est qu'un moment à passer. Au printemps nous reprendrons notre existence libre. Je te conduirai en Allemagne, en Angleterre. Voilà que tu deviens plus grand et que ton esprit s'ouvre. Je t'apprendrai bien des choses et je ferai de toi un homme. J'ai pris cet engagement devant Mme Milligan. Je le tiendrai. C'est en vue de ces voyages que j'ai déjà commencé à t'apprendre l'anglais, le français, l'italien ; c'est déjà quelque chose pour un enfant de ton âge, sans compter que te voilà vigoureux. Tu verras, mon petit Rémi, tu verras, tout n'est pas perdu.

Cette combinaison était peut-être ce qui convenait le mieux à notre condition présente. Et quand maintenant j'y songe, je reconnais que mon maître avait fait le possible pour sortir de notre fâcheuse situation. Mais les pensées de la réflexion ne sont pas les mêmes que celles du premier mouvement.

Dans ce qu'il me disait je ne voyais que deux choses :

Notre séparation.

Et le *padrone*.

Dans nos courses à travers les villages et les villes, j'en avais rencontré plusieurs, de ces *padrones* qui mènent les enfants qu'ils ont engagés de-ci de-là, à coups de bâton.

Ils ne ressemblaient en rien à Vitalis, durs, injustes, exigeants, ivrognes, l'injure et la grossièreté à la bouche, la main toujours levée.

Je pouvais tomber sur un de ces terribles patrons.

Et puis, quand même le hasard m'en donnerait un bon, c'était encore un changement.

Après ma nourrice, Vitalis.

Après Vitalis, un autre.

Est-ce que ce serait toujours ainsi? Est-ce que je ne trouverais jamais personne à aimer pour toujours?

Peu à peu j'en étais venu à m'attacher à Vitalis comme à un père.

Je n'aurais donc jamais de père.

Jamais de famille.

Toujours seul au monde.

Toujours perdu sur cette vaste terre, où je ne pouvais me fixer nulle part!

J'aurais eu bien des choses à répondre, et les paroles me montaient du cœur aux lèvres, mais je les refoulai.

Mon maître m'avait demandé du courage et de la résignation, je voulais lui obéir et ne pas augmenter son chagrin.

Déjà, d'ailleurs, il n'était plus à mes côtés, et, comme s'il avait peur d'entendre ce qu'il prévoyait que j'allais répondre, il avait repris sa marche à quelques pas en avant.

Je le suivis, et nous ne tardâmes pas à arriver à une rivière que nous traversâmes sur un pont boueux, comme je n'en avais jamais vu; la neige, noire comme du charbon pilé, recouvrait la chaussée d'une couche mouvante dans laquelle on enfonçait jusqu'à la cheville.

Au bout de ce pont se trouvait un village aux rues étroites, puis, après ce village, la campagne recommençait, mais la campagne encombrée de maisons à l'aspect misérable.

Sur la route les voitures se suivaient et se croisaient maintenant sans interruption. Je me rapprochai de Vitalis et marchai à sa droite, tandis que Capi se tenait le nez sur nos talons.

Bientôt la campagne cessa, et nous nous trouvâmes dans une rue dont on ne voyait pas le bout; de chaque côté, au loin, des maisons, mais pauvres, sales, et bien moins belles que celles de Bordeaux, de Toulouse et de Lyon.

La neige avait été mise en tas de place en place, et, sur ces tas noirs et durs, on avait jeté des cendres, des légumes pourris, des ordures de toute sorte; l'air était chargé d'odeurs fétides, les enfants qui jouaient devant les portes avaient la mine pâle; à chaque instant passaient de lourdes voitures qu'ils évitaient avec beaucoup d'adresse et sans paraître en prendre souci.

— Où donc sommes-nous ? demandai-je à Vitalis.

— À Paris, mon garçon.

— À Paris !...

Était-ce possible, c'était là Paris !

Où donc étaient mes maisons de marbre ?

Où donc étaient mes passants vêtus d'habits de soie ?

Comme la réalité était laide et misérable !

Était-ce là ce Paris que j'avais si vivement souhaité voir ?

Hélas ! oui, et c'était là que j'allais passer l'hiver, séparé de Vitalis... et de Capi...

XVII

Un « padrone » de la rue de Lourcine

Bien que tout ce qui nous entourait me parût horrible, j'ouvris les yeux et j'oubliai presque la gravité de ma situation pour regarder autour de moi.

Plus nous avancions dans Paris, moins ce que j'apercevais répondait à mes rêveries enfantines et à mes espérances imaginatives : les ruisseaux restaient gelés ; la boue, mêlée de neige et de glaçons, était de plus en plus noire, et là où elle était liquide, elle sautait sous les roues des voitures en plaques épaisses, qui allaient se coller contre les devantures et les vitres des maisons occupées par des boutiques pauvres et malpropres.

Décidément, Paris ne valait pas Bordeaux.

Après avoir marché assez longtemps dans une large rue moins misérable que celles que nous venions de traverser, et où les boutiques devenaient plus grandes et plus belles à mesure que nous descendions, Vitalis tourna à droite, et bientôt nous nous trouvâmes dans un quartier tout à fait misérable : les maisons hautes et noires semblaient se rejoindre par le haut ; le ruisseau non gelé coulait au milieu de la rue, et, sans souci des eaux puantes qu'il roulait, une foule compacte piétinait sur le pavé gras. Jamais je n'avais vu des figures aussi pâles que celles des gens qui composaient cette foule ; jamais non plus je n'avais vu hardiesse pareille à celle des enfants qui allaient et venaient au milieu des passants. Dans des cabarets, qui étaient nombreux, il y avait des hommes et des femmes qui buvaient debout devant des comptoirs d'étain en criant très fort.

Au coin d'une maison je lus le nom de la rue de Lourcine.

Vitalis, qui paraissait savoir où il allait, écartait doucement les groupes qui gênaient son passage, et je le suivais de près.

— Prends garde de me perdre, m'avait-il dit.

Mais la recommandation était inutile, je marchais sur ses talons, et pour plus de sûreté je tenais dans ma main un des coins de sa veste.

Après avoir traversé une grande cour et un passage, nous arrivâmes dans une sorte de puits sombre et verdâtre où assurément le soleil n'avait jamais pénétré. Cela était encore plus laid et plus effrayant que tout ce que j'avais vu jusqu'alors.

— Garofoli est-il chez lui ? demanda Vitalis à un homme qui accrochait des chiffons contre la muraille, en s'éclairant d'une lanterne.

— Je ne sais pas, montez voir vous-même ; vous savez où, au haut de l'escalier, la porte en face.

— Garofoli est le *padrone* dont je t'ai parlé, me dit-il en montant l'escalier dont les marches couvertes d'une croûte de terre étaient glissantes comme si elles eussent été creusées dans une glaise humide ; c'est ici qu'il demeure.

La rue, la maison, l'escalier n'étaient pas de nature à me remonter le cœur. Que serait le maître ?

L'escalier avait quatre étages ; Vitalis, sans frapper, poussa la porte qui faisait face au palier, et nous nous trouvâmes dans une large pièce, une sorte de vaste grenier. Au milieu, un grand espace vide, et tout autour une douzaine de lits. Les murs et le plafond étaient d'une couleur indéfinissable ; autrefois ils avaient été blancs, mais la fumée, la poussière et les saletés de toute sorte avaient noirci le plâtre qui, par places, était creusé ou troué ; à côté d'une tête dessinée au charbon on avait sculpté des fleurs et des oiseaux.

— Garofoli, dit Vitalis en entrant, êtes-vous dans quelque coin ? je ne vois personne ; répondez-moi, je vous en prie ; c'est Vitalis qui vous parle.

En effet, la chambre paraissait déserte, autant qu'on en pouvait juger par la clarté d'un quinquet accroché à la muraille ; mais à la voix de mon maître une voix faible et dolente, une voix d'enfant, répondit :

— Le signor Garofoli est sorti ; il ne rentrera que dans deux heures.

En même temps celui qui avait répondu se montra : c'était un enfant d'une dizaine d'années ; il s'avança vers nous en se traînant, et je fus si vivement frappé de son aspect étrange que je le vois encore devant moi : il n'avait pour ainsi dire pas de corps, et sa tête grosse et disproportionnée semblait immédiatement posée sur ses jambes, comme dans ces dessins comiques qui ont été à la mode il y a quelques années ; cette tête avait une expression profonde de douleur et de douceur, avec la résignation dans les yeux et la désespérance dans sa physionomie générale. Ainsi bâti, il ne pouvait pas être beau ; cependant il attirait le regard et le retenait par la sympathie et un certain charme qui se dégageait de ses grands yeux mouillés, tendres comme ceux d'un chien, et de ses lèvres parlantes.

— Es-tu bien certain qu'il reviendra dans deux heures ? demanda Vitalis.

— Bien certain, signor ; c'est le moment du dîner, et jamais personne autre que lui ne sert le dîner.

— Eh bien, s'il rentre avant, tu lui diras que Vitalis reviendra dans deux heures.

— Dans deux heures, oui, signor.

Je me disposais à suivre mon maître lorsque celui-ci m'arrêta.

— Reste ici, dit-il, tu te reposeras, je reviendrai.

Et comme j'avais fait un mouvement d'effroi :

— Je t'assure que je reviendrai.

J'aurais mieux aimé, malgré ma fatigue, suivre Vitalis ; mais, quand il avait commandé, j'avais l'habitude de lui obéir : je restai donc.

Lorsqu'on n'entendit plus le bruit des pas lourds de mon maître dans l'escalier, l'enfant, qui avait écouté, l'oreille penchée vers la porte, se retourna vers moi.

— Vous êtes du pays ? me dit-il en italien.

Depuis que j'étais avec Vitalis, j'avais appris assez d'italien pour comprendre à peu près tout ce qui se disait en cette langue ; mais je ne la parlais pas encore assez bien pour m'en servir volontiers.

— Non, répondis-je en français.

— Ah ! fit-il tristement en fixant sur moi ses grands yeux, tant pis ! j'aurais aimé que vous fussiez du pays.

— De quel pays ?

— De Lucca ; vous m'auriez peut-être donné des nouvelles.

— Je suis français.

— Ah, tant mieux !

— Vous aimez mieux les Français que les Italiens ?

— Non, et ce n'est pas pour moi que je dis tant mieux, c'est pour vous, parce que si vous étiez italien, vous viendriez ici probablement pour être au service du signor Garofoli ; et l'on ne dit pas tant mieux à ceux qui entrent au service du signor *padrone*.

Ces paroles n'étaient pas de nature à me rassurer.

— Il est méchant ?

L'enfant ne répondit pas à cette interrogation directe ; mais le regard qu'il fixa sur moi fut d'une effrayante éloquence. Puis, comme s'il ne voulait pas continuer une conversation sur ce sujet, il me tourna le dos et se dirigea vers une grande cheminée qui occupait l'extrémité de la pièce.

Un bon feu de bois de démolition brûlait dans cette cheminée, et devant ce feu bouillait une grande marmite en fonte.

Je m'approchai alors de la cheminée pour me chauffer, et je remarquai que cette marmite avait quelque chose de particulier que tout d'abord je n'avais pas vu. Le couvercle, surmonté d'un tube étroit par lequel s'échappait la vapeur, était fixé à la marmite, d'un côté par une charnière, et d'un autre par un cadenas.

J'avais compris que je ne devais pas faire de questions indiscrètes sur Garofoli, mais sur la marmite ?...

— Pourquoi donc est-elle fermée au cadenas ?

— Pour que je ne puisse pas prendre une tasse de bouillon. C'est moi qui suis chargé de faire la soupe, mais le maître n'a pas confiance en moi.

Je ne pus m'empêcher de sourire.

— Vous riez, continua-t-il tristement, parce que vous croyez que je suis gourmand. À ma place vous le seriez peut-être tout autant. Il est vrai que ce n'est pas gourmand que je suis, mais affamé, et l'odeur de la soupe qui s'échappe par ce tube rend ma faim plus cruelle encore.

— Le signor Garofoli vous laisse donc mourir de faim ?

— Si vous entrez ici, à son service, vous saurez qu'on ne meurt pas de faim, seulement on en souffre. Moi surtout, parce que c'est une punition.

— Une punition ! mourir de faim.

— Oui ; au surplus, je peux vous conter ça ; si Garofoli devient votre maître, mon exemple pourra vous servir. Le signor Garofoli est mon oncle et il m'a pris avec lui par charité. Il faut vous dire que ma mère est veuve, et, comme vous pensez bien, elle n'est pas riche. Quand Garofoli vint au pays l'année dernière pour prendre des enfants, il proposa à ma mère de m'emmener. Ça lui coûtait, à ma mère, de me laisser aller ; mais vous savez, quand il le faut ; et il le fallait, parce que nous étions six enfants à la maison et que j'étais l'aîné. Garofoli aurait mieux aimé prendre avec lui mon frère Leonardo qui vient après moi, parce que Leonardo est beau, tandis que moi je suis laid. Et pour gagner de l'argent, il ne faut pas être laid ; ceux qui sont laids ne gagnent que des coups ou des mauvaises paroles. Mais ma mère ne voulut pas donner Leonardo : « C'est Mattia qui est l'aîné, dit-elle, c'est à Mattia de partir, puisqu'il faut qu'il en parte un ; c'est le Bon Dieu qui l'a désigné, je n'ose pas changer la règle du Bon Dieu. » Me voilà donc parti avec mon oncle Garofoli ; vous pensez que ç'a été dur de quitter la maison, ma mère qui pleurait, ma petite sœur Cristina, qui m'aimait bien parce qu'elle était la dernière et que je la portais toujours dans mes bras ; et puis aussi mes frères, mes camarades et le pays.

Je savais ce qu'il y avait de dur dans ces séparations, et je n'avais pas oublié le serrement de cœur qui m'avait étouffé quand, pour la dernière fois, j'avais aperçu la coiffe blanche de mère Barberin.

Le petit Mattia continua son récit :

— J'étais tout seul avec Garofoli, dit-il, en quittant la maison, mais, au bout de huit jours, nous étions une douzaine, et l'on se mit en route pour la France. Ah ! elle a été bien longue la route pour moi et pour les camarades qui, eux aussi, étaient tristes. Enfin, on arriva à Paris ; nous n'étions plus que onze parce qu'il y en avait un qui était resté à l'hôpital de Dijon. À Paris on fit un choix parmi nous ; ceux qui étaient forts furent placés chez des fumistes ou des maîtres ramoneurs ; ceux qui n'étaient pas assez solides pour un métier allèrent chanter ou jouer de la vielle dans les rues. Bien entendu, je n'étais pas assez fort pour travailler, et il paraît que j'étais trop laid pour faire de bonnes journées en jouant de la vielle. Alors Garofoli me donna deux petites souris blanches que je devrais montrer sur les portes, dans les passages, et il taxa ma journée à trente sous. « Autant de sous qui te manqueront le soir, me dit-il, autant de coups de bâton pour toi. » Trente sous, c'est dur à ramasser ; mais les coups de bâton, c'est dur aussi à recevoir, surtout quand c'est Garofoli qui les administre. Je faisais donc tout ce que je pouvais pour ramasser ma somme ; mais, malgré ma peine, je n'y parvenais pas souvent. Presque toujours mes camarades avaient leurs sous en rentrant ; moi, je ne les avais presque jamais. Cela redoublait la colère de Garofoli. « Comment donc s'y prend cet imbécile de Mattia ? » disait-il. Il y avait un autre enfant qui, comme moi, montrait des souris blanches, et qui avait été taxé à quarante sous, que tous les soirs il rapportait. Plusieurs fois, je sortis avec lui pour voir comment il s'y prenait et par où il était plus adroit que moi. Alors je compris pourquoi il obtenait si facilement ses quarante sous et moi si difficilement mes trente. Quand un monsieur et une dame nous donnaient, la dame disait toujours : « À celui qui est gentil, pas à celui qui est si laid. » Celui qui était laid, c'était moi. Je ne sortis plus avec mon camarade, parce que, si c'est triste de recevoir des coups de bâton à la maison, c'est encore plus triste de recevoir des mauvaises paroles dans la rue, devant tout le monde. Vous ne savez pas cela, vous, parce qu'on ne vous a jamais dit que vous étiez laid ; mais moi... Enfin, Garofoli, voyant que les coups n'y faisaient rien, employa un autre moyen. « Pour chaque sou qui te manquera, je te retiendrai une pomme de terre à ton souper, me dit-il. Puisque ta peau est dure aux coups, ton estomac sera peut-être tendre à la faim. » Est-ce que les menaces vous ont fait faire quelque chose, à vous ?

— Dame ! c'est selon.

— Moi, jamais ; d'ailleurs je ne pouvais faire plus que ce que j'avais fait jusque-là ; et je ne pouvais pas dire à ceux à qui je tendais la main : « Si vous ne me donnez pas un sou, je n'aurai pas de pommes de terre ce soir. » Les gens qui donnent aux enfants ne se décident pas par ces raisons-là.

— Et par quelles raisons se décident-ils ? on donne pour faire plaisir.

— Ah ! bien ! vous êtes encore jeune, vous ; on vous donne pour se faire plaisir à soi-même tout d'abord ; on donne aussi à un enfant parce qu'il est gentil, et ça, c'est la meilleure des raisons ; on lui donne pour l'enfant qu'on a perdu ou bien pour l'enfant qu'on désire ; on lui donne parce qu'on a bien chaud, tandis que lui tremble de froid sous une porte cochère, c'est de la compassion. Oh ! je connais toutes ces aumônes-là ; j'ai eu le temps de les étudier ; tenez, il fait froid aujourd'hui, n'est-ce pas ?

— Très froid.

— Eh bien ! allez vous mettre sous une porte et tendez la main à un monsieur que vous verrez venir rapidement tassé dans un petit paletot, vous me direz ce qu'il vous donnera ;

tendez-la, au contraire, à un monsieur qui marchera doucement, enveloppé dans un gros pardessus ou dans des fourrures, et vous aurez peut-être une pièce blanche. Après un mois ou six semaines de ce régime-là, je n'avais pas engraissé ; j'étais devenu pâle, si pâle, que souvent j'entendais dire autour de moi : « Voilà un enfant qui va mourir de faim. » Alors la souffrance fit ce que la beauté n'avait pas voulu faire : elle me rendit intéressant et me donna des yeux ; les gens du quartier me prirent en pitié, et, si je ne ramassais pas beaucoup plus de sous, je ramassai tantôt un morceau de pain, tantôt une soupe. Ce fut mon bon temps ; je n'avais plus de coups de bâton, et, si j'étais privé de pommes de terre au souper, cela m'importait peu quand j'avais eu quelque chose pour mon dîner. Mais un jour Garofoli me vit chez une fruitière mangeant une assiettée de soupe, et il comprit pourquoi je supportais sans me plaindre la privation des pommes de terre. Alors il décida que je ne sortirais plus et que je resterais à la chambrée pour préparer la soupe et faire le ménage. Mais, comme en préparant la soupe je pouvais en manger, il inventa cette marmite. Tous les matins, avant de sortir, il met dans la marmite la viande et les légumes, il ferme le couvercle au cadenas, et je n'ai plus qu'à faire bouillir le pot ; je sens l'odeur du bouillon, et c'est tout ; quant à en prendre, vous comprenez que, par ce petit tube si étroit, c'est impossible. C'est depuis que je suis à la cuisine que je suis devenu si pâle ; l'odeur du bouillon, ça ne nourrit pas, ça augmente la faim, voilà tout. Est-ce que je suis bien pâle ? Comme je ne sors plus, je ne l'entends pas dire, et il n'y a pas de miroir ici.

Je n'étais pas alors un esprit très expérimenté, cependant je savais qu'il ne faut pas effrayer ceux qui sont malades en leur disant qu'on les trouve malades.

— Vous ne me paraissez pas plus pâle qu'un autre, répondis-je.

— Je vois bien que vous me dites ça pour me rassurer ; mais cela me ferait plaisir d'être pâle, parce que cela signifierait que je suis très malade, et je voudrais être tout à fait malade.

Je le regardai avec stupéfaction.

— Vous ne me comprenez pas, dit-il avec un sourire, c'est pourtant bien simple. Quand on est très malade, on vous soigne ou on vous laisse mourir. Si on me laisse mourir, ça sera fini, je n'aurai plus faim, je n'aurai plus de coups ; et puis l'on dit que ceux qui sont morts vivent dans le ciel ; alors, de dedans le ciel, je verrais maman là-bas, au pays, et en parlant au Bon Dieu je pourrais peut-être empêcher ma sœur Cristina d'être malheureuse : en le priant bien. Si au contraire on me soigne, on m'enverra à l'hôpital, et je serais content d'aller à l'hôpital.

J'avais l'effroi instinctif de l'hôpital, et bien souvent en chemin, quand accablé de fatigue je m'étais senti du malaise, je n'avais eu qu'à penser à l'hôpital pour me retrouver aussitôt disposé à marcher ; je fus étonné d'entendre Mattia parler ainsi :

— Si vous saviez comme on est bien à l'hôpital, dit-il en continuant ; j'y ai déjà été, à Sainte-Eugénie ; il y a là un médecin, un grand blond, qui a toujours du sucre d'orge dans sa poche, c'est du *cassé*, parce que le cassé coûte moins cher, mais il n'en est pas moins bon pour cela ; et puis les sœurs vous parlent doucement : « Fais cela, mon petit ; tire la langue, pauvre petit. » Moi j'aime qu'on me parle doucement, ça me donne envie de pleurer, et, quand j'ai envie de pleurer, ça me rend tout heureux. C'est bête, n'est-ce pas ? Mais maman me parlait toujours doucement. Les sœurs parlent comme parlait maman, et, si ce n'est pas les mêmes paroles, c'est la même musique. Et puis, quand on commence à être mieux, du bon bouillon, du vin. Quand j'ai commencé à me sentir sans forces ici, parce que je ne mangeais pas, j'ai été content ; je me suis dit : « Je vais être malade et Garofoli m'enverra à l'hôpital. » Ah ! bien oui, malade, assez malade pour souffrir moi-même, mais pas assez pour gêner Garofoli ; alors il m'a gardé. C'est étonnant comme les malheureux ont la vie dure. Par bonheur, Garofoli n'a pas perdu l'habitude de m'administrer des corrections, à moi comme aux autres, il faut dire, si bien qu'il y a huit jours il m'a donné un coup de bâton sur la tête. Pour cette fois j'espère que l'affaire est dans le sac ; j'ai la tête enflée ; vous voyez bien là cette grosse bosse blanche, il disait hier que c'était peut-être une tumeur ; je ne sais pas ce que c'est une tumeur, mais à la façon dont il en parlait, je crois que c'est grave. Toujours est-il que je souffre beaucoup ; j'ai des élancements sous les cheveux plus douloureux que dans des crises de dents ; ma tête est lourde comme si elle pesait cent livres ; j'ai des éblouissements, des étourdissements, et la nuit, en dormant, je ne peux m'empêcher de gémir et de crier. Alors je crois que d'ici deux ou trois jours cela va le décider à m'envoyer à l'hôpital, parce que, vous comprenez, un moutard qui crie la nuit, ça gêne les autres, et Garofoli n'aime pas être gêné. Quel bonheur qu'il m'ait donné ce coup de bâton ! Voyons, là, franchement, est-ce que je suis bien pâle ?

Disant cela il vint se placer en face de moi et me regarda les yeux dans les yeux. Je n'avais plus les mêmes raisons pour me taire ; cependant je n'osais pas répondre sincèrement et lui dire quelle sensation effrayante me produisaient ses grands yeux brûlants, ses joues caves et ses lèvres décolorées.

— Je crois que vous êtes assez malade pour entrer à l'hôpital.
— Enfin !

Et sa jambe traînante, il essaya une révérence. Mais presque aussitôt, se dirigeant vers la table, il commença à l'essuyer.

— Assez causé, dit-il, Garofoli va rentrer et rien ne serait prêt ; puisque vous trouvez que j'ai ce qu'il me faut de coups pour entrer à l'hospice, ce n'est plus la peine d'en récolter de nouveaux : ceux-là seraient perdus ; et maintenant ceux que je reçois me paraissent plus durs que ceux que je recevais il y a quelques mois. Ils sont bons, n'est-ce pas, ceux qui disent qu'on s'habitue à tout ?

Tout en parlant il allait clopin-clopant autour de la table, mettant les assiettes et les couverts en place. Je comptai vingt assiettes : c'était donc vingt enfants que Garofoli avait sous sa direction ; comme je ne voyais que douze lits, on devait coucher deux ensemble. Quels lits ! pas de draps, mais des couvertures rousses qui devaient avoir été achetées dans une écurie, alors qu'elles n'étaient plus assez chaudes pour les chevaux.

— Est-ce que c'est partout comme ici ? dis-je épouvanté.
— Où, partout ?
— Partout chez ceux qui ont des enfants.
— Je ne sais pas, je ne suis jamais allé ailleurs ; seulement, vous, tâchez d'aller ailleurs.
— Où cela ?
— Je ne sais pas ; n'importe où, vous seriez mieux qu'ici.

N'importe où ; c'était vague, et dans tous les cas comment m'y prendre pour changer la décision de Vitalis ?

Comme je réfléchissais, sans rien trouver, bien entendu, la porte s'ouvrit, et un enfant entra ; il tenait un violon sous son bras, et dans sa main libre il portait un gros morceau de bois de démolition. Ce morceau, pareil à ceux que j'avais vu mettre dans la cheminée, me fit comprendre où Garofoli prenait sa provision, et le prix qu'elle lui coûtait.

— Donne-moi ton morceau de bois, dit Mattia en allant au-devant du nouveau venu.

Mais celui-ci, au lieu de donner ce morceau de bois à son camarade, le passa derrière son dos.

— Ah ! mais non, dit-il.

— Donne, la soupe sera meilleure.

— Si tu crois que je l'ai apporté pour la soupe : je n'ai que trente-six sous, je compte sur lui pour que Garofoli ne me fasse pas payer trop cher les quatre sous qui me manquent.

— Il n'y a pas de morceau qui tienne ; tu les paieras, va ; chacun son tour.

Mattia dit cela méchamment, comme s'il était heureux de la correction qui attendait son camarade. Je fus surpris de cet éclair de dureté dans une figure si douce ; c'est plus tard seulement que j'ai compris qu'à vivre avec les méchants on peut devenir méchant soi-même.

C'était l'heure de la rentrée de tous les élèves de Garofoli ; après l'enfant au morceau de bois il en arriva un autre, puis après celui-là dix autres encore. Chacun en entrant allait accrocher son instrument à un clou au-dessus de son lit, celui-ci un violon, celui-là une harpe, un autre une flûte, ou une *piva* ; ceux qui n'étaient pas musiciens, mais simplement montreurs de bêtes, fourraient dans une cage leurs marmottes ou leurs cochons de Barbarie.

Un pas plus lourd résonna dans l'escalier, je sentis que c'était Garofoli ; et je vis entrer un petit homme à figure fiévreuse, à démarche hésitante ; il ne portait point le costume italien, mais il était habillé d'un paletot gris.

Son premier coup d'œil fut pour moi, un coup d'œil qui me fit froid au cœur.

— Qu'est-ce que c'est que ce garçon ? dit-il.

Mattia lui répondit vivement et poliment en lui donnant les explications dont Vitalis l'avait chargé.

— Ah ! Vitalis est à Paris, dit-il, que me veut-il ?

— Je ne sais pas, répondit Mattia.

— Ce n'est pas à toi que je parle, c'est à ce garçon.

— Le *padrone* va venir, dis-je, sans oser répondre franchement ; il vous expliquera lui-même ce qu'il désire.

— Voilà un petit qui connaît le prix des paroles ; tu n'es pas italien ?

— Non, je suis français.

Deux enfants s'étaient approchés de Garofoli aussitôt qu'il était entré, et tous deux se tenaient près de lui, attendant qu'il eût fini de parler. Que lui voulaient-ils ? J'eus bientôt réponse à cette question que je me posais avec curiosité.

L'un prit son feutre et alla le placer délicatement sur un lit, l'autre lui approcha aussitôt une chaise ; à la gravité, au respect avec lesquels ils accomplissaient ces actes si simples de la vie, on eût dit deux enfants de chœur s'empressant religieusement autour de l'officiant ; par là je vis à quel point Garofoli était craint, car assurément ce n'était pas la tendresse qui les faisait agir ainsi et s'empresser.

Lorsque Garofoli fut assis, un autre enfant lui apporta vivement une pipe bourrée de tabac et en même temps un quatrième lui présenta une allumette allumée.

— Elle sent le soufre, animal ! cria-t-il lorsqu'il l'eut approchée de sa pipe ; et il la jeta dans la cheminée.

Le coupable s'empressa de réparer sa faute en allumant une nouvelle allumette qu'il laissa brûler assez longtemps avant de l'offrir à son maître.

Mais celui-ci ne l'accepta pas.

— Pas toi, imbécile ! dit-il en le repoussant durement ; puis se tournant vers un autre enfant avec un sourire qui certainement était une insigne faveur :

— Riccardo, une allumette, mon mignon ?

Et le mignon s'empressa d'obéir.

— Maintenant, dit Garofoli lorsqu'il fut installé et que sa pipe commença à brûler, à nos comptes, mes petits anges ? Mattia, le livre ?

C'était vraiment grande bonté à Garofoli de daigner parler, car ses élèves épiaient si attentivement ses désirs ou ses intentions, qu'ils les devinaient avant que celui-ci les exprimât.

Il n'avait pas demandé son livre de comptes que Mattia posait devant lui un petit registre crasseux.

Garofoli fit un signe, et l'enfant qui lui avait présenté l'allumette non désoufrée s'approcha.

— Tu me dois un sou d'hier, tu m'as promis de me le rendre aujourd'hui ; combien m'apportes-tu ?

L'enfant hésita longtemps avant de répondre ; il était pourpre.

— Il me manque un sou.

— Ah ! il te manque ton sou, et tu me dis cela tranquillement !

— Ce n'est pas le sou d'hier, c'est un sou pour aujourd'hui.

— Alors c'est deux sous ? Tu sais que je n'ai jamais vu ton pareil.

— Ce n'est pas ma faute.

— Pas de niaiseries, tu connais la règle : défais ta veste, deux coups pour hier, deux coups pour aujourd'hui ; et en plus pas de pommes de terre pour ton audace ; Riccardo, mon mignon, tu as bien gagné cette récréation par ta gentillesse ; prends les lanières.

Riccardo était l'enfant qui avait apporté la bonne allumette avec tant d'empressement ; il décrocha de la muraille un fouet à manche court se terminant par deux lanières en cuir avec de gros nœuds. Pendant ce temps, celui auquel il manquait un sou défaisait sa veste et laissait tomber sa chemise de manière à être nu jusqu'à la ceinture.

— Attends un peu, dit Garofoli avec un mauvais sourire, tu ne seras peut-être pas le seul, et c'est toujours un plaisir d'avoir de la compagnie, et puis Riccardo n'aura pas besoin de s'y reprendre à plusieurs reprises.

Debout devant leur maître, les enfants se tenaient immobiles ; à cette plaisanterie cruelle, ils se mirent tous ensemble à rire d'un rire forcé.

— Celui qui a ri le plus fort, dit Garofoli, est, j'en suis certain, celui auquel il manque le plus. Qui a ri fort ?

Tous désignèrent celui qui était arrivé le premier, apportant un morceau de bois.

— Allons, toi, combien te manque-t-il ? demanda Garofoli.

— Ce n'est pas ma faute.

— Désormais, celui qui répondra : « Ce n'est pas ma faute » recevra un coup de lanière en plus de ce qui lui est dû ; combien te manque-t-il ?

— J'ai apporté un morceau de bois, ce beau morceau-là.

— Ça, c'est quelque chose ; mais va chez le boulanger et demande-lui du pain en échange de ton morceau de bois, t'en donnera-t-il ? Combien te manque-t-il de sous ? voyons, parle donc !

— J'ai trente-six sous.

— Il te manque quatre sous, misérable gredin, quatre sous ! et tu reparais devant moi ! Riccardo, tu es un heureux coquin, mon mignon, tu vas bien t'amuser ; bas la veste !

— Mais le morceau de bois ?

— Je te le donne pour dîner.

Cette stupide plaisanterie fit rire tous les enfants qui n'étaient pas condamnés.

Pendant cet interrogatoire, il était survenu une dizaine d'enfants : tous vinrent, à tour de rôle, rendre leurs comptes ; avec deux déjà condamnés aux lanières, il s'en trouva trois autres qui n'avaient point leur chiffre.

— Ils sont donc cinq brigands qui me volent et me pillent! s'écria Garofoli d'une voix gémissante. Voilà ce que c'est d'être trop généreux; comment voulez-vous que je paye la bonne viande et les bonnes pommes de terre que je vous donne, si vous ne voulez pas travailler? Vous aimez mieux jouer; il faudrait pleurer avec les jobards, et vous aimez mieux rire entre vous; croyez-vous donc qu'il ne vaut pas mieux faire semblant de pleurer en tendant la main que de pleurer pour de bon en tendant le dos? Allons, à bas les vestes!

Riccardo se tenait le fouet à la main, et les cinq patients étaient rangés à côté de lui.

— Tu sais, Riccardo, dit Garofoli, que je ne te regarde pas parce que ces corrections me font mal, mais je t'entends, et au bruit je jugerai bien la force des coups; vas-y de tout ton cœur, mon mignon, c'est pour ton pain que tu travailles.

Et il tourna le nez vers le feu, comme s'il lui était impossible de voir cette exécution. Pour moi, oublié dans un coin, je frémissais d'indignation et aussi de peur. C'était l'homme qui allait devenir mon maître; si je ne rapportais pas les trente ou les quarante sous qu'il lui plairait d'exiger de moi, il me faudrait tendre le dos à Riccardo. Ah! je comprenais maintenant comment Mattia pouvait parler de la mort si tranquillement et avec un sentiment d'espérance.

Le premier claquement du fouet frappant sur la peau me fit jaillir les larmes des yeux. Comme je me voyais oublié, je ne me contraignis point; mais je me trompais. Garofoli m'observait à la dérobée, j'en eus bientôt la preuve.

— Voilà un enfant qui a bon cœur, dit-il en me désignant du doigt; il n'est pas comme vous, brigands, qui riez du malheur de vos camarades et de mon chagrin; que n'est-il de vos camarades, il vous servirait d'exemple!

Ce mot me fit trembler de la tête aux pieds : leur camarade!

Au deuxième coup de fouet, le patient poussa un gémissement lamentable, au troisième un cri déchirant.

Garofoli leva la main, Riccardo resta le fouet suspendu.

Je crus qu'il voulait faire grâce; mais ce n'était pas de grâce qu'il s'agissait.

— Tu sais combien les cris me font mal, dit doucement Garofoli en s'adressant à sa victime, tu sais que, si le fouet te déchire la peau, tes cris me déchirent le cœur. Je te préviens donc, que pour chaque cri, tu auras un nouveau coup de fouet, et ce sera ta faute. Pense à ne pas me rendre malade de chagrin; si tu avais un peu de tendresse pour moi, un peu de reconnaissance, tu te tairais. Allons, Riccardo !

Celui-ci leva le bras et les lanières cinglèrent le dos du malheureux.

— Mamma ! mamma ! cria celui-ci.

Heureusement je n'en vis point davantage, la porte de l'escalier s'ouvrit et Vitalis entra.

Un coup d'œil lui fit comprendre ce que les cris qu'il avait entendus en montant l'escalier lui avaient déjà dénoncé ; il courut sur Riccardo et lui arracha le fouet de la main ; puis, se retournant vivement vers Garofoli, il se posa devant lui les bras croisés.

Tout cela s'était passé si rapidement, que Garofoli resta un moment stupéfait ; mais bientôt, se remettant et reprenant son sourire doucereux :

— N'est-ce pas, dit-il, que c'est terrible ? cet enfant n'a pas de cœur.

— C'est une honte ! s'écria Vitalis.

— Voilà justement ce que je dis, interrompit Garofoli.

— Pas de grimaces, continua mon maître avec force, vous savez bien que ce n'est pas à cet enfant que je parle, mais à vous ; oui, c'est une honte, une lâcheté, de martyriser ainsi des enfants qui ne peuvent pas se défendre.

— De quoi vous mêlez-vous, vieux fou ? dit Garofoli changeant de ton.

— De ce qui regarde la police.

— La police, s'écria Garofoli en se levant, vous me menacez de la police, vous ?

— Oui, moi, répondit mon maître sans se laisser intimider par la fureur du *padrone*.

— Écoutez, Vitalis, dit celui-ci en se calmant et en prenant un ton moqueur, il ne faut pas faire le méchant, et me menacer de causer, parce que, de mon côté, je pourrais bien causer aussi. Et alors qui est-ce qui ne serait pas content ? Bien sûr je n'irai rien dire à la police, vos affaires ne la regardent pas. Mais il y en a d'autres qu'elles intéressent, et, si j'allais répéter à ceux-là ce que je sais, si je disais seulement un nom, un seul nom, qui est-ce qui serait obligé d'aller cacher sa honte ?

Mon maître resta un moment sans répondre. Sa honte ? J'étais stupéfait. Avant que je fusse revenu de la surprise dans laquelle m'avaient jeté ces étranges paroles il m'avait pris la main.

— Suis-moi.

Et il m'entraîna vers la porte.

— Eh bien ! dit Garofoli en riant, sans rancune, mon vieux ; vous vouliez me parler ?

— Je n'ai plus rien à vous dire.

Et sans une seule parole, sans se retourner, il descendit l'escalier me tenant toujours par la main. Avec quel soulagement je le suivais ! j'échappais donc à Garofoli ; si j'avais osé, j'aurais embrassé Vitalis.

XVIII

Les carrières de Gentilly

Tant que nous fûmes dans la rue où il y avait du monde, Vitalis marcha sans rien dire, mais bientôt nous nous trouvâmes dans une ruelle déserte ; alors il s'assit sur une borne et passa à plusieurs reprises sa main sur son front, ce qui chez lui était un signe d'embarras.

— C'est peut-être beau d'écouter la générosité, dit-il comme s'il se parlait à lui-même, mais avec cela nous voilà sur le pavé de Paris, sans un sou dans la poche et sans un morceau de pain dans l'estomac. As-tu faim ?

— Je n'ai rien mangé depuis le petit croûton que vous m'avez donné ce matin.

— Eh bien ! mon pauvre enfant, tu es exposé à te coucher ce soir sans dîner, encore si nous savions où coucher !

— Vous comptiez donc coucher chez Garofoli ?

— Je comptais que toi tu y coucherais, et comme pour ton hiver il m'eût donné une vingtaine de francs, j'étais tiré d'affaire pour le moment. Mais, voyant comment il traite les enfants, je n'ai pas été maître de moi. Tu n'avais pas envie de rester avec lui, n'est-ce pas ?

— Oh ! vous êtes bon.

— Le cœur n'est pas tout à fait mort dans le vieux vagabond. Par malheur, le vagabond avait bien calculé, et le cœur a tout dérangé. Maintenant où aller ?

Il était tard déjà, et le froid, qui s'était amolli durant la journée, était redevenu âpre et glacial ; le vent soufflait du nord, la nuit serait dure.

Vitalis resta longtemps assis sur la borne, tandis que nous nous tenions immobiles devant lui, Capi et moi, attendant qu'il eût pris une décision. Enfin, il se leva.

— Où allons-nous ?

— À Gentilly, tâcher de trouver une carrière où j'ai couché autrefois. Es-tu fatigué ?

— Je me suis reposé chez Garofoli.

— Le malheur est que je ne me suis pas reposé, moi, et que je n'en peux plus. Enfin, il faut aller. En avant, mes enfants !

C'était son mot de bonne humeur pour les chiens et pour moi ; mais ce soir-là il le dit tristement.

Nous voilà donc en route dans les rues de Paris ; la nuit est noire et le gaz, dont le vent fait vaciller la flamme dans les lanternes, éclaire mal la chaussée. Nous glissons à chaque pas sur un ruisseau gelé ou sur une nappe de glace qui a envahi les trottoirs ; Vitalis me tient par la main et Capi est sur nos talons. De temps en temps seulement il reste en arrière pour chercher dans un tas d'ordures s'il ne trouvera pas un os ou une croûte, car la faim lui tenaille aussi l'estomac ; mais les ordures sont prises en un bloc de glace et sa recherche est vaine ; l'oreille basse, il nous rejoint.

Après les grandes rues, des ruelles ; après ces ruelles, d'autres grandes rues ; nous marchons toujours, et les rares passants que nous rencontrons semblent nous regarder avec étonnement. Est-ce notre costume, est-ce notre démarche fatiguée, qui frappent l'attention ? Les sergents de ville que nous croisons tournent autour de nous et s'arrêtent pour nous suivre de l'œil.

Cependant, sans prononcer une seule parole, Vitalis s'avance courbé en deux ; malgré le froid, sa main brûle la mienne ; il me semble qu'il tremble. Parfois, quand il s'arrête pour s'appuyer une minute sur mon épaule, je sens tout son corps agité d'une secousse convulsive.

D'ordinaire je n'osais pas trop l'interroger, mais cette fois je manquai à ma règle, j'avais d'ailleurs comme un besoin de lui dire que je l'aimais ou tout au moins que je voulais faire quelque chose pour lui.

— Vous êtes malade ! dis-je dans un moment d'arrêt.

— Je le crains ; en tout cas, je suis fatigué, ces jours de marche ont été trop longs pour mon âge, et le froid de cette nuit est trop rude pour mon vieux sang ; il m'aurait fallu un bon lit, un souper dans une chambre close et devant un bon feu. Mais tout ça c'est un rêve ; en avant, les enfants !

En avant! nous étions sortis de la ville ou tout au moins des maisons; et nous marchions tantôt entre une double rangée de murs, tantôt en pleine campagne, nous marchions toujours. Plus de passants, plus de sergents de ville, plus de lanternes ou de becs de gaz, seulement, de temps en temps, une fenêtre éclairée çà et là, et au-dessus de nos têtes le ciel d'un bleu sombre avec de rares étoiles. Le vent qui soufflait plus âpre et plus rude nous collait nos vêtements sur le corps; il nous frappait heureusement dans le dos, mais, comme l'emmanchure de ma veste était décousue, il entrait par ce trou et me glissait le long du bras, ce qui était loin de me réchauffer.

Bien qu'il fît sombre et que les chemins se croisassent à chaque pas, Vitalis marchait comme un homme qui sait où il va et qui est parfaitement sûr de sa route; aussi je le suivais sans crainte de nous perdre, n'ayant d'autre inquiétude que celle de savoir si nous n'allions pas arriver enfin à cette carrière.

Mais tout à coup il s'arrêta.

— Vois-tu un bouquet d'arbres? me dit-il.

— Je ne vois rien.

— Tu ne vois pas une masse noire?

Je regardai de tous les côtés avant de répondre, nous devions être au milieu d'une plaine, car mes yeux se perdirent dans des profondeurs sombres sans que rien les arrêtât, ni arbres ni maisons; le vide autour de nous, pas d'autre bruit que celui du vent sifflant ras de terre dans les broussailles invisibles.

— Ah! si j'avais tes yeux! dit Vitalis, mais je vois trouble, regarde là-bas.

Il étendit la main droit devant lui, puis, comme je ne répondais pas, car je n'osais pas dire que je ne voyais rien, il se remit en marche.

Quelques minutes se passèrent en silence, puis il s'arrêta de nouveau et me demanda encore si je ne voyais pas de bouquet d'arbres. Je n'avais plus la même sécurité que quelques instants auparavant, et un vague effroi fit trembler ma voix quand je répondis que je ne voyais rien.

— C'est la peur qui te fait danser les yeux, dit Vitalis.

— Je vous assure que je ne vois pas d'arbres.

— Pas de grande roue?

— On ne voit rien.

— Nous sommes-nous trompés?

Je n'avais pas à répondre, je ne savais ni où nous étions, ni où nous allions.

— Marchons encore cinq minutes, et si nous ne voyons pas les arbres nous reviendrons en arrière ; je me serai trompé de chemin.

Maintenant que je comprenais que nous pouvions être égarés, je ne me sentais plus de forces. Vitalis me tira par le bras.

— Eh bien !

— Je ne peux plus marcher.

— Et moi, crois-tu que je peux te porter ? si je me tiens encore debout, c'est soutenu par la pensée que, si nous nous asseyons, nous ne nous relèverons pas et mourrons là de froid. Allons !

Je le suivis.

— Le chemin a-t-il des ornières profondes ?

— Il n'en a pas du tout.

— Il faut retourner sur nos pas.

Le vent qui nous soufflait dans le dos nous frappa à la face et si rudement, qu'il me suffoqua ; j'eus la sensation d'une brûlure.

Nous n'avancions pas bien rapidement en venant, mais en retournant nous marchâmes plus lentement encore.

— Quand tu verras des ornières, préviens-moi, dit Vitalis, le bon chemin doit être à gauche, avec une tête d'épine au carrefour.

Pendant un quart d'heure, nous avançâmes ainsi luttant contre le vent ; dans le silence morne de la nuit, le bruit de nos pas résonnait sur la terre durcie. Bien que pouvant à peine mettre une jambe devant l'autre, c'était moi maintenant qui traînais Vitalis. Avec quelle anxiété je sondais le côté gauche de la route !

Une petite étoile rouge brilla tout à coup dans l'ombre.

— Une lumière, dis-je en étendant la main.

— Où cela ?

Vitalis regarda, mais, bien que la lumière scintillât à une distance qui ne devait pas être très grande, il ne vit rien. Par là je compris que sa vue était affaiblie, car d'ordinaire elle était longue et perçante la nuit.

— Que nous importe cette lumière ! dit-il, c'est une lampe qui brûle sur la table d'un travailleur ou bien près du lit d'un mourant ; nous ne pouvons pas aller frapper à cette porte. Dans la campagne, pendant la nuit, nous pourrions demander l'hospitalité, mais aux environs de Paris on ne donne pas l'hospitalité. Il n'y a pas de maisons pour nous. Allons !

Pendant quelques minutes encore nous marchâmes, puis il me sembla apercevoir un chemin qui coupait le nôtre, et au coin de ce chemin un corps noir qui devait être la tête d'épine. Je lâchai la main de Vitalis pour avancer plus vite. Ce chemin était creusé par de profondes ornières.

— Voilà l'épine ; il y a des ornières.

— Donne-moi la main ; nous sommes sauvés, la carrière est à cinq minutes d'ici ; regarde bien, tu dois voir le bouquet d'arbres.

Il me sembla voir une masse sombre, et je dis que je reconnaissais les arbres.

L'espérance nous rendit l'énergie, mes jambes furent moins lourdes, la terre fut moins dure à mes pieds.

Cependant les cinq minutes annoncées par Vitalis me parurent éternelles.

— Il y a plus de cinq minutes que nous sommes dans le bon chemin, dit-il en s'arrêtant.

— C'est ce qu'il me semble.

— Où vont les ornières ?

— Elles continuent droit.

— L'entrée de la carrière doit être à gauche, nous aurons passé devant sans la voir ; dans cette nuit épaisse, rien n'est plus facile ; pourtant nous aurions dû comprendre aux ornières que nous allions trop loin.

— Je vous assure que les ornières n'ont pas tourné à gauche.

— Enfin rebroussons toujours sur nos pas.

Une fois encore nous revînmes en arrière.

— Vois-tu le bouquet d'arbres ?

— Oui, là, à gauche.

— Et les ornières ?

— Il n'y en a pas.

— Est-ce que je suis aveugle ? dit Vitalis en passant la main sur ses yeux ; marchons droit sur les arbres et donne-moi la main.

— Il y a une muraille.

— C'est un amas de pierres.

— Non, je vous assure que c'est une muraille.

Ce que je disais était facile à vérifier, nous n'étions qu'à quelques pas de la muraille ; Vitalis franchit ces quelques pas, et, comme s'il ne s'en rapportait pas à ses yeux, il appliqua les deux mains contre l'obstacle que j'appelais une muraille et qu'il appelait, lui, un amas de pierres.

— C'est bien un mur ; les pierres sont régulièrement rangées et je sens le mortier, où donc est l'entrée ? cherche les ornières.

Je me baissai sur le sol et suivis la muraille jusqu'à son extrémité sans rencontrer la moindre ornière ; puis, revenant vers Vitalis, je continuai ma recherche du côté opposé. Le résultat fut le même : partout un mur, nulle part une ouverture dans ce mur, ou sur la terre un chemin, un sillon, une trace quelconque indiquant une entrée.

— Je ne trouve rien que la neige.

La situation était terrible ; sans doute mon maître s'était égaré, et ce n'était pas là que se trouvait la carrière qu'il cherchait.

Quand je lui eus dit que je ne trouvais pas les ornières, mais seulement la neige, il resta un moment sans répondre, puis, appliquant de nouveau ses mains contre le mur, il le parcourut d'un bout à l'autre. Capi, qui ne comprenait rien à cette manœuvre, aboyait avec impatience.

Je marchais derrière Vitalis.

— Faut-il chercher plus loin ?

— Non, la carrière est murée.

— Murée ?

— On a fermé l'ouverture, et il est impossible d'entrer.

— Mais alors ?

— Que faire, n'est-ce pas ? Je n'en sais rien, mourir ici.

— Oh ! maître.

— Oui, tu ne veux pas mourir, toi, tu es jeune, la vie te tient, eh bien ! marchons. Peux-tu marcher ?

— Mais vous ?

— Quand je ne pourrai plus, je tomberai comme un vieux cheval.

— Où aller ?

— Rentrer dans Paris, quand nous rencontrerons des sergents de ville, nous nous ferons conduire au poste de police ; j'aurais voulu éviter cela, mais je ne veux pas te laisser mourir de froid, allons, mon petit Rémi, allons, mon enfant, du courage !

Et nous reprîmes en sens contraire la route que nous avions déjà parcourue. Quelle heure était-il ? Je n'en avais aucune idée. Nous avions marché longtemps, bien longtemps et lentement. Minuit, une heure du matin peut-être. Le ciel était toujours du même bleu sombre, sans lune, avec de rares étoiles qui paraissaient plus petites qu'à l'ordinaire. Le vent, loin de se calmer, avait redoublé de force, il soulevait des tourbillons de poussière neigeuse sur le bord de la route et nous la fouettait au visage.

Les maisons devant lesquelles nous passions étaient closes et sans lumière, il me semblait que, si les gens qui dormaient là chaudement dans leurs draps avaient su combien nous, nous avions froid, ils nous auraient ouvert leur porte.

En marchant vite nous aurions pu réagir contre le froid, mais Vitalis n'avançait plus qu'à grand-peine en soufflant ; sa respiration était haute et haletante comme s'il avait couru. Quand je l'interrogeais, il ne me répondait pas, et de la main, lentement, il me faisait signe qu'il ne pouvait pas parler.

De la campagne nous étions revenus en ville, c'est-à-dire que nous marchions entre des murs au haut desquels, çà et là, se balançait un réverbère avec un bruit de ferraille.

Vitalis s'arrêta ; je compris qu'il était au bout.

— Voulez-vous que je frappe à l'une de ces portes ? dis-je.

— Non, on ne nous ouvrirait pas ; ce sont des jardiniers, des maraîchers qui demeurent là ; ils ne se lèvent pas la nuit. Marchons toujours.

Mais il avait plus de volonté que de forces. Après quelques pas il s'arrêta encore.

— Il faut que je me repose un peu, dit-il, je n'en puis plus.

Une porte s'ouvrait dans une palissade, et au-dessus de cette palissade se dressait un grand tas de fumier monté droit, comme on en voit si souvent dans les jardins des maraîchers ; le vent, en soufflant sur le tas, avait desséché le premier lit de paille et il en était éparpillé une assez grande épaisseur dans la rue, au pied même de la palissade.

— Je vais m'asseoir là, dit Vitalis.

— Vous disiez que, si nous nous asseyions, nous serions pris par le froid et ne pourrions plus nous relever.

Sans me répondre, il me fit signe de ramasser de la paille contre la porte, et il se laissa tomber sur cette litière plutôt qu'il ne s'y assit ; ses dents claquaient et tout son corps tremblait.

— Apporte encore de la paille, me dit-il, le tas de fumier nous met à l'abri du vent.

À l'abri du vent, cela était vrai, mais non à l'abri du froid. Lorsque j'eus amoncelé tout ce que je pus ramasser de paille, je vins m'asseoir près de Vitalis.

— Tout contre moi, dit-il, et mets Capi sur toi, il te passera un peu de sa chaleur.

Vitalis était un homme d'expérience, qui savait que le froid, dans les conditions où nous étions, pouvait devenir mortel. Pour qu'il s'exposât à ce danger, il fallait qu'il fût anéanti.

Il l'était réellement. Depuis quinze jours, il s'était couché chaque soir ayant fait plus que sa force, et cette dernière fatigue, arrivant après toutes les autres, le trouvait trop faible pour la supporter, épuisé par une longue suite d'efforts, par les privations et par l'âge.

Eut-il conscience de son état? Je ne l'ai jamais su. Mais, au moment où, ayant ramené la paille sur moi, je me serrais contre lui, je sentis qu'il se penchait sur mon visage et qu'il m'embrassait. C'était la seconde fois; ce fut la dernière.

Un petit froid empêche le sommeil chez les gens qui se mettent au lit en tremblant, un grand froid prolongé frappe d'engourdissement et de stupeur ceux qu'il saisit en plein air. Ce fut là notre cas.

À peine m'étais-je blotti contre Vitalis que je fus anéanti et que mes yeux se fermèrent. Je fis effort pour les ouvrir; et, comme je n'y parvenais pas, je me pinçai le bras fortement; mais ma peau était insensible, et ce fut à peine si, malgré toute la bonne volonté que j'y mettais, je pus me faire un peu de mal. Cependant la secousse me rendit jusqu'à un certain point la conscience de la vie. Vitalis, le dos appuyé contre la porte, haletait péniblement, par des saccades courtes et rapides. Dans mes jambes, appuyé contre ma poitrine, Capi dormait déjà. Au-dessus de notre tête, le vent soufflait toujours et nous couvrait de brins de paille qui tombaient sur nous comme des feuilles sèches qui se seraient détachées d'un arbre. Dans la rue, personne; près de nous, au loin, tout autour de nous, un silence de mort.

Ce silence me fit peur; peur de quoi? je ne m'en rendis pas compte; mais une peur vague, mêlée d'une tristesse qui m'emplit les yeux de larmes. Il me sembla que j'allais mourir là.

Et la pensée de la mort me reporta à Chavanon. Pauvre maman Barberin! mourir sans la revoir, sans revoir notre maison, mon jardinet! Et, par je ne sais quelle extravagance d'imagination, je me retrouvai dans ce jardinet : le soleil brillait, gai et chaud; les jonquilles ouvraient leurs fleurs d'or, les merles chantaient dans les buissons, et, sur la haie d'épine, mère Barberin étendait le linge qu'elle venait de laver au ruisseau qui chantait sur les cailloux.

Brusquement mon esprit quitta Chavanon, pour rejoindre le *Cygne* : Arthur dormait dans son lit; Mme Milligan était éveillée, et, comme elle entendait le vent souffler, elle se demandait où j'étais par ce grand froid.

Puis mes yeux se fermèrent de nouveau, mon cœur s'engourdit, il me sembla que je m'évanouissais.

XIX

Lise

Quand je me réveillai j'étais dans un lit; la flamme d'un grand feu éclairait la chambre où j'étais couché.

Je regardai autour de moi.

Je ne connaissais pas cette chambre.

Je ne connaissais pas non plus les figures qui m'entouraient : un homme en veste grise et en sabots jaunes; trois ou quatre enfants dont une petite fille de cinq ou six ans qui fixait sur moi des yeux étonnés; ces yeux étaient étranges, ils parlaient.

Je me soulevai.

On s'empressa autour de moi.

— Vitalis ? dis-je.

— Il demande son père, dit une jeune fille qui paraissait l'aînée des enfants.

— Ce n'est pas mon père, c'est mon maître; où est-il? Où est Capi?

Vitalis eût été mon père, on eût pris sans doute des ménagements pour me parler de lui; mais, comme il n'était que mon maître, on jugea qu'il n'y avait qu'à me dire simplement la vérité, et voici ce qu'on m'apprit.

La porte dans l'embrasure de laquelle nous nous étions blottis était celle d'un jardinier. Vers deux heures du matin, ce jardinier avait ouvert cette porte pour aller au marché, et il nous avait trouvés couchés sous notre couverture de paille. On avait commencé par nous dire de nous lever, afin de laisser passer la voiture; puis, comme nous ne bougions ni l'un ni l'autre, et que Capi seul répondait en aboyant pour nous défendre, on nous avait pris par le bras pour nous secouer. Nous n'avions pas bougé davantage. Alors on avait pensé qu'il se passait quelque chose de grave. On avait apporté une lanterne, le résultat de l'examen avait été que Vitalis était mort, mort de froid, et que je ne valais pas beaucoup mieux que lui. Cependant, comme, grâce à Capi couché sur ma poitrine, j'avais conservé un peu de chaleur au cœur, j'avais résisté et je respirais encore. On m'avait alors porté dans la maison du jardinier, et l'on m'avait couché dans le lit d'un des enfants qu'on avait fait lever. J'étais resté là six heures, à peu près mort ; puis la circulation du sang s'était rétablie, la respiration avait repris de la force, et je venais de m'éveiller.

Si engourdi, si paralysé que je fusse de corps et d'intelligence, je me trouvai cependant assez éveillé pour comprendre dans toute leur étendue les paroles que je venais d'entendre. Vitalis mort !

C'était l'homme à la veste grise, c'est-à-dire le jardinier, qui me faisait ce récit, et pendant qu'il parlait, la petite fille au regard étonné ne me quittait pas des yeux. Quand son père eut dit que Vitalis était mort, elle comprit sans doute, elle sentit par une intuition rapide le coup que cette nouvelle me portait, car, quittant vivement son coin, elle s'avança vers son père, lui posa une main sur le bras et me désigna de l'autre main, en faisant entendre un son étrange qui n'était point la parole humaine, mais quelque chose comme un soupir doux et compatissant.

D'ailleurs le geste était si éloquent qu'il n'avait pas besoin d'être appuyé par des mots ; je sentis dans ce geste et dans le regard qui l'accompagnait une sympathie instinctive, et, pour la première fois depuis ma séparation d'avec Arthur, j'éprouvai un sentiment indéfinissable de confiance et de tendresse, comme au temps où mère Barberin me regardait avant de m'embrasser. Vitalis était mort, j'étais abandonné, et cependant il me sembla que je n'étais point seul, comme s'il eût été encore là près de moi.

— Eh bien, oui, ma petite Lise, dit le père en se penchant vers sa fille, ça lui fait de la peine, mais il faut bien lui dire la vérité ; si ce n'est pas nous, ce seront les gens de la police.

Et il continua à me raconter comment on avait été prévenir les sergents de ville, et comment Vitalis avait été emporté par eux tandis qu'on m'installait, moi, dans le lit d'Alexis, son fils aîné.

— Et Capi ? dis-je, lorsqu'il eut cessé de parler.

— Capi ?

— Oui, le chien ?

— Je ne sais pas, il a disparu.
— Il a suivi le brancard, dit l'un des enfants.
— Tu l'as vu, Benjamin ?
— Je crois bien, il marchait sur les talons des porteurs, la tête basse, et de temps en temps il sautait sur le brancard ; puis, quand on le faisait descendre, il poussait un cri plaintif, comme un hurlement étouffé.

Pauvre Capi ! lui qui tant de fois avait suivi, en bon comédien, l'enterrement pour rire de Zerbino, en prenant une mine de pleureur, en poussant des soupirs qui faisaient se pâmer les enfants les plus sombres...

Le jardinier et ses enfants me laissèrent seul, et, sans trop savoir ce que j'allais faire, je me levai.

Ma harpe avait été déposée au pied du lit sur lequel on m'avait couché, je passai la bandoulière autour de mon épaule, et j'entrai dans la pièce où le jardinier était entré avec ses enfants. Il fallait bien partir, pour aller où ?... je n'en avais pas conscience ; mais je sentais que je devais partir... D'ailleurs, mort ou vivant, je voulais revoir Vitalis, et je partais.

Dans le lit, en me réveillant, je ne m'étais pas trouvé trop mal à mon aise, courbaturé seulement, avec une insupportable chaleur à la tête ; mais, quand je fus sur mes jambes, il me sembla que j'allais tomber, et je fus obligé de me retenir à une chaise. Cependant, après un moment de repos, je poussai la porte et me retrouvai en présence du jardinier et de ses enfants.

Ils étaient assis devant une table, auprès d'un feu qui flambait dans une haute cheminée, et en train de manger une bonne soupe aux choux.

L'odeur de la soupe me porta au cœur et me rappela brutalement que je n'avais pas dîné la veille ; j'eus une sorte de défaillance et je chancelai. Mon malaise se traduisit sur mon visage.

— Est-ce que tu te trouves mal, mon garçon ? demanda le jardinier d'une voix compatissante.

Je répondis qu'en effet je ne me sentais pas bien, et que, si on voulait le permettre, je resterais assis un moment auprès du feu.

Mais ce n'était plus de chaleur que j'avais besoin, c'était de nourriture ; le feu ne me remit pas, et le fumet de la soupe, le bruit des cuillers dans les assiettes, le claquement de langue de ceux qui mangeaient, augmentèrent encore ma faiblesse.

Si j'avais osé, comme j'aurais demandé une assiettée de soupe ! mais Vitalis ne m'avait pas appris à tendre la main, et la nature ne m'avait pas créé mendiant ; je serais plutôt mort de faim que de dire « j'ai faim ». Pourquoi ? je n'en sais trop rien, si ce n'est parce que je n'ai jamais voulu demander que ce que je pouvais rendre.

La petite fille au regard étrange, celle qui ne parlait pas et que son père avait appelée Lise, était en face de moi, et au lieu de manger elle me regardait sans baisser ou détourner les yeux. Tout à coup elle se leva de table et, prenant son assiette qui était pleine de soupe, elle me l'apporta et me la mit entre les genoux.

Faiblement, car je n'avais plus de voix pour parler, je fis un geste de la main pour la remercier, mais son père ne m'en laissa pas le temps.

— Accepte, mon garçon, dit-il, ce que Lise donne est bien donné ; et si le cœur t'en dit, après celle-là une autre.

Si le cœur m'en disait ! L'assiette de soupe fut engloutie en quelques secondes. Quand je reposai ma cuiller, Lise, qui était restée devant moi me regardant fixement, poussa un petit cri qui n'était plus un soupir cette fois, mais une exclamation de contentement. Puis, me prenant l'assiette, elle la tendit à son père pour qu'il la remplît, et, quand elle fut pleine, elle me la rapporta avec un sourire si doux, si encourageant que, malgré ma faim, je restai un moment sans penser à prendre l'assiette.

Comme la première fois, la soupe disparut promptement ; ce n'était pas un sourire qui plissait les lèvres des enfants me regardant, mais un vrai rire qui leur épanouissait la bouche et les lèvres.

— Eh bien ! mon garçon, dit le jardinier, tu es une jolie cuiller.

Je me sentis rougir jusqu'aux cheveux ; mais, après un moment, je crus qu'il valait mieux avouer la vérité que de me laisser accuser de gloutonnerie, et je répondis que je n'avais pas dîné la veille.

— Et déjeuné ?

— Pas déjeuné non plus.

— Et ton maître ?

— Il n'avait pas mangé plus que moi.

— Alors il est mort autant de faim que de froid.

La soupe m'avait rendu la force ; je me levai pour partir.

— Où veux-tu aller ? dit le père.

— Retrouver Vitalis, le voir encore.

— Mais tu ne sais pas où il est ?

— Je ne le sais pas.
— Tu as des amis à Paris ?
— Non.
— Des gens de ton pays ?
— Personne.
— Où est ton garni ?
— Nous n'avions pas de logement ; nous sommes arrivés hier.
— Qu'est-ce que tu veux faire ?
— Jouer de la harpe, chanter mes chansons et gagner ma vie.
— Où cela ?
— À Paris.
— Tu ferais mieux de retourner dans ton pays, chez tes parents ; où demeurent tes parents ?
— Je n'ai pas de parents.
— Tu disais que le vieux à barbe blanche n'était pas ton père ?
— Je n'ai pas de père, mais Vitalis valait un père pour moi.
— Et ta mère ?
— Je n'ai pas de mère.
— Tu as bien un oncle, une tante, des cousins, des cousines, quelqu'un ?
— Non personne.
— D'où viens-tu ?
— Mon maître m'avait acheté au mari de ma nourrice. Vous avez été bon pour moi, je vous en remercie bien de tout cœur, et, si vous voulez, je reviendrai dimanche pour vous faire danser en jouant de la harpe, si cela vous amuse.

En parlant, je m'étais dirigé vers la porte ; mais j'avais fait à peine quelques pas que Lise, qui me suivait, me prit par la main et me montra ma harpe en souriant. Il n'y avait pas à se tromper.

— Vous voulez que je joue ?

Elle fit un signe de tête, et frappa joyeusement des mains.

— Eh bien, oui, dit le père, joue-lui quelque chose.

Je pris ma harpe et, bien que je n'eusse pas le cœur à la danse ni à la gaieté, je me mis à jouer une valse, ma bonne, celle que j'avais bien dans les doigts ; ah ! comme j'aurais voulu jouer aussi bien que Vitalis et faire plaisir à cette petite fille qui me remuait si doucement le cœur avec ses yeux !

Tout d'abord elle m'écouta en me regardant fixement, puis elle marqua la mesure avec ses pieds ; puis bientôt, comme si elle était entraînée par la musique, elle se mit à tourner dans la cuisine, tandis que ses deux frères et sa sœur aînée restaient tranquillement assis ; elle ne valsait pas, bien entendu, et elle ne faisait pas les pas ordinaires, mais elle tournoyait gracieusement avec un visage épanoui.

Assis près de la cheminée, son père ne la quittait pas des yeux ; il paraissait tout ému et il battait des mains. Quand la valse fut finie et que je m'arrêtai, elle vint se camper gentiment en face de moi et me fit une belle révérence. Puis, tout de suite frappant ma harpe d'un doigt, elle fit un signe qui voulait dire « encore ».

J'aurais joué pour elle toute la journée avec plaisir ; mais son père dit que c'était assez, parce qu'il ne voulait pas qu'elle se fatiguât à tourner.

Alors, au lieu de jouer un air de valse ou de danse, je chantai ma chanson napolitaine que Vitalis m'avait apprise :

> Fenesta vascia e patrona crudele,
> Quanta sospire m'aje fatto jettare.
> M'arde stocore comm'a na cannela
> Bella quanno te sento anno menarre.

Cette chanson était pour moi ce qu'a été le « Des chevaliers de ma patrie » de *Robert le Diable* pour Nourrit, et le « Suivez-moi » de *Guillaume Tell* pour Duprez, c'est-à-dire mon morceau par excellence, celui dans lequel j'étais habitué à produire mon plus grand effet. L'air en est doux et mélancolique, avec quelque chose de tendre qui remue le cœur.

Aux premières mesures, Lise vint se placer en face de moi, ses yeux fixés sur les miens, remuant les lèvres comme si mentalement elle répétait mes paroles, puis, quand l'accent de la chanson devint plus triste, elle recula doucement de quelques pas, si bien qu'à la dernière strophe elle se jeta en pleurant sur les genoux de son père.

— Assez, dit celui-ci.

— Est-elle bête ! dit un de ses frères, celui qui s'appelait Benjamin, elle danse et puis tout de suite elle pleure.

— Pas si bête que toi ! elle comprend, dit la sœur aînée en se penchant sur elle pour l'embrasser.

Pendant que Lise se jetait sur les genoux de son père, j'avais mis ma harpe sur mon épaule et je m'étais dirigé du côté de la porte.

— Où vas-tu ? me dit-il.

— Je vous l'ai dit : essayer de revoir Vitalis, et puis après faire ce qu'il m'avait appris à faire, jouer de la harpe et chanter.

— Tu tiens donc bien à ton métier de musicien ?
— Je n'en ai pas d'autre.
— Les grands chemins ne te font pas peur ?
— Je n'ai pas de maison.
— Cependant la nuit que tu viens de passer a dû te donner à réfléchir ?
— Bien certainement, j'aimerais mieux un bon lit et le coin du feu.
— Le veux-tu, le coin du feu et le bon lit, avec le travail, bien entendu ? Si tu veux rester, tu travailleras, tu vivras avec nous. Tu comprends, n'est-ce pas, que ce n'est pas la fortune que je te propose, ni la fainéantise ? Si tu acceptes, il y aura pour toi de la peine à prendre, du mal à te donner, il faudra te lever matin, piocher dur dans la journée, mouiller de sueur le pain que tu gagneras. Mais le pain sera assuré, tu ne seras plus exposé à coucher à la belle étoile comme la nuit dernière, et peut-être à mourir abandonné au coin d'une borne ou au fond d'un fossé ; le soir tu trouveras ton lit prêt et, en mangeant ta soupe, tu auras la satisfaction de l'avoir gagnée, ce qui la rend bonne, je t'assure. Et puis enfin, si tu es un bon garçon, et j'ai dans l'idée quelque chose qui me dit que tu en es un, tu auras en nous une famille.

Lise s'était retournée, et, à travers ses larmes, elle me regardait en souriant.

Surpris par cette proposition, je restai un moment indécis, ne me rendant pas bien compte de ce que j'entendais.

Alors Lise, quittant son père, vint à moi, et, me prenant par la main, me conduisit devant une gravure enluminée qui était accrochée à la muraille ; cette gravure représentait un petit saint Jean vêtu d'une peau de mouton.

Du geste elle fit signe à son père et à ses frères de regarder la gravure, et en même temps, ramenant la main vers moi, elle lissa ma peau de mouton et montra mes cheveux qui, comme ceux de saint Jean, étaient séparés au milieu du front et tombaient sur mes épaules en frisant. Je compris qu'elle trouvait que je ressemblais au saint Jean et, sans trop savoir pourquoi, cela me fit plaisir et en même temps me toucha doucement.

— C'est vrai, dit le père, qu'il ressemble au saint Jean.

Lise frappa des mains en riant.

— Eh bien, dit le père en revenant à sa proposition, cela te va-t-il, mon garçon ?

Une famille !

J'aurais donc une famille ! Ah ! combien de fois déjà ce rêve tant caressé s'était-il évanoui ! Mère Barberin, Mme Milligan, Vitalis, tous les uns après les autres, m'avaient manqué.

Je ne serais plus seul.

Ma position était affreuse : je venais de voir mourir un homme avec lequel je vivais depuis plusieurs années et qui avait été pour moi presque un père ; en même temps j'avais perdu mon compagnon, mon camarade, mon ami, mon bon et cher Capi que j'aimais tant et qui, lui aussi, m'avait pris en si grande amitié, et cependant, quand le jardinier me proposa de rester chez lui, un sentiment de confiance me raffermit le cœur.

Tout n'était donc pas fini pour moi ; la vie pouvait recommencer.

Et ce qui me touchait, bien plus que le pain assuré dont on me parlait, c'était cet intérieur que je voyais si uni, cette vie de famille qu'on me promettait.

Ces garçons seraient mes frères.

Cette jolie petite Lise serait ma sœur.

Dans mes rêves enfantins j'avais plus d'une fois imaginé que je retrouverais mon père et ma mère ; mais je n'avais jamais pensé à des frères et à des sœurs. Et voilà qu'ils s'offraient à moi.

Ils ne l'étaient pas réellement, cela était vrai, de par la nature, mais ils pourraient le devenir de par l'amitié ; pour cela il n'y avait qu'à les aimer (ce à quoi j'étais tout disposé), et à me faire aimer d'eux, ce qui ne devait pas être difficile, car ils paraissaient tous remplis de bonté.

Vivement je dépassai la bandoulière de ma harpe de dessus mon épaule.

— Voilà une réponse, dit le père en riant, et une bonne, on voit qu'elle est agréable pour toi. Accroche ton instrument à ce clou, mon garçon, et, le jour où tu ne te trouveras pas bien avec nous, tu le reprendras pour t'envoler ; seulement tu auras soin de faire comme les hirondelles et les rossignols, tu choisiras ta saison pour te mettre en route.

— Je ne sortirai qu'une fois, lui dis-je, pour aller à la recherche de Vitalis.

— C'est trop juste, me répondit le brave homme.

La maison à la porte de laquelle nous étions venus nous abattre dépendait de la Glacière, et le jardinier qui l'occupait se nommait Acquin. Au moment où l'on me reçut dans cette maison, la famille se composait de cinq personnes : le père qu'on appelait père Pierre ; deux garçons, Alexis et Benjamin, et deux filles, Étiennette, l'aînée, et Lise, la plus jeune des enfants.

Lise était muette, mais non muette de naissance, c'est-à-dire que le mutisme n'était point chez elle la conséquence de la surdité. Pendant deux ans elle avait parlé, puis tout à coup, un peu avant d'atteindre sa quatrième année, elle avait perdu l'usage de la parole. Cet accident, survenu à la suite de convulsions, n'avait heureusement pas atteint son intelligence, qui s'était au contraire développée avec une précocité extraordinaire ; non seulement elle comprenait tout, mais encore elle disait, elle exprimait tout. Dans les familles pauvres et même dans beaucoup d'autres familles, il arrive trop souvent que l'infirmité d'un enfant est pour lui une cause d'abandon ou de répulsion. Mais cela ne s'était pas produit pour Lise, qui, par sa gentillesse et sa vivacité, son humeur douce et sa bonté expansive, avait échappé à cette fatalité. Ses frères la supportaient sans lui faire payer son malheur ; son père ne voyait que par elle ; sa sœur aînée Étiennette l'adorait.

Autrefois le droit d'aînesse était un avantage dans les familles nobles ; aujourd'hui, dans les familles d'ouvriers, c'est quelquefois hériter d'une lourde responsabilité que naître la première. Mme Acquin était morte un an après la naissance de Lise, et, depuis ce jour, Étiennette, qui avait alors deux années seulement de plus que son frère aîné, était devenue la mère de famille. Au lieu d'aller à l'école, elle avait dû rester à la maison, préparer la nourriture, coudre un bouton ou une pièce aux vêtements de son père ou de ses frères, et porter Lise dans ses bras ; on avait oublié qu'elle était fille, qu'elle était sœur, et l'on avait vite pris l'habitude de ne voir en elle qu'une servante, et une servante avec laquelle on ne se gênait guère, car on savait bien qu'elle ne quitterait pas la maison et ne se fâcherait jamais.

À porter Lise sur ses bras, à traîner Benjamin par la main, à travailler toute la journée, se levant tôt pour faire la soupe du père avant son départ pour la halle, se couchant tard pour remettre tout en ordre après le souper, à laver le linge des enfants au lavoir, à arroser l'été quand elle avait un instant de répit, à quitter son lit la nuit pour étendre les paillassons pendant l'hiver, quand la gelée prenait tout à coup, Étiennette n'avait pas eu le temps d'être une enfant, de jouer, de rire. À quatorze ans, sa figure était triste et mélancolique comme celle d'une vieille fille de trente-cinq ans, cependant avec un rayon de douceur et de résignation.

Il n'y avait pas cinq minutes que j'avais accroché ma harpe au clou qui m'avait été désigné, et que j'étais en train de raconter comment nous avions été surpris par le froid et la fatigue en revenant de Gentilly, où nous avions espéré coucher dans une carrière, quand j'entendis un grattement à la porte qui ouvrait sur le jardin, et en même temps un aboiement plaintif.

— C'est Capi! dis-je en me levant vivement.

Mais Lise me prévint; elle courut à la porte et l'ouvrit.

Le pauvre Capi s'élança d'un bond contre moi, et, quand je l'eus pris dans mes bras, il se mit à me lécher la figure en poussant des petits cris de joie; tout son corps tremblait.

— Et Capi? dis-je à M. Acquin.

Ma question fut comprise.

— Eh bien, Capi restera avec toi.

Comme s'il comprenait, à son tour, le chien sauta à terre et, mettant la patte droite sur son cœur, il salua. Cela fit beaucoup rire les enfants, surtout Lise, et pour les amuser je voulus que Capi leur jouât une pièce de son répertoire; mais lui ne voulut pas m'obéir et, sautant sur mes genoux, il recommença à m'embrasser; puis, descendant, il se mit à me tirer par la manche de ma veste.

— Il veut que je sorte, il a raison.

— Pour te mener auprès de ton maître.

Les hommes de police qui avaient emporté Vitalis avaient dit qu'ils avaient besoin de m'interroger et qu'ils viendraient dans la journée, quand je serais réchauffé et réveillé. C'était bien long, bien incertain de les attendre. J'étais anxieux d'avoir des nouvelles de Vitalis. Peut-être n'était-il pas mort comme on l'avait cru. Je n'étais pas mort, moi. Il pouvait, comme moi, être revenu à la vie.

Voyant mon inquiétude et en devinant la cause, le père m'emmena au bureau du commissaire, où l'on m'adressa questions sur questions, auxquelles je ne répondis que quand on m'eut assuré que Vitalis était mort. Ce que je savais était bien simple, je le racontai. Mais le commissaire voulut en apprendre davantage, et il m'interrogea longuement sur Vitalis et sur moi. Sur moi je répondis que je n'avais plus de parents et que Vitalis m'avait loué moyennant une somme d'argent qu'il avait payée d'avance au mari de ma nourrice.

— Et maintenant? me dit le commissaire.

À ce mot, le père intervint.

— Nous nous chargerons de lui, si vous voulez bien nous le confier.

Non seulement le commissaire voulut bien me confier au jardinier, mais encore il le félicita pour sa bonne action.

Il fallait maintenant répondre au sujet de Vitalis, et cela m'était assez difficile, car je ne savais rien ou presque rien.

Il y avait cependant un point mystérieux dont j'aurais pu parler : c'était ce qui s'était passé lors de notre dernière représentation, quand Vitalis avait chanté de façon à provoquer l'admiration et l'étonnement de la dame; il y avait aussi les menaces de Garofoli, mais je me demandais si je ne devais pas garder le silence à ce sujet. Ce que mon maître avait si soigneusement caché durant sa vie devait-il être révélé après sa mort?

Mais il n'est pas facile à un enfant de cacher quelque chose à un commissaire de police qui connaît son métier, car ces gens-là ont une manière de vous interroger qui vous perd bien vite quand vous essayez de vous échapper. Ce fut ce qui m'arriva.

En moins de cinq minutes le commissaire m'eut fait dire ce que je voulais cacher et ce que lui tenait à savoir.

— Il n'y a qu'à le conduire chez ce Garofoli, dit-il à un agent ; une fois dans la rue de Lourcine, il reconnaîtra la maison; vous monterez avec lui et vous interrogerez ce Garofoli.

Nous nous mîmes tous les trois en route : l'agent, le père et moi.

Comme l'avait dit le commissaire, il me fut facile de reconnaître la maison, et nous montâmes au quatrième étage. Je ne vis pas Mattia, qui sans doute était entré à l'hôpital. En apercevant un agent de police et en me reconnaissant, Garofoli pâlit; certainement il avait peur. Mais il se rassura bien vite quand il apprit de la bouche de l'agent ce qui nous amenait chez lui.

— Ah! le pauvre vieux est mort, dit-il.

— Vous le connaissiez?

— Parfaitement.

— Eh bien! dites-moi ce que vous savez.

— C'est bien simple. Son nom n'était point Vitalis; il s'appelait Carlo Balzani, et, si vous aviez vécu, il y a trente-cinq ou quarante ans, en Italie, ce nom suffirait seul pour vous dire ce qu'était l'homme dont vous vous inquiétez. Carlo Balzani était à cette époque le chanteur le plus fameux de toute l'Italie, et ses succès sur nos grandes scènes ont été célèbres; il a chanté partout, à Naples, à Rome, à Milan, à Venise, à Florence, à Londres, à Paris. Mais il est venu un jour où la voix s'est perdue; alors, ne pouvant plus être le roi des artistes, il n'a pas voulu que sa gloire fût amoindrie en la compromettant sur des théâtres indignes de sa réputation. Il a abdiqué son nom de Carlo Balzani et il est devenu Vitalis, se cachant de tous ceux qui l'avaient connu dans son beau temps. Cependant il fallait vivre ; il a essayé de plusieurs métiers et n'a pas réussi, si bien que, de chute en chute, il s'est fait montreur de chiens savants. Mais dans sa misère la fierté lui était restée, et il serait mort de honte, si le public avait pu apprendre que le brillant Carlo Balzani était devenu le pauvre Vitalis. Un hasard m'avait rendu maître de ce secret.

C'était donc là l'explication du mystère qui m'avait tant intrigué ! Pauvre Carlo Balzani, cher et admirable Vitalis ! On m'aurait dit qu'il avait été roi que cela ne m'aurait pas étonné.

XX

Jardinier

On devait enterrer mon maître le lendemain, et le père m'avait promis de me conduire à l'enterrement.

Mais, le lendemain, à mon grand désespoir, je ne pus me lever, car je fus pris dans la nuit d'une grande fièvre qui débuta par un frisson suivi d'une bouffée de chaleur; il me semblait que j'avais le feu dans la poitrine et que j'étais malade comme Joli-Cœur, après sa nuit passée sur l'arbre, dans la neige.

En réalité, j'avais une violente inflammation, c'est-à-dire une fluxion de poitrine causée par le refroidissement que j'avais éprouvé dans la nuit où mon pauvre maître avait péri.

Ce fut cette fluxion de poitrine qui me mit à même d'apprécier la bonté de la famille Acquin, et surtout les qualités de dévouement d'Étiennette.

Bien que chez les pauvres gens on soit ordinairement peu disposé à appeler les médecins, je fus pris d'une façon si violente et si effrayante, qu'on fit pour moi une exception à cette règle, qui est de nature autant que d'habitude. Le médecin, appelé, n'eut pas besoin d'un long examen et d'un récit détaillé pour voir quelle était ma maladie; tout de suite il déclara qu'on devait me porter à l'hospice.

C'était, en effet, le plus simple et le plus facile. Cependant cet avis ne fut pas adopté par le père.

— Puisqu'il est venu tomber à notre porte, dit-il, et non à celle de l'hospice, c'est que nous devons le garder.

Le médecin avait combattu avec toutes sortes de bonnes paroles ce raisonnement fataliste, mais sans l'ébranler. On devait me garder, et on m'avait gardé.

Et, à toutes ses occupations, Étiennette avait ajouté celle de garde-malade, me soignant doucement, méthodiquement, comme l'eût fait une sœur de Saint-Vincent-de-Paul, sans jamais une impatience ou un oubli. Quand elle était obligée de m'abandonner pour les travaux de la maison, Lise la remplaçait, et bien des fois, dans ma fièvre, j'ai vu celle-ci aux pieds de mon lit, fixant sur moi ses grands yeux inquiets. L'esprit troublé par le délire, je croyais qu'elle était mon ange gardien, et je lui parlais comme j'aurais parlé à un ange, en lui disant mes espérances et mes désirs. C'est depuis ce moment que je me suis habitué à la considérer, malgré moi, comme un être idéal, entouré d'une sorte d'auréole, que j'étais tout surpris de voir vivre de notre vie quand je m'attendais, au contraire, à la voir s'envoler avec de grandes ailes blanches.

Ma maladie fut longue et douloureuse, avec plusieurs rechutes qui eussent découragé peut-être des parents, mais qui ne lassèrent ni la patience ni le dévouement d'Étiennette. Pendant plusieurs nuits, il fallut me veiller, car j'avais la poitrine prise de manière à croire que j'allais étouffer d'un moment à l'autre, et ce furent Alexis et Benjamin qui, alternativement, se remplacèrent auprès de mon lit. Enfin la convalescence arriva ; mais, comme la maladie fut longue et capricieuse, il me fallut attendre que le printemps commençât à reverdir les prairies de la Glacière pour sortir de la maison.

Alors Lise, qui ne travaillait point, prit la place d'Étiennette, et ce fut elle qui me promena sur les bords de la Bièvre. Vers midi, quand le soleil était dans son plein, nous partions, et, nous tenant par la main, nous nous en allions doucement, suivis de Capi. Le printemps fut doux et beau cette année-là, ou tout au moins il m'en est resté un doux et beau souvenir, ce qui est la même chose.

C'est un quartier peu connu des Parisiens que celui qui se trouve entre la Maison-Blanche et la Glacière ; on sait vaguement qu'il y a quelque part par là une petite vallée, mais, comme la rivière qui l'arrose est la Bièvre, on dit et l'on croit que cette vallée est un des endroits les plus sales et les plus tristes de la banlieue de Paris. Il n'en est rien cependant, et l'endroit vaut mieux que sa réputation. La Bièvre, que l'on juge trop souvent par ce qu'elle est devenue industriellement dans le faubourg Saint-Marcel, et non par ce qu'elle était naturellement à Verrières ou à Rungis, coule là, ou tout au moins coulait là au temps dont je parle, sous un épais couvert de saules et de peupliers, et sur ses bords s'étendent de vertes prairies qui montent doucement jusqu'à des petits coteaux couronnés de maisons et de jardins. L'herbe est fraîche et drue au printemps, les pâquerettes émaillent d'étoiles blanches son tapis d'émeraude, et dans les saules qui feuillissent, dans les peupliers dont les bourgeons sont enduits d'une résine visqueuse, les oiseaux, le merle, la fauvette, le pinson, voltigent en disant par leurs chants qu'on est encore à la campagne et non déjà à la ville.

Ce fut ainsi que je vis cette petite vallée – qui depuis a bien changé – et l'impression qu'elle m'a laissée est vivace dans mon souvenir comme au jour où je la reçus. Si j'étais peintre, je vous dessinerais le rideau de peupliers sans oublier un seul arbre – et les gros saules avec les groseilliers épineux qui verdissaient sur leurs têtes, les racines implantées dans leur tronc pourri – et les glacis des fortifications sur lesquels nous faisions de si belles glissades en nous lançant sur un seul pied – et la Butte-aux-Cailles avec son moulin à vent – et la cour Sainte-Hélène avec sa population de blanchisseuses – et les tanneries qui salissent et infectent les eaux de la rivière – et la ferme Sainte-Anne, où de pauvres fous qui cultivent la terre passent à côté de vous souriant d'un sourire idiot, les membres ballants, la bouche mi-ouverte montrant un bout de langue, avec une vilaine grimace.

Dans nos promenades, Lise naturellement ne parlait pas, mais, chose étonnante, nous n'avions pas besoin de paroles, nous nous regardions et nous nous comprenions si bien avec nos yeux que j'en venais à ne plus lui parler moi-même.

À la longue les forces me revinrent, et je pus m'employer aux travaux du jardin; j'attendais ce moment avec impatience, car j'avais hâte de faire pour les autres ce que les autres faisaient pour moi, de travailler pour eux et de leur rendre, dans la mesure de mes forces, ce qu'ils m'avaient donné. Je n'avais jamais travaillé, car, si pénibles que soient les longues marches, elles ne sont pas un travail continu qui demande la volonté et l'application; mais il me semblait que je travaillerais bien, au moins courageusement, à l'exemple de ceux que je voyais autour de moi.

C'était la saison où les giroflées commencent à arriver sur les marchés de Paris, et la culture du père Acquin était à ce moment celle des giroflées; notre jardin en était rempli; il y en avait des rouges, des blanches, des violettes, disposées par couleurs, séparées sous les châssis, de sorte qu'il y avait des lignes toutes blanches et d'autres à côté toutes rouges, ce qui était très joli ; et le soir, avant que les châssis fussent refermés, l'air était embaumé par le parfum de toutes ces fleurs.

La tâche qu'on me donna, la proportionnant à mes forces encore bien faibles, consista à lever les panneaux vitrés le matin, quand la gelée était passée, et à les refermer le soir avant qu'elle arrivât ; dans la journée je devais les ombrer avec du paillis que je jetais dessus pour préserver les plantes d'un coup de soleil. Cela n'était ni bien difficile, ni bien pénible ; mais cela était assez long, car j'avais plusieurs centaines de panneaux à remuer deux fois par jour et à surveiller pour les ombrer ou les découvrir selon l'ardeur du soleil.

Pendant ce temps, Lise restait auprès du manège qui servait à élever l'eau nécessaire aux arrosages, et, quand la vieille Cocotte, fatiguée de tourner, les yeux encapuchonnés dans son masque de cuir, ralentissait le pas, elle l'excitait en faisant claquer un petit fouet ; un des frères renversait les seaux que faisait monter ce manège, et l'autre aidait son père : ainsi chacun avait son poste, et personne ne perdait son temps.

J'avais vu les paysans travailler dans mon village, mais je n'avais aucune idée de l'application, du courage et de l'intensité avec lesquels travaillent les jardiniers des environs de Paris, qui, debout bien avant que le soleil paraisse, au lit bien tard après qu'il est couché, se dépensent tout entiers et peinent tant qu'ils ont de forces durant cette longue journée. J'avais vu aussi cultiver la terre, mais je n'avais aucune idée de ce qu'on peut lui faire produire par le travail, en ne lui laissant pas de repos. Je fus à bonne école chez le père Acquin.

On ne m'employa pas toujours aux châssis ; les forces me vinrent, et j'eus aussi la satisfaction de pouvoir mettre quelque chose dans la terre, et la satisfaction beaucoup plus grande encore de le voir pousser. C'était mon ouvrage à moi, ma chose, ma création, et cela me donnait comme un sentiment de fierté : j'étais donc propre à quelque chose, je le prouvais, et, ce qui m'était plus doux encore, je le sentais. Cela, je vous assure, paie de bien des peines.

Malgré les fatigues que cette vie nouvelle m'imposa, je m'habituai bien vite à cette existence laborieuse qui ressemblait si peu à mon existence vagabonde de bohémien. Au lieu de courir en liberté comme autrefois, n'ayant d'autre peine que d'aller droit devant moi sur les grandes routes, il fallait maintenant rester enfermé entre les quatre murs d'un jardin, et du matin au soir travailler rudement, la chemise mouillée sur le dos, les arrosoirs au bout des bras et les pieds nus dans les sentiers boueux ; mais autour de moi chacun travaillait tout aussi rudement ; les arrosoirs du père étaient plus lourds que les miens, et sa chemise était plus mouillée de sueur que les nôtres. C'est un grand soulagement dans la peine que l'égalité. Et puis je rencontrais là ce que je croyais avoir perdu à jamais : la vie de la famille. Je n'étais plus seul, je n'étais plus l'enfant abandonné ; j'avais mon lit à moi, j'avais ma place à moi à la table qui nous réunissait tous. Si durant la journée quelquefois Alexis ou Benjamin m'envoyait une taloche, la main retombée je n'y pensais plus, pas plus qu'ils ne pensaient à celles que je leur rendais ; et le soir, tous autour de la soupe, nous nous retrouvions amis et frères.

Pour être vrai, il faut dire que tout ne nous était pas travail et fatigue ; nous avions aussi nos heures de repos et de plaisir, courtes, bien entendu, mais précisément par cela même plus délicieuses.

Le dimanche, dans l'après-midi, on se réunissait sous un petit berceau de vignes qui touchait la maison ; j'allais prendre ma harpe au clou où elle restait accrochée pendant toute la semaine, et je faisais danser les deux frères et les deux sœurs. Ni les uns ni les autres n'avaient appris à danser ; mais Alexis et Benjamin avaient été une fois à un bal de noces aux *Mille Colonnes*, et ils en avaient rapporté des souvenirs plus ou moins exacts de ce qu'est la contredanse ; c'étaient ces souvenirs qui les guidaient. Quand ils étaient las de danser, ils me faisaient chanter mon répertoire, et ma chanson napolitaine produisait toujours son irrésistible effet sur Lise :

Fenesta vascia e patrona crudele.

Jamais je n'ai chanté la dernière strophe sans voir ses yeux mouillés.

Alors, pour la distraire, je jouais une pièce bouffonne avec Capi. Pour lui aussi ces dimanches étaient des jours de fête ; ils lui rappelaient le passé, et, quand il avait fini son rôle, il l'eût volontiers recommencé.

Ces dimanches étaient aussi pour moi le jour de Vitalis. Je jouais de la harpe et je chantais comme s'il eût été là. Bon Vitalis ! à mesure que je grandissais, mon respect pour sa mémoire grandissait aussi. Je comprenais mieux ce qu'il avait été pour moi.

Deux années s'écoulèrent ainsi, et, comme le père m'emmenait souvent avec lui au marché, au quai aux Fleurs, à la Madeleine, au Château-d'Eau, ou bien chez les fleuristes à qui nous portions nos plantes, j'en arrivai petit à petit à connaître Paris et à comprendre que, si ce n'était pas une ville de marbre et d'or comme je l'avais imaginé, ce n'était point non plus une ville de boue, comme mon entrée par Charenton et le quartier Mouffetard me l'avait fait croire un peu trop vite.

Je vis les monuments, j'entrai dans quelques-uns, je me promenai le long des quais, sur les boulevards, dans le jardin du Luxembourg, dans celui des Tuileries, aux Champs-Élysées. Je vis des statues. Je restai en admiration devant le mouvement des foules. Je me fis une sorte d'idée de ce qu'était l'existence d'une grande capitale.

Heureusement mon éducation ne se fit point seulement par les yeux et selon les hasards de mes promenades ou de mes courses à travers Paris. Avant de s'établir jardinier à son compte, le père avait travaillé aux pépinières du Jardin des Plantes, et là, il s'était trouvé en contact avec des gens de science et d'étude dont le frottement lui avait donné la curiosité de lire et d'apprendre. Pendant plusieurs années il avait employé ses économies à acheter des livres et ses quelques heures de loisir à lire ces livres. Lorsqu'il s'était marié et que les enfants étaient arrivés, les heures de loisir avaient été rares. Il avait fallu avant tout gagner le pain de chaque jour ; les livres avaient été abandonnés, mais ils n'avaient été ni perdus, ni vendus, et on les avait gardés dans une armoire. Le premier hiver que je passai dans la famille Acquin fut très long, et les travaux de jardinage se trouvèrent sinon suspendus, au moins ralentis pendant plusieurs mois. Alors, pour occuper les soirées que nous passions au coin du feu, les vieux livres furent tirés de l'armoire et distribués entre nous. C'étaient pour la plupart des ouvrages sur la botanique et l'histoire des plantes avec quelques récits de voyages. Alexis et Benjamin n'avaient point hérité des goûts de leur père pour l'étude, et régulièrement tous les soirs, après avoir ouvert leur volume, ils s'endormaient sur la troisième ou la quatrième page. Pour moi, moins disposé au sommeil ou plus curieux, je lisais jusqu'au moment où nous devions nous coucher. Les premières leçons de Vitalis n'avaient point été perdues, et en me disant cela, en me couchant, je pensais à lui avec attendrissement.

Mon désir d'apprendre rappela au père le temps où il prenait deux sous sur son déjeuner pour acheter des livres, et, à ceux qui étaient dans l'armoire, il en ajouta quelques autres qu'il me rapporta de Paris. Les choix étaient faits par le hasard ou les promesses du titre ; mais enfin c'étaient toujours des livres, et, s'ils mirent alors un peu de désordre dans mon esprit sans direction, ce désordre s'effaça plus tard, et ce qu'il y avait de bon en eux me resta et m'est resté ; tant il est vrai que toute lecture profite.

Lise ne savait pas lire, mais, en me voyant plongé dans les livres aussitôt que j'avais une heure de liberté, elle eut la curiosité de savoir ce qui m'intéressait si vivement. Tout d'abord elle voulut me prendre ces livres qui m'empêchaient de jouer avec elle ; puis, voyant que malgré tout je revenais à eux, elle me demanda de les lui lire, et puis de lui montrer à lire dans l'imprimé. Grâce à son intelligence et malgré son infirmité, les yeux suppléant aux oreilles, j'en vins à bout. Mais la lecture à haute voix, qui nous occupait tous les deux, fut toujours préférée par elle. Ce fut un nouveau lien entre nous. Repliée sur elle-même, l'intelligence toujours aux aguets, n'étant point occupée par les frivolités ou les niaiseries de la conversation, elle devait trouver dans la lecture ce qu'elle y trouva en effet : une distraction et une nourriture.

Combien d'heures nous avons passées ainsi : elle assise devant moi, ne me quittant pas des yeux, moi lisant ! Souvent je m'arrêtais en rencontrant des mots ou des passages que je ne comprenais pas, et je la regardais. Alors nous restions quelquefois longtemps à chercher ; puis, quand nous ne trouvions pas, elle me faisait signe de continuer avec un geste qui voulait dire « plus tard ». Je lui appris aussi à dessiner, c'est-à-dire à ce que j'appelais dessiner. Cela fut long, difficile, mais enfin j'en vins à peu près à bout. Sans doute j'étais un assez pauvre maître. Mais nous nous entendions, et le bon accord du maître et de l'élève vaut souvent mieux que le talent. Quelle joie quand elle traça quelques traits où l'on pouvait reconnaître ce qu'elle avait voulu faire ! Le père Acquin m'embrassa.

— Allons, dit-il en riant, j'aurais pu faire une plus grande bêtise que de te prendre. Lise te paiera cela plus tard.

Plus tard, c'est-à-dire quand elle parlerait, car on n'avait point renoncé à lui rendre la parole, seulement les médecins avaient dit que pour le moment il n'y avait rien à faire et qu'il fallait attendre une crise.

Plus tard était aussi le geste triste qu'elle me faisait quand je lui chantais des chansons. Elle avait voulu que je lui apprisse à jouer de la harpe, et très vite ses doigts s'étaient habitués à imiter les miens. Mais naturellement elle n'avait pas pu apprendre à chanter, et cela la dépitait. Bien des fois j'ai vu des larmes dans ses yeux qui me disaient son chagrin. Mais, dans sa bonne et douce nature, le chagrin ne persistait pas ; elle s'essuyait les yeux et, avec un sourire résigné, elle me faisait son geste : plus tard.

Adopté par le père Acquin et traité en frère par les enfants, je serais probablement resté à jamais à la Glacière sans une catastrophe qui tout à coup vint une fois encore changer ma vie, car il était dit que je ne pourrais pas rester longtemps heureux, et que, quand je me croirais le mieux assuré du repos, ce serait justement l'heure où je serais rejeté de nouveau, par des événements indépendants de ma volonté, dans ma vie aventureuse.

XXI

La famille dispersée

Il y avait des jours où, me trouvant seul et réfléchissant, je me disais :

« Tu es trop heureux, mon garçon, ça ne durera pas. »

Comment me viendrait le malheur, je ne le prévoyais pas, mais j'étais à peu près certain que, d'un côté ou de l'autre, il me viendrait.

Cela me rendait assez souvent triste; mais, d'un autre côté, cela avait de bon que, pour éviter ce malheur, je m'appliquais à faire de mon mieux ce que je faisais, me figurant que ce serait par ma faute que je serais frappé.

Ce ne fut point par ma faute; mais, si je me trompai sur ce point, je ne devinai que trop juste quant au malheur.

J'ai dit que le père cultivait les giroflées; c'est une culture assez facile et que les jardiniers des environs de Paris réussissent à merveille : témoin les grosses plantes trapues garnies de fleurs du haut en bas qu'ils apportent sur les marchés aux mois d'avril et de mai. La seule habileté nécessaire au jardinier qui cultive les giroflées est celle qui consiste à choisir des plantes à fleurs doubles, car la mode repousse les fleurs simples. Or, comme les graines qu'on sème donnent dans une proportion à peu près égale des plantes simples et des plantes doubles, il y a un intérêt important à ne garder que les plantes doubles; sans cela on serait exposé à soigner chèrement cinquante pour cent de plantes qu'il faudrait jeter au moment de les voir fleurir, c'est-à-dire après un an de culture. Ce choix se nomme l'*essimplage*, et il se fait à l'inspection de certains caractères qui se montrent dans les feuilles et dans le port de la plante. Peu de jardiniers savent pratiquer cette opération de l'*essimplage,* et même c'est un secret qui s'est conservé dans quelques familles. Quand les cultivateurs de giroflées ont besoin de faire leur choix de plantes doubles, ils s'adressent à ceux de leurs confrères qui possèdent ce secret, et ceux-ci « vont en ville », ni plus ni moins que des médecins ou des experts, donner leur consultation.

Le père était un des plus habiles *essimpleurs* de Paris ; aussi, au moment où doit se faire cette opération, toutes ses journées étaient-elles prises. C'était alors pour nous, et particulièrement pour Étiennette, notre mauvais temps, car entre confrères on ne se visite pas sans boire un litre, quelquefois deux, quelquefois trois, et, quand il avait ainsi visité deux ou trois jardiniers, il rentrait à la maison la figure rouge, la parole embarrassée et les mains tremblantes.

Jamais Étiennette ne se couchait sans qu'il fût rentré, même quand il rentrait tard, très tard.

Alors, quand j'étais éveillé, ou quand le bruit qu'il faisait me réveillait, j'entendais de ma chambre leur conversation.

— Pourquoi n'es-tu pas couchée ? disait le père.

— Parce que j'ai voulu voir si tu n'avais besoin de rien.

— Ainsi Mlle Gendarme me surveille !

— Si je ne veillais pas, à qui parlerais-tu ?

— Tu veux voir si je marche droit ; eh bien ! regarde, je parie que je vais à la porte des enfants sans quitter ce rang de pavés.

Un bruit de pas inégaux retentissait dans la cuisine, puis il se faisait un silence.

— Lise va bien ? disait-il.

— Oui, elle dort ; si tu voulais ne pas faire de bruit.

— Je ne fais pas de bruit, je marche droit ; il faut bien que je marche droit, puisque les filles accusent leur père. Qu'est-ce qu'elle a dit en ne me voyant pas rentrer pour souper ?

— Rien ; elle a regardé ta place.

— Ah ! elle a regardé ma place.

— Oui.

— Plusieurs fois. Est-ce qu'elle a regardé plusieurs fois ?

— Souvent.

— Et qu'est-ce qu'elle disait ?

— Ses yeux disaient que tu n'étais pas là.

— Alors elle te demandait pourquoi je n'étais pas là, et tu lui disais que j'étais avec les amis ?

— Non, elle ne me demandait rien, et je ne lui disais rien ; elle savait bien où tu étais.

— Elle le savait, elle savait que... Elle s'est bien endormie ?

— Non, il y a un quart d'heure seulement que le sommeil l'a prise ; elle voulait t'attendre.

— Et toi, qu'est-ce que tu voulais ?

— Je voulais qu'elle ne te vît pas rentrer.

Puis après un moment de silence :

— Tiennette, tu es une bonne fille ; écoute, demain je vais chez Louisot, eh bien ! je te jure, tu entends bien, je te jure de rentrer pour souper ; je ne veux plus que tu m'attendes, et je ne veux pas que Lise s'endorme tourmentée.

Mais les promesses, les serments ne servaient pas toujours, et il n'en rentrait pas moins tard, une fois qu'il acceptait un verre de vin. À la maison, Lise était toute-puissante, dehors elle était oubliée.

— Vois-tu, disait-il, on boit un coup sans y penser, parce qu'on ne peut pas refuser les amis ; on boit le second parce qu'on a bu le premier, et l'on est bien décidé à ne pas boire le troisième ; mais boire donne soif. Et puis, le vin vous monte à la tête ; on sait que, quand on est lancé, on oublie les chagrins ; on ne pense plus aux créanciers ; on voit tout éclairé par le soleil ; on sort de sa peau pour se promener dans un autre monde, le monde où l'on désirait aller. Et l'on boit. Voilà.

Il faut dire que cela n'arrivait pas souvent. D'ailleurs la saison de l'*essimplage* n'était pas longue, et, quand cette saison était passée, le père, n'ayant plus de motifs pour sortir, ne sortait plus. Il n'était pas homme à aller au cabaret tout seul, ni par paresse à perdre son temps.

La saison des giroflées terminée, nous préparions d'autres plantes, car il est de règle qu'un jardinier ne doit pas avoir une seule place de son jardin vide ; aussitôt que des plantes sont vendues, d'autres doivent les remplacer.

L'art pour un jardinier qui travaille en vue du marché est d'apporter ses fleurs sur le marché au moment où il a chance d'en tirer le plus haut prix. Or, ce moment est celui des grandes fêtes de l'année : la Saint-Pierre, la Sainte-Marie, la Saint-Louis, car le nombre est considérable de ceux qui s'appellent Pierre, Marie, Louis ou Louise, et par conséquent le nombre est considérable aussi des pots de fleurs ou des bouquets qu'on vend ces jours-là et qui sont destinés à souhaiter la fête à un parent ou à un ami. Tout le monde a vu la veille de ces fêtes les rues de Paris pleines de fleurs, non seulement dans les boutiques ou sur les marchés, mais encore sur les trottoirs, au coin des rues, sur les marches des maisons, partout où l'on peut disposer un étalage.

Le père Acquin, après sa saison de giroflées, travaillait en vue des grandes fêtes du mois de juillet et du mois d'août, surtout du mois d'août, dans lequel se trouve la Sainte-Marie et la Saint-Louis, et pour cela nous préparions des milliers de reines-marguerites, des fuchsias, les lauriers-roses, tout autant que nos châssis et nos serres pouvaient en contenir ; il fallait que toutes ces plantes arrivassent à floraison au jour dit, ni trop tôt, elles auraient été passées au moment de la vente, ni trop tard, elles n'auraient pas encore été en fleurs. On comprend que cela exige un certain talent, car on n'est pas maître du soleil, ni du temps, qui est plus ou moins beau. Le père Acquin était passé maître dans cet art, et jamais ses plantes n'arrivaient trop tôt ni trop tard. Mais aussi que de soins, que de travail !

Au moment où j'en suis arrivé de mon récit, notre saison s'annonçait comme devant être excellente ; nous étions au 5 août et toutes nos plantes étaient à point. Dans le jardin, en plein air, les reines-marguerites montraient leurs corolles prêtes à s'épanouir, et dans les serres ou sous les châssis, dont le verre était soigneusement blanchi au lait de chaux pour tamiser la lumière, fuchsias et lauriers-roses commençaient à fleurir ; ils formaient de gros buissons ou des pyramides garnies de boutons du haut en bas. Le coup d'œil était superbe, et, de temps en temps, je voyais le père se frotter les mains avec contentement.

— La saison sera bonne, disait-il à ses fils.

Et en riant tout bas il faisait le compte de ce que la vente de toutes ces fleurs lui rapporterait.

On avait rudement travaillé pour en arriver là et sans prendre une heure de congé, même le dimanche ; cependant, tout étant à point et en ordre, il fut décidé que pour notre récompense nous irions tous dîner, ce dimanche 5 août, à Arcueil chez un des amis du père, jardinier comme lui ; Capi lui-même serait de la partie. On travaillerait jusqu'à trois ou quatre heures, puis, quand tout serait fini, on fermerait la porte à clef, et l'on s'en irait gaiement, on arriverait à Arcueil vers cinq ou six heures, puis, après dîner, on reviendrait tout de suite pour ne pas se coucher trop tard et être au travail le lundi de bonne heure, frais et dispos.

Quelle joie !

Il fut fait ainsi qu'il avait été décidé, et, quelques minutes avant quatre heures, le père tournait la clef dans la serrure de la grande porte.

— En route tout le monde! dit-il joyeusement.

— En avant, Capi!

Et, prenant Lise par la main, je me mis à courir avec elle, accompagné par les aboiements joyeux de Capi qui sautait autour de nous. Peut-être croyait-il que nous nous en allions pour longtemps sur les grands chemins, ce qui lui aurait mieux plu que de rester à la maison, où il s'ennuyait, car il ne m'était pas toujours possible de m'occuper de lui – ce qu'il aimait par-dessus tout.

Nous étions tous endimanchés et superbes avec nos beaux habits à manger du rôti. Il y avait des gens qui se retournaient pour nous voir passer. Je ne sais pas ce que j'étais moi-même, mais Lise, avec son chapeau de paille, sa robe bleue et ses bottines de toile grise, était bien la plus jolie petite fille qu'on puisse voir, la plus vivante. C'était la grâce dans la vivacité ; ses yeux, ses narines frémissantes, ses épaules, ses bras, tout en elle parlait et disait son plaisir.

Le temps passa si vite que je n'en eus pas conscience ; tout ce que je sais, c'est que, comme nous arrivions à la fin du dîner, l'un de nous remarqua que le ciel s'emplissait de nuages noirs du côté du couchant, et, comme notre table était servie en plein air sous un gros sureau, il nous fut facile de constater qu'un orage se préparait.

— Les enfants, il faut se dépêcher de rentrer à la Glacière.

À ce mot, il y eut une exclamation générale :

— Déjà!

Lise ne dit rien, mais elle fit des gestes de dénégation et de protestation.

— Si le vent s'élève, dit le père, il peut chavirer les panneaux ; en route.

Il n'y avait pas à répliquer davantage ; nous savions tous que les panneaux vitrés sont la fortune des jardiniers, et que, si le vent casse les verres, c'est la ruine pour eux.

— Je pars en avant, dit le père ; viens avec moi, Benjamin, et toi aussi, Alexis, nous prendrons le pas accéléré. Remi viendra en arrière avec Étiennette et Lise.

Et, sans en dire davantage, ils partirent à grands pas, tandis que nous les suivions moins vite, réglant notre marche, Étiennette et moi, sur celle de Lise.

Il ne s'agissait plus de rire, et nous ne courions plus, nous ne gambadions plus.

Le ciel devenait de plus en plus noir, et l'orage arrivait rapidement, précédé par des nuages de poussière que le vent, qui s'était élevé, entraînait en gros tourbillons. Quand on se trouvait pris dans un de ces tourbillons, il fallait s'arrêter, tourner le dos au vent, et se boucher les yeux avec les deux mains, car on était aveuglé; si l'on respirait, on sentait dans sa bouche un goût de cailloux.

Le tonnerre roulait dans le lointain, et ses grondements se rapprochaient rapidement, se mêlant à des éclats stridents.

Étiennette et moi nous avions pris Lise par la main, et nous la tirions après nous; mais elle avait peine à nous suivre, et nous ne marchions pas aussi vite que nous aurions voulu.

Arriverions-nous avant l'orage?

Le père Benjamin et Alexis arriveraient-ils?

Pour eux, la question était de tout autre importance; pour nous, il s'agissait simplement de n'être pas mouillés, pour eux de mettre les châssis à l'abri de la destruction, c'est-à-dire de les fermer pour que le vent ne pût pas les prendre en dessous et les culbuter pêle-mêle.

Les fracas du tonnerre étaient de plus en plus répétés, et les nuages s'étaient tellement épaissis qu'il faisait presque nuit; quand le vent les entrouvrait on apercevait, çà et là dans leurs tourbillons noirs, des profondeurs cuivrées. Évidemment ces nuages allaient crever d'un instant à l'autre.

Chose étrange! au milieu des éclats du tonnerre, nous entendîmes un bruit formidable qui arrivait sur nous, et qui était inexplicable. Il semblait que c'était un régiment de cavaliers qui se précipitaient pour fuir l'orage; mais cela était absurde: comment des cavaliers seraient-ils venus dans ce quartier?

Tout à coup la grêle se mit à tomber; quelques grêlons d'abord qui nous frappèrent au visage, puis, presque instantanément, une vraie avalanche; il fallut nous jeter sous une grande porte.

Et alors nous vîmes tomber l'averse de grêle la plus terrible qu'on puisse imaginer. En un instant la rue fut couverte d'une couche blanche comme en plein hiver; les grêlons étaient gros comme des œufs de pigeon, et en tombant ils produisaient un tapage assourdissant au milieu duquel éclataient de temps en temps des bruits de vitres cassées. Avec les grêlons qui glissaient des toits dans la rue tombaient toutes sortes de choses, des morceaux de tuiles, des plâtras, des ardoises broyées, surtout des ardoises qui faisaient des tas noirs au milieu de la blancheur de la grêle.

— Hélas! les panneaux! s'écria Étiennette.

C'était aussi la pensée qui m'était venue à l'esprit.

— Peut-être le père sera-t-il arrivé à temps?

— Quand même ils seraient arrivés avant la grêle, jamais ils n'auront eu le temps de couvrir les panneaux avec les paillassons; tout va être perdu.

— On dit que la grêle ne tombe que par places.

— Nous sommes trop près de la maison pour qu'elle nous ait épargnés; si elle tombe sur le jardin comme ici, le pauvre père va être ruiné; oh! mon Dieu, il comptait tant sur la vente, et il avait tant besoin de cet argent!

Sans bien connaître le prix des choses, j'avais souvent entendu dire que les panneaux vitrés coûtaient quinze ou dix-huit cents francs le cent, et je compris tout de suite quel désastre ce pouvait être pour nous, si la grêle avait brisé nos cinq ou six cents panneaux, sans parler des serres ni des plantes.

J'aurais voulu interroger Étiennette, mais c'était à peine si nous pouvions nous entendre, tant le tapage produit par les grêlons était assourdissant; et puis, à vrai dire, Étiennette ne paraissait pas disposée à parler; elle regardait tomber la grêle avec une figure désolée, comme doit l'être celle des gens qui voient brûler leur maison.

Cette terrible averse ne dura pas longtemps, cinq ou six minutes peut-être, et elle cessa tout à coup comme tout à coup elle avait commencé; le nuage fila sur Paris, et nous pûmes sortir de dessous notre grande porte. Dans la rue, les grêlons durs et ronds roulaient sous les pieds comme les galets de la mer, et il y en avait une telle épaisseur que les pieds s'enfonçaient dedans jusqu'à la cheville.

Lise ne pouvant marcher dans cette grêle glacée, avec ses bottines de toile, je la pris sur mon dos; son visage, si gai en venant, était maintenant navré, des larmes roulaient dans ses yeux.

Nous ne tardâmes pas à arriver à la maison dont la grande porte était restée ouverte; nous entrâmes vivement dans le jardin.

Quel spectacle! tout était brisé, haché: panneaux, fleurs, morceaux de verre, grêlons formaient un mélange, un fouillis sans forme; de ce jardin, si beau, si riche le matin, rien ne restait que ces débris sans nom.

Où était le père ?

Nous le cherchâmes, ne le voyant nulle part, et nous arrivâmes ainsi à la grande serre dont pas une vitre n'était restée intacte ; il était assis, affaissé, pour mieux dire, sur un escabeau au milieu des débris qui couvraient le sol, Alexis et Benjamin près de lui immobiles.

— Oh ! mes pauvres enfants ! s'écria-t-il en levant la tête à notre approche, qui lui avait été signalée par le bruit du verre que nous écrasions sous nos pas, oh ! mes pauvres enfants !

Et, prenant Lise dans ses bras, il se mit à pleurer sans ajouter un mot.

Qu'aurait-il dit ?

C'était un désastre ; mais, si grand qu'il fût aux yeux, il était plus terrible encore par ses conséquences.

Bientôt j'appris par Étiennette et par les garçons combien le désespoir du père était justifié. Il y avait dix ans que le père avait acheté ce jardin et avait bâti lui-même cette maison. Celui qui lui avait vendu le terrain lui avait aussi prêté de l'argent pour acheter le matériel nécessaire à son métier de fleuriste. Le tout était payable ou remboursable, en quinze ans, par annuités. Jusqu'à cette époque, le père avait pu payer régulièrement ces annuités à force de travail et de privations. Ces paiements réguliers étaient d'autant plus indispensables, que son créancier n'attendait qu'une occasion, c'est-à-dire qu'un retard, pour reprendre terrain, maison, matériel, en gardant, bien entendu, les dix annuités qu'il avait déjà reçues. C'était même là, paraît-il, sa spéculation, et c'était parce qu'il espérait bien qu'en quinze ans il arriverait un jour où le père ne pourrait pas payer qu'il avait risqué cette spéculation, pour lui sans danger – tandis qu'elle en était pleine, au contraire, pour son débiteur.

Ce jour était enfin venu, grâce à la grêle.

Maintenant qu'allait-il se passer ?

Nous ne restâmes pas longtemps dans l'incertitude, et, le lendemain du jour où le père devait payer son annuité avec le produit de la vente des plantes, nous vîmes entrer à la maison un monsieur en noir, qui n'avait pas l'air trop poli et qui nous donna un papier timbré sur lequel il écrivit quelques mots dans une ligne restée en blanc.

C'était un huissier.

Et, depuis ce jour, il revint à chaque instant, si bien qu'il finit par connaître nos noms.

— Bonjour, Rémi, disait-il ; bonjour, Alexis ; cela va bien, mademoiselle Étiennette ?

Et il nous donnait son papier timbré, en souriant, comme à des amis.

— Au revoir, les enfants !

— Au diable !

Le père ne restait plus à la maison, il courait la ville. Où allait-il ? je n'en sais rien, car, lui qui autrefois était si communicatif, il ne disait plus un mot. Il allait chez les gens d'affaires, sans doute devant les tribunaux.

Et à cette pensée je me sentais effrayé ; Vitalis aussi avait paru devant les tribunaux, et je savais ce qu'il en était résulté.

Pour le père, le résultat se fit beaucoup plus attendre, et une partie de l'hiver s'écoula ainsi. Comme nous n'avions pas pu, bien entendu, réparer nos serres et faire vitrer nos panneaux, nous cultivions le jardin en légumes et en fleurs qui ne demandaient pas d'abri ; cela ne serait pas d'un grand produit, mais enfin cela serait toujours quelque chose, et puis c'était du travail.

Un soir, le père rentra plus accablé que de coutume.

— Les enfants, dit-il, c'est fini.

Je voulus sortir, car je compris qu'il allait se passer quelque chose de grave, et, comme il s'adressait à ses enfants, il me semblait que je ne devais pas écouter.

Mais d'un geste il me retint :

— N'es-tu pas de la famille ? dit-il, et, quoique tu ne sois pas bien âgé pour entendre ce que j'ai à te dire, tu as déjà été assez éprouvé par le malheur pour le comprendre ; les enfants, je vais vous quitter.

Il n'y eut qu'une exclamation, qu'un cri de douleur.

Lise sauta dans ses bras et l'embrassa en pleurant.

— Oh ! vous pensez bien que ce n'est pas volontairement qu'on abandonne de bons enfants comme vous, une chère petite comme Lise.

Et il la serra sur son cœur.

— Mais j'ai été condamné à payer, et, comme je n'ai pas l'argent, on va tout vendre ici ; puis, comme ce ne sera pas assez, on me mettra en prison, où je resterai cinq ans ; ne pouvant pas payer avec mon argent, je paierai avec mon corps, avec ma liberté.

Nous nous mîmes tous à pleurer.

— Oui, c'est bien triste, dit-il, mais il n'y a pas à aller contre la loi, et c'est la loi.

— Cinq ans ! Que deviendrez-vous pendant ce temps-là ? Voilà le terrible.

Il se fit un silence.

— Vous pensez bien que je n'ai pas été sans réfléchir à cela ; et voilà ce que j'ai décidé pour ne pas vous laisser seuls et abandonnés après que j'aurai été arrêté.

Un peu d'espérance me revint.

— Rémi va écrire à ma sœur Catherine Suriot, à Dreuzy, dans la Nièvre ; il va lui expliquer la position et la prier de venir ; avec Catherine qui ne perd pas facilement la tête, et qui connaît les affaires, nous déciderons le meilleur.

C'était la première fois que j'écrivais une lettre ; ce fut un pénible, un cruel début.

Bien que les paroles du père fussent vagues, elles contenaient pourtant une espérance, et, dans la position où nous étions, c'était déjà beaucoup que d'espérer.

Quoi ?

Nous ne le voyions pas, mais nous espérions. Catherine allait arriver, et c'était une femme qui connaissait les affaires ; cela suffisait à des enfants simples et ignorants tels que nous. Pour ceux qui connaissent les affaires, il n'y a plus de difficultés en ce monde.

Cependant elle n'arriva pas aussitôt que nous l'avions imaginé, et les gardes du commerce, c'est-à-dire les gens qui arrêtent les débiteurs, arrivèrent avant elle.

Le père allait justement s'en aller chez un de ses amis, lorsqu'en sortant dans la rue il les trouva devant lui ; je l'accompagnais, en une seconde nous fûmes entourés. Mais le père ne voulait pas se sauver, il pâlit comme s'il allait se trouver mal et demanda aux gardes, d'une voix faible, à embrasser ses enfants.

— Il ne faut pas vous désoler, mon brave, dit l'un d'eux, la prison pour dettes n'est pas si terrible que ça, et on y trouve de bons garçons.

Nous rentrâmes à la maison, entourés des gardes du commerce.

J'allai chercher les garçons dans le jardin.

Quand nous revînmes, le père tenait dans ses bras Lise, qui pleurait à chaudes larmes.

Alors un des gardes lui parla à l'oreille, mais je n'entendis pas ce qu'il lui dit.

— Oui, répondit le père, vous avez raison, il le faut.

Et, se levant brusquement, il posa Lise à terre ; mais elle se cramponna à lui et ne voulut pas lâcher sa main.

Alors il embrassa Étiennette, Alexis et Benjamin.

Je me tenais dans un coin, les yeux obscurcis par les larmes ; il m'appela :

— Et toi, Rémi, ne viens-tu pas m'embrasser ? n'es-tu pas mon enfant ?

Nous étions éperdus.

— Restez là, dit le père d'un ton de commandement, je vous l'ordonne.

Et vivement il sortit après avoir mis la main de Lise dans celle d'Étiennette.

J'aurais voulu le suivre, et je me dirigeai vers la porte, mais Étiennette me fit signe de m'arrêter.

Où aurais-je été ? Qu'aurais-je fait ?

Nous restâmes anéantis au milieu de notre cuisine ; nous pleurions tous, et personne d'entre nous ne trouvait un mot à dire.

Quel mot ?

Nous savions bien que cette arrestation devait se faire un jour ou l'autre ; mais nous avions cru qu'alors Catherine serait là, et Catherine, c'était la défense.

Mais Catherine n'était pas là.

Elle arriva cependant, une heure environ après le départ du père, et elle nous trouva tous dans la cuisine sans que nous eussions échangé une parole. Celle qui, jusqu'à ce moment, nous avait soutenus, était à son tour écrasée ; Étiennette, si forte, si vaillante pour lutter, était maintenant aussi faible que nous. Elle ne nous encourageait plus, sans volonté, sans direction, toute à sa douleur qu'elle ne refoulait que pour tâcher de consoler celle de Lise. Le pilote était tombé à la mer, et nous enfants, désormais sans personne au gouvernail, sans phare pour nous guider, sans rien pour nous conduire au port, sans même savoir s'il y avait un port pour nous, nous restions perdus au milieu de l'océan de la vie, ballottés au caprice du vent, incapables d'un mouvement ou d'une idée, l'effroi dans l'esprit, la désespérance dans le cœur.

C'était une maîtresse femme que la tante Catherine, femme d'initiative et de volonté ; elle avait été nourrice à Paris, pendant dix ans, à cinq reprises différentes ; elle connaissait les difficultés de ce monde, et, comme elle le disait elle-même, elle savait se retourner.

Ce fut un soulagement pour nous de l'entendre nous commander et de lui obéir ; nous avions retrouvé une indication, nous étions replacés debout sur nos jambes.

Pour une paysanne sans éducation comme sans fortune, c'était une lourde responsabilité qui lui tombait sur les bras, et bien faite pour inquiéter les plus braves ; une famille d'orphelins dont l'aîné n'avait pas dix-sept ans et dont la plus jeune était muette. Que faire de ces enfants ? Comment s'en charger quand on avait bien du mal à vivre soi-même ?

Le père d'un des enfants qu'elle avait nourris était notaire ; elle l'alla consulter, et ce fut avec lui, d'après ses conseils et ses soins, que notre sort fut arrêté. Puis ensuite elle alla s'entendre avec le père à la prison, et, huit jours après son arrivée à Paris, sans nous avoir une seule fois parlé de ses démarches et de ses intentions, elle nous fit part de la décision qui avait été prise.

Comme nous étions trop jeunes pour continuer à travailler seuls, chacun des enfants s'en irait chez des oncles et des tantes qui voulaient bien les prendre :

Lise chez tante Catherine, dans le Morvan.

Alexis chez un oncle qui était mineur à Varses, dans les Cévennes.

Benjamin chez un autre oncle qui était jardinier à Saint-Quentin.

Et Étiennette chez une tante qui était mariée dans la Charente au bord de la mer, à Esnandes.

J'écoutais ces dispositions, attendant qu'on en vînt à moi. Mais, comme la tante Catherine avait cessé de parler, je m'avançai :

— Et moi ? dis-je.

— Toi ? mais tu n'es pas de la famille.

— Je travaillerai pour vous.

— Tu n'es pas de la famille.

— Demandez à Alexis, à Benjamin, si je n'ai pas du courage à l'ouvrage.

— Et à la soupe aussi, n'est-il pas vrai ?

— Si, si, il est de la famille, dirent-ils tous.

Lise s'avança et joignit les mains devant sa tante avec un geste qui en disait plus que de longs discours.

— Ma pauvre petite, dit la tante Catherine, je te comprends bien, tu veux qu'il vienne avec toi ; mais vois-tu, dans la vie, on ne fait pas ce qu'on veut. Toi, tu es ma nièce, et quand nous allons arriver à la maison, si l'homme dit une parole de travers, ou fait la mine pour se tasser à table, je n'aurai qu'un mot à répondre : « Elle est de la famille, qui donc en aura pitié, si ce n'est nous ? » Et ce que je te dis là pour nous est tout aussi vrai pour l'oncle de Saint-Quentin, pour celui de Varses, pour la tante d'Esnandes. On accepte ses parents, on n'accueille pas les étrangers ; le pain est mince rien que pour la seule famille, il n'y en a pas pour tout le monde.

Je sentis bien qu'il n'y avait rien à faire, rien à ajouter. Ce qu'elle disait n'était que trop vrai. « Je n'étais pas de la famille. » Je n'avais rien à réclamer ; demander, c'était mendier. Et cependant, est-ce que je les aurais mieux aimés, si j'avais été de leur famille ? Alexis, Benjamin, n'étaient-ils pas mes frères ? Étiennette, Lise, n'étaient-elles pas mes sœurs ? Je ne les aimais donc pas assez ? Et Lise ne m'aimait donc pas autant qu'elle aimait Benjamin ou Alexis ?

La tante Catherine ne différait jamais l'exécution de ses résolutions ; elle nous prévint que notre séparation aurait lieu le lendemain, et là-dessus elle nous envoya coucher.

À peine étions-nous dans notre chambre que tout le monde m'entoura, et que Lise se jeta sur moi en pleurant. Alors je compris que, malgré le chagrin de se séparer, c'était à moi qu'ils pensaient, c'était moi qu'ils plaignaient, et je sentis que j'étais bien leur frère. Alors une idée se fit jour dans mon esprit troublé, ou, plus justement, car il faut dire le bien comme le mal, une inspiration du cœur me monta du cœur dans l'esprit.

— Écoutez, leur dis-je, je vois bien que, si vos parents ne veulent pas de moi, vous me faites de votre famille, vous.

— Oui, dirent-ils tous les trois, tu seras toujours notre frère.

Lise, qui ne pouvait pas parler, ratifia ces mots en me serrant la main et en me regardant si profondément que les larmes me montèrent aux yeux.

— Eh bien ! oui, je le serai, et je vous le prouverai.

— Où veux-tu te placer ? dit Benjamin.

— Il y a une place chez Pernuit ; veux-tu que j'aille la demander demain matin pour toi ? dit Étiennette.

— Je ne veux pas me placer ; en me plaçant, je resterais à Paris ; je ne vous verrais plus. Je vais reprendre ma peau de mouton, je vais décrocher ma harpe du clou où le père l'avait mise, et j'irai de Saint-Quentin à Varses, de Varses à Esnandes, d'Esnandes à Dreuzy ; je vous verrai tous, les uns après les autres, et ainsi, pour moi, vous serez toujours ensemble. Je n'ai pas oublié mes chansons et mes airs de danse ; je gagnerai ma vie.

À la satisfaction qui parut sur toutes les figures, je vis que mon idée réalisait leurs propres inspirations, et, dans mon chagrin, je me sentis tout heureux. Longtemps on parla de notre projet, de notre séparation, de notre réunion, du passé, de l'avenir. Puis Étiennette voulut que chacun s'allât mettre au lit ; mais personne ne dormit bien cette nuit-là, et moi bien moins encore que les autres peut-être.

Le lendemain, dès le petit matin, Lise m'emmena dans le jardin, et je compris qu'elle avait quelque chose à me dire.

— Tu veux me parler?

Elle fit un signe affirmatif.

— Tu as du chagrin de nous séparer; tu n'as pas besoin de me le dire, je le vois dans tes yeux et le sens dans mon cœur.

Elle fit signe que ce n'était pas de cela qu'il était question.

— Dans quinze jours, je serai à Dreuzy.

Elle secoua la tête.

— Tu ne veux pas que j'aille à Dreuzy?

Pour nous comprendre, c'était généralement par interrogations que je procédais, et elle répondait par un signe négatif ou affirmatif.

Elle me dit qu'elle voulait que je vinsse à Dreuzy; mais, étendant la main dans trois directions différentes, elle me fit comprendre que je devais, avant, aller voir ses deux frères et sa sœur.

— Tu veux que j'aille avant à Varses, à Esnandes et à Saint-Quentin?

Elle sourit, heureuse d'avoir été comprise.

— Pourquoi? Moi je voudrais te voir la première.

Alors de ses mains, de ses lèvres et surtout de ses yeux parlants, elle me fit comprendre pourquoi elle me faisait cette demande; je vous traduis ce qu'elle m'expliqua :

— Pour que j'aie des nouvelles d'Étiennette, d'Alexis et de Benjamin, il faut que tu commences par les voir; tu viendras alors à Dreuzy, et tu me répéteras ce que tu as vu, ce qu'ils t'ont dit.

Chère Lise!

Ils devaient partir à huit heures du matin, et la tante Catherine avait demandé un grand fiacre pour les conduire tous d'abord à la prison embrasser le père, puis ensuite chacun avec leur paquet au chemin de fer où ils devaient s'embarquer.

À sept heures, Étiennette à son tour m'emmena dans le jardin.

— Nous allons nous séparer, dit-elle; je voudrais te laisser un souvenir, prends cela : c'est une ménagère; tu trouveras là-dedans du fil, des aiguilles, et aussi mes ciseaux, que mon parrain m'a donnés; en chemin, tu auras besoin de tout cela, car je ne serai pas là pour te remettre une pièce ou te coudre un bouton. En te servant de mes ciseaux, tu penseras à nous.

Pendant qu'Étiennette me parlait, Alexis rôdait autour de nous; lorsqu'elle fut rentrée dans la maison, tandis que je restais tout ému dans le jardin, il s'approcha de moi :

— J'ai deux pièces de cent sous, dit-il ; si tu veux en accepter une, ça me fera plaisir.

De nous cinq, Alexis était le seul qui eût le sentiment de l'argent, et nous nous moquions toujours de son avarice ; il amassait sou à sou et prenait un véritable bonheur à avoir des pièces de dix sous et de vingt sous neuves, qu'il comptait sans cesse dans sa main en les faisant reluire au soleil et en les écoutant chanter.

Son offre me remua le cœur ; je voulus refuser, mais il insista et me glissa dans la main une belle pièce brillante ; par là je sentis que son amitié pour moi devait être bien forte, puisqu'elle l'emportait sur son amitié pour son petit trésor.

Benjamin ne m'oublia pas davantage, et il voulut aussi me faire un cadeau ; il me donna son couteau, et en échange il exigea un sou « parce que les couteaux coupent l'amitié ».

L'heure marchait vite ; encore un quart d'heure, encore cinq minutes, et nous allions être séparés. Lise ne penserait-elle pas à moi ?

Au moment où le roulement de la voiture se fit entendre, elle sortit de la chambre de tante Catherine et me fit signe de la suivre dans le jardin.

— Lise ! appela tante Catherine.

Mais Lise, sans répondre, continua son chemin en se hâtant.

Dans les jardins des fleuristes et des maraîchers, tout est sacrifié à l'utilité, et la place n'est point donnée aux plantes de fantaisie ou d'agrément. Cependant dans notre jardin il y avait un gros rosier de Bengale qu'on n'avait point arraché parce qu'il était dans un coin perdu.

Lise se dirigea vers ce rosier auquel elle coupa une branche, puis, se tournant vers moi, elle divisa en deux ce rameau qui portait deux petits boutons près d'éclore et m'en donna un.

Ah ! que le langage des lèvres est peu de chose comparé à celui des yeux ! que les mots sont froids et vides comparés aux regards !

— Lise ! Lise ! cria la tante.

Déjà les paquets étaient sur le fiacre.

Je pris ma harpe et j'appelai Capi, qui, à la vue de l'instrument et de mon ancien costume, qui n'avait rien d'effrayant pour lui, sautait de joie, comprenant sans doute que nous allions nous remettre en route et qu'il pourrait courir en liberté, ce qui, pour lui, était plus amusant que de rester enfermé.

Le moment des adieux était venu. La tante Catherine l'abrégea ; elle fit monter Étiennette, Alexis et Benjamin, et me dit de lui donner Lise sur ses genoux.

Puis, comme je restais abasourdi, elle me repoussa doucement et ferma la portière.

— Embrassez le père pour moi ! m'écriai-je, puisque...

Un sanglot étouffa ma voix.

— En route ! dit-elle.

Et la voiture partit.

À travers mes larmes, je vis la tête de Lise se pencher par la glace baissée et sa main m'envoyer un baiser. Puis la voiture tourna rapidement le coin de la rue, et je ne vis plus qu'un tourbillon de poussière.

C'était fini.

Appuyé sur ma harpe, Capi à mes pieds, je restai assez longtemps à regarder machinalement la poussière qui retombait doucement dans la rue.

Un voisin avait été chargé de fermer la maison et d'en garder les clefs pour le propriétaire ; il me tira de mon anéantissement et me rappela à la réalité.

— Vas-tu rester là ? me dit-il.

— Non, je pars.

— Où vas-tu ?

— Droit devant moi.

Sans doute, il eut un mouvement de pitié, car, me tendant la main :

— Si tu veux rester, dit-il, je te garderai, mais sans gages, parce que tu n'es pas assez fort ; plus tard, je ne dis pas.

Je le remerciai.

— À ton goût, ce que j'en disais, c'était pour toi ; bon voyage !

Et il s'en alla.

La voiture était partie ; la maison était fermée.

Je passai la bandoulière de ma harpe sur mon épaule. Ce mouvement que j'avais fait si souvent autrefois provoqua l'attention de Capi ; il se leva, attachant sur mon visage ses yeux brillants.

— Allons, Capi !

Il avait compris ; il sauta devant moi en aboyant.

Je détournai les yeux de cette maison où j'avais vécu deux ans, où j'avais cru vivre toujours, et je les portai devant moi.

Le soleil était haut à l'horizon, le ciel pur, le temps chaud ;

cela ne ressemblait guère à la nuit glaciale dans laquelle j'étais tombé de fatigue et d'épuisement au pied de ce mur.

Ces deux années n'avaient donc été qu'une halte ; il me fallait reprendre ma route.

Mais cette halte avait été bienfaisante.

Elle m'avait donné la force.

Et ce qui valait mieux encore que la force que je sentais dans mes membres, c'était l'amitié que je me sentais dans le cœur.

Je n'étais plus seul au monde.

Dans la vie j'avais un but : être utile et faire plaisir à ceux que j'aimais et qui m'aimaient.

Une existence nouvelle s'ouvrait devant moi. J'évoquai le souvenir de Vitalis, et je me dis en moi-même : En avant !

Table des matières

Préface 5

Première partie 13

I. Au village 15
II. Un père nourricier 23
III. La troupe du signor Vitalis 31
IV. La maison maternelle 41
V. En route 49
VI. Mes débuts 55
VII. J'apprends à lire 67
VIII. Par monts et par vaux 75
IX. Je rencontre un géant chaussé de bottes
de sept lieues 79
X. Devant la justice 87
XI. En bateau 99
XII. Mon premier ami 121
XIII. Enfant trouvé 135
XIV. Neige et loups 143
XV. Monsieur Joli-Cœur 165
XVI. Entrée à Paris 177
XVII. Un « padrone » de la rue de Lourcine 185
XVIII. Les carrières de Gentilly 201
XIX. Lise 209
XX. Jardinier 221
XXI. La famille dispersée 229

Dans la même collection

Honoré de Balzac, *Le Père Goriot*
Honoré de Balzac, *Eugénie Grandet*
Honoré de Balzac, *Le Cousin Pons*
Honoré de Balzac, *La Cousine Bette*
Honoré de Balzac, *Le Lys dans la vallée*
Charles Baudelaire, *Les Fleurs du mal*
Beaumarchais, *Le Mariage de Figaro*
Pierre Corneille, *Le Cid*
Alphonse Daudet, *Lettres de mon moulin*
Denis Diderot, *Jacques le Fataliste*
Gustave Flaubert, *Madame Bovary*
Gustave Flaubert, *Bouvard et Pécuchet*
Victor Hugo, *Les Misérables (3 vol.)*
Jean de La Bruyère, *Les Caractères*
Jean de La Fontaine, *Fables*
Guy de Maupassant, *Bel-Ami*
Guy de Maupassant, *Une vie*
Guy de Maupassant, *Contes du jour et de la nuit*
Guy de Maupassant, *Boule de suif*
Molière, *L'Avare*
Molière, *Le Tartuffe*
Molière, *Le Bourgeois gentilhomme*
Edgar Allan Poe, *Histoires extraordinaires*
Jean Racine, *Phèdre*
Arthur Rimbaud, *Poésies*
Edmond Rostand, *Cyrano de Bergerac*
George Sand, *La Mare au diable*
Stendhal, *La Chartreuse de Parme*
Stendhal, *Le Rouge et le Noir*
Jules Verne, *Le Tour du monde en quatre-vingts jours*
Jules Verne, *Michel Strogoff*
Villiers de L'Isle Adam, *Contes cruels*
Émile Zola, *L'Assommoir*
Émile Zola, *La Bête humaine*
Émile Zola, *Germinal*
Émile Zola, *Nana*

Distribution

Allemagne :
Buchvertrieb O. Liesenberg
Grossherzog-Friedrich-Str. 56
D-77694 Kehl

Algérie :
Exfree International
165, Avenue de Versailles
75016 Paris

Angleterre :
Sandpiper Books
24, Langroyd Road
London SW17 7PL

Chine :
CNPIEC
16, E. Gongti Road
100020 Beijing

Égypte :
El Dorado
167, rue Guers el Suez
Héliopolis
Le Caire

Espagne :
Ribera Libros
Poligono Martiartu, Calle 1, N° 6
48480 Arrigorriaga – Vizcaya

États-Unis :
Powell's Books Wholesale
1500 S. Western Avenue
Chicago IL USA 60608

Italie :
Inter Logos
Strada Curtatona 5/J
41100 Loc. Fossalta, Modena

Lituanie :
Humanitas
Donelaicio Str. 52
3000 Kaunas

Maroc :
Librairie des Écoles
12, avenue Hassan II
Casablanca

Russie :
Magma
P.O. Box 71/24
117296 Moscou

Syrie :
Librairie Avicenne
P.O. Box 2456
Damas

Tunisie :
L'Univers du livre
39, rue Naplouse
1002 Tunis

Achevé d'imprimer en janvier 2001
sur les presses de l'imprimerie Mondadori – Italie
Dépôt légal 1er trimestre 2001